MALCOLM
BLACK

TASK
FORCE
Gleneagles

CRINAN BOOKS

Copyright © Malcolm Black 2005

First published in Great Britain in 2005
By Crinan Books

The right of Malcolm Black to be identified as the Author of
the Work has been asserted by him in accordance with the
Copyright, Designs and Patents Act 1988.

1 3 5 7 9 10 8 6 4 2

All characters in this publication are fictitious and any
Resemblance to real persons, living or dead, is purely coincidental

A CIP catalogue for this title is available from the British Library

ISBN 0 9550171 0 6

Printed by
William Culross & Son Ltd
Queen Street, Coupar Angus, Perthshire PH13 9DF
Tel: 01828 627266   Fax: 01828 627146
E-mail: admin@culross.co,uk   www.culross.co.uk

Crinan
30 Buchanan Gardens
ST ANDREWS
KY16 9LU

The author and publisher gratefully acknowledge the co-operation of
The Sunday Times in giving permission for the use of the article from The
Sunday Times of 9th October, 1983, printed on both sides of the back cover,
and
The British Library for providing photocopies.
The author also expresses his gratitude to
The Museum of
The Argyll & Sutherland Highlanders for information provided.

CHAPTER 1

Glen was awake before the handle of his bedroom door had begun to turn. His acute hearing had alerted him to the slight pressure on the maple flooring of the adjacent open-plan living room.

A minute wafting of air across his face told him that the door had opened without further sound.

His heavy breathing continued, and his eyes remained closed.

A faint shadow spread slowly across his eyelids, came closer and remained fixed.

He concentrated on the one sense that would not betray his alertness and tried to pick up some trace of smell that would give him a clue as to the identity of his intruder. There was only the hint of a freshly laundered garment.

Suddenly the shadow swooped. At the last moment he opened his eyes to see the glint of disappointment in the unblinking eyes of the beautiful face whose lips were inches from his cheek.

The lips edged towards his own, brushing them so lightly that he could feel the difference between the warmth of her mouth and the coolness of the skin at the edges of the lips, cool even in comparison with the air-conditioned atmosphere.

The young woman lifted her head, leaned on her elbow and studied him as he sighed and stretched.

"You knew. Didn't you?" she accused.

"Sort of," he admitted.

"How?"

"I don't know. I'm just like that," he apologised.

"I did everything you told me to, and you still wakened," she challenged.

"Maybe I was on the point of wakening," he reasoned.

"Funny thing, you are on the point of wakening no matter when I sneak in here. I think you're scared of me," she pouted.

"I even showered for half-an-hour in cold water so that there would be no scent of soap or perfume. I left my shoes outside the apartment, and you can't say I have too many clothes on to crease, far less rustle as I move."

He gave an appraising look at the sun-top and the brief shorts, designed to derive maximum benefit from the Florida sun, and said, "Whatever your clothes sound like, no one can deny that they look gorgeous." He stretched his face towards her and was rewarded with a peck on the lips.

She swung her legs off the bed in a parabola of exquisite symmetry and promised, "I'll fix breakfast while you shave."

Colin Glen, at thirty-four, retained the fresh complexion of his native Northwest, where he had been as adept in the pursuits of the great outdoors of Washington, Oregon and Idaho as he was in more academic activities, first of all at his local state university and later at Mexico City University, the oldest in the Western Hemisphere.

His natural aptitude for languages, which had earlier given him a special relationship with the Nez Perce Indians and an insight into their culture and field-craft skills, enabled him to become fluent in Spanish to the extent of being an expert in several of the main dialects of Latin America. His first interest in the culture of Iberia came from a few words he had picked up from shepherds when he had been trekking in Idaho.

His determination to master Spanish only came later, when he discovered that the shepherds had been teaching him the totally unrelated language of Basque. By a strange twist of fate, this unique language of very limited distribution had almost certainly saved his life years later when he had been captured by Argentine soldiers in San Sebastian, Tierra Del Fuego, during the Falklands War.

Although he took his language studies seriously, he considered himself an economist rather than a linguist. His professional interest in the language was to help him unravel the manifold economic problems stretching from the Rio Grande to Cape Horn.

His knowledge of Latin America and the flexibility with which he was able to move about the continent brought him to the attention of his country's diplomatic service, which found him an invaluable consultant.

It was not long before these consultations became assignments of an escalating strategic nature.

His present involvement as director of tourism research at the University of Florida, although superficially a home posting, owed as much to the federal government's concern about the political activities of the burgeoning Hispanic population in that state, both refugee and transient.

As Glen buzzed his razor over his face he mused to his reflection. In his mid-thirties he was little older than his senior students, and, like any presentable academic of reasonable appearance, was a focal point for the romantic attentions of not a few attractive young women. As he stroked his chin to test the efficacy of the razor he admitted to himself that part of his success in that area was probably due to the flutter of interest he aroused when he turned up in an academic department half way through a semester.

His reverie was interrupted by a call from Kathy, "Coffee's ready. Come and get it."

"Hey! This grapefruit's terrific. I love the way you cut the fleshy parts so that I can scoop them out with no chewy bits."

....

Glen let Kathy drive them out to Cape Canaveral Space Centre so that he could spend his time enjoying her profile instead of keeping his eye on a monotonous road.

She smiled at him, "Stop looking at me like that. I can't concentrate on my driving."

"Why do you try to sneak into my apartment and take me by surprise?" he countered.

2

"Partly because it seems to be impossible, and partly to find out if you ever lapse into being untidy."

"You wouldn't know it was difficult if you didn't keep trying. Why do you do it?"

She smiled at him quizzically. "I think it's because the first time I did it on impulse, I seemed to get a glimpse of a different you – a more alert, tense person than you are normally. It frightened me at the time. Now to help me get over it, I try to make a joke of it. Maybe I want to find out if your Dr Jekyll has a Mr Hyde before I come completely under your spell." She was speaking part seriously and part teasingly.

"I didn't know it showed," he answered with a grin.

"It shows a little. It showed then and it showed when you told me all the things I should not do if I wanted to take someone by surprise. It sounded a bit professional – not at all academic and theoretical."

She concentrated on her driving again for a few moments before turning and looking at him straight in the eye. "It's showing again."

"What?"

"Mr Hyde. You're moping about what I said. It's your other personality coming through. Your Dr Jekyll doesn't mope."

"Nothing of the kind! It's your ravishing beauty that puts guilty thoughts into my head, and I'm just embarrassed when you catch me out."

She laughed, and her softly waved brunette hair bobbed across her forehead. "You sure can cover up quickly and please the girls at the same time," she scolded, but her eyes sparkled and her lips parted in a wide smile.

Her quick glimpse confirmed for her his physical attractiveness. Just under six feet, he had a power and vibrancy that gave her goose pimples.

CHAPTER 2

"Dr Glen, please go to the Director's office. Dr Colin Glen." The attractive female voice made the invitation sound personal over the public address system, a tribute to some of the technological spin-off from the locally based space programme.

Turning to his assistant, Glen asked rhetorically, "Will you manage on your own for a few minutes, Kathy?"

Kathy was holding a clipboard containing a sheaf of questionnaires where she recorded answers from some of the tourists milling around the concourse.

With her long, slender legs attractively exposed in brief shorts and her sleek, tanned shoulders glinting above a smooth sun-top, Kathy had little difficulty in persuading male tourists to answer her questions.

She nodded, "Sure, Dr Glen," and seemed mainly concerned with keeping her clipboard in a position in which it was possible to continue writing. The present interviewee was meanwhile doing his best to frustrate this objective by standing as close to her as possible.

Glen strode across the vast concrete square where hundreds of tourists were milling about, some gazing up at a couple of gleaming space rockets, which were already museum pieces, while others were trying more mundanely to provoke an alligator in a large compound into causing some misdemeanour.

The majority seemed committed to the great American tradition of converting junk food into obesity. The catering equipment at Cape Canaveral vied seriously with that of space technology in terms of efficiency. Stainless steel self-service carousels enjoyed a popularity never dreamed of by the old fashioned fair-ground variety. Staff were hard-pressed to replenish stocks on their side as the consuming masses responded slavishly to their voracious appetite.

Beyond the tourist throngs, Glen opened the door of the administrative building, releasing a blast of cold, dry air from its insulated efficiency.

In the Director's office on the second floor Joseph McKane leaned back in his chair, as Glen entered. He seemed more affable than usual, although his welcome did not extend to removing his favourite Tampa cigar from his clenched teeth, as he spoke.

"Hi, Colin. Ya di'n't waste any time. Good. They bin callin' ya fr'm Cocoa. Ya gotta call straight back to the Dean's office. Jus' ya use ma phone."

Glen smiled and accepted the offer.

Joe, it should be explained, was not the Director of Cape Canaveral's Space Programme. He was Director of probably its least prestigious, but, until the commercial viability of Columbia's space shuttle, its most profitable enterprise – tourism, a position to which he had risen from his astute use of the opportunities put in his way as one of the first security supervisors.

As he pushed the phone across the desk to Glen he muttered, not for the first time, "Ah don' know why ya gotta study tourism at a university."

To Glen's surprise, before he could answer Joe, he was connected immediately to the Dean, without the usual interception by an ever-vigilant secretary.

"Hi, Paul, What's new?" he asked.

"Colin, you must have impressed someone with a recent paper. I've had a call from the President of the University about you. You're required for some consultation. I said you were out supervising a survey with some of your seniors and I'd let you know when you got back, but he told me that wasn't fast enough."

Detecting some annoyance in the Dean's tone, Glen tried to mollify him with a diplomatic, "Sorry for the hassle, Paul."

It worked, and the onus lay with the Dean as he explained, "It's just that I never thought anything in your line of tourist research could possibly be so urgent."

"It plays a big part in the budget of some states, and some Congressman is impatient for a quick answer to a big hotel group, I guess."

"That figures. Call in and see me when you get back to campus," he invited.

"Sure. Thanks, Paul. See you."

Glen replaced the receiver and smiled at Joe, "I think I'll be leaving you for a little while."

"Too bad," Joe grinned, betraying a lack of the professional hospitality, which was so fundamental to his position. "We'll try to manage for a few days on our own."

As he rose, Glen said, "The work to date has been useful, and whether or not I'm able to continue with it personally, someone will have to take it up."

Joe didn't agree. "We're doin' swell our own way."

CHAPTER 3

Once outside again, he went straight across to Kathy, who seemed to have found a niche for herself as the only analyst of tourist attractions who had actually become a tourist attraction in her own right.

"Kathy, I'm afraid today's session is going to have to be cut short. Something has cropped up at the Department," he said as he circumnavigated a couple of avocado-shaped questionnaire volunteers.

"Do you want me to continue on my own? I'd be glad to."

"Afraid not. I have a lot to discuss with you. I'll tell you in the car."

The urgency of his tone alerted Kathy to the thought that Mr Hyde was nearer the surface than at any time since she had known him.

She smiled apologetically to the two men, "I'm afraid I'll have to leave you, gentlemen. I'm sorry to have taken up your time."

Their smiles of acknowledgement and their scowl towards Glen's back showed that they were sorry too and whom they held to blame.

Before Kathy's thanks were finished, Glen had her by the elbow and was ushering her across the tarmac to the car park.

"What is it, Colin?" she asked anxiously.

He looked down at her, and his face relaxed into its habitual slow smile. "Jealousy! I'm jealous of all those men who queue up to be interviewed by you."

But the smile did not reach his eyes, and his pace did not slacken.

She tried to make light of his compliment as usual, although she would have loved to think that he really was jealous. "I bet you say that to all your postgrad girls."

"True," he teased, "but I never mean it as a rule."

As they reached the car, he opened the driver's door and motioned her in.

"You drive," he commanded.

"Back to campus?"

"I'll tell you as we go along."

As they pulled out from the car park, Kathy flicked her indicator to show that she was about to turn left on to NASA Causeway.

"The other way," Glen ordered peremptorily.

"Kennedy Parkway?"

"Take the road east. We're going to Complex 36."

Instead of taking either the NASA Causeway across India River or Kennedy Parkway towards Merritt Island, Kathy swung the car eastwards towards the isolated launch pads.

"I know! You can't resist me any longer and you're carrying me off to an isolated corner of this sub-tropical paradise to make mad passionate love." She smiled invitingly.

"What an excellent idea," he agreed, "but that will have to wait."

Then for the first time since she had known him Kathy recognised a hesitancy and lack of confidence in his voice, as he said, "That is, if you will wait."

"What on earth do you mean?" Anxiety sharpened her voice and dulled her eyes.

"Mr Hyde, Kathy."

"I knew it," she gasped.

"I'll try to explain as much as I can. Please listen. We have no time for a discussion. I shouldn't be telling you any of this and it's pointless to try swearing you to secrecy. The onus is on me."

She did not answer, and, with both of them staring straight ahead as though driving in thick fog instead of under a brilliant Florida sky, he spoke mechanically.

"You're an excellent student, Kathy. You could've done your master's in a wide choice of research projects, but you thought this one would make use of your knowledge of Spanish. Since we started, you've kept noticing things, especially the attention we've been paying to Hispanics. You'd begun to appreciate that I could pick out different nationalities by their accents, be they Venezuelan, Mexican or Chilean. I shouldn't've let that be so obvious, because then you started to analyse certain factors separately from their tourism value. You correctly perceived differences between short-term tourists, would-be immigrants, over-confident, new Americans, etc., etc., and you began to ponder aloud what national interests other than the economy could benefit from what we were doing.

"It was partly my fault for not making the work more demanding for someone as bright as yourself.

"You were right. I have a separate remit. I spent time in Argentina before and during the invasion and liberation of the Falkland Islands. The Pentagon had a powerful interest in that conflict. The Argentines suspect it might have been more direct than it was, and some of their hotheads are regarded as a security risk to our country should they try to set up any terrorist cells here.

"Now you know why I'm a relatively light sleeper," he added with a half-hearted attempt to be frivolous.

Kathy gave him a wan smile and said, "Gee, I'm sorry".

"No need to apologise. I wouldn't have missed those close encounters for the world.

"You are intelligent enough to understand immediately that I wouldn't be telling you this as a tribute to your powers of observation.

"I've been in and out of situations like this for more than a decade and move on to the next assignment just as suddenly as I moved into the Florida Faculty with no emotional qualms or hang-ups. But this time it's different.

"I decided this morning that I would have to come out into the open with you and discuss it with you tonight, or tomorrow or next week at the latest. I must have been here too long and becoming complacent, for I was forgetting that I can't plan ahead that far. We don't even have tonight now.

"From the moment I was called to Joe's office, I've been on my way to be briefed about my next assignment. I'm committed now. There's no way I can say, 'Get someone else because I have this great girl.'

"Hey! This is getting maudlin. The real secret is my weakness for your grapefruit special. Who knows what other domestic attributes you have hidden away?"

The timbre of his voice had visibly raised goose-flesh on Kathy's arms before he had deliberately introduced a bit of levity.

They were speeding along the straight embanked road showing only emptiness in both windscreen and mirror. The neatly trimmed verges merged into uniform slopes on either side of the road to slip symmetrically down to ditches, ominous with the memory of the alligator compound back at the Centre. Beyond the ditches, unseen from the car, the tall, monotonous swamp vegetation obliterated the road from any possible observers except airborne ones.

"I had to keep those things from you, not only for security reasons, but also because such knowledge can make life dangerous for you."

Kathy drew the car to a halt, gave Glen a twinkling, demure smile. "Sir, I do declare you say the most romantic things to a girl, like she reminds you of a sour, old grapefruit. How can you say you love her all that much?"

"I'll show you," he said, drawing her towards him and kissing her on her willing, upturned mouth until she drew slowly away.

"Your work can have your undivided attention now, on condition that I get your undivided attention when it comes my turn."

He didn't protest, but gazed admiringly at her as she accelerated the car. But a sudden shadow across her face gave warning a moment before she took her foot off the gas pedal and allowed the car to slow slightly. He looked ahead and saw a figure on the road, which had been deserted seconds before. The man was waving at them to stop and pointing to the ditch.

"His car seems to have gone off the road," Kathy guessed as she continued to slow down.

Glen's eye caught a glimpse of something in the man's hand.

"Don't stop," he yelled. "He's armed. Put your foot down."

Kathy's reflexes were quick, and the car surged forward.

When the man realised they were not going to stop he gesticulated threateningly and stood his ground in the middle of the road, as the car raced towards him. At the last moment he leapt aside.

As they passed, Glen looked over his shoulder and, through the rear window, saw the man assume a crouching position and hold his pistol in both hands as he aimed at the back of the car.

"Duck!" he shouted at Kathy, but even as the word rose in his throat, he heard the explosion of a bursting tyre and felt the jolt as it staggered the car.

Kathy gave a scream as the wheel jumped in her hands. The force of the acceleration outstripped her capacity for recovery, and, before she could correct the skid, the car was on to the verge where the soft surface increased the drag on the flat tyre.

Glen tried to grab the wheel, but their combined efforts at correction against the built-up inertia only exaggerated it, and the car began, very slowly it seemed, to roll on to its near side.

Glen felt the motion quite gradual and comfortable, as his weight moved from his seat to his side and then his shoulder, before he ended up swinging gently from his seat-belt, from which position he was able to see the murky water of the drainage canal seep in at the top of the open window, which was slipping inexorably deeper into the opaque slime.

As he struggled to open his buckle, impeded by the strain put on the belt by his own weight, he asked Kathy, "Are you OK?"

The only reply was a dull moan.

He freed himself at last, but was in such a tangle that he could do nothing more until he opened the door. Despite the slow-motion impression of the crash, the side of the car was severely damaged, and the door was jammed tight in the twisted frame.

He grabbed the handle to wind the window down. It moved painfully slowly, but the resistance built up and, after the gap had reached no more than five inches, it stuck completely.

The trickle of translucent green water became a stream as it flowed through his hair and round his shoulder to the lower side of the car where it was already lapping the top of Kathy's forehead.

Its tepid wetness seemed to bring her round, and the gentle moaning stopped. In a dazed voice she asked, "What happened?"

The relief in hearing her voice drove Glen's frantic efforts to new heights as he struggled with the window.

"You OK?" he gasped between clenched teeth.

A feeble "Yes," gave him all the encouragement he needed.

He contorted himself into position to drive his right heel against the resistant window, but the length of the jab was too short, and the fact that he hit the glass close to the doorframe meant that it absorbed most of the energy. The window remained intact.

He swore and tried again, aiming his kick close to the open edge of the window. There was a splintering of glass, which left a hole large enough for him to squeeze through, but jagged enough to extort a toll of blood and shredded clothes.

As he pulled his legs free he could hear voices shouting from the road. It was no surprise to him that the language was Spanish. He scrambled over the upturned chassis to reach Kathy's door, the window of which was almost completely covered by water. If it had been open, they would both have been drowned before he was able to untangle himself.

Fortunately, since the car had not rolled on the driver's side, the door was undamaged. He studied Kathy's position through the narrow slit of glass remaining uncovered by the water.

He had seconds to unharness her, but if he knew exactly where her buckle was he would not have to grope for it in the dark water.

Kathy's eyes were open.

Mouthing the words as clearly as he could so that she could lip-read, he asked, "Are you alright?"

"Fine apart from a sore neck," she answered faintly through the glass.

He realised the danger involved in moving someone with a sore neck following the accident they had just had. He would have given anything not to have to pull her out of the car without medical help, but he had no option.

The footsteps on the road above were getting closer, but they were slow and deliberate and the voices were more hushed. There was no prospect of help from that source – only greater danger.

He wrenched the door open, and the fetid water rushed in. He snatched her buckle open, ensuring as he did so that he was able to support Kathy's weight. To absorb it he had to crouch under water in an almost impossible position. Holding the door open with his hip against the force of the water, he pulled her out, his left hand round her waist and his right hand supporting her neck and head.

He floated her across the ditch and scrambled into the reeds on the other side. He spread the support of his arms wide along her back and neck and lifted her the minimum amount to pass her smoothly from water to land.

Through the reeds he could see a head bob above the horizon of the grass verge and subside below it again. A moment later it cautiously emerged again close to the same spot.

As soon as it went out of sight again, he drew Kathy a few more inches into the depth of the reeds.

Two heads appeared this time, and then the men stood up. Only the chassis and the two rear wheels remained above the water. The men whispered to each other and then, emboldened by the silence, began to talk more loudly. They wondered if the people in the car had escaped. There was no way they could check inside the car without getting very wet. If the occupants had escaped and were hiding in the reeds, they would have all the advantage, if they were armed. For the same reason, pursuit into the reeds was also ruled out.

One of them asked, "Do you think we got him this time?"

"I'm sure we did," his companion affirmed.

"Let's go back to the car before someone else comes along. That was a good idea to hide it on the other side of the embankment. Nobody would expect a car to be hidden on this featureless road."

"Maybe not, but that damned gringo guessed pretty quickly that you were up to something. Let's hope that's the last we'll see of him."

The two men turned away, and Glen could hear nothing more of their conversation. He knew from their accents that they were Argentines, although their blatant action had at first suggested to him that they might have been Cuban, since they had greater numbers in the state to back up such an attack.

He remained absolutely still for almost ten minutes. Then he whispered to Kathy, "Can you move? We'll have to do a little walking."

Her eyes filled with tears, and she said in a tremulous voice, "I don't think so. I've tried. My arms and legs are all pins and needles. I can move my head. That's all."

With a reassuring smile, Glen lied to her, "You've been concussed. You must have knocked your head when we crashed."

He said, "We've a couple of miles to go across country. The road takes a loop round and is much longer, but we'll have to keep clear of it in the meantime. We just go south-west from here. If the ground was firm I could carry you, but it's soft and we'd make very slow progress. It's best you stay here while I go get some help."

She nodded, but her eyes betrayed her apprehension.

Glen kissed her and then plunged into the tangle of reeds, unnavigable except for the occasional glimpse of the sun.

Kathy lay completely immobile. Fortunately, her lack of feeling in her limbs had saved her from the knowledge that she was being colonised by the first adventurous leech. Although she could turn her head and nod, she was unable to lift it off the ground.

A slithering noise caused her heart to miss a beat. Another wriggle and a rustle. Her imagination began to run riot. In an outburst of pent-up trauma she screamed hysterically.

Glen had only penetrated about two hundred yards of dank vegetation when he heard the piercing scream. Immediately, he turned and blundered as fast as his flailing arms and squelching feet would allow.

He yelled at the top of his voice, "Hold on Kathy! I'm coming! I'm coming!"

He reached the featureless drainage canal, but could not see where he had left her. "Kathy?" he yelled. "Kathy? Where are you?"

From about fifteen feet away she called gently, "Over here."

He thrashed his way towards her and was horrified by what met his eyes.

She was smiling foolishly at him and apologising, "I'm sorry for being such a silly. I was alright on my own. Really I was."

But Glen was not listening. An alligator had stopped on its tracks about a yard from her right foot, its gauntleted front leg held in mid-air like the arm of a foppish swordsman, while it considered its next move in the light of the unexpected intrusion.

Without looking at her and keeping his voice as calm as possible, he soothed her gently, "It's alright, my love. I'm here now. I shouldn't have left you in this place," as his eyes locked on those of the reptile.

He moved forward very, very slowly, then suddenly lunged at its midriff with a ferocious kick, as it turned its leering jaws at him.

The brute was much more solid than Glen had realised, but he was impervious to the pain in his ankle. Fortunately, the creature had not been motivated by undue hunger and slithered back into the water to search for an easier prey.

11

"What is it? Why aren't you speaking?" Kathy asked querulously.

"It's OK," he soothed her as he bent over her. "I was just making sure there was nothing to harm you. I'll stay here and try the road later when I'm sure it's safe to do so. It was too difficult going through the swamp anyway."

"I was so frightened," she whimpered. "I never felt so lonely in my life. Hold me close. Lift me so that I can see where I am."

He put both arms round her head and shoulders and, with the gentleness of a doting parent, began to ease her upwards.

She murmured, "You have the kindest hands."

As she finished, there was the slightest click as she turned her head to look at him, and she went completely limp.

For several minutes Glen held her, scarcely daring to breathe and terrified to look at her face to confirm the truth.

CHAPTER 4

Glen remained reverentially bowed over Kathy's inert body, bidding her a silent farewell and committing himself anew to a more effective protection of the innocents.

With no option but to carry Kathy's body across his shoulders, he winced as he lifted her, realising for the first time that he had injured his own back.

The burden on his back, even with the physical pain, was nothing compared with the burden he carried on his conscience.

Exhausted and dishevelled, he eventually reached the edge of the clearing that comprises Complex 36.

The soft ground, the resistant vegetation, Kathy's body and the insects had all taken their toll.

Still under cover, he laid her body on the ground and scrutinised the open space carefully to ensure that nobody was watching.

A bus and a grey Chevrolet sedan, each bearing NASA logos, were the only vehicles on the scruffy expanse of reddish wasteland that surrounded the deserted Space Museum, an unprepossessing building similar to a World War II pillbox, which was the focal point of the site.

But the blast-proof doors and the thick walls bespoke the need to withstand forces greater than any known in that era. This building was designed to survive the rage of space rocket engines on the adjoining launch pad.

It was the farthest point to which tourists were brought from the concourse in a perfectly planned itinerary designed to educate and entertain the public, but above all to keep them under control without their being aware of it. The next tour would arrive fifteen minutes after the departure of this one, give or take a couple of seconds.

As he watched, Glen saw the first of the passengers emerge from the north-west corner of the building and return to their bus, which, from this point, would take them straight back to the Visitor Centre where he and Kathy had been busy such a short life-time ago.

From that distance he was unable to distinguish any faces, but felt sure he would have recognised Kathy's assassin at almost any distance. The man's image was permanently emblazoned on his mind.

He waited a further minute after the bus had left, listening to the silence that droned in at the end of the bus's diminishing engine throb.

He rose, brushed down his clothes to make them presentable at any distance beyond a hundred yards. He strode across the intervening space, as though it was the most natural thing in the world for pedestrians to disport themselves on a surface which was the virtual domain of the wheeled vehicle.

The exposed environment was the very antithesis of the claustrophobic swamp.

The utilitarian ugliness of the coarsely shuttered concrete, the mottled surface of roughly poured cement and the neglected weathering confirmed that crude strength denied all aesthetic considerations in the building's concept.

He passed through the recessed heavy steel doors and the cave-like thick, concrete walls. The ugliness was so overwhelming, he found himself apologising under his breath, "To think, Kathy, that one man could have built the Taj Mahal for love and this is what I bring you to."

Inside, the lighting, subdued to ease the reading of bank upon bank of illuminated instrument control panels, reduced the harshness of the concrete.

He walked along a short passage and into a small lecture theatre where the lighting was even dimmer. He had to feel for the tip-up theatre seats in the back row and began to edge along to his left.

Expecting to meet a colleague, he sensed his presence before he could see him.

A female voice came from the shadows. "It's a lot easier to see your way about when you've been inside for a few minutes. Two more paces and you'll be right beside me."

"I don't need to see. I'd recognise that voice anywhere. It's good to hear from you, Del. What's new?"

"Let's clear the preliminaries first," the voice replied.

Del was one of the most dependable agents Glen had ever worked with, but that did not prevent both of them taking all prescribed security precautions on every occasion. Once these were confirmed, Del gave Glen his instructions.

Suspected security leaks at a US Navy listening station in Scotland were being checked by another agent, who, believing he was himself being spied upon, had asked for back-up.

Glen's cover would be the usual academic assignment, this time to observe a tourism phenomenon in Scotland from the security of one of its most ancient ivory towers.

The instructions, although cryptic, were clear. It was time to move on even before his eyes had become accustomed to the poor light.

Glen's last duty was to explain about Kathy's death and describe where her body lay. He omitted his emotional involvement except to say, "She deserves a lot of respect. Please make sure her body is recovered and well treated, when, as the Company puts it, matters are regulated."

It was the first time Glen had ever had to ask for the drill practised by the CIA when a non-involved civilian became an innocent victim of its activities. He fervently hoped it would be the last.

He put his right hand on his forehead and drew it down over his eyes with his thumb and forefinger along either side of his nose, trying to wipe away the involuntary tears and blessing the dull lighting, which he hoped hid his distress.

He rose. "I'll need a car."

"Take mine. Here are the keys. It's the Chevy. I'll go out on the next tour."

"Thanks. See you," was all he could trust himself to say. "Take care."

"And you." The soft reply came from the opposite end of the row.

It was easier to find his way out of the room. The intricate instrument panels had switched on automatically to provide atmosphere for the next batch of tourists, who would see how the earliest rockets had been controlled from that very room, now relegated to obscurity if not oblivion by the dizzy pace of technology. The luminous green digits and diagrams spread their eerie glow.

Minutes later Glen was off the Space Centre territory. He turned south to Cocoa Beach and then right at Ron Jon's – 'the Largest Surf Shop in the World'.

A couple of skyway bridges took him over the Banana and Indian Rivers.

On his way to the Dean Glen slipped into his own office for a quick change of clothes, which was normal procedure for anyone doing outside work in the sub-tropical climate.

Thirty minutes after leaving Del he entered the Dean's office.

"Hi, Paul. You got some instructions for me?" he opened.

"I sure have," the Dean replied. "You have a pretty tight schedule. You have a reservation on a British plane out of Miami this p.m. and a connecting flight to Brussels. Trish has your documents in her office. I guess you enquired about the work, so you know what's waiting for you?" he added interrogatively.

"It's a project rather similar to the one I was on here," Glen obliged, only dissembling to the extent of omitting the parallel security similarities. "I start in Brussels because it's an EC sponsored project." He did not elaborate on the Scottish connection.

"Florida to the French Riviera via Brussels, if I know my man," the Dean smiled sagely. "You have the right idea for a career. Choose your climate, season, hotels, restaurants, beach, snow or mountains and you call it work."

Glen gave an apologetic shrug, which seemed to acknowledge that, unlike the bureaucrat in front of him, he was not a serious academic.

"You'll excuse me if I rush now. These Europeans are a bit sensitive if we don't jump when they crack the whip. It could set me back weeks in terms of co-operative attitudes if I don't show immediate interest in their project."

"What about your work here?" Paul wanted to know.

"There's a straightforward statistical-gathering programme followed by analysis which is already programmed. Two or three of the postgrads are well briefed to supervise."

The Dean's remark of, "Good luck, then," was interrupted by the phone, which Glen seized as a good opportunity to withdraw.

As he reached the door he looked over his shoulder to give a flick of a wave, but his hand stopped halfway. Paul looked suddenly pale and drawn as he beckoned him to wait.

Glen closed the door softly and returned to the front of the desk.

The Dean put down the phone and looked up at Glen, his face ashen. "You'll have to disappoint the Europeans this time. That was the police. Kathy was killed in a car accident a few minutes ago."

CHAPTER 5

In situations like this a secret agent's cover becomes very vulnerable. All Glen's training and instincts told him he had to take urgent action, but he was inhibited by the thought that Paul would realise that his behaviour was suddenly out of character.

In the Dean's office Paul still looked shocked. He had worries which the whiz-kid administrator doesn't look for in his fast-track race to the top – human relations, especially the possibility that Kathy's wealthy father might cut off the generous donations, about which Kathy and Glen had known nothing.

Glen took advantage of Paul's torpid state. "May I phone Joe McKane?"

Paul nodded.

As soon as he got through on the Dean's direct line he asked in urgent undertones. "Glen here. What's happened to Kathy?"

Give him his due, Joe's innate skill and long experience came up trumps. He had already checked with the head of military security. "Kathy finished an interview and took off in your car. Ten minutes later she appears to have driven off the NASA Causeway, down an embankment and into the drainage canal. Nobody saw the accident. Fortunately, the windows were closed, presumably for the air-conditioning. So the 'gators haven't complicated the identification process." It was amazing how Joe's spoken English had improved for this semi-official report. Del had played her part well.

"Thanks, Joe. We'd appreciate at this end, if you could let us know what develops," he asked without indicating that he would not be around to hear any further information.

But Joe had given away a lot and wanted something in return. "Say, Colin, there's a lotta loose ends here. They say she was in your car. Why was that, and how did you leave? And what's this with you getting urgent phone calls to take off?"

"Joe, the phone messages couldn't have been related. I'm in the Dean's office, and Kathy sure wasn't contacted from here. I borrowed one of your pool cars. I'll send it back immediately and another car to bring the team back. They'll be traumatised by the news."

"You took one of my staff pool cars!" Joe exploded, but his temper subsided as quickly. "In the circumstances, I'll overlook it, but only this once."

Glen hung up and turned to the Dean. "She seems to have run off the road, but they have nothing more than that at the moment."

"You'll postpone your trip now?" the Dean ventured.

Glen was non-committal as he replied, "It will certainly affect my plans."

The Dean nodded dumbly.

"I'll find out what plans Trish had on hand for me," Glen said and quietly left the office.

The atmosphere in Trish's office was completely different from that of the one he had just left. The Dean knew how to pick a super-efficient secretary who was, in addition to being very attractive to look at, also a bright personality. She, of course, knew nothing yet of Kathy's death, and Glen did not break the news to her.

She smiled in a lively way as she drew out a wallet of flight tickets from a slender drawer unit and handed it over with a cheery, "Have a nice vacation in Europe!"

"We'll see," he said.

Retaining his slightly distracted air and without further attempt at conversation, he left her office and went straight to his own.

His academic and administrative work was always kept very organised and up-to-date exactly for eventualities such as this. Anyone required to take up his work at short notice could do so very easily, as far as clarity of progress and records were concerned.

He opened a cupboard door and took out an overnight bag, which always lay there ready packed, as did another at his flat in Titusville. He opened it, went to one of his filing cabinets and took out four folders containing duplicates of the administrative and research documents in his desk and a selection of lecture notes which would tide him over in any university economics department for the first week.

From another locker he took another complete change of clothes including a casual coat and a pair of fawn pants. A short-sleeved shirt, cotton pants and open sandals would not be the best protection against the elements in Scotland, even in July.

When he had changed into the fresh clothes he placed all those he had taken off into a plastic carrier bag.

He gave the room a quick survey again, took his passport from his overnight bag, closed it and put the passport inside his coat pocket. He picked up his case and the plastic bag with his laundry in it and left. On the way out he handed his laundry bag to a janitor with a ten-dollar bill, and asked to have the clothes cleaned and left in his room for his return.

Outside, he ignored the Faculty car park and scanned the student vehicles, which reflected a greater spectrum of wealth and style than did those of the staff. With a grim smile he spotted Kathy's red Corvette and went over to it. He felt under the rear fender and retrieved her spare keys, for, like other members of Faculty, he had benefited from Kathy's delight in offering her tutors the occasional lift in a more exciting vehicle than they would normally aspire to. The powerful engine growled its response to the ignition.

Kathy would forgive him, he told himself, for continuing to work as he had been trained to do.

Driving out of the campus he turned left, then right again to take him on towards the Interstate 95. He did not join it at the first opportunity, but took a slight diversion to the west and just beyond the flyover turned right into a quiet road that led to Cocoa Holiday Inn.

Luis was on duty at the reception desk. His face lit up as he recognised the man whom he credited with solving his Green Card problems when he had started work without due consultation with the US government's Immigration Service.

17

"Meester Glen, what a pleasure to see you!"

"Nice to see you too, Luis," Glen replied, and without further preliminaries asked, "Can you give me a line outside, please? I want to phone long distance. I also need two envelopes and two sheets of notepaper. Can you oblige?"

"Sure," Luis grinned back, and turned to the switchboard. "Look. That's the first booth round the corner connected up."

"Thanks, Luis."

He dialled a Washington number, which was answered immediately. He identified himself by code and similarly indicated a change of plan. Without going into any detail, he asked for a colleague to meet him in Seattle Airport. He looked at his watch. It was just coming up for noon, less than two hours since he had been called from the tourist concourse at Cape Canaveral. He did a quick calculation. His very best travelling time including a car to Orlando Airport, plane from Orlando to Atlanta and another flight on to Seattle, would take five hours. He allowed for the difference in time zones, but gave the minimum for any hitches or delays.

"ETA – fifteen hundred hours," he reckoned and rang off.

Back at the reception desk he collected the stationery, thanked Luis and offered to pay.

"Certainly not," Luis protested.

"If you don't let me pay, how can I ask you a favour again? Come on. Take it. Besides, I've got to rush. I'm late for a date".

"OK, but only this once," Luis conceded.

Glen gave him a five-dollar bill, a thumbs-up and a conspiratorial wink and retreated to the Corvette.

He left the car park, turned right and joined the Interstate 95 within a couple of hundred yards. Three miles farther north he joined the Bee Line Expressway and took advantage of its speed potential as he streaked along the fifty miles to Orlando Airport.

He parked the car as close as possible to the terminal, noted the number of the bay on the notepaper, folded the paper, placed it in one of Luis' envelopes, put the key in the other envelope, folded it three times and put it in the envelope with the notepaper, wrote a name on the envelope, and left it and a five-dollar bill with a smiling girl at the information desk.

He turned and checked the departure information screen. The first flight to Atlanta was due to leave in ten minutes. It was Eastern Airways. He raced to their desk.

"Have I time to catch the 12.50 for Atlanta?" he asked.

"You sure can, sir," the clerk replied in an over-leisurely manner, which tried Glen's patience somewhat. "Is Atlanta your destination, or do you require a through ticket for a connecting flight?"

"I'm stopping in Atlanta," Glen improvised. "I'll have to make arrangements for Mexico City once I'm there, but I don't think we have time right now."

The clerk nodded in agreement. As he took Glen's American Express card he spoke to a colleague, "Vince, ask the driver to hold the loading coach for the 12.50

to Atlanta. We have another passenger coming through." Turning to Glen he asked, almost in the same breath, "Have you any more luggage, sir?"

Glen shook his head as he picked up the completed Credit Card Debit form to sign. The clerk scrutinised signatures. He was the kind of person who would be able to give a vivid description of all his customers days after they had passed through. A flight to the busy hub Atlanta Airport gave no indication of a passenger's final destination unless the passenger chose to do so. In Glen's case he had chosen to misinform.

As Glen picked up his bag, the clerk waved his arm to the right. "The departure gate is right over there, sir. You'll see the bus, which has just loaded, waiting for you. Have a good flight, sir."

The flight to Atlanta on an elongated DC 10 was smooth and uneventful apart from a welcome coffee, which became more difficult to appreciate as his inactivity allowed his mind to dwell on the tragedy that had struck Kathy.

Glen disembarked via a telescopic tunnel and down an escalator to the automated shuttle train in a transparent tunnel, which took him from Concourse B to the Main Hall.

Once more he checked the battery of flight information screens. The time was 1.55, and the next flight he could identify to Seattle was the 2.45 by Delta.

He phoned the Company in Arlington and arranged for a ticket to be waiting for him at the boarding gate.

He had forgotten about food, but decided a black coffee could be forced into his churning stomach and headed for the nearest cafeteria.

As he sat nursing the warm cup, his training switched on automatically and he scanned those around him indirectly on glass or polished surfaces, always avoiding eye contact.

A momentary lapse almost betrayed him. His eyes had zoomed telephoto-like on another pair of scanning eyes belonging to a figure lurking behind a newspaper. The two pairs transected on a glazed door panel.

Fortunately, the shock of what he had seen triggered an aversion in the nick of time.

He suppressed a nausea that had taken away all thought of coffee.

These were eyes he would never forget. These were the eyes transfixed in his memory as they had gazed over their wrecked car, as Kathy lay beside him moments from death.

Two possibilities flashed into his mind. It could be pure coincidence and perfectly rational that one of the assassins was making his escape through Atlanta Airport. Most likely they would have split up. On the other hand, one or both may have been tailing Glen. If the latter was the case, they must have been very lucky, very clever or amazingly well informed.

Glen had two courses of action. The first professional choice was to evade the surveillance. The second choice, only to be taken as a last resort, was to terminate the surveillance.

Without compunction, Glen opted for the latter solution. His only regret was that Kathy's assassin would not know his execution was imminent.

If his plans had been discovered from the desk clerk in Orlando, one might already be preparing to board the flight to Mexico City, while this one was watching in case Glen was planning a re-route.

Glen looked at the departure screen, noted quietly that his Seattle flight was on time. The next flight to Mexico City left in fifteen minutes. The last call had gone out for passengers.

He leapt to his feet with an exclamation of concern and almost ran towards the escalators, but not so fast as to miss his adversary immediately discard the Washington Post, in which, moments ago, he had been feigning such interest.

Glen heard the gentle murmur of the automatic train's approach, but instead of keeping his place at the head of the surge, he looked down, cursed and bent to retie an already perfectly tied shoelace. At the same time he pressed the stopwatch button on his watch the second the train stopped.

He rose more clumsily than usual and apologised more elaborately than necessary to two separate passengers who paid not the slightest attention. Inevitably, he had no option but to obey the metallic voice's warning that the train doors were closing.

He stood back from the train, which was already moving. He recognised the blurred outline of his tail reflected in the train's shiny side panels. If Glen was to be the next assassination victim, he had made a bad move in making himself so vulnerable between his potential attacker and the electric track. It might just be sufficiently tempting for him to take the bait.

The automatically operated trains on their limited closed circuit journey within the airport followed a predetermined timetable to the split second. Glen felt the slight movement of air on his cheek, telling him that the next train was approaching. Ten seconds to go. He began counting at seven.

He moved to where the first door would open two seconds after the train had stopped.

He was at the very edge of the platform. His hands were sticky. He blinked, as the sweat glands leaked above his eyebrows. It was impossible for him to focus on reflections. There was a lot of jostling and movement behind him. His senses were giving him no information. All he could do was count. Five seconds, four, three …

He felt someone tense at his shoulder and heard an intake of breath, which presaged an energising surge of oxygen for the bloodstream. Two. The last second expanded into a microcosm of eternity.

Like a matador, he timed his minute body swerve to perfection and instantaneously twisted his left knee outwards in a move he had learned on the soccer field in the mild winters of north-western Oregon.

There was a violent scuff against his side, for which he had braced himself, and a bony knock of unsupportive knee against his own tensed one.

An off-balance figure carried forward by its own momentum stumbled past his field of vision and into the path of the train.

The passing body grunted partly with exertion and partly with surprise, but it was bludgeoned into oblivion before another sound passed its lips.

Glen saw the staring eyes of the shocked passengers and heard the crescendo of screams from several female throats. The attention of the public was drawn inexorably forward with the hypnotic horror of what was going on under the front of the train.

The doors opened as the train stopped, exactly as the second hand on Glen's watch passed the apex of the dial.

He clasped his free hand to his mouth as though to stifle nausea before turning aside and retreating to mingle with the passengers emerging from the opposite side of the train.

He did not indulge himself in the satisfaction of looking back to see the well-deserved violent fate of Kathy's killer.

CHAPTER 6

Within four hours of take-off from Atlanta they were descending at Seattle as gently, in the zephyr breeze from Puget Sound, as if the plane knew it was coming back home to its Boeing birthplace.

With cabin luggage only, Glen did not need to waste time at the giant carousel where all the hold baggage would be disgorged. He looked at his watch, which he had turned back four hours aboard the plane to allow for the difference between Eastern and Pacific Time. It was five past three.

He went straight to the message board. Although there appeared to be nothing on it for him, he stood close scrutinising it as he ran his right finger tips along the bottom of the frame. They touched a thumbtack, which he pulled out and pocketed.

He went to the washroom. Behind a locked door he examined the thumbtack. A tiny piece of tightly folded paper pressed right against the head of the tack.

Opened out, it gave the simple message, table 5.

Lunchtime had peaked in the restaurant, and the majority of the tables were free of customers, but a few remained to be cleared of dishes and napkins. Table 5 had one occupant and two neatly prepared place settings. He approached the table and asked the husky-looking customer if he could join him.

"I've just arrived from Atlanta. Someone was due to meet me, but I guess he'll know where to find me."

The husky-looking fellow nodded, "Perhaps you should leave a message on the board for him. I usually do that for anyone I am expected to meet, especially if I don't know what he looks like. Have you met this person before?"

"No. I just said I would be here at 3 p.m. It was a bit of a rush at the time. It would be a coincidence, if you were the person I was supposed to meet?" Glen hazarded.

His new acquaintance looked at him fixedly. "If I was the guy you were to meet, you'd have found a message on the board. I just said so." He pressed his thumb on the table-cloth and seemed to screw it into the table without taking his eyes off Glen's.

"In that case, it's no coincidence I'm at table 5," Glen responded.

The stranger leaned back in his seat, brandished his right palm and stretched across the table. "Glad to meet you. Chuck's the name."

"Nice to know you, Chuck," Glen grinned as he grasped the hand.

"You had some kind of emergency up to Seattle, I believe. In what way can I help?"

"I got an assignment signal, and almost within minutes an assistant, who was entirely outside the Company, came to an untimely end at the wheel of my car. That decided me to take another route. I was in fairly deep cover, and my lines of communication were over-stretched," Glen explained.

"The first thing I can confirm is that you do have an assignment in Scotland. You can fly there from Seattle by North Western with one stop Stateside."

"I think I'll cut out a flight from the US and travel by road a little farther north to Canada. I think I can get a flight from Vancouver."

"And that way you can cover your exit from the States for a little bit longer. Good thinking. You had me guessing when I heard you were coming this far west. I'll check on reservations right away."

Moments later he was back, just as Glen was enjoying his first bite of blueberry muffin.

"A Wardair Jumbo leaves at 19.30. We'll just make it if we leave now."

Before Glen was up from the table, Chuck had paid the waitress, and with a strong grip on Glen's elbow was ushering him out of the restaurant.

As they climbed into the parked Pontiac, Chuck explained, "Right now we have three hours to get to Vancouver. That's a hundred and fifty miles and a few towns to pass. We'll make it, but you'll have to hang on to your britches."

Chuck took the harbour expressway, explaining, "This is the most direct route, even if it does go through the city. It also gives a view of the Waterfront. It's quite picturesque at this time of year with the pleasure craft. You can see the Skylon on the right just ahead of us. It was part of the 1962 World Fair. You may get a glimpse of the Monorail transport system, which goes to it from Downtown. When you get over to the UK you can tell the Limeys about it. Their Queen rode on it when she visited the city four months ago."

"You sound as if you're in the tourist business too," Glen jested.

"No way!" Chuck replied seriously. "You hide tourist people in Florida. If you want to hide agents in Seattle you put them into logging or aviation. My speciality is aerodynamics. That can get you into fairly sensitive areas when you have to be posted on a Company job."

They were cruising fast along US Highway 99 with the scenic waters of Puget Sound on the left and the forested slopes on the right covered with giant hemlock, Douglas fir and cedar. It was scenery on the grand scale, a complete contrast to the monotony of flat Florida.

Chuck looked at his watch. "Good, we're ahead of schedule. We won't have so much traffic ducking on and off the highway between here and Bellingham, so I can concentrate on passing on your orders, as far as I know them.

"Your flight goes direct to Scotland. It lands at a very quiet airport called Prestwick. However, that's only a stopover. The flight terminates at Amsterdam.

"Your destination in Scotland is an RAF station on the east of the country. It's pronounced Loo..chers, spelt L e u c h a r s. It's a front line station equipped with Phantoms. They spend their days and nights intercepting Soviet Bears and Badgers whenever they get too far west across the North Sea. We frequently have people there on exchange. Our nearest permanent presence on the ground is a listening station at a former US Navy base about forty miles to the north, called Edzell. Any initiative for contact will remain yours, but you can depend on maximum co-operation as soon as you require it."

"What about my cover?" Glen wanted to know.

"The usual," Chuck replied. "Five miles from Leuchars is a real quaint old town called St Andrews. It's just a little place, but it has a very ancient, and incidentally very good, university with a respectable economics school, that's just made for you.

"St Andrews is a unique tourist spot with tremendous potential – history, beaches, style, culture and so on, but above all golf. The headquarters of British golf is there. The Limeys think it's the world centre for the game. It's called the Royal and Ancient. They run several events, but the daddy of them all is the Open. It's in a different location each year on an irregular rotation of about seven or eight top courses. This year it comes home to St Andrews. Basically, that's your cue for a study. Sorry, maybe I should have called it a research project. It's to be held next week.

"Don't let the golf get to you. Leuchars is your baby. It's home to a strategic strike force and therefore a prime nuclear target.

"The urgency is because it is to be the reception point for NATO defence ministers who are holding a conference in nearby Gleneagles. Their arrival coincides with the final day of the Open.

"We have an agent in place who will be your contact. His recent signals are ringing alarm bells in Virginia. He is working in the math department of the university in conjunction with some wind power project. Stefan Zelinsky is his name.

"Oh, I almost forgot. Nobody is expecting you in St Andrews. So the first thing you do is establish your status on the Faculty as of right. There was no time to go through the normal channels."

Suddenly they were out of the trees, and Glen could see the sparkling sea with the islands in the distance and small craft dotted on the water. Moments later they were passing Bellingham and the scenery had changed again to much flatter agricultural land.

"One thing I'd like, but I know it's difficult to find at short notice," Glen ventured. "Have you any written material on which I can bone up?"

"I got a St Andrews University Calendar from Washington State, a book called 'St Andrews, Home of Golf', from a friend in real estate, who's fanatical about the game, and some tourist material from various travel agents. Anything else?"

"Yes. Who has the Company decided should be expecting me at the university and how will he be expected to accept me at such short notice?"

"Your academic contact is Campbell MacLaren, a senior lecturer in the Economics Department. He has done several regional analyses including some specific to tourism, is a consultant to the Scottish Tourist Board, and has several publications to his credit, mainly on regional development. Just as well you know your stuff."

As soon as they rejoined Highway 99 on the Canadian side of the Peace Arch, it became the Sovereign's highway, and to prove it, a crown topped the signpost, and, even better, the name became 'King George Highway'.

Without any prompting Chuck continued, "You are going there as the first Bobby Jones Foundation Fellow. If you don't know about Bobby Jones, you better learn fast.

"Obviously, a lot of these arrangements had to be made retrospectively. The Fellowship smoothed things a lot. Tomorrow we quote from fictitious correspondence. Your first job is to put files in place so that the correspondence is no longer fictitious. They're in that package I prepared for you." Chuck paused for breath.

They sped across the flat Fraser Delta, minutes relentlessly ticking away. The road merged into the Vancouver-Blaine Freeway and flew over the Fraser River as elegantly as any Florida skyway.

One more bridge and they reached Vancouver Airport on Sea Island with bilingual signs everywhere indicative of Canada's distinctive culture – French to placate the nearest Quebecois over two thousand miles away, but no native language for the Airport's nearest neighbours.

It was 7.15 as they drove up the ramp to the departure gates.

"No need to bid fond farewells," Chuck grinned. "Your luggage is light. Go straight to the Wardair desk. You're expected."

He drew up at the kerb. Then he stretched over to the back seat, clutched at something and handed Glen a plastic carrier bag.

"Here's your reading material and the correspondence files you have to burgle in reverse."

Glen scrambled out of the car, clutching his small bag, his coat and Chuck's tourist pack.

CHAPTER 7

Glen tested the next position on the wall with his foot and stretched towards the roof of the single-storey sandstone projection. Taking a firm grip on the rone-pipe to steady himself, he paused to make certain that his spine did not jar and sure-footedly completed his move.

Crouched in the shadow where the roof abutted the higher wall, he scanned the marquees and trailer vans cluttering the landscape between his position and the beach a hundred yards to the north. Nothing stirred. No one challenged him.

The transcontinental and transatlantic flight into Prestwick that morning, followed by a two-hour drive in a small car on the wrong side of the road had not helped his injured spine. He flexed and relaxed his back muscles as he watched and listened.

No alarm came from the inexperienced security guards, hired only for the duration of the Open.

Assured that he was unobserved, he straightened, grabbed the next rone-pipe and hauled himself on to the roof of the Royal and Ancient Golf Club.

Hidden from most directions by the irregular silhouette of the roof, he stole wraith-like to the south-east corner.

The bright foil round the edge of the fanlight glass proclaimed a deterrent to all would-be burglars. Glen was undeterred.

Before tackling the security catch, he scrutinised the bus parked fifty yards away on a roped-off area of grass. From its black and white diced waistline he identified it as the mobile police headquarters despite its archaic self-description of Fife Constabulary.

Glen wondered whether such a force would be able to cope with security at the Open, if the latter event turned out to be as big an affair as Chuck had suggested. Glen satisfied himself that the vehicle was unoccupied.

The only sound, as he lifted the heavy fanlight, was his own breathing. He slipped silently through the narrow gap and dropped lightly to the floor.

From the full description of the building in one of the booklets he had read on the plane, he knew the exact position of the strong-room on the ground floor crammed with its valuable collection of silver and gold trophies. Plenty of wealthy collectors would be prepared to pay a king's ransom for the old claret jug that came out once a year to be awarded to the Open winner, not to mention the other baubles, such as the gold golf balls presented to the Club by its Royal Captains.

More accessible valuables were the paintings. Top of the list was the one presented to the club by Lord Boothby.

Ignoring them all, he glided to the administration area.

Inside the Secretary's office, he inspected the filing cabinets before choosing one. He picked the lock in the top right-hand corner of the unit and pulled open the second drawer.

The files were neatly labelled. With the help of a minute pencil torch, he picked out one marked 'R.A. Jones – Exchange Students'.

From his inside jacket pocket he took a slim plastic tube and, with his index finger, withdrew a single sheet of typed A4 paper. It was crease-free. He laid it on the Secretary's wide desk and folded it neatly in three, typed surface inside, as though ready for an envelope. He opened it out again, slipped it into the 'R.A. Jones' file, closed the drawer and locked the cabinet before leaving the building as silently and unencumbered as he had entered it.

Fifteen minutes later and a quarter of a mile away, he had made a much simpler forced entry; on this occasion, into a much less secure building of the University of St Andrews.

His advance information was every bit as reliable as it had been for his visit to the R&A.

Making straight for the general office of the Economics Department, he opened the door with minimum difficulty and crossed to the stationery cupboard. He scanned the shelves and picked out a box of new folders for the filing system. He took one and, from a box beside it, a plastic label-holder and a leaf of labels.

Seated at the nearest desk, he took the cover off a typewriter, wound the top label into place and typed out, 'R.A. Jones Fellowship'.

He replaced the remainder of the labels and locked the cupboard door.

From his pocket he took the plastic tube, removed a second letter, scanned it quickly and folded it as before. Opening it out, he inserted it in the file he had labelled.

He opened the correspondence filing cabinet, made a space among the files and slotted the 'R.A. Jones Fellowship' in the correct alphabetical sequence.

He made one further visit on his way back to his hired Ford Sierra parked inconspicuously by the quaint old harbour, nestling under the high walls of the once magnificent cathedral.

As he drew away he checked his watch. Half-past two, and already he could see the sheen of dawn above the North Sea. His timing had needed every minute of the short hours of darkness in a Scottish July. He still had half-an-hour drive across the Tay Bridge to Dundee.

CHAPTER 8

Glen spent the remainder of the night in the Earl Grey Hotel on the edge of Dundee's waterfront.

To cover his tracks he phoned Hertz and asked them to collect the Sierra he had hired at Prestwick Airport.

Half-an-hour later Avis brought a blue Cavalier 2.0Gli to where we was waiting outside Dundee railway station.

At 11 a.m. Glen drove back into St Andrews past the silver and gold sandstone facades of North Street.

He parked his car on the cobbled area of pavement outside Deanscourt, a residence for postgraduate students at St Andrews University.

He closed the car door firmly and picked up his flight bag, taking care not to jerk his back.

It would take more than a sore back to detract from his finding out why Zelinsky had sent his urgent message to the Company in Arlington.

July was a good month to be away from Florida's humid heat. In fact, next to September it was the best month to be out of Florida, since humidity was preferable to hurricanes.

In the hallway, without pausing, he checked Zelinsky's name on the in/out board. It was an easy name to find on an alphabetical list. He was out, but Glen made a mental note of his room number.

There was no sign of a reception desk in the medieval-style vestibule with its scaled down baronial sandstone walls and oak panels, recessed doors and arches. He took a few steps on the bare wooden boards before moving on to the small oriental-style rug in the middle of the floor to reduce the echoing clatter of his shoes.

Light footsteps sounded on the stair, and a maid appeared round the corner, her arms laden with linen.

She smiled, "Good morning," her voice giving the final syllable a distinctive lilt. "Can I help you?"

"My name's Glen – Colin Glen. I'm supposed to be moving in."

"Of course! I should have known. In fact, I've just been getting your room ready. I should have recognised your accent, but we get so many Americans here, sometimes I don't notice."

She put the linen down on a table. "I'll show you where your room is."

It was smaller than he was accustomed to, but with the charm of irregular shapes and sizes of walls and a window made up of tiny panes of glass deeply set in a thick stone Gothic arch.

"You mentioned lots of Americans. Are there any here now?" he asked.

"Plenty in St Andrews, but we've only one staying in Deanscourt. He's Dr Zelinsky. I never thought names like that were American until I heard of Kojak and Starsky."

"And now I'll leave you to settle in," she added as she made for the door.

As soon as her footsteps had faded on the stairs, Glen went to Zelinsky's room and slipped a plain, sealed envelope under the door.

Inside was a piece of paper marked in advance with ten digits. Only Zelinsky would know they were a six-figure map reference followed by a specific time on the twenty-four-hour clock.

Downstairs again, Glen made a point of asking the first person he met how to get to the Economics Department and listened attentively as though he had never been there before.

Within five minutes he was being ushered into Campbell MacLaren's office, two doors along from the general office where he had made his additions to the files a few hours earlier.

MacLaren stood up formally as his secretary introduced Glen. As their eyes met, Glen automatically registered that MacLaren was of similar height to himself, neither of them quite making the six-foot mark.

"Dr MacLaren, this is Dr. Glen from the University of Florida."

"Colin," Glen added, extending his hand. "Please call me Colin."

"How do you do?" MacLaren murmured.

As his secretary withdrew, MacLaren's face, as he gestured Glen towards a deep leather chair, although solemn, was as uncreased as his impeccably cut tweed jacket.

"Please sit down," he invited, and waited for Glen to be seated before resuming his own upright chair behind the heavy oak desk, carefully hitching his trousers to protect the sharp crease. Before he settled in his chair he smoothed the hacking tails of his jacket with the backs of his hands. Glen noted that, like himself, MacLaren lacked the pallor of the academic. His choice of tweed suit was suggestive of the businessman on a leisure visit to the country, but the variegated mahogany brown shoes that twinkled below the pedestal desk betrayed a military fondness for spit and polish.

His hair was neatly trimmed as though to curb its natural waves. The intrusion of grey helped Glen to estimate the man opposite to be about fifty.

With a touch of reprimand in his voice, MacLaren said, "You have us at a bit of a disadvantage. Afraid there has been a breakdown in communications somewhere. No recollection of the arrangement here. Fortunate your colleague phoned from Florida to say you were on your way. As it is, preparations are rather tentative."

"I'm sorry to be a nuisance. I don't know what could have happened. I made my application for the Bobby Jones Fellowship real early and had confirmation months ago," Glen lied with the confidence of one who knew he had all the necessary evidence in place.

"More distressing for you than for us. Never mind. We'll iron it out."

"Miss Fleming, my secretary, was willing to swear it was the University's central administration to blame for not consulting us. Couldn't believe her eyes when she discovered a copy of the arrangements on file in her own office."

Glen clucked sympathetically in an effort to prevent himself smiling at the thought of Miss Fleming's consternation caused by his nocturnal filing.

"Checked with central office at College Gate. Had a full file on your application."

"Certainly shouldn't have forgotten a Bobby Jones Fellow," MacLaren continued. "First one we've had in Economics, you know. Come to think of it. Quite appropriate - the work you'll be doing."

Glen agreed, "The impact of the Open Championship on the vicinity of St Andrews is a neat exercise and ties in with the tourism project I was doing at Cocoa."

"Rather interested in this line of work myself," MacLaren continued. "Yes, indeed. Conducted a fairly big survey in conjunction with the 1978 Open here. Lots of material and resources ready to hand. Make up for our shortcomings on preparation for you. Growth industry this leisure. Lots of scope for our discipline."

Glen thanked him, but the last thing he wanted was to have a locally based colleague breathing down his neck. "I'll be glad of any help, but I don't wish to impose."

"Too many plus points to call it imposition. Working in golf is a pleasure. A double pleasure with the name of Bobby Jones. You know, he was a freeman of St Andrews. The greatest honour a city can bestow. A brilliant golfer and a perfect gentleman. Take it you're a golfer - choosing this Fellowship, and it choosing you, so to speak?"

"I play, but I'd hardly describe myself as a golfer."

"Not so modest now. What's your handicap?"

"Well, I did get it down to four at one time, but I guess I'm out of practice right now."

"Practice can easily be provided here. Older than you. Fifty-five next birthday. Still play below double figures. Probably give you twenty years in age. Could have a good round together."

"You're dead right about my age, but I'd placed you at least five years younger."

"No point in letting yourself go to seed if you've led an active life. Golf and squash nowadays. Used to be skiing and climbing. Still do a little. Picked them up in the army. First time I met your chaps - Americans. Went to the other side of the world. Korea. Good bunch."

"Did you teach or do research in Korea?"

"Hardly. Fought. In the Argylls. Infantry regiment, you know. Korean War. Before your time. Did intelligence work with some of your chaps. Debriefing and that. More exciting than this job. What an upturn in their economy! Fine study for you there. Wouldn't mind going back. Showing my age. Nostalgic. Sorry. Back to business. Get you set up here in no time. Office, materials, resources, contacts. You name it. No problem. First things first, though. Take you to the R&A - Royal and Ancient. Golf Club, you know. They'll want to meet you, of course. You're their guest as well as ours."

"That would be just dandy, but right now I'm a bit jet-lagged. Can we leave it for a day?"

"Certainly. Very thoughtless. Time to unpack and all that."

Miss Fleming opened the door, knocking on it as she did so.

"I've been on the phone to the R & A. Part of the mystery is solved. They hadn't opened a file for the Fellowship. They had just put the correspondence into the R.A. Jones – Exchange Students file. You would think they would have been more careful, since Dr Glen is the first Fellow."

CHAPTER 9

The central heating had long been switched off at the University, and the last thing St Andrews needed was air-conditioning, even in the middle of summer. Nevertheless, MacLaren was sweating profusely when Glen left.

He mopped his brow with a large colourful handkerchief, which he had drawn from the left sleeve of his tweed jacket. His concave back sagged and his shoulders hunched, as he slumped forward on his desk as though completely exhausted.

"Thank God," he whispered. "Thank God, I kept control long enough till he left."

A sob racked his body, and he began to shake. The tremors lasted for about five minutes.

There was a light tap on the door, and Miss Fleming looked in, but seeing the state of MacLaren, she withdrew silently except for a final click of the door handle.

The slight noise penetrated MacLaren's consciousness and he looked up. His face was haggard, his mouth drooped and his eyes were lifeless. The shaking stopped, and the eyes began to focus. At first, they looked exhausted and uncomprehending as he stared at the door, his face a picture of terror.

Gradually some kind of awareness began to dawn on him. He sighed heavily and pushed himself into an upright position.

"Pity he turned up from nowhere like that without any real warning. I need to prepare myself. It brings it all back. I don't like those Americans taking me by surprise like that."

He picked up his handkerchief from the floor where he had knocked it as he had sprawled across his desk and began to push it back into his sleeve. He was clumsier than usual and pushed back the double cuff of his shirt, exposing a cicatrice between it and his watch. He stared fixedly at it, then opened his cufflinks and pushed both sleeves almost to his elbow.

He stood admiring the grotesque pattern of discoloured weals and ridges that replaced the flesh of a normal limb. It was as though he was using this unsightly mess to restore his peace of mind.

As his shoulders squared again, and his haggard face became grim, then resolute and finally content, he muttered, "Damned napalm."

He deliberately focused his mind on the horror of that far-off day in that far-off country – 23rd September, 1950, on Hill 282 in Korea. What pride he had felt as a 22-year-old National Service subaltern leading his platoon consisting mainly of National Service personnel even younger than himself. Only the platoon sergeant and the corporal of number two section were older than him. Only the sergeant had been in action before Korea, but what action!

Although he had no gallantry medals, he had a chest-full of campaign ribbons. His drill instructions were inextricably interwoven with recollections of history, legend and myth of the regiment and the clans that had gone before.

He had regaled the impressionable young crofters from the Western Isles and Highlands of Scotland, shepherds from the Banks of Loch Lomond, ship-yard apprentices from the Clyde, miners from Bannockburn and clerks from Kinross with the most ferocious tales of one of the world's most renowned fighting regiments, the Argyll and Sutherland Highlanders.

He drew few distinctions in his anecdotes between those exploits, which had been reported to him and those in which he had probably taken part, but they were all imbued with a highly personalised pride and an infectious esprit de corps. But he had not told them of napalm.

He knew all the pipe tunes of the regiment, all the VCs, all the heroic battles, all the associated regiments in Canada, Australia, South Africa, New Zealand and the Indian sub-continent. But he had never heard of napalm.

What he had told them and how he had trained them helped them to fight as hard as any of their forebears to reach the top of Hill 282 against far greater numbers.

Having taken the hill they had to hold it against a counter-attack. Their ammunition was low and their casualties were high. Their position was overlooked by the enemy on higher ridges on neighbouring hills.

An air strike was called against the enemy. Recognition panels were spread out on the hill. At 12.15 three American Mustangs attacked Hill 282 with napalm and made a further attack with machine-guns. For many of the Argylls festering to death the machine guns were humanitarian aid on that unnamed hilltop. But not for the Sergeant. He was spared the impossible task of finding thoughts, far less words, to give any meaning of gallantry or bravery in face of napalm.

MacLaren had lain like the other charred corpses when the counter attack took the hill back into enemy hands.

A day passed before a knock from a spade of the burial party elicited a groan. Fortunately, the burial party had time to consider his future, time that would have been too much of a luxury in the heat of battle twenty-four hours earlier. His lieutenant's two shoulder pips were recognised. A decision was made, and MacLaren's fate was sealed.

MacLaren had difficulty in distinguishing how much of his suffering derived from the burns he had received and how much was subsequently contrived by his captors. For many months he had at least as much difficulty as the sergeant in distinguishing what he had actually experienced and what he had learned from the experience and opinions of others.

One thing he had worked out for himself after he was returned from the prisoner-of-war camp was that he had to concentrate his mind very positively before meeting Americans or before thinking about anything to do with America. Without forearming himself in this way, he found such meetings or topics always brought out the worst in him.

He sighed to himself, "Maybe I can't cure it, but I know how to make it feel better."

He unlocked the little door in the right pedestal of his desk and asked himself, "Which one will it be – Macallan, Highland Park or Laphroaig? I think it better be the Argyll one this morning." So saying, he lifted the dark bottle of Islay malt whisky and poured a moderate measure into a five-ounce Edinburgh Crystal tumbler. He savoured the vapours that rose from it, redolent with memories of peat from the island moors and seaweed from the Atlantic shores.

CHAPTER 10

Glen leaned on the railing, which ran along the edge of the tiny harbour. He was at the six-figure map reference he had slipped under Zelinsky's door at the time notified.

He was looking at the reflection of the motley collection of yachts and dinghies on the glassy water, but his attention was fixed on the fact that Zelinsky had not turned up. He scanned the faces about him again. Although he had never met Zelinsky, he had studied his photograph and knew he could pick him out in a crowd. Zelinsky was a second generation American Pole, and Glen had put him down in his memory as a typical Slav clone of Dubjek or Jaruzelski.

Five minutes having passed since their appointed time, Glen had moved to a vantage point where he could keep his eye on the opposite embankment.

Since Zelinsky's plea for assistance had brought Glen to St Andrews, he should have made every effort to contact him as arranged. But Zelinsky would not have pressed the alarm button unless he was encountering real difficulties. That knowledge added to Glen's anxiety.

He knew that Zelinsky had been placed as a research assistant in the Department of Applied Mathematics at St Andrews to give him a cover for his security role at RAF Leuchars, Britain's front line air station in the north. The RAF were more than capable of fulfilling their military role, but a political one had been thrust upon them, as Leuchars was to be the arrival point for the forthcoming meeting of NATO Defence Ministers at Gleneagles Hotel near Perth.

It was normal procedure for the Americans at least to have a counter-intelligence agent on the ground well in advance of the movement of high security VIPs. With access to the RAF Station because of the relevance of his work on wave patterns to aeroplane design, Zelinsky was an ideal man for the job.

The routine bit was easy. Now Glen had to know what had gone wrong, and only Zelinsky could tell him. Despite his impatience for Zelinsky to show, Glen reluctantly began to walk slowly up the ancient narrow road known as The Pends from the harbour to Deanscourt.

As he entered the grounds of Deanscourt, his senses were alerted to the suppressed tension within the tight little knots of academics gossiping in the courtyard.

From the first group beside the gate, he demanded, "What's up?"

One of the young men raised his head, showing hurt in his gentle, dark eyes. "It's Zelinsky," he said softly. "He's had an accident. He's dead."

Hiding his shock, Glen took the news with the solemnity to be expected of a stranger.

"What happened?" he asked.

"Fell from St Rule's Tower."

"More likely jumped," interjected a bearded opinionist. "That's it over there." He jabbed with his pipe towards the tall, isolated square tower that could be seen between the remnants of the flying buttresses in the Cathedral grounds across the road. "It happens from time to time."

"What do you mean, 'It happens from time to time'?" Glen demanded.

"Students have been known to fall. Depression. Disappointment. Failure. Bored. You name it."

"You think it was suicide?"

The cynic shrugged and gave a non-committal gesture with his pipe, "I'm only a psychologist, after all."

Glen gave a sympathetic mutter. As a stranger, it was simple enough for him to withdraw once he heard the facts. He had to use the time, while everyone was outside and before the police arrived, to examine Zelinsky's room.

The housemaids had a small service-room for linen and cleaning-equipment on each floor. There was one near Zelinsky's room. Glen tried the door. It was unlocked. There was no-one about. He went in. Overalls were hanging on the back of the door. He put his hand in the pocket of one. Nothing. He tried the next one and found what he was looking for - a pass key.

He closed the door and crossed to Zelinsky's room.

He inserted the key in the lock. It turned. He moved quickly into the room and locked the door behind him. He pocketed his own brown envelope still lying on the floor.

One look told him that Zelinsky had been playing it by the book. The room was neat and apparently undisturbed.

But a faint dusting of talcum powder on the floor had been smudged. He checked the pillow carefully. A tell-tale white thread had been moved.

Zelinsky had taken the prescribed precautions when he had realised that the opposition were about. It showed that he had expected his room to be searched.

It had been. By another expert who had got there before Glen.

Opening the top right-hand drawer in the chest below the window, Glen removed a piece of soap still apparently in its original wrapping and slipped it into his pocket. He took the shaving head off the electric razor, examined it and put it back. He knelt down at the washbasin and with his knife as a spanner removed a screw from the bottom of the U-bend, catching the trickle of water that escaped in a tumbler. As he drew out the screw, an attached piece of fuse wire came with it. He drew the wire gently and gave a sigh of satisfaction as a tiny plastic bag emerged at the end of it.

He put the plastic bag and the fuse wire in his pocket before replacing and tightening the screw. He emptied the tumbler into the basin and rinsed both.

He retreated to the door, but, before opening it, he crouched and blew the remains of the talcum powder so that no distinguishable footprints remained.

Listening for a moment, he took the pass key in his right hand and opened the door. A quick look. An empty corridor. He slipped the key into the lock on the outside. Stepped into the corridor, door closed, key turned, all in one quick movement.

Ten minutes later he was standing at the reception desk of the local police station reading posters about rabies, Colorado beetles and water safety while he waited for

Inspector Gordon to appear. Despite reminders of increasing frequency to the desk staff, it was a good half-hour before Glen's evaporating patience was rewarded.

"Good evening, sir. What can I do for you?"

Glen turned to face the Inspector, who had entered from a door behind him.

For a policeman, Glen reckoned, Gordon was on the small side. Dapper, a quaint word Glen had read some place and had never used before in his life, could describe him, his slight frame accentuated by his neat uniform, his sharp features underlined by a precisely trimmed moustache.

Glen hesitated. "I've just arrived in this country and am staying at Deanscourt. I heard about this unfortunate business concerning Zelinsky. I thought that as a fellow American I might be able to offer some help."

"That's a fine display of good citizenship. Did you have anything particular in mind that you were afraid we might omit?"

Glen recognised the defensiveness of professional pride. If Gordon's attention to his duties was anything like his attention to his uniform, all the formalities would be correctly attended to.

At his most self-effacing Glen said, "I was thinking of the personal side, Inspector, contact with the man's family, or his university, or, from the international point of view, it might be of interest to our Embassy to know that I am available. They will have a record of my proposed work here. It may just be that I could help to reduce the amount of correspondence."

Reduction in correspondence, especially with a foreign power concerned about the sudden death of one of its citizens, has a certain appeal to the official mind. Gordon was no exception.

"You'd better come into my office," he invited peremptorily, holding the door open for Glen to squeeze past him. "Upstairs at the end of the corridor."

Glen had established some usefulness and therefrom a privilege. Inside Gordon's office he took the next step, "So far, people seem to believe this is an open and shut case of suicide."

"Mr. Glen, that's my department. I don't intend discussing the matter until our investigations are complete. You gave me the impression that you had non-police tasks that you were prepared to undertake. Perhaps this meeting is premature, and you should come back later."

Glen had wasted too much time already. This policeman was going to have to be much more helpful. Glen began to press. "That's a fair observation, but I think if you contact my Embassy, they will indicate that I am an acceptable person to be consulted on their behalf - to begin with anyway."

"We are already in communication with your consul general's office in Edinburgh."

Glen waited.

Gordon hesitated, cleared his throat to assert his authority. "Aye, well, the main thing is we're both wasting each other's time and not doing the unfortunate Mr. Zelinsky any good at all."

Glen persisted, "Everyone I've heard mention Zelinsky's death takes for granted it was suicide. Is that how the police are treating it?"

Gordon's frustration showed as he lapsed into the vernacular, "Man, can you no' take a hint? I'm trying to tell you that you're not involved. I don't discuss police business with anyone that cares to walk in off the street."

He rose. If Glen would not leave of his own accord, Gordon was prepared to escort him to the door.

Glen did not follow his example. Instead he leaned back in his chair and held Gordon's angry glare with his own determined stare.

"Inspector, it will only take a few minutes to dial the Embassy and ask for this extension," he said scribbling a number on a scrap of paper torn from the Inspector's desk pad. "You will be assured I am not 'anyone off the street' and that if I offer to be involved in what you correctly regard as confidential enquiries, you will find that authorisation will be immediately forthcoming."

Gordon replaced his hat on the peg behind the door and resumed his seat. His eyes did not leave Glen's as he stretched across the desk for the scrap of paper on which Glen had written a London telephone number and extension.

He did not look at it. His eyes kept locked on Glen's.

He lifted his internal phone and pressed a button. When it was answered, he said quietly, "What is the number of the American Embassy?" He listened to the instrument, then said stiffly, "In London. All the embassies are in London." Taking the phone from his ear he held it in front of him, his left hand over the mouthpiece as he leaned forward, his elbows lightly on the table. Neither of the men spoke.

In the silence of the office, it was easy to hear when a voice came through the phone again.

Gordon lifted it to his ear. "Go ahead," he said.

Holding Glen's scrap of paper in front of him, he checked it against the number coming over the phone.

"Right. Ring that number and ask for extension ...."

But seeing Glen shake his head, he changed his instruction. "Just get that number."

He hung up.

"No need to let that extension number get to anyone else."

"That could be construed as a lack of confidence in my staff, but I'll not take umbrage on their behalf - yet," Gordon stated sardonically.

The phone rang. Gordon's hand shot out and snatched it up. His tension was showing.

"American Embassy?" Pause. "Put me through to this extension." He read out the number.

The extension was answered the moment it rang.

"Good evening. Inspector Gordon of Fife Police. I'm phoning from St Andrews. I have with me in my office a Mr. Colin Glen. One of your citizens has been involved in a fatality. Mr. Glen is also American. He is trying to persuade me that in some way he should be involved on your behalf and has asked me to telephone you."

Gordon listened attentively for a moment.

"Are you a doctor?" Gordon asked Glen.

"I have a doctorate - not medical, of course."

"He's Dr. Glen," Gordon confirmed.

Gordon's expression changed for the first time. He raised his eyebrows in surprise as he handed the phone across the desk to Glen. "Your friend wants to hear your voice."

Glen took the phone and spoke impersonally. "This is Dr. Colin Glen, at present on a Bobby Jones Fellowship at St Andrews University," and handed the phone straight back to Gordon, and whispered to Gordon, "I can be identified by my voice print."

Glen watched Gordon's jaw tightening as he absorbed the reply from the Embassy.

"That may be so, but it doesn't give me any reason for discussing a case with him while it is still under investigation," Gordon replied tartly.

Gordon was silent and attentive to the instrument again.

"I'll need more than that," he snapped.

Consternation was beginning to show on Gordon's face.

"They seem to know you; they seem to approve of you; they even seem to think you can be useful in some way. But I still have no justification, or, from my point of view, any reason whatsoever for discussing this matter or any other matter with you, Dr. Glen."

"It may take a few minutes. After all, the wheels have just been set in motion. While we're waiting, I wonder if I may use your washroom?"

"Why not?" Gordon sighed. "You'll see it at the end of the corridor."

When he had locked the toilet door behind him, Glen took from his pocket the bar of soap and the tiny plastic bag he had retrieved from Zelinsky's room. He unwrapped the soap and slipped the wrapper back into the same pocket. He took out his knife, opened it and gently probed the 'o' of toilet. Nothing happened. He probed the 'o' of soap. It moved. A little gentle persuasion with the end of the blade and he eased out a minute plug of soap followed by a tiny roll of microfilm.

Picking up the film he opened it out. It was covered with microfiche script. It would have to wait till he took it to an appropriate instrument in the University Library. He took out a box of matches, wound the film round a single match, returned it to the box and put the box back in his pocket.

Cutting the bar of soap into several pieces, he dropped them into the bowl of the toilet. He took the wrapper from his pocket and tore it up before dropping all the pieces in beside the soap.

Then he turned his attention to the little plastic bag and withdrew a piece of paper that had been folded several times. Opened out, it was much bigger than the film, and the minute writing could be read by the naked eye.

He scanned the writing, quickly at first, then more carefully, mouthing some of the words as he committed them to memory.

It was dated four days earlier and must have been written at the same time as Zelinsky had signalled Washington for support. The Company had moved fast to get Glen into position, but not fast enough. The only clue was mention of doubts about security at Edzell, wherever that was.

He read the message once more, then tore up the paper and flushed it away with the rest of the debris in the bowl.

He waited till the water settled to make sure that nothing remained.

Gordon was leaning on his desk, his left hand supporting his forehead, as he completed a form. He looked up as Glen entered, and at the same moment the phone rang.

"Gordon here."

He paused and listened.

"Good evening, Superintendent."

Glen watched intently as Gordon's face puckered in surprise as he listened to his superior.

"If the Home Office is really involved, we'll need written confirmation. I needn't remind you, sir, that we should make sure no lines are crossed or omitted with the Scottish Home Office. Sometimes London tends to forget we have our own hierarchy up here."

Gordon nodded, looking slightly less tense. "Thank you, sir."

The indignation had left his expression, and he was nodding again, apparently more at home with the tone of the conversation now. "That was my impression, sir. Very much a routine matter."

"Very good, sir. I'll ensure that he knows he must deal only with me and not in front of any other officers." He hung up.

Gordon leaned his elbows on his desk and clasped his hands in front of his chin. He looked almost complacent compared with his earlier tension.

"Well, Dr. Glen, it seems I am authorised to tell you about investigations concerning Zelinsky's death, though I can't for the life of me see why you're so interested."

It was Glen's turn to assert his authority. "Depend upon it. Otherwise, would you have received that kind of clearance so quickly, if at all?"

"Accepted. To put it bluntly, everything points to suicide. We are proceeding on that assumption, but nothing is taken entirely for granted. I have an open mind as to whether it was suicide or accident. There were no witnesses, and it is difficult to fathom possible motives when he was a relative stranger."

Gordon leaned back as though, having discharged all the duties assigned to him by his superior, he was going to relax, but Glen was far from satisfied.

"There must be some people who knew him well enough to say whether he was depressed or in any kind of difficulty."

"His research supervisor tells us that his thesis was proceeding well. Outside his work he spent a lot of time on his own. He seemed to do a lot of walking."

"Do you pass this information to the coroner for him to take into account in his court?"

"We don't have coroners in this part of the world," Gordon retorted briskly.

"Do the police have full jurisdiction, then?"

"In Scotland these matters go to the procurator fiscal. He initiates an inquiry if he is not satisfied with the evidence presented in the first instance. He is also responsible for prosecuting on behalf of the Crown, or, as you would say, on behalf of the State. In this respect your system of a district attorney has much more in common with Scotland than with England, although there is a move afoot at present to bring England into line with our more progressive nations."

The twinkle in Gordon's severe blue eyes betrayed the pleasure his little homily had given him.

"Is the procurator likely to accept your suggestion that this was suicide?"

"I'm not suggesting to him that it is suicide. My report will indicate that there were no suspicious circumstances, which means no involvement of a third party. He died as the result of a fall from a tower 180 feet high. There were no witnesses. He could easily have been taking photographs and overbalanced. His camera was found on the observation platform. It was ready for use. It's up to the fiscal to record that he died by misadventure. If there was any doubt and the possibility of a prosecution later, he would ask for an open verdict."

Gordon evidently wanted something in return now and stabbed in the sudden policeman's question, "Would you recommend an open verdict?"

It was the second last thing Glen wanted. With criminal enquiries going on, life could become very complicated for counter-espionage.

He replied with conviction, "I don't see any call for that. Why not settle for a suicide verdict and stop pussyfooting around?"

Gordon seemed to switch the subject completely when he asked with dead serious face, "Are you a religious man?"

Glen was taken aback. "I've been to church. I guess nowadays I'm a vague kind of Protestant; part Episcopal, part Presbyterian, maybe Lutheran, most of it inherited from my parents."

"However unattractive suicide may be to these Christian traditions, it would not be held to be a mortal sin. In Scotland, because we don't have such a variety of religions as I believe you have in America, we can keep a track of how these things affect people. Zelinsky was a practising Roman Catholic. The local Catholic population has many ex-patriate Poles. There is no point in the police saying suicide when we are not one hundred per cent certain and would have great difficulty in proving it. Therefore the outcome is not changed by a verdict of misadventure and no unnecessary offence caused.

"Besides, I believe his mother is alive in Chicago and presumably will be seeking the solace of her church and religion. He was unmarried and didn't carry significant life insurance. So his insurance company is unlikely to complain or mount an investigation which would cost them far more than they could possibly save.

"I try to take as much as possible into account. As I said at the outset, if you know of anything I may have omitted which you consider pertinent to the cause of death, I'm prepared to reassess everything."

Glen was struck by the humanity of the man as well as his efficiency. In a very short time he had put together a remarkable number of facts about Zelinsky. No doubt, given any hint of Zelinsky having a more complex life, he would have been determined to do more unravelling. Glen had no intention of giving such a hint. He also knew it would be tactically sound to share some confidence with Gordon. After all, the place would be crawling with police during the Open, and a good relationship with the local chief could do no harm.

"You realise my excuse for a private conversation was just to get us out of the public office. Besides, you would not have been very impressed by 'anyone off the street' demanding that you phone the American Embassy. You see, Zelinsky's research had a military side to it in aircraft design. He wasn't tops, but you can't ignore anything in that field. It's also important to get his papers and records back as quickly as possible to his own research director in the States. May I ask you to attend to that as a priority?"

Gordon's piercing blue eyes sparkled as he proffered his hand. "Aye, you wouldn't have got over the doorstep if you'd started with the second part of the story. But mind, as well as the official bit, I would be quite happy if you wrote one or two of these letters you offered to."

After Glen left his office, Gordon sat in silence for a couple of minutes before lifting his phone and speaking to the desk sergeant. "Has he left?"

"Just out the door, sir."

He pressed the telephone rest and released it, then dialled HQ at Dysart.

A female voice answered, "Fife Police Headquarters. Can I help you?"

"Inspector Gordon for the Superintendent."

The phone at the other end was lifted the moment it rang. "Miller here."

"Good evening again, sir. Glen has the gist of the report I submitted verbally to you earlier. He seemed satisfied with everything I said, and maybe a wee bit relieved. My men are all off the case now as you instructed. I'm just finishing my report. Do you wish me to mention Glen in it?"

"No, his visit was after the event. Keep the Home Office approval in your personal file. It's only to indemnify you. You'll be going off duty now. Will you be at home if I want to contact you?"

"Aye. It's too late for a round of golf at this time, "Gordon replied ruefully.

"Don't complain. I never had the luck to be posted to St Andrews."

CHAPTER 11

Throughout the telephone conversation between Miller and Gordon, the eyes of the second man in Miller's shabby office never left Miller's face.

He leaned forward intently as Miller put down the phone and changed his tone from one of command to one of deference. "Gordon's local lads won't cause you any trouble now. It could have been awkward if that American had wanted to stir up the Zelinsky death. Do you think he's in the same team? No need to ask. You wouldn't tell me even if you knew - which you probably do."

"Thanks, John," was all that Commander Donald Ross from Special Branch at New Scotland Yard was prepared to say.

Although he had a high professional regard for the tall, gangling man opposite him, Ross always found him a difficult conversationalist unable to pitch the tone at the right level, his mobile Adam's apple and flushed cheeks giving him the appearance of being constantly embarrassed.

Ross was a tall, straight-backed man with the complexion of a healthy farmer and the responsibility for the security of the nation's most prominent people and most important overseas visitors.

"I can't rise to your bait, John, but you know who we're expecting, and we can't afford to let anything go wrong. You've already put a stop to all leave for the middle of July."

"That's for the Open," Miller replied mischievously, and his Adam's apple shot all over the place like a ball on a bagatelle board.

"Aye, part of it, but remember to keep the piggy-bank full," he warned as he rose.

"You'll need every penny for the extra overtime," was his parting shot. Metropolitan life had not robbed Ross of his native Scottish canniness.

It was second nature for Ross to move on quickly to avoid protracted conversations even with senior colleagues. As a man of few words himself, he regarded unguarded confidences as among the greatest unintended dangers to his clients.

An unmarked Rover sat in the corner of the visitors' car park, a civilian driver behind the wheel.

As Ross moved quietly into the nearside back seat, the driver said, "The Under-Secretary wants you to call him. He says he likes to keep tabs on you when you operate north of the Border."

Ross sighed. The Under-Secretary of State for Scotland with responsibility for the Scottish Department of Home Affairs couldn't care less about the separation of police powers between Scotland and England. He was an avid Westminster careerist who interfered only to be officious and try to put himself on a par from time to time with the Home Secretary.

Ross guessed that the telephone exchange with the American Embassy had reached his ears. Since he had almost as much contact with the Foreign Office as with the Home Office, Ross thanked his lucky stars that Scotland did not have an Under-Secretary of State for Foreign Affairs.

He lifted the car phone and dialled a London number.

"Get me all you can on a Dr. Colin Glen, an academic economist employed by the CIA, at present on exchange at St Andrews University. Urgent."

He put the phone back in its cradle and lifted it again. This time he dialled an Edinburgh number.

A dull bureaucratic voice answered.

"Commander Ross here. The Under-Secretary wants me to contact him. Ask him if I can have ten minutes of his time tomorrow morning. He has my number."

He replaced the phone, unzipped a briefcase that lay on the seat beside him, switched on a light on a flexible metal stem, adjusted it, and began to study a thick sheaf of papers.

He was halfway through page seven as the car sped on to the Forth Road Bridge. He looked out the window. Below, on the west side of the Fife shore, in the slightly fading light, grey ships blended with the shore installations of Rosyth Royal Naval Dockyard. Opposite, on the south shore, the glow of the north-westerly sun silhouetted the irregular heights and shapes of Grangemouth refinery.

To the east, the Rail Bridge shone with an enhanced ruddy glow, and, beyond it, near the southern shore, a super-tanker was discharging its cargo of North Sea Oil. When Ross considered the amount of organisation and co-operation necessary to achieve such development he had no doubt in his mind that he would always strive to maintain a well-ordered world.

The phone's bleep distracted him from the scene.

"Ross," he answered.

"Good evening, Commander. This is Philips, Department of Home Affairs. The Under-Secretary would like you to meet him in the Holiday Inn, Glasgow, tomorrow at 4.30 p.m."

Ross muttered something rude.

"Pardon?" Philips asked primly.

"Just checking my diary," Ross explained. "Sorry, I can't make it then."

"The Under-Secretary will not be very pleased about that."

"Possibly, but I'll be in Perthshire with the Secretary of State at three. That's why I asked for a morning appointment with your man."

"I'll see what I can do," offered Philips, and the phone clicked.

"Pompous ass!" Ross complained to himself.

The car reached a tollbooth at the southern end of the Bridge, and the driver was handing over the 30p charge, when the phone bleeped again. The toll-collector looked surprised as he heard the sound through the driver's open window.

Ross waited until the car had pulled away before he answered.

A voice, which did not identify itself, said, "A preliminary enquiry has been made concerning Dr. Colin Glen. American citizen, born Oregon. Father born

43

Britain, emigrated as child with parents. Mother American born. Bachelor's degree in economics 'summa cum laude' at age twenty. Started doctorate on Mexican migration to Southern California.

"Gave up to study Spanish at the University of Mexico. Appears to have worked on doctorate concurrently with studies in Mexico City, for he completed it one year after graduating in Spanish. Expert on Spanish American dialects. Involved in covert activities on behalf of US government in Latin America and within the US. Has acted as consultant at highest level. Believed to have been partially responsible for lack of enthusiasm shown by some US officials at UN for British stance during Falklands crisis. Assigned to Europe for short spells, mainly Spain.

"Uses academic cover. Respected economic authority on regional development, migration and tourism. Publications in learned journals creditable, but not outstanding. Last known assignment Cocoa Campus of the University of Florida - academic: tourism and the space programme, security: Cuban militants. Question. Is a more extensive investigation required?"

"Hold on." Ross clamped his large hand over the mouthpiece. He leaned back in the corner of his seat and mused to himself, "What the blazes is someone with his background doing over here?" His frown intensified for a minute. Then it unfurled like a sail unreefed after a storm. Taking his hand away from the mouthpiece, he spoke into the phone. "Two points. One, get me his golf handicap. Repeat, golf handicap. Two, maximum details of travel to and work to do in St Andrews."

The car sped past the entrance to Army Headquarters (Scottish Command) and crossed the city boundary into Edinburgh.

44

CHAPTER 12

Ten minutes after leaving Inspector Gordon, Glen knocked on the presbytery door of St James' Catholic Church on The Scores. He was about to knock again, when the door was opened by a tiny floral extravaganza of a woman.

"Good evening?" she lilted interrogatively.

"Is the priest available, please? I'd like to have a word with him."

"No. He's at a Parish Council meeting, but he won't be long. It's usually over by this time. Would you like to come in and wait?"

Glen accepted the invitation and the offer of a cup of tea, which followed.

"If you'd like to wait in the sitting-room," she said, leading him into a small hallway and opening a door for him. "I'll have the tea in a jiffy, and Father Mackellar will almost certainly be back in time to join you in a cup."

Only when he sat down in the comfortable armchair did Glen realise how tired he was. He had lost all track of time and felt like a gyro spinning independent of the earth's time zones.

His sense of time was not helped by the speed with which she returned laden with a tray heaped with scones, cakes, pancakes, butter and jam as well as teapot, sugar, cream jug, cups, plates, knives and teaspoons.

"I didn't mean to put you to any trouble," Glen apologised.

She beamed at him with great satisfaction. "I was right. Father Mackellar's just finished his meeting."

"I didn't hear him come in."

"Oh, the meeting was just next door in the Church."

A round-faced man in a cassock appeared through the door, rubbing his hands briskly as though he was cold.

"Good evening, good evening," he chirruped. "I'm glad to see Mrs. MacDonald is looking after you."

"You smelt the tea as usual, Father," she teased him. "Now, I'll leave you both to enjoy it." And she withdrew.

The priest dispensed the hospitality of Mrs. MacDonald's laden tray with liberality and enjoyed his own share with gusto. With a wave of his hand and the refrain, "We can't be expected to work on an empty stomach," he dismissed all Glen's attempts to explain the purpose of his visit.

At last, while he supped his third cup of tea, he was ready to discuss Glen's business.

Glen explained that he had been shocked by Zelinsky's death and upset by the dismissive way it had been passed off by one or two people. Having learned that Zelinsky had attended St James', he wondered if the priest could help him come to terms with their apparent callousness.

The spark in Father Mackellar's little eyes changed voltage, betraying the shrewdness of one who had entered a guessing game, despite his amiable hospitality.

"Stefan was a good boy and a clever scientist, and, in the best sense of the words, he was a good Catholic. Having said that, I think I have told you an enormous amount about him, but perhaps you had something more specific in mind." He paused. "But before you ask your other questions, you must judge how dependable my answers may be. The best way for you to judge my knowledge of Stefan is for you to decide whether I can tell you anything about yourself.

"You are not one of our Faith. You have not been entirely truthful in your reasons for wanting to know about Stefan, but you are genuine in your concern. You share something with Stefan - a sense of duty. If what I say is true, it may be worth your while to ask me your questions, if not, you can dismiss them as the foolish talk of a doddering old man."

Glen smiled. "If I was as smart as you, I wouldn't have to ask others for the answers."

Glen knew from his briefing that St Andrews had a large population of Polish ex-servicemen who had settled there after the war, but he framed his question to avoid betraying this knowledge. "Back home in the States there would be plenty people of Polish extraction to rally round, but he might have felt isolated here if he had no-one of his own people to turn to."

Mackellar sighed. "Ah, that's where you are mistaken. There is a plaque on the wall of the town hall and a statue to General Sikorsky, the wartime Polish leader, in Kinburn Park. This was an important base for the Polish army during the war, and many ex-servicemen stayed on here rather than return to a Russian-occupied Poland. Their community is now becoming less homogeneous. The original ex-servicemen and their families are growing older. Their forms of nostalgia and loyalty are less relevant to the young people who have lived all their lives in this country and in many cases married into Scottish families. It's sad to see differences of opinion hurt the older people harder than the normal generation gap because they are cut off from their roots and remember a Poland which most of their own generation living in Poland today would have difficulty in recalling." He sighed heavily. "I should know. I have the same difficulty when I visit my native land of Morar in the West Highlands and see the changes, and even hear them in the lack of Gaelic spoken there today compared with sixty years ago."

While he spoke, Glen's linguistic ear puzzled over Mackellar's speech, not just the distinctive accent, but the form of delivery. He had seemed foreign, but his name was Scottish. There was the explanation. He was not a native English speaker, although British born and bred.

"I say this, so that you won't make the mistake of regarding anything said by one or two members of the Polish community as being a consensus. In fact, it is wrong of me to talk about 'the Polish community'. It is entirely integrated and completely accepted by the indigenous population. Some of them are involved in very Scottish institutions like the Robert Burns Club, the Scottish National Party and so on.

"Stefan did visit one or two homes and I'll give you the names and addresses, and he had other invitations, but he didn't have time to take up all the offers.

"There has also been a temporary or transient Polish population, probably drawn to St Andrews by the permanent contacts here. It is interesting to note the degree of acceptability, which the local Poles extend to them. If there is any hint that they are sponsored in the slightest way by the present communist regime, or are sympathetic towards it, they are virtually ostracised by the locals, sometimes, I know for a fact, with no justification. At other times, I am in no position to say.

"There is one Polish national in Scotland at present who claims that he cannot return to Poland because of his activities in Solidarity before he came to study for a year in the Department of Slavonic Studies at Glasgow University. He comes through to St Andrews occasionally, but he seems to suffer from a credibility gap with the locals. I mention him because he visited Stefan several times.

"Now I must ask you a serious question. Is it at all possible that Stefan might have been less than surprised by your visit and the interest you are showing in his affairs? You see, it is part of my business to understand what people are trying to say despite the obscure way in which they sometimes weave their words. It is rather like recognising a man by the tartan he is wearing. The weave of your tartan, or as you would call it, plaid, is very similar to Stefan's."

"Stefan and I had never met, but he knew that I would be coming to St Andrews. If he had lived, we would have been helping each other."

The priest nodded slowly. "I should probably never have noticed it, if you had not talked of Stefan, but, as soon as you did, I could sense you had some common purpose." The priest lapsed into a thoughtful silence, which Glen respected.

Then he said, his face screwed up with exaggerated anguish, "The only other person I should mention to you is Major diMaggio who is stationed with the American Navy at Edzell. He was important in some way to Stefan, but I cannot say how, and I can only pray that I am doing the right thing for all three of you in mentioning his name."

Edzell! This was the kind of break Glen was looking for. He watched Father Mackellar's face relax into its former glow as he sensed some easing of the burden weighing on the man opposite him.

Glen tried not to betray his sudden interest, as he said, "I'll try to make a point of contacting him."

"Before you go," Mackellar ventured, "remember that I am here to offer moral support as well as spiritual. You would be more comfortable with yourself if you were less intense."

Glen tried to laugh it off. "I didn't know it showed."

"It shows. And remember, if I can see it, others, perhaps less well disposed, may as well."

CHAPTER 13

When Glen arrived at the Economics Department, Miss Fleming was tidying the mail. She looked up and smiled.

"Dr MacLaren will be in at nine. He's always very punctual," she said with a touch of pride in her voice. "I'll show you the room you'll be using."

It was a small office made by dividing a larger room with thin partition walls. The window gave an uninspiring view of slated roofs crowding close to the glass. The buildings might be quaint on the outside, he mused, but you sure have to pay for it in cramped quarters.

He pointed to the phone on the desk and asked, "Is that an outside line?"

"Oh, yes. As a visiting researcher your calls will go through the University's central switchboard, of course. Senior members of staff have their own direct lines, but everyone else has to use this system. You can dial any number in the local area direct, but if a number begins with a zero, you have to ask the internal exchange to connect you. You dial zero and, when the telephonist answers, you give the number you want and your own extension number. You hang up the receiver, and she rings back when she's made the connection.

"It's an economy measure," she added, with a nod.

Glen could tell that Miss Fleming approved of economy measures. He also realised he had to change his working and living accommodation, if he was to have privacy.

There was a sharp rap of fingertips outside, and MacLaren put his head round the door.

"Hope the room is acceptable," he greeted. "Won't compare with what you're used to. Best we could do in the time. Didn't expect someone as senior as yourself."

He ignored Miss Fleming, whose worshipping eyes never left his face.

"Let's pop along to mine for a minute," he invited.

When they entered the office, MacLaren took a bundle of newspapers from under his arm and laid them on his desk. "Like to keep in touch, you know," he explained as he signalled with his free hand for Glen to take a chair.

"Very unfortunate business - that young fellow-countryman of yours."

"Yes, it was real upsetting."

Glen could not leave the topic without turning it to his advantage. Zelinsky would not have objected to the lack of reverence uppermost in his mind.

"I feel I got off to a bad start. Being the only other American in Deanscourt, people may subconsciously identify me with Zelinsky. The relationship I was looking forward to with the other residents is not likely to normalise in the short time I'm going to be here. I'd like to move into other accommodation and make a fresh start."

"Quite understand. Afraid halls of residence are a bit cluttered. People on summer courses and so on. Student flats probably all let to summer visitors. All be

48

making a fortune on the Open. Note that for your report. Tell you what, I'll phone my wife."

Glen hadn't bargained for being kept under MacLaren's wing. He had wanted to choose a place for himself, but he was only too aware of the problems, which MacLaren had outlined.

MacLaren spoke to his wife. He looked doubtful for a minute. Then his face lit up and he exclaimed, "Excellent! The very thing."

He put down the phone and turned to Glen. "My wife suggests a friend's bungalow, about two miles out of town on the west side. He's going off at short notice to Cambridge for the remainder of the summer. My wife will contact them and get back to us."

"I sure appreciate that. I don't want to appear ungrateful for the arrangements you made. It's just the way circumstances have come about."

"Not at all. Understand only too well. Now you know your way about, you'll want to straighten out your thoughts and start planning your programme.

"Miss Fleming will take responsibility for any secretarial work - she'll farm it out, of course. You know the system in the departmental library. University Library is no distance away. And, of course, I am always available."

Glen rose to leave, but MacLaren had not finished. "Here's a useful list of telephone numbers and addresses I've compiled to give you a start: economists and geographers sharing our interests - Edinburgh University Geography Department is especially involved in this sort of work. You should visit them. Local golf clubs, R&A, Scottish Tourist Board and so on," he enumerated as he handed the typewritten pages to Glen.

His own room looked less stark when he returned to it. Miss Fleming must have been hoping that MacLaren would look favourably on those who helped Dr. Glen. Folders, files, paper, stationery and writing materials lay in neat piles on the desk. Several useful reference books lined a shelf at the window. A covered typewriter stood on a small table by itself. On the middle of the desk was a University Diary and Staff Handbook. Beside them lay a miniature cassette recorder with spare cassettes.

Glen quickly redistributed the items according to his own preference. He was well practised at settling into new premises. There was an organised simplicity about his work-style. It included the appearance of a management pattern which could best be summed up as mess, the heart-ache of many a secretary conditioned to believe that a systematic approach meant that information should be easily retrieved. Glen agreed, except that he was selective about who should do the retrieving. This included unwitting help by a conscientious secretary showing off her professional skill in knowing where to put her hand on everything, regardless of who asked.

He pursed his lips at the thought of the unfavourable comparison Miss Fleming was bound to make between himself and MacLaren.

He lifted the phone, dialled zero and asked for the Embassy number, which he had given Gordon the previous night. When the call was put through, he slipped a small scrambling device between the phone lead and the junction box, then asked for the same extension.

He identified himself and added, "Keep my voice profile up-to-date in case I develop a Scotch accent up here."

A drawl came back with a deliberate burr, "All phones have a Scotch accent. The pesky machine was invented by a Scotchman. Dae ye no rrememberrr?"

"OK. Here are a few things I want you to do for me," and his voice crackled with energy. "Get me a summary of the financial state of the Open Championship since 1978 when it was last held in St Andrews, any reports on its local impact at Turnberry, Lytham, Gullane and so on. Prepare comparisons between its impact on places which are primarily tourist orientated and those which are not; a report on the phenomenon of golf in Scotland; maps of golf facilities in Scotland in various hierarchies of exclusivity, access - social, physical and economic, comparative land-use values, etc.; turnover on equipment, clothes, coaching, etc.; tourism's contribution to the St Andrews area, the impact of golf on it, and the interaction between golf and other tourist attractions; complete breakdown on climate and weather as they affect golf and its seasonality, including assessment of compatible activities in the golf low season. Put a good team on to it. The material has to be written up both as an academic research paper and as a document for the European Common Market bureaucrats and politicians.

"There has been a break in continuity here and I am having difficulty in picking up the threads, so I need the department to do more than usual at this stage. But remember, I'll go through it with a fine toothcomb when I've time. I won't put my name to anything that's not first class.

"I've got to use the library here. Send me titles, authors, etc. of all books, papers, documents the team digs out, including access numbers. I don't know yet which system they use here. Give me both Dewey and Congressional till I find out. I'll also need summaries of every printed source you recommend.

"All correspondence must go out as from me in St Andrews. I'll send you a copy of the Department's notepaper. Use that format all the time. All replies to correspondence will come here, as this is the originating address. It will be photocopied and the copies sent to you daily. I'll have to keep the originals on file here.

"I'll send you some addresses to contact in the search. We must use them, since they've been recommended by the local Department chief.

"Any questions?"

Glen was agitated. He had done the one thing which he believed he was never entitled to do. He was setting up what amounted to a ghost research team. The facility was always there for him whenever he wanted to use it. In the past he resorted to some back-up when under pressure, like getting research papers annotated for him, but never before had he asked for the bulk of the work to be done from the outset.

"It's a pretty tall order," the voice at the other end observed with resignation.

"It may be a tall order to you." In the instrument at his ear Glen's voice sounded sharper than he intended, and he remembered Father Mackellar's warning, 'It shows'. He brought his voice under control and said calmly, "but to me it's a lifeline, while I swim in murky waters. I don't want to be the next guy lying on a slab. Have you any helpful suggestions?"

The voice betrayed no emotion as it replied, "I would suggest that correspondence going out from this end should have a reference to distinguish it from anything you may send out direct."

"Good idea. Something simple. Tell you. Add the initials B.J. for Bobby Jones. Also send me copies of all outgoing correspondence immediately it is sent. Vary the postal frank on the mail you send here.

"Next, get a photographer who knows golf to provide clearly annotated photos of all golfing facilities within a fifty-mile radius of St Andrews so that, if need be, I can do some simulation field studies without travelling all over the place. I want different angles, not just the postcard variety.

"Finally, arrange for me to have satellite pictures with full interpretations of defence and security installations within fifty miles of St Andrews.

"I'll leave you to get on with that. My only phone contact at present is 0334 76161. Ask for me at the Economics Department. If I'm not present, which is more than likely, Miss Fleming will take a message for me.

"Have a good day."

He hung up.

He closed his eyes meditatively and tried to relax in a yoga trance, but he didn't know the first thing about yoga and little more about relaxing.

The agent who had asked for help had not indicated what he was up against and had inconsiderately got himself killed. His academic contact was a pompous militarist, determined to get a piece of the action. His living quarters and his office had people crowding him all the time. He was increasingly coming to the opinion that he was the wrong agent in the wrong place. What on earth did his Latin American expertise have to do with this outpost on the North Sea?

CHAPTER 14

After a few moment's reflection, Glen put another call through to his Control at the Embassy.

"What gen can you give me on Marine Major diMaggio, Edzell Air Force Base?"

After a moment's hesitation, the voice at the other end replied, "Sorry. Can't help you on that one."

"That's good enough for me. You've just told me a mouthful."

"Hold on!" the voice exclaimed. "I never told you nothing."

"Don't argue. I've got to have a word with him."

"You can't."

"I can and I will. There's trouble at Edzell and I aim to find out what's causing it."

He rang off, removed and pocketed the scrambler before reconnecting the line and leaving his office.

Glen entered the grounds of the ancient cathedral for the first time and made for St Rule's Tower, the most complete surviving remnant of the huge medieval building which had once dominated the landscape and much of the seascape besides. The remaining crumbling pillars and flying buttresses, still stretching their emaciated appeal to heaven to be mindful of their former ecclesiastical glory, bore witness to its scale.

Two stone steps led to a wooden door set in the west side of the Tower. It stood ajar and creaked grudgingly wider as though objecting to the fact that he had ignored the entrance fee of fifty pence. He entered and climbed the spiral steel stair, more suited to a ship's engine-room than a national monument.

With a secular efficiency, it carried the twentieth-century pilgrim to the lowest safe step of the original stone staircase, still winding tightly upwards as it had done for pre-Reformation sandalled feet.

The claustrophobic walls and the steep climb were well designed to induce an apprehensive breathlessness to be relieved by gasps for oxygen when the climber reached the open platform at the top - the very thing to persuade the devout of their spontaneous exultation at being so close to God.

Being fitter than the original users and more intent on the ground than on the heavens, Glen was far from breathless as he examined the details of the wooden platform on which he had emerged.

It was protected by a wooden rail a little above waist height, level with the original stone wall beyond. There was nothing to prevent anyone foolhardy enough or determined enough to go right over the edge, or, for that matter, being forced over by an assailant.

Four sightseers were intent on taking full advantage of the complete panorama, from ancient man-made harbour in the east to sophisticated golf extravaganza in the west. With their clicking cameras, they ignored Glen, but being ignored was no guarantee that none of these people had any interest in him.

Out of the corner of his eye, Glen noted each of them, including a young woman, as he followed their shuffling progress round the platform. None of them registered as familiar, as he processed their features through the files of his memory while scrutinising the rails and stonework as meticulously as the others did the scenery. There were no fresh marks to indicate anyone had scrambled or been forced over the parapet.

Back at ground level, Glen sought out the caretaker in his little wooden booth.

As he handed over his pound note, he apologised, "I guess I should have paid before I went in the Tower. Can I put it right now?"

"Better late than never," replied the elderly attendant, handing him his ticket and his change.

Glen turned away, and then as an afterthought said, "I heard that some guy fell from the top yesterday. Is that true? "

"Somebody fell, right enough," came the taciturn reply.

"That's difficult to understand. It seemed perfectly safe to me," Glen countered

"The Tower's safe enough for anyone who takes the least bit of care."

"Where did he fall from?"

"He must have fallen from the other side. His body was found there, in a little corner where a wall comes out at the foot of the Tower."

By a roundabout way he got to the spot where Zelinsky's body had been discovered. On the east side of the Tower was a small grassy area enclosed on three sides, the only opening obscured by large, upright tombstones.

If Zelinsky had fallen, his body could have lain there for some time without anyone noticing from the ground or from the unsighted platform. On the other hand, it was an ideal spot to leave a body killed elsewhere. The time lapse between the killing and the discovery could be accounted for by the possibility that the body had lain unnoticed in that hidden spot.

Glen could see from the trampled grass that there had been a lot of activity there recently. He was mainly interested in the area close to the foot of the wall where the body would have struck. Considering that Zelinsky's 180-odd pounds was supposed to have fallen over a hundred feet, there were no marks on the grass or ground to indicate such an impact.

The suspicion floating in Glen's mind came closer to the surface. Zelinsky would not have committed suicide somewhere else and then gently laid himself well out of view at the foot of the Tower. He had been murdered elsewhere and his body left here by his killer or killers.

The police should also be very well aware of this. Much would depend on the nature of the injuries. Perhaps they were consistent with a fall, in which case the police might have overlooked the ground evidence. On the other hand, they might believe that the death had not been accidental, but had their own reasons for not publicising their suspicions. He assumed the latter explanation and decided that British intelligence was also hovering around Zelinsky's death and his own activities. Otherwise his approach to the police might not have gone as smoothly as it had.

Worst of all he had lost confidence in his own Controller, who had been evasive and misleading about diMaggio.

....

Two miles west of St Andrews, Glen stepped out of the passenger door of MacLaren's Rover, and MacLaren joined him from the other side.

They were in the pebble driveway of a single-storey traditional stone cottage, which bore all the hallmarks of extension and modernisation. A faded blue Mini stood in front of the garage.

"Good. My wife's arrived here ahead of us," MacLaren intimated, nodding towards the Mini. "She has the keys."

He led the way through the front door straight to the lounge.

The room, disproportionately large compared with the exterior of the house, was dominated by a huge picture window taking in the wide sweep of the Eden Valley and north to the Firth of Tay, but for once Glen's attention for detail was arrested without seeing the window, for its only significance to him was that it provided the frame for an elegant young woman in her twenties.

The vision moved and in doing so made viewing even more compulsive for Glen.

His momentary trance was shattered by MacLaren's voice, and shattered again by what it said. "My wife."

"Isobel," she murmured, her voice as smooth as velvet, extending her hand to Glen.

As he took it he felt the long slender fingers, as smooth as the voice, wrap round his hand and give a distinctive intimate pressure, as her vivid blue eyes pierced his own with a laser compounded of challenge and innocence.

If his response had not been a reflex one, he might have been lost for words. But he managed to answer, "Colin Glen."

Her hand disengaged slowly and reluctantly. If MacLaren had not been beside him Glen would have stopped its slow withdrawal.

But his host seemed oblivious to his wife's magnetic femininity, or its possible effects. He had moved over to the window and was pronouncing on the view.

"Fine view. Mustn't let it distract you. Inspires old Stevenson, but then he's Eng. Lit."

Glen joined him by the window, having run the seductive gauntlet of Isobel's tactile fragrance.

Compared with Isobel, the view was not quite so enchanting; nevertheless it had its merits. The gradient from town, although gradual, had been constant, and their drive had brought them high enough to look across north Fife to the estuary of the Tay, with Dundee and the Sidlaw Mountains beyond.

On the northern shore of the Eden Estuary, less than three miles away, Glen recognised Leuchars RAF Station with its main runway stretching the length of the pine forest to the edge of the sea. This house was the perfect location.

For the second time in as many minutes, MacLaren broke the spell, "Done quite well, my wife. Got this place at the last minute. Stevensons off on the London train already. Friends of ours. Delighted to oblige. Glad to have the place looked after at short notice."

CHAPTER 15

MacLaren led the way into the shabby grey building which houses the world's most prestigious golf club. He spoke to the uniformed attendant in his tiny office inside the main door.

"Afternoon, Davie. Signing in a friend, Dr. Glen from the United States."

"Good afternoon, Dr. MacLaren," greeted Davie with the formality of one who keeps at arm's length from his collective employers. "Dr. Glen."

MacLaren signed the visitors' book on the oak ledge beside Davie's window. "Are we still in time for a bite to eat?"

"Oh, yes, sir."

"Good. We'll have something in here." He nodded towards the door on his left. "We only want a snack."

Inside the panelled room he pressed one of the white buttons on the wall, as he said over his shoulder, "No need to stand on ceremony in this room, but don't take your cue from Seamus over there."

He nodded towards a bushy-haired man sporting an unkempt sandy-coloured moustache and wearing a patterned pullover between his loudly-checked shirt and his green tweed jacket.

MacLaren cleared his throat and raised his voice. "Might have known you were here, Seamus. Place is deserted. Everyone else's fled."

Seamus paused and listened. He seemed to realise from his companion's expression that someone had come into the room.

When he turned round and saw MacLaren, he swore. "Good God, MacLaren, are you still here? The only decent thing this government is doing is closing down universities. Why haven't they sacked you yet? It just goes to show how bloody incompetent they are! And you needing all the time you can get to improve that ridiculous golf handicap!"

MacLaren explained to Glen, more for Seamus' benefit than Glen's, "Seamus is a one-man Highland Clearance in reverse. He makes occasional forays into the Lowlands to frighten the natives."

"Highland Clearances are no laughing matter," Seamus bristled. "Do you realise that it was only two hundred years ago this year that the English Government allowed some of the clan chiefs to go back to take possession of their own lands? That was thirty-eight years after Culloden. In that time they had brain-washed the next generation into becoming a bunch of English nyaffs and that's what they still are today."

"Don't be so hard on your own class," MacLaren tormented him.

"Class is an alien concept in the clan system. My solidarity is with my clan and kin, not with a spineless sycophantic set of anglicised morons."

"Dr. Glen," MacLaren began punctiliously, "may I introduce you to Sir Seamus Breck, the last genuine eighteenth-century clan chief? Seamus, say hello to Colin."

"If you must be sarcastic, get your centuries right. I'd rather be seventeenth-century and be done with it. The rot started in the eighteenth."

Glen offered his hand, but Breck only glowered at him. "Colin?" he mused. "Colin! Have you got Campbell blood in you?"

"Not to my knowledge, I'm afraid."

"Don't apologise for that, man! Only, you see, Colin is a common name among that tribe. If I've got your oath on it, we'll shake hands."

He grasped Glen's hand suddenly and squeezed it fiercely. An appreciative glimmer came into his eye when Glen returned the grip strength for strength without flinching.

"Never mind MacLaren. Come and sit at our table," he invited, putting his arm round Glen's shoulder.

Ignoring Breck, MacLaren drew a fourth chair to the table and placed himself between Breck and the hitherto silent observer and introduced himself and Glen to the fourth man.

The stranger's eyes crinkled at the corners, as Glen mentally noted other features, which stamped the man as amiable and uncomplicated. Apart from the lines around his twinkling eyes, his round face was tightly packed into a taut skin with a smooth, shiny complexion. He wore a bright green blazer of unconventional style over a shirt with clashing green stripes and a red and white tie. His hair was unfashionably short. He shook hands with both newcomers, and Glen could feel the dimples in his plump hand.

Before he could give his name, Breck interrupted, "You teachers should pay proper respect to Captain Schultz here. Like myself, he is a man of action. It is service men like himself who ensure that people like you can sleep o' nights." He grinned expansively, as Schultz tried to smile away his embarrassment.

Schultz protested, "My work is closer to academic quiet than hand-to-hand fighting. You know that, Seamus."

A club steward entered in a white drill jacket and stood at a respectful distance.

MacLaren brought him forward by raising his index finger to shoulder height. "Jack, bacon roll for me. Cold ham roll for Dr. Glen. Two pints of Special, Whisky number two for Sir Seamus, and a refill for Captain Schultz. What's your pleasure, Captain?"

"I'd like a malt, again, please."

MacLaren turned back to Jack, "That's another whisky number two."

Breck frowned at the steward. "And don't offer him ice in it this time."

As Jack left, MacLaren addressed Schultz, "Captain Schultz ..."

"Call me Fred."

Breck interjected, "If you have a perfectly decent name like Ferdinand, why reduce it to something wet like Fred?"

"Never mind him, Fred. Just want to ask what you do. Seamus is only a tax-gatherer among his peasantry for two or three days a week. Likes to rub shoulders with real working people like ourselves the rest of the time. Gives him an air of respectability."

While Breck spluttered, Schultz answered, "I'm with the US Navy, stationed at a small post in Angus called Edzell."

"He's helping to protect the bloody English by listening to the Russians. They always get someone else to do their dirty work. It was the Scots in the past and sometimes the Germans who built up the British Empire, and it worked until the English went out to administer it with their jumped-up civil servants. Now they've got some of their colonials back from America to wet-nurse them again."

Breck's blustering helped Glen to cover any interest he might have shown in the mention of Edzell, but his thoughts were interrupted when the drinks arrived.

"You're a bit quiet for an American," Breck accused him. "What have you to say for yourself?"

"I just got here yesterday. I'm still finding my bearings."

"Couldn't do better than find them on a golf course. Have you booked a time for this afternoon?"

MacLaren overheard the question and answered for Glen. "No, we haven't. Have you?"

"No. Blast! This GI beat me in the morning, and I want to get my revenge fast. I'd even make up a four with you! I'll play with anyone who has a booking just to beat this damn Yank before nightfall."

"We haven't even discussed golf."

"How can you have somebody in St Andrews since yesterday and not discuss golf? It's uncivilised - only to be expected from a man with Campbell for a name."

MacLaren looked at Glen, "If it suits you, we could ask if there's a free time this afternoon. I have no other plans."

A game of golf was low on Glen's list of priorities, but it offered a unique opportunity to find out more about Edzell, and he replied without hesitation, "Excellent idea. I guess I can hire clubs here?"

"I'll see what Davie can do for us," offered MacLaren, rising and leaving the room.

"We'll all go through to the main lounge and watch the activity outside on the Old Course," Breck announced.

"We'll follow you," Schultz agreed, "but I think Colin may be interested in looking at the trophies in the strong room here."

Colin nodded. He would have Schultz alone.

"Baubles!" Breck exploded, using the word like an expletive.

As he reached the door, MacLaren returned and announced, "Cancellation on the Old for three o'clock. Booked it."

....

As Schultz pointed out the different trophies in the glass-fronted display between the open strong-room doors he explained, "Always remember that's the Open Cup - not the British Open. Theirs was the first - so it's THE Open. You got to hand it to these Brits. They sure like their traditions."

Then he chuckled. "Say, that Seamus sure is one walking tradition all of his own. What a helluva guy!" And he shook his head wistfully.

"He sure can project himself," Glen agreed with enthusiasm. "How come you met up with a guy like that?"

"He has a small estate close to Edzell and is very hospitable to us American servicemen. Invites us to shoot from time to time and fish in his river, but our guys who are real hunters back home are looking for moose or brown bear, not jack rabbits. One guy said that to Seamus once. Seamus just about bust a gut. So we're only invited to stalk the occasional stag nowadays. Myself, I prefer golf. He and I play at Edzell. It's a fine course, but if he's coming to St Andrews he takes me as his guest to the R&A, and we have a round or two on the Old Course."

"How long have you known him?" Glen quizzed, making the most of Schultz's talkativeness.

"I met him as soon as I took over command at Edzell eighteen months ago. It might be more correct to say he introduced me to my command. He was in the CO's office with my second-in-command, Frank diMaggio, when I arrived to take over. It was pouring wet outside. I hadn't seen anything for miles because of the mist. It was like arriving at Brigadoon. This guy is standing there in his kilt with pools of water forming at his feet. Then he puts his hand in his sporran and pulls out a flask of whisky. He passes it to myself and then diMaggio before saying something incomprehensible and taking a slug from it himself. It got us off to a great relationship. We've been buddies ever since."

With his antennae already on the alert about Edzell and diMaggio, Glen was less than assured by the station commander's account of the freewheeling security that seemed to prevail. Schultz appeared to be a sincere man, but he would check on him with his own Control and hope that he got more co-operation than he had over diMaggio. Breck was worrying though. He was all bluster and gesture. Maybe too conspicuous to be a genuine security risk, but if he carried his machismo act too far he could do damage in a sensitive electronic outpost like Edzell.

While they were talking, Davie had looked round the door a couple of times.

"I guess he's trying to tell us we shouldn't be in here on our own without a member," Schultz said uncomfortably.

Schultz led the way back to the lounge.

They walked the length of the room under the great brass chandeliers dangling from the delicate Wedgwood ceiling to where MacLaren was sitting in the window bay.

"Pity about all that ironmongery out for the Open," he apologised, nodding towards the banks of scaffolding which provided the temporary grandstands laid out at strategic points all over the well-manicured, gently undulating landscape beyond the window. "Usually more peaceful than this."

"Don't mention it. Just standing here, we're so close to the first tee I feel I'm actually on it," Glen assured him "That's good enough for me."

Under a larger than life portrait of the Queen halfway along the room, Breck was in conversation with an elderly gentleman in navy-blue blazer and regimental tie.

"About the only place Seamus behaves himself," MacLaren muttered.

Glen wanted to find out as much as he could about Breck. "Who's he speaking with now?"

"Brigadier Farquharson, Seamus' battalion colonel when he did his National Service as a subaltern in the early fifties. Brilliant war record, marred by political repercussions following Suez in 'fifty-six. Fine strategist, brave soldier. Perfect military operation. Maximum ground taken, minimum casualties both sides, but a political cock-up. Heroes had to remain unsung. Compare the decorations dished out for Falklands with those for Suez operation. No comparison.

"Regiment distinguished itself at Suez - Argylls, same as myself. Seamus demobbed a month before the invasion. Still can't hide his frustration at missing the action. Kept volunteering for excitement. Never got farther from UK than Gibraltar on Governor's staff."

To Glen, Breck's aggressive superiority complex was consistent with behaviour subconsciously trying to cover up for inadequacies and disappointment. Perhaps MacLaren's tale accounted for it.

CHAPTER 16

As Glen and his companions were winding their way up from the locker-room in the basement of the R&A to take their place on the first tee of the Old Course, Commander Donald Ross was passing the first tee of the famous King's Course at Gleneagles in Perthshire.

The Rover accelerated from the intersection, but the driver had to brake again, for most of the west side of the road was taken up with parked cars, leaving little room for two cars to pass on what remained. A chocolate-coloured Mercedes coupé backed suddenly into their path opposite Dormy House with all its facilities for Gleneagles golfers. The Rover stopped on the proverbial sixpence.

"Sorry, sir," the driver apologised through gritted teeth.

"Not your fault. You did well to save his paint-work," Ross complimented.

A frail, elderly man grinned sheepishly from the driver's seat of the Mercedes, before shifting the automatic control lever. His powerful toy lurched forward.

The Rover surged past his rear bumper as soon as there was an inch of clearance.

"I should have let him finish his manoeuvre, sir, but we're pretty neat for time."

"Quite right. We can't keep the Secretary of State waiting."

"There's a small roundabout in a little over a hundred yards. Go three-quarters of the way round, and the hotel entrance is just in front of you. Don't wait in the car-park at the entrance, but come back here and park in line with this lot. It will be less noticeable for you to wait in the car here. Quite a few people change into their golf shoes in their cars, and it will be more comfortable for yourself to be in the shade.

"I'll take this," he said holding up an electronic paging device, "and bleep you when we need to be picked up."

He turned to the man in the back seat beside him. "We can't have this lot cluttering up the place next week," he said, pointing to the indiscriminately parked cars.

Their own car swung round the tight roundabout and moved sedately up to the entrance of the luxury hotel.

Ross and his companion climbed out of the back, and a third large man emerged from the front passenger door of the Rover, which discreetly glided away.

It was one minute to three. On the top step, Ross paused and cast his eyes over the panorama of southern Perthshire.

To the man who had been beside him in the back seat, he said, "Iain, you must have about the most beautiful beat of any policeman in the world. I hope we can keep it as peaceful as it is right now."

Then he went through the door and spoke quietly to the porter at the desk on the right.

The porter nodded and caught the eye of a man standing diagonally across the hall. The man moved towards Ross.

As he and Ross met in the middle of the foyer below the incongruous moose head among the red deer antlers decorating the walls, the man bent towards Ross and asked very quietly, "Commander Ross?"

Ross gripped his elbow, and, although he was the one to be conducted to his appointment, guided the man towards the stairs without any further words or gestures between them.

At the foot of the stairs, a television flickered as it turned another page of Oracle.

Ross' two companions from the car fell neatly into step behind. Ross winced inwardly and deliberately broke step at the first corner. He hated plain-clothes officers marching as though they were on uniformed parade.

Going one pace ahead when they reached the landing, Ross' guide knocked on the first door he reached, his head inclined as he waited for an answer. When he heard it, he opened the door to usher in the visitors.

Without looking at his watch, Ross knew automatically that it was exactly three o'clock.

The room was the sitting room of a spacious suite. Ross recognised the Secretary of State for Scotland, The Right Honourable James MacEwan, Privy Councillor and Member of Her Majesty's Cabinet.

He was a tall, thin man with the frank expression of a politician whose greatest obstacle in public life had been to charm the selection committee of a safe Conservative constituency into offering him their sinecure despite the disadvantage of a titled mother and a millionaire father, it being a well-known fact that Conservative Selection Committees prefer to have these parental roles reversed.

Ross knew better than to dismiss the man's ability simply because he had luck on his side. He also knew him as ambitious. Sooner or later, he wanted to have one of the top ministerial posts that pave the way to Number Ten, Downing Street. That meant a two-to-one chance that Ross would be working with him again, at the Home Office or the Foreign Office, unless, of course, he became Chancellor of the Exchequer.

Both men knew of their importance to each other's careers, but both also knew that the politician held the upper hand in the long run, and therefore Ross had to keep his political wits about him as well as his professional ones.

The Cabinet Minister was standing beside the tall windows draped with plush curtains. He was leafing through a sheaf of papers. One of the two men with him was talking to him and pointing out different passages in the papers. The other man made occasional notes. Although he looked towards the door as Ross and his two companions came in, he made no other gesture and didn't speak. With head bent he seemed absorbed by what he was listening to and oblivious to the other people in the room.

Advancing to the centre of the room, Ross stood on the large central medallion in the middle of the carpet, whose colour and design would have delighted Barbara Cartland. His companions stood silently behind him, one at each shoulder - an impressive trio.

From his position, Ross saw an unmarked white Granada negotiate the tight roundabout beside the Balmoral Drive entrance to the time-share complex and accelerate along the drive towards the hotel entrance. Without moving his head, he followed it with his eyes until it disappeared out of sight below the window frame.

MacEwan handed the file to the man who had been doing most of the talking, said something to him and nodded to the third man who closed his note-book. Once the two men were dismissed he paid no further attention to them.

He began to cross towards Ross, his hand extended, all his attention focused on his latest visitor. Knowing better than to wait for his political master to reach him, Ross moved quickly to grasp the proffered hand.

MacEwan pushed a lank strand of hair from his brow with his free hand and greeted Ross affably, "Very good of you to come along, Commander Ross. I thought it would be best to meet on location, so-to-speak."

"Thank you, Secretary of State."

As their hands met, the white Granada stopped at the hotel entrance. Three men stepped out, and the driver pulled away to the parking lot, locked the doors and followed his companions inside.

Upstairs Ross asked, "May I present my colleagues?"

MacEwan smiled his approval.

First, he introduced the man who had been sitting beside him, then his other companion, "Superintendent MacNab of Tayside Police, Chief Inspector Duncan of Fife Police, The Right Honourable Mr. MacEwan."

MacEwan shook hands with both policemen.

Downstairs the three Granada passengers walked purposefully past the stairs, turned right and reached two display cases containing valuable pieces from the collection of an exclusive jeweller.

MacEwan said to Ross, "I think we can have our discussion here. We have the room to ourselves, and there's a man posted at the door."

"I'm sure you're right, sir, but may I be excessively cautious? It's quite possible for someone to pick up our conversation with highly sensitive microphones from a variety of positions within sight of this window," Ross said, trying to keep melodrama out of his voice.

MacEwan had not reached his present high office without knowing how to delegate and when to listen. Without hesitation he retorted, "You're the expert. What do you recommend?"

"I would suggest, sir, that we go down to the Eagle's Nest. It's a small room just off the main dining room with no external walls or windows. We will also have plenty of table tops on which to spread out our maps."

"Good thinking, Commander. Let's do just that."

At the foot of the stair, they turned left and moved towards the display cases the men from the Granada had passed. Although Ross noticed one of the men at the door of the Eagle's Nest as he passed, he made no remark as the man stood aside to let them enter. Inside the room MacEwan saw another figure lurking outside the door on the west wall which gave access from the passage leading to the Ballroom.

"Are these your men, Commander?"

"I took the precaution of posting them in the hope that you might agree to the suggestion of using this room."

"What would they have done if we had not come down?"

"They would have waited five minutes and then gone out among the shrubs, trees and buildings which could have given shelter to any electronic eavesdropper."

"Why didn't they carry out that search anyway before they came in?"

"Our job is still prevention, sir. We want to keep the level of activity as low as possible. We want interested parties to believe that we have no idea of their interest. That way they conduct themselves much more quietly. Otherwise, it would be cowboys and Indians all over the place."

"With that kind of attention to detail, Commander, we shouldn't have anything to worry about for our visitors." MacEwan chose his seat at the table and beckoned the others to take theirs, Ross on his right.

"I never take anything for granted, sir. If any element of the opposition decided to escalate the scale of intervention, we would have to make a fundamental reappraisal. We base our calculations on variations on the conventions, not having them overturned altogether."

"Give me an example."

"Well, sir, we've used the SAS. from time to time to restore normality. The best known example is the siege of the Iranian Embassy. The West Germans did the same when they freed an airliner in Somali. If you postulate a scenario where such forces are used first, you get what I mean. The SAS could be in and out of a situation so quickly that witnesses would swear there were fewer of them than the gang in the Great Train Robbery. Nobody would say it was an intervention by part of a nation's armed forces."

"Fortunately, that doesn't happen."

Without losing his concentration, Ross noted that MacEwan, with his economy of words, could have become a good TV chat-show host, eliciting maximum information from his guest - so much better than his own garrulous, opinionated political master at the Home Office.

"With respect, sir, the problem is that it does happen. Israel is so adept at it that no one notices. In fact, the only time it is seen to work in this way nowadays is when they mount a rescue operation as they did of their hijacked airliner at Kampala. Our own people mounted the same sort of raids on the Argentine mainland. You remember the helicopter that came down in Chile. Nobody heard about the damage that we did in Argentina, because the people with the right to object did not want to lose face."

"What would you see as posing the greatest threat to this conference?"

Again crisp and to the point. Ross approved

"Well, sir, that takes us into two areas in which I have no expertise: politics and military. You know the politics, and Colonel Sinclair will be responsible for the military. But in terms of who has the military skill, there is no doubt that the British are outstanding. Unfortunately, this country is probably the most expert in the world with its involvement, since the end of the war, in places stretching from Malaya and

Cyprus to Kenya and Ulster. Since the end of National Service we have had the best trained and, sadly, the most experienced professional army in the world. We fought so many guerrillas from the Troodos Mountains to the Falls Road and from the Stern Gang to Mau Mau, that we have become the greatest experts in this kind of warfare."

MacEwan smiled wistfully. He had been a lieutenant with a Highland regiment in Cyprus during the Enosis trouble. "We don't need to worry about the British, since we're on the same side."

"That depends on the politics, sir."

"What do you mean by that?"

"A hint of political opinion from an official always gets a minister's full attention," Ross mused to himself.

"I can't discount the British trying to disrupt a NATO conference just because it's in Britain. If I get into that line of thinking, I start to eliminate others. That way our guard is lowered. I operate the other way round. I think, how would the best in the world do it - the SAS. Then I pose all the political grudges that may be harboured. If a terrorist outrage happened in Britain, we might be the least likely to be suspected. It could be a golden opportunity to settle old scores."

"That's preposterous. You have no justification for saying any such thing." For the first time MacEwan showed a trace of impatience.

Ross stood his ground. "It's not my job to justify it, sir. In fact, I condemn it, but I must consider the possibility. But can I make the point that, for a variety of reasons, we don't want Spain in the Common Market or NATO? You know the political and economic arguments much better than I do about agricultural support for another Mediterranean producer of olive oil or grapes, from which support prices our farmers get nothing, or Gibraltar, or the Spanish attitude to the Falklands. It is my job to consider the possible implications in a security context."

"Our government would never contemplate such a thing. While I agree about our reservations on Spanish membership of the EEC and NATO, it is totally insupportable to suggest that we would use the SAS like that in the middle of Perthshire."

A challenge like that always put Ross on his toes. Despite his irreproachable civility, one of his little pleasures in life was being able to refute such attacks. That was one reason only that his preparation was always impeccable.

"From my point of view, sir, as an impartial observer with a job to do, I believe it is supportable. Otherwise, I should never have mentioned it. May I ask why the conference is being held at Gleneagles?"

The look in MacEwan's eyes told him that he had struck a chord.

The Secretary of State hesitated. "Since your work frequently brings you into contact with the Home Secretary and the Foreign Secretary, I can tell you that both of these colleagues discussed the proposal with me personally and, after agreement, put the idea to the Cabinet."

"I understand, sir. I was just wondering why these gentlemen gave this prestigious but onerous task to the Scottish Office."

That was the nearest Ross could go to political innuendo. With a General Election in the offing and a Cabinet reshuffle imminent, Ross knew that the publicity of the forthcoming meeting could play a big part in the ambitions of these three powerful Cabinet Ministers. If the two more senior Secretaries of State had handed this opportunity to MacEwan, they must have had their reasons.

But his only outward manifestation was a blink, as he said with less conviction, "You're barking up the wrong tree this time. Can't you make some more likely suggestions?"

Ross allowed no flicker of satisfaction to cross his face, but he knew his information about internal Cabinet manoeuvrings and jealousies had been sound.

"Of course, sir. France has a similar ability, partly because of her decolonisation problems as well, but her romantic attachment to the Foreign Legion and her paramilitary Gendarmerie have prevented the development going as far as we have. They are still relatively conventional.

"West Germany has developed the capacity for low-profile military intervention because she still suffers a guilt complex from her former overt militarism. The Munich Olympics attack also alerted her authorities to the need for that kind of force."

Ross was uninterrupted as he kept the facts flowing and had finished all he was going to say about internal politics.

"The United States certainly has the hardware, but the hardware probably exceeds the capacity to operate it on a scale compatible with the small numbers which are a prerequisite of such activities. In any case, the United States is more committed to Spanish membership of EEC and NATO than any of the other countries and it can turn economic screws much tighter than anyone else. So I'm not worried about the Americans."

Aware of the distractions of body language, Ross kept his hands clasped in front of his chin and his eyes fixed on the Minister.

"We mustn't forget that Spain is just emerging from a military dictatorship and has a tradition for the army to be more interventionist in its society and politics than is the case in the existing NATO countries. It also has national service for all young men, and their training is pretty efficient.

"The tourists on the beaches may not see much of the army and may think of Spaniards only as waiters and chambermaids, but, if they take a trip into the mountains around such places as Ronda, they'll see plenty of fit young men being rigorously and skilfully trained.

"Remember that the right-wingers in Spain are implacably opposed to both international groupings, and the new socialist government is not very enthusiastic about NATO. In fact, it has serious doubts about continuing to allow the Americans the use of the bases they already have.

"These considerations I can balance fairly rationally. What really concerns me are the fanatics for whom I can form no logical patterns, but for whom I must be ready.

"I'm sorry, sir. I'm going on at length." But Ross had made sure he had finished before inviting a response.

"Not at all. I'm a good listener. I have to be to take decisions. But right now, it's time we got down to practicalities."

The emphasis on the last word was not lost on Ross.

CHAPTER 17

The next afternoon Ross called by appointment on Malcolm Munro, Under Secretary of State for Scotland, at New St Andrews House in Edinburgh, with his report on proposed security measures, which MacEwan had indicated, should be authorised by Munro's signature. But when Ross offered his report to Munro, he was disinclined to accept it.

"The Secretary of State told me you would be bringing this report. He and I are of the opinion that it should go to the Home Secretary."

Ross was less than surprised. MacEwan had already passed the buck to Munro, and now he was trying to wriggle out of it.

He put a great deal of doubt into his single, respectful answer, "Sir?"

"You heard."

"Why, sir?"

"We believe that since the various ministries involved - Home Office, Foreign Office, Defence and so on - are all in London, and since all the embassies are in London, it would be tidier if you reported to the Home Office."

"And the Canadian High Commission?"

"The Canadian High Commission!"

"Yes, sir, as well as the foreign embassies."

"Of course, I'd forgotten about the Commonwealth High Commissions. Yes, of course."

"I'm sorry, sir. I can't"

"What do you mean, can't?"

"The Secretary of State gave me to understand that it was still very much a Scottish Office affair, and I had to report to you. I cannot disregard his direct instruction."

"He has authorised me to re-instruct you."

"Is it in writing, sir?"

"Why do you need it in writing?"

"Because the Home Secretary was most emphatic that I must refer everything done in Scotland to the Scottish Office, as he believes that is procedurally correct. Besides, sir, you summoned me yourself to remind me of an avoidable indiscretion on a former occasion. I stood in this office only two days ago and gave you my solemn oath I would not do such a thing again. Have you forgotten, sir?"

"Of course, I haven't forgotten. Give me that damned report!"

"Certainly, sir."

....

At two minutes to ten the next morning, MacEwan was sitting at his place in the Cabinet Room, when the Home Secretary came in, smiling benignly on all and sundry. His eye caught MacEwan's and he lifted his index finger with a little gasp as though he had just remembered something. He laid his red despatch box on the table at his place next to the Prime Minister's and stole round to MacEwan's side like a furtive schoolboy afraid of being caught out of his place. He leaned over until his everted lips almost touched MacEwan's ear and whispered, "Excellent work yesterday. Munro sent me Ross' report. Read it at breakfast. Congratulations," and he squeezed MacEwan's shoulder affectionately like a proud father and gave a cherubic smile to MacEwan's upturned face.

MacEwan felt a pang of conscience at having thought such a genuine old statesman could possibly have placed him in a political trap.

The Home Secretary tip-toed back to his own place, opened his despatch box, took out the top manila file, looked at it and clucked vexatiously. He almost ran back to MacEwan.

"Munro forgot to sign it," he fussed, "and the PM requires it from me immediately. Could you possibly oblige?"

All the ministers except the Prime Minister were in the room and seated. The door handle turned. Only one person could be coming in now. The clock showed nine seconds to ten.

MacEwan signed.

The Home Secretary raced back to his place in time to give the Prime Minister his usual effusive greeting.

When they had both sat down and the Prime Minister's head was bent over the first report of the day, the Home Secretary looked at MacEwan, pursed his lips and puckered his chin to increase the gravitas of his reassuring nod to MacEwan.

The only comfort MacEwan took from it was the knowledge that it would pay him to keep a close watch on the wily old bird, not because he distrusted him, but because he knew there was so much to learn from him.

CHAPTER 18

At his second attempt Glen found the small harbour at the end of the maze of narrow streets that make up the township of Tayport. The street nameplate on the last house, President Grant Place, set the tone for a secret meeting between two Americans.

He drove past the white line of houses still bright in the gathering dusk and parked close to the edge of the harbour wall, alongside another couple of cars, forlorn on the wide empty space. The location had been diMaggio's choosing.

He got out of the car and walked along the grit-covered track to the end of the harbour and the derelict buildings where diMaggio had promised to be waiting. At the end he turned left, but his next step warned him that the surface had changed. Wood planking gave a loud echo in the silence of the gloaming. He stepped back onto the stone pier-work and continued to the small block that crouched in the gloom at the far corner.

He tapped lightly on the door. There was no response. He tried again. Still no response.

He stood back to wait in the shadows, blending into the murk of industrial dereliction whose profile was criss-crossed by disapproving strokes of mooring ropes belonging to the new generation's leisure craft at their languid ease in the limpid waters.

From the north, the lights of Dundee flickered across the river on the rippling backs of intervening wavelets.

Without warning something hard pressed into his back and a gravelly voice croaked in his ear, "Freeze, buddy."

"diMaggio?"

"Yeah, diMaggio. And who the hell are you?"

"I told you."

"So? Some guy sniffing around Zelinsky?"

"What do you know about Zelinsky?"

"I'm the guy asking the questions. Remember? Where did you come from all of a sudden asking all them damn fool questions?"

"If you knew Zelinsky, you know he must have back-up."

"Sure he has back-up!" diMaggio sniffed. "But not from you. The moment you show, he snuffs it. How come you're asking all these questions around town? And who put you on to me?"

"I came to help Zelinsky. He signalled to Washington that he was on to something important. Before I could talk to him, he died. I knew there was a contact at Edzell, but I didn't know who. Zelinsky was the only one who knew. I met Schultz by chance and was pretty sure it wasn't him. Then your name turned up."

diMaggio growled contemptuously, "You'll have to do better than that, buddy boy. If you had checked with the proper minder you would have been told to stay right away from yours truly. Zelinsky came barging into my life and caused me almost as much trouble as he caused himself in the end. Now I'm wondering if it would be a kindness for me to end it all for you right here and now."

"Look, we're both Americans. We're on the same side. We need to co-operate. I need to know what Zelinsky turned up."

"The hell you do! You don't know whose side I'm on. When did someone stop wiping your nose? You don't even know whose side you're on. I stopped trusting the other guy a long time ago. Fellow Americans are the most dangerous of the lot when they go off."

"If you are on our own country's side, and I think you are, we can both check together with our Embassy."

"You really are green! Some guys are so deep, their own side would disclaim them without hesitation to protect the line. You sure are fresh in the field - worse even than Zelinsky. We're wasting time. I want you to start moving very slowly across the wharf."

"Why?"

"One, because I'm holding the gun, and two, because by the time you reach the edge, I'll have decided how I'm going to kill you."

Glen's instinct hadn't let him down yet. He obeyed.

The moment he took his first cautious step forward, his brain moved up a gear. There was a risk that military intelligence and his own outfit had got their wires crossed. Whether or not they were on the same side in the grand super-power strategy, there was little doubt that the immediate future would only have one of them as a survivor. Despite his present disadvantage, Glen made up his mind it was going to be him.

He calculated the number of paces to the edge of the pier. The gun in diMaggio's hand was a last resort. The resourceful marine was undoubtedly planning to make his death look like an accident.

From the direction of diMaggio's voice and the position of the gun in his right kidney, Glen reckoned that the gun was in his right hand. diMaggio would be at his most alert for a false move as they started to walk forward and again when anticipating his own move in the last few paces.

Glen had to act before the edge, for he calculated the most likely plan was to strike him from behind and throw him over the side of the pier.

Ten feet from the nearest bollard marking the perimeter of the wooden edge, Glen moved like lightning. He dropped to the left and brought his right elbow up from ankle height with explosive force into diMaggio's groin. Simultaneously he felt the burn of a bullet crease the flesh of his hip as diMaggio involuntarily pressed the trigger.

As the noise of the shot rang out, he swung his left hand and grabbed the gun-hand before diMaggio could turn it on him, not that he was in any condition to do other than writhe in a foetal position, as the pain in his lower abdomen occupied his whole existence.

Glen grabbed diMaggio's gun hand with both of his, thumbs pressed hard against the back of his adversary's hand, his fingers against the gun enclosed in the palm. With all his strength he began to twist diMaggio's hand anti-clockwise.

The new source of pain brought diMaggio back from the abyss of his first agony. He swung his left fist at Glen's ear. Unconcentrated as it was, it did little damage, but forced Glen to use his right arm to defend himself.

A shout came from one of the yachts in the harbour. "Is anything wrong up there?"

Glen managed to gasp back, "It's OK. My friend here's had a little too much to drink."

The voice came back, "I thought I heard a shot."

"Yeah!" Glen panted in staccato intervals. "This nut ... fired ...our ...Very pistol ... into the water."

With that he changed his tactic and used diMaggio's strength against him by pulling in the same direction as diMaggio and cracking his gun-hand hard against the bollard. The pistol clattered on the planks.

"It's OK ...I've got it ... from him now."

The interruption had given diMaggio time to recover. He grabbed for the pistol, but Glen reached it first with his foot and flicked it over the edge.

diMaggio was a ferocious fighter and, without his gun, became desperate. The fury of his attack took Glen by surprise. The pain and viciousness of Glen's first blows had maddened him, so that skill gave way to brute force.

He pinned Glen against the bollard and lashed wildly with his fists. Glen wove skilfully but left himself exposed on the outer plank of the pier. Oblivious to his own safety, diMaggio butted him in the midriff. The impetus launched Glen into space and carried diMaggio with him.

With his back to the water, Glen felt himself cascading into a void. He prayed that the tide was in and the water deep. The splash was a relief, but the water was shallow, and most of the air was knocked out of his lungs by a sickening thud on his back. He surfaced spluttering, but before he could draw breath, a black figure rose beside him and hurled itself upon him, burying him in the opaque darkness.

His struggle used up the remnants of oxygen in his shattered lungs. He did the only thing he could. He grabbed diMaggio's head and held it under water cheek to cheek with his own, until he felt his adversary's grip weaken. But still he held on despite the throb of black and scarlet in his head as his whole being screamed for life-saving oxygen. Then diMaggio began to struggle to free himself. Glen pulled with all his weight and thrust the other man beneath him.

Forcing his feet against the muddy bottom, he pushed himself hard for the surface and the pier.

Furiously he pumped air into his lungs until his sight cleared and he became giddy with the new surge of energy. As soon as he could pick out the outline of the piles supporting the pier, he lunged at the nearest horizontal girder. As he grabbed at it he felt a vice-like grip round his legs, and his hands slipped on the greasy seaweed.

Once more diMaggio plunged him below the surface, this time pinning him painfully against a stone on the seabed. The agony in his spine was inevitable. Frantic to relieve it he grappled desperately below his distorted back. He was sure he was being deceived by delirium when he felt his hands fasten round the barrel of a gun. His reason told him it must be diMaggio's.

He writhed sufficiently to free it, and, bringing his hand round close to diMaggio's ear, he pressed the trigger.

He felt as though a miniature depth-charge had gone off inside his head. What it did to diMaggio he had no idea, but the effect was electric.

He felt diMaggio's grip go limp instantly and he surfaced to see diMaggio with his hands over his ears, swinging his head from side to side. The water was shallow enough for them to stand. Glen pointed the gun at diMaggio.

"Walk slowly away from me," he hissed.

As his eyes adjusted, he was able to focus on a ladder running up the front of the pier about six feet from where he stood.

"Stay absolutely still where you are," he ordered diMaggio. He tried to walk towards the ladder, but his buoyancy hindered him. Keeping his gun trained on diMaggio all the time, he felt his way up the ladder with his free hand. At the top he said, "Your turn now," as he swung himself onto the pier.

When diMaggio's head appeared over the parapet, Glen was twelve feet back with the gun levelled at his protagonist's head.

"This isn't the time or the place, but you have a helluva lot of explaining to do. I aim to get you into a corner where you can't turn or squirm, and so many people will be squeezing you that you'll spew your guts out. Remember I know where to find you. Never try to pull anything like this on me or my department again," Glen gritted through clenched teeth.

"You bastard! You've been lucky this time, but remember what Zelinsky got when he fouled up my patch. Some things are bigger than our small departments, and individuals have to be sacrificed."

"Did you kill Zelinsky, then?" demanded Glen, his finger tightening involuntarily on the trigger.

"Did I hell! He was a good kid, but he crossed some ruthless bastards, and they rubbed him out. I don't want you starting up where he left off. I had to scare you off. Keep me out of your plans or everything will blow up in our faces."

"I'll be in touch," Glen promised. "In the meantime, you just wait right where you are until I hit that road over there."

Soaking wet and wracked with pain, Glen needed every ounce of his remaining strength and resolve to squeeze himself into his car.

His numbness and stiffness denied him his usual co-ordination, and his car shot into the darkness as though driven by a demon.

CHAPTER 19

One week earlier in an apartment on the third floor of one of the blocks of flats overlooking the tree-shaded promenade of San Sebastian in northern Spain three men were engaged in an animated discussion. More correctly, one of them was animated and the other two were trying to placate him. All three were oblivious to the sparkling water of the horseshoe bay enfolded in the protective arms of two tree-clad headlands whose fingertips almost touched the small island nestling between them.

A portly man was furiously exercising his heavy jowls as he gave vent to his feelings, a dangerous glint in his dark eyes. His neat moustache bristled as his lips quivered in an effort at self-control. He sat erect on the edge of a large armchair.

His companions, both younger men in their mid-thirties with all the appearance of prosperous businessmen, seemed more comfortable in their chairs.

The portly man fulminated, "It is with extreme misgivings that I even consider thinking of these murderers as being of any use whatsoever to our cause. The thought of actually associating with them nauseates me. They represent all that I abhor and have spent my life fighting against under Generalissimo Franco. They are anti-Spanish. They oppose everything I hold dear. My mind, my breeding, my training, my very blood all tell me this is wrong. Yet the alternative is so damnable that I must compromise my soul."

"General Lopez, sir, it is all as you say," soothed one of the other men, his accent softer with a Gallician lilt still underlying the polished tones of a Madrid education. "We share your sentiments entirely, and it is even more repulsive for us, for these people live among us in our daily lives and are responsible for atrocities against our friends and colleagues, but we believe they can serve our purpose in this matter."

The general was not to be easily won. "Don Ramon, it is such short-term expedients I despise. The Generalissimo was a strategist whose tactics had to fit into overall principles. My fear is that I am betraying that trust which I inherited as a subaltern who had the privilege of being close to him from the moment he returned from Africa to lead our country with his nobility of mind and purpose."

The third man entered the conversation. "It is exactly because what he built up so tenaciously is now at risk that we wish to intervene.

"His Majesty was too protected by the ever-loving Caudillo from the vicious realities of democracy to understand how underhand its machinations are, and especially the excesses of socialism which have been forced on us by a malevolent proletariat. It is in our anguish that we implore you to give your personal endorsement to the plans we have laid with the Basque terrorists in their hateful ETA separatist organisation."

"Don José," the general interrupted, "I agree with almost everything that you say. I appreciate that the Basques have the manpower, and, God knows, more guts than our own people who go along with this festering sore of democracy so that they can lick the pus that suppurates from the wounds of taxation. But when the rest of the people of Spain come to their senses and rise against this tyranny of mediocrity and inefficiency, the Basques will still have to be brought to heel, and I do not wish my name to live in infamy, as one who collaborated with them."

"At present," Don José pointed out, "the Basques are divided by the frontier between ourselves and France. How much more mischief can they get up to when that frontier is eroded after we are in the Common Market? They will cross backwards and forwards with virtually no control. They will join up with the French Basques. They will appeal to the European Court for all sorts of ethnic minority rights and redress of imaginary grievances. They choose not to invest in business and then jeopardise the profitability of others with their outrages. They will frighten away foreign investment. It is difficult enough to compete with other parts of Spain for funds from Madrid banks who see this as a high risk area."

"Don José, you are talking about profits. I am talking about patriotism and principles."

"You are right, of course, general," interposed Don Ramon, and cleverly diverted the conversation to a patriotic cause célèbre. In your own part of the country we prove time and time again that principle is more important than profit to our national pride. We rightly forego the latter in order to squeeze the British from what is rightfully Spanish territory."

The general could not ignore the bait. His eyes blazed as he spluttered, "Gibraltar!" In his excitement, the word came out with the strong guttural accent of Andalucia whose Moorish background made the garrison rock sound more Arabic than Spanish.

As his apoplexy subsided, he screamed, "Gibraltar must be returned to Spain before we enter the Common Market, if that fate is inevitable. It is unthinkable that Spaniards will have equal rights with British on Gibraltar simply because they are Europeans and not because they are Spaniards. It must become sovereign Spanish territory."

Don Ramon fuelled the fire. "It is not only the Common Market countries, but even NATO countries, like Canada and the United States, and, after all, they are just an extension of British influence. Then there's Turkey ..."

"Infidels!" The general was literally bouncing in his chair. "It's as though we had never won Lepanto. Those trash should be kept at their own filthy end of the Mediterranean. Only Spain can keep the Faith pure. They're pirates. Just like the English. Profit! That's all they're interested in! Profit! The Americans are only English who stole their land from Spain.

"NATO is a conspiracy to protect their continuing piracy. It is English dominated with their lick-spittle lackey of a Germany. What a blessing Hitler and Franco are no longer alive to see what has become of their dreams.

"This Common Market is only the beginning. It is only a contrivance to drag Spain into NATO. We have compromised too much already in letting the Americans have bases here. We did it for money. They are corrupting us already. We must have nobler objectives. The King must be protected from bad advisers."

"And the Spanish-speaking peoples of the world must lead the resistance against this corrosive English influence," Don Ramon goaded.

"Of course! The Americans stamp on Mexico, Panama and now Nicaragua ..."

"And the Malvinas ..."

His voice broke, and he screamed, "The Malvinas! There was perfidy and collusion between the English and the Americans. I cannot and will not stand by while there is any device at my disposal which I can manipulate to save Spain from their domination."

Don Ramon seized the opportunity he had contrived, "Then you believe we must avoid entry to the Common Market by any means available?"

"Yes!"

"Has anyone else approached you with a foolproof plan?"

"No."

"Has anyone approached you with any plan?"

"No."

"Then we have the only plan?"

"Yes."

"Will you put your name to it? That is all we ask."

"Yes."

Don Ramon sighed with relief, and his eyes sparkled a message of triumph to Don José over the general's bowed head.

"Will you commit your supporters to active service?"

"I must. They depend on my judgement and I know many of them are desperate to prove their loyalty to Spain. But we need money to fight."

The others smiled confidently, and Don José assured him, "Money will be no object in this noble cause."

Don Ramon began to outline the plan. "The supporters of the former Junta in Buenos Aires will only join us if they have your personal assurance that you are co-ordinating all military elements of the operation. This can be passed through certain members of the Embassy in Madrid. Our own Embassy in Buenos Aires also has some well-placed staff who can be trusted absolutely."

"The air attaché in Madrid is a vital contact, but his involvement must be protected with the utmost secrecy, for a successful outcome depends on him almost more than on anyone else.

"The task assigned to your forces will be entirely outwith Spain, so that there will be no possibility of conflict of interest in encountering units known to your men.

"You will, however, be required to elicit a considerable amount of military intelligence, and remember, the more accurate the intelligence and the more of it we have, the less prospect of bloodshed.

"Manoeuvres must be contrived to reduce security forces in certain areas at given times. All activities in Spain will be the responsibility of ETA guerrillas so that there may be no breath of collusion or conspiracy within the armed forces. That is why we must have ETA's co-operation as well as the manpower they can muster.

76

"Basically, there will be no need for contact between anyone in your organisation and ETA except yourself and one representative of ETA. We shall co-ordinate such meetings and ensure that the same representative of ETA acts on their behalf every time."

"That is small concession to my conscience," said the General with resignation, "but I will try to think of the overwhelming justice of our cause."

"It is our moral duty to lead our country to a finer destiny than is currently being prepared for it," Don José encouraged.

"We have many moral duties to perform for Spain," the general declared, "and one of the first is to restore morality. There are actually women lying on that beach outside exposing their breasts to the lascivious eyes of any degenerate, and there are men gazing lustfully on them while supposedly relaxing with their wives and their children. This is the kind of immorality to which Spain has been subjected by those northern Europeans who think they can bring in their godless wantonness with impunity to a country which has always been in the thrall of the Holy Mother Church and her true teachings.

"Everything I see convinces me that this is a struggle for good against evil. To me it has the justification of a crusade, and I shall prosecute it with the same dedication."

"Even so," Don Ramon advised, "we must be circumspect, for our good works will not always be appreciated by those who have ulterior motives. Our meetings, for instance, must be varied in their locations and timings. It is a risk for someone as well known as yourself to come here on so short a visit. Our next meeting will be at Estepona. Don José and I have already booked a golfing holiday at the Atalaya Park Hotel for the weekend after next. We have the use of a villa, which belongs to a friend, and will meet you there on the Saturday evening. We shall have our Basque contact with us."

"Don't worry. I learned to cover my tracks a long time ago. At this very moment I am scarcely interrupting a visit to an old comrade-in-arms whom I have to rejoin in fifteen minutes' time at the Yacht Club. For safety's sake I chose someone who not only accepts democracy but actually advocates it. I can't understand how such a dolt ever became a Colonel."

"The Yacht Club is scarcely five minutes' walk from here."

"A lifetime habit of punctuality is not to be lost. I shall leave now and be in good time."

When the general had gone, Don José smirked to his companion. "Perhaps he wants to walk slowly and leer at all those naked women who get him so excited."

"It's all in the mind."

"Anyway, I think we have done a good day's work to get the crusty old devil to join our noble cause."

"And the nobler the cause, the bigger the percentage."

CHAPTER 20

That evening a very different group of men assembled in a room of the Hotel Central overlooking the Nive River beside the main bridge which helped to make the small fortified town of St-Jean-Pied-de-Port one of the strategic route centres of the Western Pyrenees. It is a focal point for the Basques of France with access via the quiet mountain pass of Alto Ibaneta to Spain and its more significant communications centre of Pamplona.

Some of the men were known to the security forces of France or Spain. Some of the more renowned, or notorious, dependent on one's point of view, were known to the security forces of both countries, but the most influential were those whose names and faces were not recorded by either force.

Ostensibly, two recreational and cultural interests accounted for their presence in St-Jean-Pied-de-Port. One was a meeting earlier in the day concerning the Jai Alai championships, that fastest of ball games, universally loved and played by Basques from the Pyrenees to the Philippines. The meeting had been at the rooms of the local club in the Place de Trinquet.

The other was to make final arrangements for the traditional Basque Sports Day, or Kermesse Garazi, which had been organised on a regular basis for the past fifteen years for the benefit of tourists. But those sports sprang from competitions lost in the mists of antiquity, when men pitted their strength against each other in Soka-Tira, Orga Joko or Zakulari.

To these men who carried on these traditions the presence of alien tourists from France or Spain or even farther afield was an unavoidable encroachment largely ignored.

However, what they chose not to ignore was the outside political power. The great mountains from which the Basques drew their strength and inspiration had been used as a divisive boundary between France and Spain, regardless of the consequences for the Basques whose home the mountains are.

The chairman spoke in their beloved language, "You all know why we are gathered here. We have been approached by what can only be described as reactionary right-wing elements in Spain. They want our co-operation to mount some kind of insurrection, which will discredit Spain in the eyes of the rest of Europe. That, of course, would be quite in accord with our own view of Spain.

"Their purpose, however, is to make Spain less acceptable to the European Community. We have to decide our own position on that first."

There were some enthusiastic murmurings. Then someone called from the back, "What's in it for us?"

"A promise," the chairman replied. "A promise of autonomy within Spain if it does not proceed with its application to join the Economic Community and rejects totally the prospect of joining NATO."

There was some interest, but many scoffed.

"It sounds like an attempt at a right-wing overthrow of the government," called one, "and the last time they were in power, we learned all about vicious repression."

"What have we to gain from another civil war?" shouted another. "Remember the Falangists and the Nazi air-raids on Guernica."

"Democracy is bad enough in Spain, but at least there is some prospect of being allowed to talk and being listened to," yelled a third.

The chairman hushed them with a gentle wave of his hand.

"Every Basque agrees with these views. But there is more. I don't have the full details, but there's a plan afoot for an enterprise that will so embarrass the government that Spain will be despised by the rest of the European nations. This would bring about the short-term objective of the right-wing conspirators, but I believe Spain cannot remain as isolationist as she has done in the past. Therefore I believe she would have to improve her image very quickly, and a form of devolution for Basques would become a priority.

The exercise I mentioned is to take place in a foreign country and will not compromise us."

"It can only be in France," the delegate from Oloron complained, "and in that case it will compromise us."

"It's all very well for you in France where you're so much better off with your oil and natural gas in Pau not to mention your fat cheques from Brussels for your farmers. What about us from places like Fuenterrabi where life is much harder? This is a Spanish matter. You French should keep out of the discussion."

"Friends," the chairman appealed, "we're all Basques first and foremost. It serves only the interests of our enemies if we quarrel among ourselves."

One young man stood up and addressed them. Although they found his accent grate on their ears, they nodded encouragement. "I agree that Spanish interests in this affair are paramount, but our common brotherhood requires that we put collective interest above all others. However, we must ensure that the relative peace in France is not endangered."

One of the men sitting beside the chairman congratulated him, "Well said, Joel."

Then Laxalt enquired, "Is there anyone totally opposed to continuing the discussion to the next stage?"

After a silent pause, he said, "Very well. I propose this meeting adjourns and the Strategic Council assumes authority."

Whatever their misgivings, the assembly knew that since they were in a struggle with the authorities they had to sacrifice some of the privilege of democratic debate. They also knew that the fewer involved, the smaller the security risk. Some muttered, some nodded, some sat impassive, but no-one opposed the suggestion.

The meeting broke up as informally as it had begun. The chairman scraped back his chair, but, instead of declaring the meeting closed or where the Strategic Council should meet, he chatted amiably with his companions. The man on his left went over to the group where Joel was listening attentively. He engaged Joel in conversation for a couple of minutes. When Joel looked over at where the chairman had been sitting, he was gone, and Joel knew that once more he had lost his lead to the Strategic Council.

It seemed to him strange that although he was a delegate and although the assembly chose the Council, he did not know the seven members of the Council nor where they met. He assumed the chairman must be a member and that if he watched him at the end of an assembly he would find out the next stage in the organisation of which he had become an established member.

As it was, the chairman was on his way with the other members of the Council to the back of a baker's shop in the Rue d'Espagne, a narrow street of multiple shadows from recessed doorways and protruding windows. Within some of these doorways at the end of the street next to the Pont d'Eglise and again at the intersection with the Rue d'Uhart lolled two or three idle youths. Had Joel or anyone else succeeded in following any member of the Council, these young men would have sprung into action.

As soon as the chairman arrived, the meeting got under way with the same informal approach, but this time there was a greater alertness in the proceedings.

He began by asking, "Are there any views on the progress to date?"

"What I can't understand, Laxalt, is why we still burden ourselves with that traitor, Joel." There was pent-up fury in Uberuga's voice.

Laxalt replied nonchalantly, "To begin with, he's not a traitor. He's not one of ours and that's a comfort. For one thing, we know who to watch. For another, it would be more dangerous and more damaging if Joel was exposed and the Ministry of the Interior put pressure on one of our own people. It would be much more difficult to find him. Think of the distrust. It would spread like a cancer. Besides, Joel's accent is so terrible it always gives me a good laugh. Think of the damage that would be done to our language if more undercover agents had to learn it every time we uncovered one of them. I feel sorry for Joel. He has put so much effort into the role he is playing. It also helps them to believe that we are even more stupid than they take us for already."

"But tonight," Uberuga persisted, "we discussed something on the kind of scale we have never dreamt about before, far less tackled, and there was Joel hearing every word of it."

"And what's he going to do with every word?"

"Run straight to the Deuxième Bureau."

"And whose ears will this news get to?"

"The President himself."

"And does he want Spain to join the Community?"

"Of course not. Everyone knows that."

"Then will he help us or hinder us?"

"Laxalt, you're a genius."

"I try to keep my eyes and ears open and my mouth shut, and I've kept it shut on one or two things so far tonight. But before I begin, I want to hear your views."

Aguirre spoke for all of them, "We cannot really trust these right-wingers."

They all nodded.

"Is that your only fear? Not the bank raids? Not capturing and holding a military base?"

The physical danger did not worry them. They simply did not wish to form an alliance with people they believed were using them for their own ends.

Laxalt sighed. "I think that's the greatest fear that all small isolated groups have. Whichever side wants their help initially has as a long-term objective the complete annihilation of any minority which has distinctive traditions and culture."

"I trust those with fascist ideals no more than you do, but I trust even less those with no ideals at all."

"What do you mean?" Aguirre demanded.

"I mean that the men who made the initial contact are not men of principle or ideal. They're not in this to help anyone but themselves. They're the worst kind of mercenary because they'll not carry the guns, only point the guns of those who do. They will change their mind and their sides the moment a higher offer comes along. They're extremely clever and know the weaknesses and ambitions of everyone they deal with. But like our friend Joel, I feel they are less dangerous because I have their measure.

"The rest is more promising. For the first time ever we have people outside our own Basque nation who will be on our side. It is up to us to maximise the impact, especially since most of them will be very reluctant allies.

"Second, as you will see, we are going to provide funds for years to come without the risk of normal bank raids. As substantial funds will be necessary for the scale of this enterprise, we would be expected to use our expertise to carry out several bank and bullion raids. For this we are to expect co-operation from right-wing sympathisers at the very highest level.

"We'll be advised of locations, critical timings and movements, safe combinations and so on. Security will be rendered ineffective one way or another when a raid is due. We have a target of two hundred million pesetas to meet. Our contacts say they have a fixed requirement of seventy-five million pesetas. The greatest problem - if we can trust them - is that the whole operation has to be completed within ten days. The raids will also take place outside our normal operational radius.

"To protect us from a double-cross by them none of the money will be handed over until after the last raid. To protect them against a double-cross by us they insist on holding five of our members whom they shall name."

There was uproar from the men at this suggestion.

The chairman held up his hand. "You can readily appreciate that if and when we reach agreement there will be many details to work out.

"Third, we are required to attack a military installation ..."

This time he was interrupted by loud cheering.

He smiled grimly and joked, "I thought that motion would be carried, but there is even better to come. Because of the help we are to receive, all our targets will be weakened before we strike."

There were more loud cheers and triumphant laughter.

"On the other hand, it is a fairly big base. We have to hold it for half-an-hour.

When we leave we have to take certain hostages, but we only hold them until nightfall and release them unharmed."

"Third, most of the activity will take place outside our own territory and it will therefore be less easy for the government to justify reprisals.

"Fourth, and this is news to you, part of the campaign will be conducted well outside Spain. We will make an impact on the international scene, and attention will be focused on our cause."

"Where?" Uberuaga demanded. "If it's Paris, we've tried that before, but the government pretends it was Palestinians or Algerians or Armenians. They make sure we get no publicity."

"Better than Paris. Where would we get maximum publicity?"

"The United States?"

"You're on the right track. The most widely read or heard news is in their language ..."

"England!"

"Near enough. In fact, the northern part of that country - Scotland."

"But we've tried them before," Juan complained. "That Scottish National Party is too wishy-washy. They no longer seek independence. They like being a part of England. It makes them feel big to call themselves democrats and talk about working through the ballot box. That's no way to fight for independence when the Civil Guard have their heel on your neck. We've invited them to come to our conferences, but they keep us at arm's length."

"This is a different group who are prepared to fight. They are a very small group, but we only need them to provide local knowledge. They have no qualms about becoming involved in a real battle. They call themselves the SPA, the Scottish People's Army."

CHAPTER 21

Glen oozed out of the soaking wet driving seat of his hired car and distorted his shoulders into a Quasimodo hunch of relief for his agonised back.

He squelched up the steps into his temporary home, rented from the Stevensons, stumbled through to his bedroom, where his sparse luggage lay unopened on the floor, and sat on the edge of the bed as he tugged at his reluctant, soggy clothes, oblivious at first to the damp seeping into the quilt and the puddles forming on the carpet.

He got up carefully from the bed and walked erect, shoulders stiff, to the bathroom. He leaned on the wash-hand basin and viewed his face in the mirror. It was unmarked by blows, but its ashen, grey colour surprised him. To cheer up his reflection he congratulated it aloud on the successful outcome of the fight.

He began to peel his jacket by pushing it slowly off one shoulder. From there to the elbow it behaved like a straight-jacket, but managed by manipulating the cuff slowly between finger-tips and heel of hand until he had dragged it free from one arm. The other side was easier. Once he had pushed it from the inside to the shoulder, he let his slack arm hang straight, and the jacket, weighed down by its own wetness, dropped leadenly to the cork floor.

His shirt clung to him like a second skin. He gave up the struggle and managed to remove the rest of his clothes instead.

Knowing how temperamental plumbing can be outside the United States, he turned the shower on from a safe distance and checked the water temperature with his fingers. The shock of a sudden change from hot to freezing could cause a spine-jarring jerk. Not until he was certain that the thermostat really worked did he venture under the stinging hot spray.

When the combination of water jet, warmth and steam had soothed him back to a semblance of normality, he tackled his shirt again. He faced the shower and bent his neck so that the water squirted below his collar and lubricated between skin and fabric. With a little extra persuasion, the shirt dragged itself from his back. He trampled it under his feet as he stretched his skin towards the invigorating spray.

Fifteen minutes later, when he sensed the British domestic supply of hot water must be running out, he emerged from the shower. Thank god the Stevensons had installed a proper shower and not one over the bath!

He was physically at ease, and mentally on the stable side of euphoria. He plundered Mrs Stevenson's airing cupboard for a bath towel, which he wrapped round himself as he padded through to the lounge and stood in front of the large picture window.

There was a lot of activity at RAF Leuchars. Two Phantoms were practising instrument circuits and bumps. They took off towards the west in a tight pair and climbed steeply over Ludlow Hill before banking north over Tentsmuir Forest and completing the rectangle by racing in at wave-level, lowering their undercarriage as they reached the strand, stalling inches above the blurred surface of the runway and boosting themselves forward instantly with a roar from their after-burners to hurtle them into their next circuit.

Sighing at his forgetfulness, he went back to his soaking clothes to extract his phone scrambler. Back in the lounge he inserted it between phone lead and jack.

He dropped the towel on the chair next the phone and, still damp, sat down on it.

He dialled his Controller at the Embassy and identified himself.

"Have you got my satellite pictures yet?" he demanded.

"They're on their way to you by Securicor. You'll have them by eleven hundred hours tomorrow."

"Where did you address them to?"

"Yourself, at the Economics Department."

"Correct. Continue to use that as my mail-box, but here are details of my new domestic arrangements," he said, giving his new address and phone number.

"But the best part is the superb view I have of our main centre of interest."

"Yes, we thought it would be useful."

"You know?"

"Yes, Zelinsky set it up for you. How do you think Stevenson managed to get called to Cambridge for the summer? He's years past it, and he knows it. We were worried he might turn it down, but a little judicious flattery overcomes the resistance of the most modest men."

"Did you arrange for MacLaren's wife to recommend it to me?"

"No. That was pure luck. Probably the last for a while."

"Pity. I could do with someone like her on my side. Since you know so much, you'll know what else I need."

"Night glasses, an infra-red camera, a gun because you're feeling lonely out there in the country?"

"Right. And a set of golf clubs."

"Golf clubs?"

"You guys set it up. Have you forgotten I'm on a golf foundation exchange? How inefficient can you be, letting me turn up here without a set of clubs? I had to tell friends at the Royal and Ancient Club today that mine had gone missing at the airport. Get someone to burgle my apartment in Titusville and send me my own clubs. I hired a set here and was hard put to break ninety."

"What it takes to put an agent in the field nowadays! Anything else?"

"There was another American in our foursome - Captain Schultz, US Navy, CO at Edzell. More an electronics whiz kid than a seaman. Zelinsky guessed Edzell is leaky. Can you run a check on Schultz for me?

"He has as a buddy a wild Highland chieftain called Seamus Breck. He seems to have freer access to Edzell than is healthy for a civilian. You should have a file on him by this time. Also the second-in-command, Major diMaggio.

"Finally, how sound is this communication system? Stevenson broadcast to the telephone company that he was going away. He was afraid I wouldn't pay my phone bill, I guess. Rumour might spread that I'm here. That could provide employment for eavesdroppers. If I see any plumbers up telegraph poles, I'll know someone's interested."

"Yeah, wilco. You're alright for friendly incoming calls, but I'll give you a signal for priority ones. But you shouldn't have tried to slip one in about diMaggio again. You tried a routine check on him this morning and you got thumbs down. He's purple code. No way can you get a fix on him."

"Our side or theirs?"

"Don't even ask that much. But I hear there's pressure for the reintroduction of crucifixion for guys like you who tangle with guys like diMaggio. You're lucky you weren't killed. He never takes prisoners."

"Then he's been in touch with you already? He must have a helluva lot of clout to pull!"

"Just leave him alone. It's healthier that way."

"He was the only lead I had. Apart from him, I've made zero progress."

The voice at the other end ignored the plea and went off at a tangent. "I hope you can sleep in spite of these circuits and bumps up there."

"You got someone else on the ground? Come clean."

"Not on the ground. In space. I've just seen a computer analysis of air movements in your part of the world based on satellite feed-back."

"Tell the satellite to keep an eye on me as well. I need all the protection I can get."

Glen put down the phone and, abandoning his towel, padded from the darkened lounge through the hall on his way to the bedroom. The light shining under the bathroom door made the details of the hall clear compared with the lounge.

As he pushed the bedroom door open he heard the handle of the front door turn slowly. As he looked round with eyes dilated by the darkness in which he had been sitting, he could make out the levers of the Mortise retract into the lock.

His soft bare feet pressed into the polished parquet flooring as he took up position at the back of the opening door, his pain temporarily forgotten.

He wished he had a gun in his hand. He felt vulnerable in his nakedness.

How many were there? Could he tackle the first one? Was it an ordinary burglar who knew that the Stevensons were away? Or was it Zelinsky's murderer or murderers?

A right hand spread its fingers round the edge of the door. The knuckles took a grip, and the shoulder appeared. The intruder's back remained to Glen.

He waited until the figure was right inside before he lunged and fastened a lethal lock around the neck. The slightest pressure from Glen and the precious vertebra pinpointed by the more humanitarian hangman would have cracked with supreme prejudice to his prisoner.

His surprise was almost as great as his victim's. The delicate perfume and the soft body told him that he was holding a woman. He had no intention of letting her go in a futile gesture of gallantry. He was aware that the female of the espionage species was more deadly than the male. His only concession was to allow her to breathe.

Fine, slender fingers tried to prise his fingers open. This woman was no professional. She had no idea where to start attacking a man. For this Glen was most grateful, considering how exposed his tender parts were.

"What are you doing here?" he hissed.

"I only came to help," panted his victim.

There was something familiar about the voice. He had heard it recently. It was frightened now and not provocative. There was no trace of implied tease or flirtation, only fear. It took no concentration of memory to recognise the delectable Isobel MacLaren.

Retaining a firm grip, he took his arm from her throat and gruffly demanded, "What the hell do you think you're playing at, coming creeping in here like that? I could have killed you. Do you realise that?"

There was little trace of shock or fear in her voice, as she explained, "I only came to see if I could do anything in the house for you. I have a key. The Stevensons left it with me once when they went away so that I could come up and check the place for them. When I offered to return it that time, they asked me to keep it. I've had it ever since."

Her voice was so matter-of-fact, and the reason so mundane, that Glen didn't know whether to laugh or cry.

He relaxed his grip entirely, and his body shook with laughter.

She made no attempt to move from his slackened arms. If anything she was closer to him now than when he was holding her in a death-grip. The length of her body touched him in more places and nestled itself intimately against his flat belly.

His hands moved to give her arms a reassuring squeeze, but she locked them under her elbows and drew them slowly round her body, one at her waist and one higher till he could feel the feminine softness over her heart. She pressed his hands against her body and tensed firm against him before subsiding in a feverish shiver.

She turned and clung to him, pressing herself into him, hungry for his touch, oblivious to his nakedness.

Glen could feel his interest being aroused, but her desperation and willingness warned him that this could be the oldest form of deception in the world, the latest Mata Hari.

But this was not a woman offering her treasures. It was a wild, hungry female, desperate for a mate.

"Easy now," he soothed with gentle caresses. "It's all over. You had a bad fright. That's all."

A spasm passed through her and total relaxation spread throughout her body as she collapsed into gentle sobs.

If this had been acting, Glen had never seen anything like it in his life before. He was convinced that her orgasmic frenzy had been spontaneous and without any premeditated plan. If, in fact, she had been sent to set him up, her organisation was at a considerable disadvantage, if it had to depend on agents who were more easily sensually provoked than provocative. But it was strange how she had led him to this house in the first place, just happened to have a spare key, and then came sneaking in at dead of night.

He took her to the couch, half leading her, half supporting her. As she sank into it, she looked up at him, her large eyes, soft and vulnerable from her weeping, looked straight into his, and he could see no guile in them. With the same open honesty they ran over his body, taking in his nakedness with the frankness of a primitive innocent.

Without comment he went and picked up his towel from the chair where he had left it and wrapped it round his waist.

He went back to her and gently stroked her hair.

"I'm sorry to have given you such a fright, but I must admit you frightened me too."

She gazed back.

"Let me get you a coffee. Or would you like something stronger?"

She nodded.

"Do you know where the Stevensons keep their brandy?"

Again she nodded and, crossing to the sideboard, opened a door and took out two glasses and a bottle.

She poured two generous measures and asked him, "Water or lemonade?"

"What is it?"

"Whisky."

"I'll take water."

She went through to the kitchen, and he heard her fill a little water in the glasses direct from the tap.

As she handed it to him her fingers lingered on his, tingling with sensual awareness. But there was no deliberate provocation in her eyes or guile in her movements as her lips caressed the rim of the glass, everything about her rejoicing in the essence of natural female invitation.

They sat together on the couch, comfortable in each other's presence like old comrades, oblivious to the possibility of tension between the sexes. Without invitation or stealth they moved close to each other.

"I'm sorry about attacking you just now," he murmured.

"It was a pleasure - after the initial shock. You must keep very fit. Your hands are strong. I could feel all your muscles tense as you held me - even after you realised I was a woman. But your hands changed. Your muscles were as strong as ever, but your hands were definitely more gentle and sensitive."

Reluctant as he was to break the spell, Glen had to find out why she was here.

At last he said, "Shouldn't we phone Campbell? He'll be worried about you."

"Not a chance! This is his bridge night. He never misses it. The other three are just as fanatical. They even arrange their holidays so that they are away at the same time. If one is ill, the bridge is held in his bedroom."

"That's enthusiasm for you."

"Misplaced enthusiasm as far as I'm concerned. Imagine! On our first night home from our honeymoon he went round for his game of bridge and didn't get home until two in the morning. I never forgave him for that, especially when I learned that the honeymoon had been timed to finish so as not to hinder the bridge arrangements.

"Part of the trouble was that he had been a widower for two years before we married. He's much older than me, you know. I was a junior honours student when his wife died. I was infatuated. He's always so proper and correct. He's charming to the students and makes them all feel so important. They adore him. He's a walking textbook of all that's correct in his subject, academic life and social life. I could almost say, in domestic life as well, but there are one or two chapters missing from that one. I was so flattered and thrilled when he paid any attention to me.

"As you know, he has a formidable academic reputation although he has not bothered to climb the academic ladder, partly because he prefers to do the things he's interested in like teaching, research and writing, and, of course, his private pursuits like his golf and his bridge. He's also a consultant and is often called upon by the government to work on various bodies. He says, the fact that he doesn't have administrative responsibility apart from his department gives him greater freedom."

"You're very proud of him."

"I admire him greatly. I used to believe I loved him, but I realise now I was in love with an image I had of him. I even believed he loved me, but I think it was a kind of mutual respect. You may not believe it now, but I was a very good student. Campbell still says I was the brightest student he's ever had. Alright, I was intelligent, and that man inspired me. Part of it was the tragedy he suffered when his wife died."

"What happened?"

"A car accident. There were rumours at the time that it had been deliberate. He seemed so strong at the time, I was mesmerised by him, but it may be another part of the textbook by which he lives. He has very strong codes, but no feelings."

"He has a military background. Perhaps that has something to do with his highly organised life-style. He spent time in Korea, didn't he?" Glen probed.

"Oh, that was well before my time. I wasn't even born when he was in Korea. But, you know, he does keep in touch with a lot of people from those days. Camaraderie is one thing, but the letter-writing he keeps up is exceptional. He's the one who keeps everyone else in touch. He gets phone calls from people who want to find out about so-and-so from the old days. He made a lot of friends among Americans too. When did you and he first meet?"

"We never did. What gave you the impression that we had?"

"Oh, just something he said, I suppose. He seemed to talk a lot about you just before you arrived and I gathered that he was very interested in finding out exactly what you would be doing. I know. He phoned some of his old army friends and asked them about you. It was after one of these phone calls that he mentioned this house might suit you. Oh! I wasn't supposed to tell you it was his idea," she exclaimed, putting her hand to her mouth.

Glen felt a greater relief than he had anticipated, when his nagging doubts about her integrity towards himself were answered. At the same time the collegiate ties of loyalty to MacLaren were conveniently diminished to the point where they would be no obstacle to intensifying his relationship with Isobel. What did worry him, however, was that MacLaren had talked about him before he had arrived. That required clarification.

CHAPTER 22

General Lopez did not believe in wasting time. He cut short his holiday with his democratic friend in the north. It was not difficult for them to find something to disagree about, and his early departure was as acceptable to host as it was to guest.

Next morning he flew direct from Bilbao to Madrid by an internal flight of Iberian Airways. He was met by a corporal driver with a car bearing the insignia of a two-star general and was driven to a military base on the outskirts of the city. One of the regimental boards at the entrance carried the insignia of the Corps of Engineers.

A guard checked driver and passenger and signalled to a colleague to raise the barrier and let them through. The car glided towards the entrance of the main administration block. The driver drew up at the steps and ran round to the nearside door to hold it open for Lopez to push himself out of the large Seat. He straightened himself and swept a hand downwards over his jacket to smooth any creases before climbing the short flight of steps.

Although he was bareheaded and in civilian clothes he saluted smartly when two immaculate guards snapped to attention and presented arms with a crack of the palm on the magazines of their rifles.

Inside, an orderly sergeant conducted him to the office of General Commanding, Major General Mendez.

As soon as they entered Mendez sprang to his feet and with a wave of his hand dismissed the staff captain with whom he had been conferring.

"Captain Anaya," he ordered, "have breakfast served in here for myself and General Lopez."

The moment the door closed behind the captain and sergeant, Mendez clasped Lopez by his shoulders, and with his eyes glistening, demanded, "Mission accomplished?"

"A singularly distasteful mission, but nonetheless accomplished. We are obliged to deal with ETA and with even less savoury, unscrupulous self-seekers. I shall take great pleasure, when this affair is over, in seeing that they are all brought to book. I feel sullied by being in contact with such people."

"Console yourself with that thought. More important, does their plan sound feasible?"

"Not only is it feasible! It is beautiful! On a much larger scale than we had anticipated. We shall have our own volunteers backed up by ETA guerrillas, and ... wait for it ... Argentina regulars, including some of their best pilots!

"General Lami Dozo has many supporters in Argentina who believe that he was betrayed by Galtieri militarily and politically. They believe that the two men should not be spoken of in the same breath, and the present Junta is too cowardly to rehabilitate Lami Dozo openly. Even the British were impressed by the skill and bravery of the Argentine Air Force. It is universally agreed that they were inspired and their strategy masterminded by Lami Dozo.

Dependable elements in Argentina are in a much stronger position than we are with this government of ragbag socialists. They ..."

He was interrupted by a knock at the door.

"Come!" Mendez barked.

Two orderlies entered, each carrying a tray.

"Over there," growled Mendez pointing to a heavy table at the side of his large, ornate office.

....

Lopez was taken back to Madrid International Airport by the same driver and delivered to the departure lounge. He waited until the car had driven away before he entered the foyer and looked at the flight information screen. He was more interested in arrivals than departures.

He noted that there was a little over an hour to wait for the next flight from Bilbao.

He made his way to the arrival terminal to wait for it.

He stood at the observation window as it touched down, watched it taxi to the gate and went down to join the passengers as they emerged from the luggage collection carousel and walked among the first of them to the exit.

An Airforce NCO was anxiously scrutinising the passengers as they emerged.

Lopez went over to him and asked, "Are you waiting for me? I am General Lopez."

The airman saluted smartly. "Yes, sir. I have a car right over here."

He drove Lopez swiftly to the Airforce base at Getafe and delivered him to the office of the commanding officer, Colonel Alcazar.

Together they discussed the disposition of Spain's air power as though they were moving chessmen about a board.

Lopez declined the offer of lunch and was driven back to Madrid by the Airforce car, from which he alighted at the Central Station.

A large black Mercedes glided over from the restricted parking area where it had been waiting with its engine purring. Before it reached the general, the back door opened and he was swept inside.

A glass partition separated the rear compartment from the driver. The sole occupant pressed an intercom switch and gave the driver his next destination. He was a man in his late forties or early fifties. It was difficult to think of him being so young, for his face had all the exuberance of the late Paul Getty on a bad day. His clothes, his furtiveness and his frown spoke volumes for the relief from care that only vast wealth can buy.

His first words to Lopez were in keeping with his appearance. "I'm not at all happy.

"Your proposals to handle much greater sums of cash in the National Lottery fill me with forebodings. Why do you want the money to be moved in larger quantities on fewer occasions? It's dangerous."

Lopez's curt answer made him wince. "To save bloodshed!

"It is the most efficient way of providing funds for our cause without hurting the business community. They help us, so we should protect them. We don't want to be greedy. We need a lot more money than usual this time. It wouldn't be fair to ask the same people again and again."

"But the veterans will suffer. The money is for them."

"The money had better come out of profits and prizes. Make sure the veterans do not suffer by this."

Lopez always found his temper difficult to control when he was with businessmen. Although their politics were sensible in the main, they lacked the open-handedness of the military when it came to spending money on essentials like armaments and defence.

As a sop to his companion's aversion to violence he had come prepared. Handing him a slip of paper, he commanded, "The first prize this month and next month will go to these numbers."

One with such a vivid pallor as the general's new accomplice would not easily be seen to blanch, but the deterioration in his complexion was as though someone had switched off all the disco lights on his face.

"It's impossible," he gasped.

Lopez knew he was as compassionate as the next man, but he positively snapped at the trembling spectre beside him, "Make it possible. You made us the laughing stock of the world when you used the equipment to draw the teams for the World Cup Soccer Finals. You fixed that, not once, but twice, in front of millions. Don't tell me it's impossible. Only this time, do it with some finesse."

CHAPTER 23

MacLaren handed Glen a note when he joined him at the bar of the Staff Club at lunchtime.

"From Miss Fleming."

Glen read, 'Father Mackellar has been phoning for you. Please contact him as soon as you can.'

When Glen looked up, his attention was caught by two newcomers. One was a tall bearded man of about thirty with craggy appearance and sturdy outdoor clothes. At first glance, Glen put him down as some foraging species of natural scientist. His companion was a much neater man, not much over five feet eight, with small, pointed features and dark wavy hair.

"Here's someone you should meet," said MacLaren and stretched on his toes to wave them over to the bar.

He introduced Glen to the tall man first, "Dr. Glen from America."

The stranger's eyes glittered as he said, "Como esta Usted?"

Glen's presence of mind stopped him answering in Spanish. He'd come across the trick before - speak to someone suddenly in a language to see if they understand it. Instead, he stuck out his hand as he heard MacLaren say, "David Johnson."

Glen beamed at him, more overtly friendly than ever, because this man could be an enemy. "Good to know you, David."

Johnson then introduced his companion, "Antonio Hernandez, also from America."

"One of my little foibles," Johnson explained off-handedly. "Being involved in what might be called Latin America, I refuse to take for granted that someone described as American is necessarily a citizen of the United States. After all, from a Spanish point of view, or any objective point of view, come to that, English is hardly the first language of the Americas. The gringos don't even have a proper name for their country. What's the correct name for their citizens - United Statesers?"

Johnson's manner was designed to offend, but Glen was happy that the burst of Spanish had only been an excuse for him to pursue a hobbyhorse and not an astute attempt to find out if he spoke the language.

MacLaren ordered drinks for Johnson and Hernandez.

He then explained to Glen, "Main interest of the Spanish Department here in St Andrews is Latin, or, more precisely Hispanic America.

"Don't know if you would guess, but David's great hobby is mountaineering. By charging off to South America to work on mountain dialects he gives himself an excuse to sling his ropes and spikes all over the Andes."

Glen asked, "Are you a mountaineer too, Antonio?"

"No. My hobby at present, as well as trying to improve my English while I am here, is tracing certain British migrations to South America."

"If your research compares with your English, you should be a happy man. How long have you been here?"

"Only since May."

Johnson had moved away while they were talking and called Hernandez to meet someone else.

MacLaren and Glen helped themselves to the cold buffet and retired to a low table to enjoy it.

Minutes later, Glen's ear automatically tuned in to a Spanish conversation at a table behind, as Johnson and Hernandez talked earnestly.

Hernandez spoke in his low intense voice, made almost unintelligible by the general hum of background noise. Two distinct words that leapt out at Glen were 'Malvinas' and 'revenge', but he could make no sense of the isolated words he picked up.

....

Back at the office, Glen's first task was to phone Mackellar.

"Ah! Dr. Glen, my son, it's good to hear from you. The reason I've been troubling all these nice people with phone calls is that I've heard from one of my parishioners that the young man of whom we spoke two nights ago is coming through this weekend. Would you like me to arrange a meeting between the two of you?"

"That's very kind of you, Father. I'm sure most grateful."

He hung up and thought for a moment before redialling.

"Hi, Antonio. Gee, I was sorry we didn't have longer to talk when we met. This is Colin Glen. Remember? The guy from the country with no name. The other American from the other America."

Antonio remembered without enthusiasm.

Glen persevered. "I was interested in your work on migration. I've done some demographic studies too. Perhaps we could get together and compare notes. I'm not pretending we can help each other, but at least we have a common interest. What do you say?"

"I suppose we could meet."

"Say, that's great! How about a beer in the Staff Club around five tonight? We can talk around the subject and see if we want to share any ideas that could be of mutual benefit."

"I think we can have a beer, but I do not think we shall want to co-operate in any work."

"Don't worry. We'll have a get-together anyway."

As soon as he hung up, the phone rang. A familiar voice said, "Engineering department. We've had a complaint about your extension. Have you had any problems?"

Glen recognised his Embassy control. "Not to my knowledge, but I'll hang up, and you can ring again to make sure."

Quickly he stretched behind and inserted the scrambler before the phone rang again.

The familiar voice was sharper than usual. "Communications problem. At 8pm a blue Sierra will pass your door driving westwards. A hundred and fifty yards farther on opposite the next farm road on the right it will stop and flash its brake lights twice. As soon as it moves off, follow it."

The phone clicked.

CHAPTER 24

A wire hawser scraped across the submarine's steel deck, as she moored in the naval dockyard of Santa Cruz, Tenerife. Orders were shouted in English, but the white ensign was nowhere to be seen. The captain gave the order, 'finished with engines,' before speaking in a guttural language to the coxswain, "Timing couldn't have been better. Walvis Bay extends our field enormously. We couldn't have reached this far if we had to operate from Cape Town."

The coxswain grinned. "It's a good feeling to have this kind of mobility. The lads will enjoy their shore leave in a friendly port. It does a lot for morale to know we are within sailing distance of an ally."

"For god's sake, man, don't be too enthusiastic, not just yet anyway. Things look promising, but don't spoil our chances by jumping the gun." The Afrikaans reprimand sounded harsh.

The submarine was made fast alongside an identical vessel flying the Spanish flag.

The captain turned to his navigating officer. "I'll step across and pay our compliments informally to our neighbour. But I won't waste any time. This is an operational visit not a courtesy one. And that applies to all members of the shore party. They must be reminded they are on duty."

As the other two descended from the conning-tower back inside the submarine, the captain climbed down the outside on to the deck, where the bo'sun was checking the rigging of a flimsy gangplank joining them to the vessel berthed on the inside.

The captain saluted his own vessel's South African ensign as he crossed the plank, and immediately touched the peak of his cap again with flattened finger-tips in recognition of the Spanish ensign.

Within minutes crew members in civilian clothes were scrambling on to the wharf with the usual cheery abandon of naval ratings coming ashore after a long voyage. They were nodded through the barrier manned by Spanish Naval Police who gave their pay-books only a cursory inspection.

Once in the town the men dispersed in groups of twos and threes.

One pair took a taxi to the Avis car rental office and collected a Seat, which had been reserved by a German tourist firm on behalf of two of its nationals. For identification purposes, the two seamen produced West German Passports, which contained their photographs, but described them as an architect and a surveyor. They paid their deposit in American Express Travellers' Cheques in multiples of West German Marks.

They drove across the island to Puerta de la Cruz and checked into the Atlantis Hotel which had a room reserved in the names of the men described on their passports.

A trio took a bus to mountain-perched Tenerife Airport and disappeared into a bar where they quenched their salty thirst with orange juice. Half-an-hour later a KLM Jumbo Jet landed from Amsterdam with a complement of Dutch holidaymakers which would have been full, had not three passengers failed to check in. The three sailors mingled with the hordes emerging from customs and clambered onto a bus to be taken to Playa de Las Americas. The courier ticked their names off. One was described as a bank clerk from Delft, and the other two as employees of Netherlands radio in Hilversum.

These identities were confirmed by the passports they presented at the reception office of the apartment block in the southern tip of the island where they were booked in for a week.

Twenty of the men who had come ashore were thus dispersed throughout the islands of the Canaries, for some of them had travelled by local air-service or ferry to Gran Canaria and Lanzarote. None of them acknowledged his South African citizenship. Most were described as German or Dutch, but Austria, Switzerland and even Zimbabwe figured on passports. All accommodation had been booked and paid for in advance through a variety of travel agents. Travellers' cheques and currency were in marks, guilders, Swiss francs, schillings, dollars and pesetas, but nowhere was there a rand in sight.

By early evening the one third of the liberty party still in Santa Cruz had returned to their ship and their less fortunate shipmates, who had not enjoyed shore-leave. As hand-picked volunteers, their total sobriety was the only characteristic that might have distinguished them from typical naval revellers at the end of a night in town.

The cramped quarters of the ratings' mess in a submarine can well do without shipmates who have over indulged. On this occasion they were conspicuous by their absence. With so many empty bunks, the silence was sepulchral, for everyone aboard, with the exception of the officer of the watch and the master-at-arms, was asleep in his bunk.

The crew needed to make the most of their rest, for there were only enough ratings to man one watch, although there was a full complement of officers and petty-officers.

By ten o'clock only one person had not returned. The submarine captain, Commander Zeitsmann, left the ship when the last rating was back aboard. A private car drew up, as he stepped ashore, and whisked him into the darkness.

Its destination was a discreet villa nestling high above the harbour and protected by a dense screen of trees.

At the door of the spacious lounge illuminated by the lights from the harbour and the reflection of the moon, he was greeted in English by the bulkier of the two men there ahead of him. "You have done well, Commander. Your voyage has been a great success and augurs a new era for our country in international relations. Let me introduce you right away to Señor Velasquez."

His white suit enveloped in cigar smoke gave him a ghostly appearance as he led Zeitsmann across the twilit room to the shadowy veranda where Velasquez was waiting.

"Señor Velasquez is the Air Force Attaché at the Argentine Embassy in Madrid. His colleagues are the imaginative originators of this enterprise for which you and your crew have volunteered."

Velasquez was a slender man with elegant gestures. He bowed formally as they shook hands, and his English was less heavily accented than either Swartz or Zeitsmann as he said, "It is a privilege to meet you, Commander. We are indebted to you for your efforts on our behalf in the attempted liberation of the Malvinas."

"Don't thank me. If it were not for Colonel Swartz here and his colleagues in the Bureau of State Security using their good offices, the hands of people like myself would be completely tied. In fact, we have to thank him for the present arrangements. It's very difficult for a serving officer like myself to say so, but the South African government, I believe, does not know the full implications of this exercise any more than does your own government. I am happy to volunteer because I am certain that when we prove the success of the operation, our governments will come more into the open and we shall achieve popular support for such co-operative ventures between our two countries."

Swartz intervened. "All your crew members who are staying ashore have reported back that all is going according to plan. My own men who are operating a precautionary surveillance have confirmed this.

"I had a signal from the 'Tafelberg' that she is in position for your rendezvous as scheduled. I take it that all bunkering and revictualling is complete and you are ready to sail at midnight."

"I'm ready as soon as I receive my orders, Colonel," Zeitsmann replied.

"Here they are," said Swartz, drawing a small envelope from the inside of his linen jacket.

....

In accordance with the orders passed on by Swartz, the South African submarine, on the stroke of midnight, hauled the last mooring line inboard and slipped quietly from its berth. Six miles out and still within Spanish territorial waters, contrary to maritime law, it submerged. Within minutes of disappearing below the surface, it changed course.

Four hours later, Zeitsmann was at the raised periscope scanning the dark surface water. He hesitated and his shoulders tensed as he held the periscope steady and concentrated on focusing it on a distant, distinctive configuration of lights.

When he was certain of his identification he gave his orders, and the hunter closed on its quarry.

CHAPTER 25

Hernandez was late. Glen had been waiting fifteen minutes, positioned in a corner from which he could watch the door.

Hernandez entered, his sharp features tightly set. His bright dark eyes swept the room with the minimum movement of his head. As the room was almost deserted, he must have seen Glen right away, but he ignored him and went direct to the bar and ordered a lager.

Glen got up to protest that he was buying, but saw from the look in Hernandez' eyes that the gesture was not appreciated.

When Hernandez came over to where he was sitting, Glen opened affably, pointing at his own drink, "I see you prefer lager too. I can't enjoy that dark beer at all. I don't like the taste, and, if anything is going to be cold in a bar here, the best chance is it'll be lager."

He raised his glass in a toast, although it was nearly empty. "Here's to success."

Hernandez did not respond. He continued to stare at Glen, his eyes blazing.

"Dr. Glen, you have not been honest with me. You are much more familiar with South America than you pretended."

"What do you mean?"

"As soon as you phoned me this afternoon, I thought you were being very kind and, so that I should know exactly what you had published, I checked with the Library."

"But I've no work in the Library," Glen protested.

"Perhaps not in the University Library, but certainly in our Department Library - for obvious reasons, since you are such an expert on Hispanic America. I was impressed to find you are an authority on many parts of South America, including my own country of Argentina, which most North Americans have never visited. The references you quote suggest you must speak very competent Spanish. Why, I ask myself, did this man not speak Spanish to my friend, David?"

"I can read Spanish very well. I knew what David said to me, but I've been caught out before when I tried to show off by speaking it, only to discover that so many people around me spoke it fluently. It's no big deal. Lots of people speak Spanish. Why get so excited about it?"

"That is not so. Very few people here understand Spanish."

"Oh, I guess I'm thinking of the States. I assumed the same thing here. It's the main foreign language taught in America ... Sorry, the States. I guess it's French or German over here. Could be Latin for all I know!" He tried to make light of it and sound vague, but he knew Hernandez should be worried about the conversation he'd had with Johnson.

"That may be, and possibly I am over-sensitive to what I thought was a deception." He accepted his share of the blame unconvincingly.

"There is the other matter," he continued by way of justification. "You mentioned only Mexico and the Caribbean, but yet you know much about Argentina. Why did you not say so?"

"Look. I'm a bit older than you, Antonio. I learned a long time ago that no matter how much we may flatter ourselves that we have some knowledge, there is always someone who is a greater authority. If you were an expert on the United States and taught about it for years in Buenos Aires, you would never presume to tell a native of any part of the United States all about his hometown. You would just look foolish. That's the way I operate, Sure, I know more about Argentina than most Americans - sorry, most people in the United States - and therefore I can write about the tiniest parts of that huge country for specialised interests.

"Antonio, I'll gladly talk with you all night about Argentina. You may learn a little from me. I will learn a lot from you. Partly, I guess, I had that in mind when I suggested we talk."

Having accepted these explanations, Hernandez appeared to lapse from aggression into stiff formality, and for twenty minutes they exchanged reserved anecdotes about their work.

Hernandez explained his interest in British migration to Argentina. "You see, I went to St George's College, a beautiful school at Quilmes, a rich suburb of Buenos Aires. It is regarded by many as the finest school in the whole of Argentina." There was a mixture of pride and bitterness in his voice.

"My parents were comfortable, but not rich and had to make sacrifices. But it is a prestigious thing to do. I loved the school, and I thought I admired and liked the British. That was why I started this study. That is why I have reasonably good English."

Glen took him up on a point, "You said you thought you liked the British? Have you changed your mind?"

Hernandez' whole attitude stiffened. "Dr. Glen," he said formally, "the Malvinas was worse than a disaster for us. It was a national humiliation. The British - and your people, who turned out not to be the friends of their fellow Americans - could have solved the problem by political, diplomatic or economic measures. It would have taken a little longer. That is all. By the end of the century, the Malvinas will belong to Argentina. Britain will be relieved and even happy, but there will always be a bitter taste in the mouths of Argentines. Your country and the British were already looking for oil on the continental shelf before the war. The profit from that, for surely there will be profit, would pay many times over for the cost of forcing peace on Argentina by economic means. Only you and the British have the technology to exploit that oil. We could all have worked as friends. Now we cannot forget. You have visited my country. You know my people are not warmongers."

Glen's glass had been empty for some time before Hernandez finished his drink.

"Let me buy you another," Glen offered, "to show there are no hard feelings."

"No, thank you. I must keep a clear head. I have more work to do this evening."

He got up to leave, and Glen asked as an apparent afterthought, "By the way, I hope I didn't cause any misunderstanding with David over this matter of Spanish."

"He does not know of it. I have not seen him since I found out these matters. He has gone away for a few days."

"Oh! Where to?" asked Glen innocently.

"Glencoe. The call of the mountains is very strong for him, and he has gone climbing with friends."

"Do you not climb?"

"I do. With me it is a sport. For David it is a passion."

....

On his way home through Strathkinness village, Glen noticed a yellow Telecom van beside an open manhole. A man in blue overalls was packing his equipment into the van.

As he unlocked the front door, the telephone rang. He reached it at the third ring.

The gently undulating tones of Father Mackellar wafted along the line. "Good evening, my son. You must think me a pestilential old nuisance to trouble you so soon again.

"I just wanted to tell you that our expected guest will not be through in St Andrews this weekend. When I took the liberty of telling him that you wished to soften the blow of the bereavement for our friend's mother, he said he would like to contact you. I gave him your number. Have I done right?"

"Yes, indeed."

"Bless you, my son. You're so easy to please. Don't hesitate to ask for any help I can give."

Only when they rang off did it occur to Glen that Mackellar's message, although entirely intelligible to himself, would have made little sense to anyone listening in. He wondered if the wily old cleric had an idea that he might be under surveillance.

CHAPTER 26

Glen chose to use the Stevensons' ancient Mini to throw possible watchers off his tracks.

At two minutes to eight he left the house, opened the garage, started the temperamental machine at the third attempt, reversed it out of the garage and turned it to face the drive exit with the engine running.

At ten seconds to eight a blue Ford Sierra passed the gate travelling west.

Glen accelerated, or at least he pressed the accelerator, but the engine stalled. He turned the ignition several times but only succeeded in flooding the carburettor. He struggled out of the little door and peered round the wall to see if the Sierra had stopped. It had. Its brake lights winked once, and it drove on. Glen assumed that the first signal from the brake lights had been given before he was in a position to see it.

He scrambled back into the car, switched on the ignition and prayed to the profane god of internal combustion. The engine cleared its throat and purred into life. He revved it gently. It sounded perfect. He let out the clutch and the four-wheeled mule jumped into the middle of the road. The Sierra was disappearing over the brow of the hill. He shot after it, regardless of the clutch's reluctance to establish a reliable relationship with the engine.

In a quarry on the south side of the road, opposite where the Sierra had stopped, a long-wheel-base Land Rover was parked. A combination of his rush to catch up with the Sierra, now out of sight, and the camouflage of the Land Rover prevented its registering on his eye.

He raced over the brow of the hill like a mechanised Don Quixote. The road dipped to the right, then turned to the left in a precipitous downhill gradient. A large tractor was coming towards him where the road narrowed from its twelve feet. Several cars belonging to anglers in the stream below were parked partly on the verge, partly on the road.

Two of the parked cars had left a bigger space between them than the others, the ground between them consisting of a large, hostile rock. The tractor was passing the space barely five feet longer than itself. Glen couldn't have braked in time, even if the braking system had been in perfect condition. He had no time to think, but acted instinctively. He called for everything the engine had. The car leapt for the gap on the wrong side of the road. He saw the tractor driver close his eyes. The car bounced into space, hit the rocky obstruction with screams of neglected machinery protesting at this further abuse, and bounced back onto the road at the behest of the wheel that Glen was wrenching frantically from one full lock to another. Incredibly, the little car responded.

His foot was still pressing the accelerator as the wheels renewed their grip on the tarmac and carried him at breakneck speed down the one-in-six gradient on the wrong side of the road.

He touched the brakes. Nothing happened. His only scope for manoeuvre was being on the right hand side of the road, which took a sharp bend to the right at the bottom of the hill. His eye caught a grass embankment on the outside of the corner. He used the full width to take the corner like a racing cyclist moving to the top edge of a velodrome. He stamped on the brake pedal. No response. He crashed into third gear and the engine raced violently, but it slowed him down.

Two farmyards stood on opposite sides of the road. One of them enjoyed free-range eggs from hens that free-ranged on to the road. Glen's noisy approach persuaded some of them to extend their freedom to the air. Amidst their squawking and fluttering, his attention was taken from the declining revs. By the time the mini emerged from the shower of feathers, it had recovered its composure and was rolling along sedately in the calm sylvan setting of the valley floor with the Eden winding its tranquil way in the opposite direction.

One advantage of the frantic descent was that he had the Sierra in sight and was able to see it turn on to the narrow bridge, which crossed the stream at right angles to the road. Left and up the hill past the quaint old church prominent on the river terrace. A short distance along the main road, then up the winding hill to the radio station, advertising its secret presence for miles with its mega-web of poles and aerials.

The welcome sign read, 'Ministry of Defence - Keep Out'. Despite it, the gate opened for the Sierra. Glen followed and parked beside it.

The driver got out, grinning from ear to ear. "It's as well James Bond's retired. He couldn't stand the competition. Is that car one of Q's secret weapons?"

"I borrowed it from a friend. That's why I treated it with care," Glen retorted.

The man laughed as he led Glen into the administrative building and introduced him to a military-looking official, who said without preamble, "I believe you need a scrambler phone. I'll show you where you can use one. It should be available to you whenever you need it. The only thing I would ask of you is to make your arrivals and departures here as inconspicuous as possible."

Glen hid a smile as he said, "I deliberately chose a vehicle with that end in view."

He used the phone as he would a normal instrument, but its internal electronics distorted everything into an unintelligible cacophony of metallic babble for anyone without a pre-set descrambler.

"You're just in time with this arrangement," Glen told his controller. "The plumbers were busy. I saw them on my way home an hour ago. Switching to business ... I came across a Spanish connection, an Argentine called Antonio Hernandez and a Brit called David Johnson. Hernandez is emphatically a hostile. I guess Johnson may be. They seem very close. The Falklands, or as they call them, the Malvinas, seem to rankle. Is this why I'm on this job - to act as baby-minder to guys who might lapse into Spanish, or have you anything Zelinsky told you that you haven't passed on to me yet from that microfiche I sent?"

"Zelinsky had bad vibes from these guys. That's all. It was a long shot, getting you over, but it may be the right one. We'd have had to get someone to replace him anyway. Hernandez came over at short notice after the decision was made about the venue for the NATO defence ministers. That's caused some escalation in our apprehensions. Johnson was instrumental in making the arrangements. We have no intelligence specific to security operations, but Johnson's passport record shows no evidence of entry to Chile, whereas we have affirmative advice that he has been there on more than one occasion."

"He's an expert mountaineer. He could have crossed the Andes in several places without going anywhere near manned posts."

"Yeah."

"Chile's political dynamite. Did he interfere?"

"Not super-powerwise, not left or right, but the international boundary between Chile and Argentina still has a few disputed points, as you know. Chances are he was trying to gain ground for Argentina while Chile was in political turmoil. All kinds of definitions of boundaries are still being fought over like watersheds, native ethnic groupings, settlement and so on. It's easy to plant evidence in remote areas. We figure he may have been so engaged."

"That makes it more serious. I aimed to get closer to Hernandez, but it was blown. He went to work quickly on my bona fides and discovered my background in Spanish-American economics through a simple library routine."

"But we checked out the library - both main one and economics one. We evacuated everything; likewise the indices. Thank god for computers! That file was easier to wipe than the ledger one. We only left what your record here has non-categorised. You're clean."

"Not so! Nobody thought about the Hispanic American Department Library. He also noticed that I had evaded Johnson's attempt to catch me with a Spanish phrase. I thought it was a trick at the time, now I'm beginning to think so again. I managed to explain it away. It meant that they were slightly off-guard in a conversation in Spanish, but I didn't get more out of it than cause for further worry. They won't expose themselves in Spanish now that they know I understand it. The only other lead I have at the moment is a Polish visitor who seems to be persona non grata with the local Polish community. Zelinsky had contact with both."

"What have you on Schultz, diMaggio and Breck?"

"Affirmative your opinion re Schultz. Technologist - a good one. Rank and years' service justify command. Electronics skill is integral to work of the base. Security clearance as white as the driven snow.

"Repeat previous message re diMaggio. His book is permanently closed - with extreme prejudice. He died today in a situation described as a mountaineering accident; incompatible with confidential information available to us. Reassessment of views on crucifixion here. Now regarded as excessively humane. Terminal risk is highly communicable."

There was a pause for Glen to absorb the news, which he did with difficulty. diMaggio had been as hard as nails. Whoever could kill someone like him had to be a very dangerous adversary.

The voice continued without change in tone or inflection. "Breck is more difficult. Politics are erratic. Not red by conviction, but could be manipulated. Militarily gained commission on good old British class preference during national service. Endangered his platoon by issuing live ammunition against orders and without warning, to add realism, he claimed. Hushed up because of social connections, but he was restricted to office work until he left the army.

"He's chief of the Breck Clan, and a substantial landowner. Idiosyncrasies include flirting with a minority nationalist group in Scotland. MI6 have surveillance on this aspect. They play a dangerous game with it. They don't squash it, but contain it like a small fire that can flare up and discredit the main body of nationalists from time to time. That's OK, if its isolated, but it could cause a conflagration if it is associated with an international organisation. That's one reason we want to go parallel with the Brits on this one. They internalise some issues we see as international. We don't like him at Edzell one tiny bit, but we won't clamp down now. We don't want to drive him underground, if he's going to give us a lead. Anything else we can do for you this end?"

"There sure is. Campbell MacLaren, the guy who's setting up this programme for me at the university here, told me he worked with our boys in Korea during the war there. He keeps in touch with a lot of contacts. Could be helpful if I knew how I stand with him."

"As good as done. Anything else?"

"Yes. My golf clubs."

"You'll have them tomorrow by Securicor."

"The satellite pictures were just dandy."

The military gentleman was waiting outside the soundproofed door. With minimum conversation he escorted Glen to his car.

As Glen approached the gate, a man in plain clothes emerged from a doorway and opened the barrier for him.

CHAPTER 27

On his return journey he noticed the Land Rover parked in the quarry.

Inside his letterbox was a note from Hernandez, 'Phone when you return.'

A number was scribbled at the top of the paper.

The fewer calls he made from the house the better.

He returned to the car and, minutes later, was on the phone to Hernandez from his office.

Hernandez' voice was colder than ever. "I should like to continue our conversation of this afternoon."

"Sure. How about the Staff Club again?"

"If it is as convenient for you, I should prefer if you would come round to our department. I shall be in my study, and we could talk more privately - perhaps even in Spanish."

"Sure, if it's not too far. How do I get there? I'm in my office at Economics."

"Do you know where the Castle is?"

"No."

"When you come out of the Economics building turn right. Our department is about one hundred metres along The Scores on the left, just before the Castle. One block, not too much for an American to walk, I trust."

"Give me twenty minutes."

He left immediately and diverted only slightly to call at the presbytery of St James'. Father Mackellar answered the door himself.

"What a pleasure to see you again! Won't you come in?"

"Only for a moment."

As they stood in the little sittingroom, Glen explained, "I have to ask you for more help. I've come across two men, who might be dangerous to me, as they would have been to Stefan. You may know something about them. They are Antonio Hernandez, an Argentine, and David Johnson, a Briton. Hernandez is most likely a member of your Church. Johnson may be."

"Bless me! You surely aren't going to ask me to spy on everyone in my flock for you?"

"Father, I'm only asking you this because you understand the seriousness of my work and Stefan's. Time may be short, and a lot of lives at stake, important lives with great responsibility for the lives of others."

"They have never attended my church here nor used me as a priest, but I have met them through the Students' International Society. It's a Society which does a lot of good work for students from all over the world and who are far from home, often for the first time. It grieves me when people use contacts made through it to defame other countries and their citizens. That is why I remember these men. They are older than the average student member, and it was quite clear to me that they were doing their best to sow discord.

"Apart from that, I don't really know anything about them ...except an unusual biographical detail about Johnson. It probably lingers because of an appeal to an idiosyncrasy in my own folk memory. David Johnson has Basque blood in him. He is half Basque. As one of the ethnic minorities of Europe whose culture is driven into a corner, I feel a certain affinity with him."

"You never know what turns out to be significant in these matters."

"By the way, the visitor from Glasgow is called Wladyslaw."

"I'll remember. Thank you for omitting names and places when you spoke to me on the phone. If you did it deliberately you were more than justified."

"One tries to keep up with the times," the old priest smiled, but for the first time Glen detected a weariness and sadness in his eyes.

....

As his feet crunched on the gravel of the drive, his attention was focused on the impending confrontation with Hernandez. Before him lay the Scottish baronial mansion which housed the Department of Hispanic American Studies in place of the original wealthy merchant and his family.

Hernandez was waiting for him at the door which gave entry via a multi-level gazebo along the front of the house, its glass panels rising with each short flight of steps interrupted by longer horizontal lines parallel to the lengths of intermittent passageway.

Hernandez greeted him. "You have had a walk. I too should like a little walk. Shall we stretch our legs within the grounds?"

"Why not? Life's pretty sedentary for me too."

Hernandez got to the point very quickly. "Dr. Glen, I find that you know even more about my country than you revealed. I cannot help wondering how deep your interest goes."

"What do you mean?"

"I have it on very good authority that you visited my country in April of 1982. This, of course, you were entitled to do, and I am sure you would have been welcomed - as an economist. But you chose to visit in a different capacity. You came as a member of a diplomatic mission direct from the President of the United States. While other members of the mission spoke with representatives of our government, you managed to slip away and visit Rio Gallegos in the south, an area, which was part of the strategic war zone. To have reached such a place you could not have travelled as an American diplomat."

Glen recognised that Hernandez had exposed his own cover. His preoccupation with Glen, the kind of information he was able to obtain, and the speed with which he had obtained it, all pointed to his involvement in his country's secret service.

Glen could not give up the struggle, because the person questioned gains from the interrogator. The more the latter has to convince his adversary that he is unmasked, the more evidence he is forced to bring out. Somewhere in that evidence may lie the clue as to where a deception took place or a mistake was made.

107

"Are you trying to tell me that you read all this in your library as well?"

They were standing glaring at each other under one of the tall sycamore trees beside the heavy wooden gates by which Glen had entered the drive.

Hernandez retorted, "No matter where I learned it, do you deny it?"

"Tell me, why should I confirm it or deny it to you? What interest is it of yours?"

"I do not like someone to pose as my friend when he is treacherous to my country."

"That's a bit of a contradiction coming from you. Look at yourself. You're accepting the hospitality of a country with which your own country refuses to confirm the cessation of hostilities. Is that not treachery on your part?"

"My friend, Johnson, invited me. He is an invaluable ally to my country. He is a man Argentines are proud to call friend. When I work with him, it does not matter what soil is under my feet."

Glen started to move forward. "Let's get on with our walk instead of arguing here like a couple of little boys."

Hernandez declined the obvious part of the proposal. "Let us walk within the grounds. We can argue without disturbing neighbours."

His white teeth flashed a smile, but his eyes were as cruel as a kite's. He turned right towards the inner side of the high stone wall that secluded the grounds.

Glen fell into step beside him. Neither spoke.

At last Glen asked, "Supposing I was with an American mission in Argentina as you said, what was the purpose of the mission?"

"It was one of those so-called attempts to find a peaceful solution to the Malvinas affair."

"Then, would it not have been in the interests of your country, especially on the basis of what you said earlier about economic and political strategies being as effective as a military one?"

"It might have been, but, as it turned out and as we felt all along, your country did not behave as impartial neutrals. In fact, your country found the war a very useful exercise in terms of techniques and materials, which they are still analysing. It was for your naval and military strategists a perfect simulation exercise. The fact that two of their friends were involved did not detract from their morbid interest."

"It may be that most of the people outwith a small group preoccupied with military games were genuinely interested in bringing about a peaceful solution."

Hernandez remained silent.

"All right," Glen said in exasperation. "I was with that group and I did go to Rio Gallegos. I went incognito because it would have been impossible otherwise."

A glint of triumph sparked in Hernandez' glittering, black eyes.

Glen continued, going for the opposite effect known as the pre-emptive cringe, "We believed it was important to know the kind of support the Junta enjoyed in different parts of the country, what military morale was like, how efficient the military logistics were on the nearest part of the mainland. All these things were important to help us in our bargaining position. All our negotiations had to be geared to the extent of determination and resources of both countries. The more accurate and up-to-date our information, the more effectively we could bring about a lasting solution by peaceful means."

The two men had passed the second corner of the wall and were heading back towards the large, gaunt house about which the evening shadows were settling. The wall on their left was the sea-facing, north wall and they could hear the force of the North Sea swell breaking on the rocks below.

"It is a pity," Hernandez observed dryly, his sharp chin cutting the air like a chisel, "that your pious aspirations are not supported by the facts."

"What do you mean by that?"

"Within days of your visit to our base, it was attacked by a British Special Boat Squadron. Their information was very precise and, as you say, up-to-date. The damage done to our surface craft and submarines meant that Britain had only to deal with our air force. You can appreciate how much differently the war could have turned out if our navy, which was as well prepared as our air force, had been able to operate with the same skill, expertise and bravery. Your visit was the turning point of the war."

"And now you have come to Scotland to see whether or not it is true that we can carry the war to the very shores of Britain. Come ... I will show you something."

They had reached the end of the wall. The remaining part of the boundary was protected by a chain-link fence five feet six high. Where it adjoined the wall, the latter had come down from ten feet to six feet. At the corner of the wall were two metal rings cemented into the stonework, one of them two feet above the ground, the other four feet. Hernandez indicated the rings, which had at one time supported a flagpole.

"Come. Use these as steps, and I will satisfy your curiosity," he invited.

Glen's senses tingled in anticipation, for he had learned never to offer to satisfy the curiosity of an adversary if he believed there was any chance of him living to tell the tale. For this reason as well as the success of Isobel's comforting ministrations the previous night, he climbed nimbly to the flat top of the thick wall. It provided an excellent vantage point over the seascape lurking in the gathering dusk.

The tide was low, and the tireless sea lashed the outer edges of the rocky wave-cut platform, which, between high tides, protected the base of the cliffs from the sea's continuous onslaught.

Hernandez followed with a lithe, effortless movement and stood beside Glen who had moved away from the protection of the abutting higher section of wall to make way for him. Glen's face was faintly illuminated by the glow of the setting sun.

Hernandez was almost completely hidden in the shadows of the wall. Although nothing could be seen of his expression, his voice was growing in confidence. "You can now see where our invasion will take place. Can you make an educated guess?"

"Leuchars!"

"You are very quick. Too quick! You didn't even have to look at the place. You do not know where the Castle is, but you know where Leuchars is. You even pronounce it correctly like a Scotsman, or perhaps it is your fluent Spanish that helps you with the non-English sounds, or perhaps you were carefully schooled in its pronunciation before you left Florida so suddenly."

"Now, Dr. Glen," Hernandez' voice began to gloat, "you are very reluctant to show me what a clever man you are and how much you know. Perhaps this will persuade you to tell me exactly why you are in St Andrews and why you have tried to worm yourself into my confidence."

The voice came from the shadows, and Glen could not see how he was being threatened.

"What do you mean - persuade me?"

"This!"

Hernandez brandished his left hand. As it emerged from the shadows, Glen saw it was clutching a gun.

"Don't talk nonsense. I have no interest in you other than what I've told you already. For both our sakes, put that thing away. It's dangerous."

"I'll say what's to be done. First, what do you know about Leuchars?"

"It's a strategic air base. Part of Britain's first line of defence against Russia. It sometimes has our forces stationed there on exchange."

"Keep talking, Dr. Glen."

"It's planned to be kept operational in event of a nuclear war. Underground headquarters are being built to protect strategic command personnel and equipment against nuclear blast."

"You do not have to come to Scotland to find out that. You know it from your photographs taken from space, in the same way as you told the British what we were doing in the South Atlantic. What else?"

"NATO defence ministers will be arriving there in a few days' time."

"Ah. We are on the same wavelength after all. Have you come to protect your own Secretary of State from revenge?"

"You're talking nonsense. Are you and Johnson going to rush Leuchars and take on the RAF Regiment? They're a tough bunch, you know."

"We have more resources than that at our disposal. Johnson is with a few of our helpers at this moment."

"In Glencoe?"

Glen could hear the shrug in Hernandez' voice although he could not see it, as he said, "It does not matter what you know now. This building here is only an outpost. My office is not so useful. Someone kindly decided to give me a south-facing window so that I should not miss the sun, but Johnson has a study at the north-west corner giving him an ideal view over Leuchars. It compares very favourably with your own prospect from the Stevensons' house."

"How did you know to deliver your note there?"

"Your friend, MacLaren, told me. He even offered to drive me to the house. In the end he took the note himself."

"Is MacLaren involved with you and Johnson?"

"Not in the slightest. Johnson meets him through a mutual friend."

"Who's the mutual friend?"

"It is not important."

"It is to me."

"But you are not important. You might have been up to now, but now your assignment is over." His voice was cold and determined as he brought his gun closer to his body.

Glen could sense him steadying his elbow against his side.

His mind flashed to Johnson. Obviously the dominant partner. He whipped out, "Johnson wouldn't approve. Think of the mess. A bullet would lead to too many questions. It's got to be cleverer." Then he fired the words, "Like Zelinsky."

"What do you know about Zelinsky?"

"A lot more than you think. Remember, you're the one who says I'm so clever."

Hernandez uttered an oath in Spanish. Glen's acute hearing distinguished a minute change in the position of its source. He noticed Hernandez' gun hand had disappeared in the darkness. The last remnants of the sun's glow left the sky. Glen's face and body were blacked out. The sudden contrast confused Hernandez' senses more than Glen's.

Glen lifted his right foot and in the blanket of darkness silently took one pace backwards to the end of the wall. He balanced there on the balls of his feet, his heels overhanging the abyss not daring to breathe.

Suddenly, he felt the swish of air as Hernandez swung with all his force at the black velvet emptiness, which had a moment ago contained Glen.

Glen knew better than to swing to left or right. He brought his hand straight down in a ferocious karate chop which connected with the base of Hernandez' skull and made certain he had no chance of recovering from the inertia he had set in motion.

A muted cry was followed by a dull thump from the grass embankment beside the wall, then a sickening crash from the rocks far below.

Glen slipped over the wall, hanging initially by his fingertips, then dropped the last few inches to the steeply sloping ground outside the wall.

As he went down he grabbed wildly for the chain-link fence in the darkness to arrest his slide down the steep, slippery grass, only to jam his fingers painfully in the joint-jerking mesh that tore at his spine.

Once he had stopped his headlong plunge he was able to slither along the slope at the base of the wall to where he had seen some roughly-hewn steps before the light had faded. More from memory than feel, he made his perilous journey along the lip of the cliff.

With light only a memory, the darkness was less stark, and he managed to find the steps and make his way to the bottom of the cliff. He glided cautiously among the rocks to where he reckoned Hernandez had crashed. He stiffened when he thought he heard a sound. Sure enough, he heard it again - a faint moan. He went closer, conscious that Hernandez might still be armed, until he saw, his eyes now accustomed to the dark, the form of Hernandez' body lying on its back at an impossible angle across a boulder. It emitted another moan, fainter this time.

Glen leaned closer and peered at the distorted face for signs of recovery.

There was a different sound. He put his ear to Hernandez' mouth.

A panting whisper came from his lips, "You are a dead man too. It is all written down for Johnson."

Ignoring the sentiment, Glen said, "I'll ease you into a more comfortable position."

But, gentle as he tried to be, no sooner had he lifted Hernandez by a fraction of an inch, than he felt him twitch and go limp. His spinal cord had been hanging by less than a fibre of the proverbial thread.

Even if Hernandez had been his best friend, he would have had no more time to spare for him. There was too much to do.

Police investigation would not be a problem, but Johnson finding out about him was a risk of a higher dimension.

It would be impossible to find the gun in the dark, but that was not his problem, as it had only been handled by Hernandez.

He scrambled back up the rocky path, but since he could not get over the fence or wall he took a longer way round, through a large private garden. He hesitated to go along the street, but had little option, and kept as close as possible to the shadows. When he reached the entrance to the drive, he avoided the gravel and kept to the grass.

A light shining in the glass porch warned that someone might be in the building. Glen became more cautious. On the right of the drive was a sunken lawn, which had formerly boasted a private tennis court. He scrambled into it in a crouching run and lay on the grassy bank, studying the house.

It didn't take his expert eye long to recognise that it was a security light designed to deter prowlers, a term which he would not have contemplated as descriptive of his own profession.

He rose, and keeping within the shallow gully stole to the shelter of the bushes and trees at the north end. Through them he blended like a shadow to the side of the house and along it to the door.

The purpose of the light misfired, for it gave him a better view of the lock, so that he was able to pick it more quickly than he could have done in the dark. Once inside he flitted up the gazebo stairs, keeping well to the inside to prevent shadows flickering on the glass wall.

The staff board told him Hernandez' room was number 33, which meant it was on the third floor by British convention, fourth floor by American reckoning. He raced up the stairs as lightly as he had taken the precarious backwards step on the wall minutes earlier. Floorboard squeaks were to be avoided on pain of death.

He picked out the room quickly, thanks to the light streaming under the door. He crept forward, knelt silently and looked through the keyhole. Within the limits of the aperture, he confirmed that the room was empty. He listened patiently, turned the handle with the touch of a brain surgeon and pushed the door softly inwards.

The room was empty.

The light from the anglepoise lamp on the desk enabled him to search more quickly than he could have done with his small pencil torch. He found no message for Johnson. Several neat piles of learned journals were systematically laid out on the desk with slips of paper sticking out of the covers showing Hernandez' scribbled annotations marking the articles contributed by Glen. He collected all the notes and stuffed them deep into his pocket and left the room with the light on.

He went down one flight of stairs and across the landing to a door marked 'Dr. D.X. Johnson'. He watched and waited before trying the door. It was locked. He took out a plastic card, inserted it at the lock between door and doorpost. Slight pressure and the door swung open.

Without a light, his search was slower, but no less meticulous. He drew a blank. He took a quick second look at the line of books with unpronounceable syllables on their spines and covers. Basque was a language apart. What he was looking for was not in Johnson's room.

He went downstairs to start at the beginning.

There was nothing in the entrance hall. He tried the staff common room opposite the main entrance stairway. Nothing there. He found the door marked 'Office', used his little plastic card and let himself in. Part of one wall was taken up with pigeonholes identified by the names of staff members. They were arranged in alphabetical order, but Hernandez was at the bottom of the unit, his name typed on a fresh white card.

He sifted through the material in the boxes belonging to both Hernandez and Johnson. Cards, periodicals, old letters and a circular from American Express he returned to their boxes. Everything else he pocketed. A reminder from the departmental librarian gave him an idea.

He went back up to Hernandez' room, took all the periodicals and a couple of books containing articles by himself and carried them down to the library, where he overcame the lock in his usual way and laid them, minus Hernandez's notes, neatly on the desk for returns.

A few minutes later he was back at his own desk in the Economics Department.

He lifted the phone and dialled Isobel's number.

She answered by giving the five digits he had dialled. As soon as she stopped, he whispered, "Colin."

He heard her repeating, "Hello. This is Mrs. MacLaren. Hello?"

Glen held the receiver in his hand, momentarily oblivious of all except his vision of Isobel. With a sigh he replaced the instrument.

He took out the envelopes and notes he had appropriated from the pigeonholes, scrutinised them and sorted them into two piles - one to be studied more closely, and the other to be destroyed. He put the papers he wanted to keep in his inside jacket pocket and carried the others in his hand.

....

Almost an hour later a gentle tap on the front door brought Glen quickly from the lounge. He was well-groomed and clean shaven, looking as though he'd done nothing all day more strenuous than a game of squash. He wore matching grey teeshirt and cotton slacks with red trim. He opened the door with his accustomed caution. A smile of welcome lit up his face.

"Great, Isobel. I couldn't be sure you'd really come."

"Wild horses wouldn't keep me away after last night. You made a woman of me - not an honest one, perhaps, but a fulfilled one."

"You know, you are so open and honest about yourself, you must be the most liberated woman in the world." He took her hand and drew her into the hall, his eyes dancing over the new vitality of her beauty and the thrusting confidence of her body. " Hasn't Campbell noticed how different you look?"

"He wouldn't. I tried to show him. I dressed up. I've been singing all day. I didn't want to hide anything from him. I don't want to cheat on him, but he doesn't want into the game. He is uninterested and disinterested. I'll tell him as soon as you like."

"Don't waste time talking about him. I can work with him because he's such a cold fish. I don't feel I've stolen you from him. Rather, I hope I've rescued you and he doesn't even know what an ogre of indifference he is. But, please believe me when I tell you the next few days may be critical and I can't afford any avoidable friction. It will only be a few days, I promise."

"As long as you won't send me away, I'll do whatever you say," she murmured, turning her big gentle blue eyes on him.

Holding hands, they went into the bedroom.

"It's unfair," she pointed out, "that you should have that gorgeous tan, and my poor pale body is so dull by comparison."

CHAPTER 28

Glen was wakened by the phone ringing.

A deep voice at the other end said, "Good morning, sir. I'm sorry to trouble you so early. This is St Andrews Police Station. Is that Dr. Colin Glen?"

Glen looked at his watch. It was eight-thirty. It wasn't an unreasonable time, especially if they were investigating a death.

"Good morning. No problem about calling at this time. I'm Dr. Glen. What can I do for you?"

"We've had a complaint about a car being driven recklessly last night, sir. It was identified as belonging to Professor Stevenson, and we have reason to believe that you might have been using it. Is that correct?"

"Yes."

"The person who reported it claims that you killed two of her hens yesterday evening about eight o'clock. We tried your number several times last night, sir, but we were unable to contact you."

"Sorry about that. Yes, I did run into some chickens and it's possible that I did kill one or two. I can assure you I was more alarmed at the time than any of the chickens. The car was doing the most unpredictable things."

"We can appreciate that, sir. Professor Stevenson's car is quite notorious about town, but he does drive it with a slightly finer touch than you were reportedly showing last night."

"What's the charge?"

"At the moment, there's no charge, sir. The lady who complained did not want to pursue the matter when we explained it was probably an American who had just arrived in the country."

"Well, that sure is most generous. The least I can do is go and pay for the chickens and offer my apologies."

"I'm sure that would be most appreciated, sir. The lady's name is Robertson - Mrs. Robertson. You know where she stays."

As he pushed the downy aside, Isobel's provocative perfume wafted through his senses and into his mind. She had left hours ago, but the room vibrated with her vitality and empathy.

....

Having carried out his promise to visit Mrs. Robertson, Glen was about to drive past his home on his way to the University when he noticed he had visitors. A car was sticking out of his drive. As he slowed down and turned in, it drew forward to make room for him.

Inspector Gordon emerged from the driver's door, clutching his hat to his head so that he retained his impeccable uniformed smartness. A civilian got out on the passenger side.

115

"Good morning, Dr. Glen. Can I introduce my colleague, Inspector Smith?"

The two men shook hands, and Gordon asked, "May we come in for a few minutes?"

"Of course," Glen joked, "but isn't this taking the deaths of a couple of chickens a bit seriously? I've already been to see Mrs. Robertson and paid her my fine, as it were."

"Yes, we know about that, Dr. Glen. But this is a bit more serious. It concerns the death of a man."

"Have you found out something new about Zelinsky?"

"I'm afraid it's a new case. A body has been found on the beach. It's been identified as that of an Argentine lecturer who was on an exchange visit similar to your own. His name was Dr. Antonio Hernandez of the University of Buenos Aires. We are trying to trace all his contacts. We believe you spent some time with him yesterday evening."

"This is shocking news. Yes, he and I spent almost half an hour in the Staff Club."

As the two men followed him into the lounge, Glen reflected how Smith's chubby cheeks reminded him of a cherub in a religious painting.

They stood in the middle of the lounge, having declined Glen's offer of a seat.

Gordon began, "I believe you were introduced to Hernandez at lunch-time yesterday. Then you met him again later about five-fifteen, and you talked for some time, at least half-an-hour. You must have had something in common. What did you talk about?"

"I told him that I had done work in Latin America and we discussed the possibility of exchanging material."

"Did you meet after that?"

"No."

"Did you speak?"

"No."

"Phone calls?"

"I received a note to call him."

"Did you?"

"Yes, I phoned him from my office in the Economics Department. He wanted to ask me for the title of a book I had recommended."

"And you didn't see him again?"

"No."

"Thank you, Dr. Glen."

"What happened to him? Was he drowned? Did he fall from a boat? Where was he found - which beach?"

"He was found on the West Sands. His injuries suggest he fell onto rocks at some point, possibly close to where he worked. He was not drowned."

"When did it happen?"

"We haven't the time exactly yet, but it must have been at low tide. If the tide had been in at all, the water would have cushioned his fall. You've been very helpful, Dr. Glen. It's sad that you're being consulted about a second tragic death and it's scarcely four days since you came to the place. It's usually so quiet here, too. Well, we had better get back to the office and co-ordinate the investigation. I just wanted to visit you myself since we had spoken previously."

Smith spoke for the first time. "If Dr. Glen is going into town within the next few minutes, perhaps I could travel back with him?"

Despite the confidence of his smart uniform, Gordon's expression showed that he feared he had missed something, which his detective colleague had noticed. All he said was, "You're your own boss here. Take as long as you like, but the station is my responsibility.

"Dr. Glen, would you let me out on to the road? Your car was parked behind mine when we came in."

Having helped with the necessary reshuffling of cars, Glen came back in to find Smith gazing out of the window. He turned with his unfathomable smile and said, "You must find this view fascinating." Then he sat down.

Glen nodded, and Smith continued, "There are one or two things that puzzle me, but I didn't want to bring them up in front of Gordon. He might have jumped to awkward conclusions. As soon as the body was discovered, I visited the building where Hernandez had worked. A member of the janitorial staff let me in. The light was still on in Hernandez' room, as if he had been interrupted in the middle of some work, but his desk was bare. I thought, where does an academic get his working materials? Answer, library. I went there, and imagine my surprise when I found several items which, according to the records, had only been taken out hours earlier! The library door was locked. The janitor had to unlock it for me. When she arrived, the librarian swore the books had not been there when she locked up the night before. And you know how well organised librarians normally are.

"Hernandez had a system of reporting to his research supervisor, Dr Johnson, a summary of everything he had done each day. It was slightly unusual, I believe, but it was imposed on him by his government as a condition of the scholarship he held. There was no trace of yesterday's report in Dr. Johnson's office, in Hernandez' office, nor in Johnson's mailbox. In addition, a communication placed in Johnson's box by another member of staff had disappeared. It seems to me that someone may have conducted a search of Hernandez' effects when he knew Hernandez was safely out of the way. Perhaps he even killed Hernandez to get him out of the way."

As an afterthought he added, "A strange coincidence you'll be interested in! Each of the books and magazines returned to the library had one thing in common - an article written by you, Dr. Glen."

Glen cut in blandly, "If we are going to sit here talking, I'd rather be drinking a cup of coffee. How about you? My breakfast was slightly curtailed this morning."

Still beaming, Smith accepted, "That's very kind of you. My breakfast was non-existent this morning."

Glen filled the percolator and switched it on. Then he returned to his guest who sat there radiating goodwill and good health.

"You were saying?" Glen prompted.

"According to Dr. MacLaren, Hernandez sounded quite agitated when he was trying to get hold of you yesterday evening. That is why MacLaren delivered the note to your home himself. Did you know it was MacLaren who had left it?"

"Yes."

"Perhaps I could see that note?"

Glen had destroyed it with the other papers. "I don't think I would have kept it. In fact I didn't. I went straight to the washroom when I got in, read it there and flushed it down the toilet. I don't know how it could have helped. Just asked me to phone him."

"What bothers me is why was he so upset? Even if he was desperate to have the title of a book, he would not have been able to get it from the library until the morning. Are you sure it was only a book title he wanted?"

"You know these Latins. They get so easily excited. Academics anywhere can be the same. A simple thing may be puzzling them, but they can't rest until the question is answered. Happens to me."

"Yes, of course. But the steward at the Staff Club said that he seemed rather unfriendly when he came to join you in the afternoon. The librarian says that he mentioned your name when he withdrew the books and magazines that were so quickly returned."

"Excuse me. The percolator's ready now."

When Glen returned with the coffee, Smith continued as affably as before, "Dr. Glen, I must admit I have a strong case of circumstantial evidence, which, if I felt so inclined, I could build into a fully substantiated case of murder against you with all the necessary witnesses and so on."

Glen ignored the main import of what had been said and challenged him on the minor point. "What do you mean, 'if you felt so inclined'?"

Smith relaxed back in his chair, sipped his coffee and smacked his lips appreciatively. "You make an excellent up of coffee. I do so admire the Americans for their coffee."

He took another mouthful and savoured it before answering Glen. "Perhaps I was overestimating my own importance when I said, 'if I had the inclination'."

He sipped his coffee. "The discretion, of course, lies exclusively with my superiors."

"You mean the police in this country only prosecute on a whim?"

"No. Not at all. And may I say you seem extraordinarily keen to be prosecuted? Your reactions are not at all those of the ordinary citizen, albeit an American, being faced with the prospect of spending a long time as a guest at Her Majesty's expense. Now this brings me to my next thought. Perhaps, if you are not an ordinary citizen, you are an extraordinary one. Let me just give you one or two examples of what I mean. Anyone who can order the American Ambassador to fly his golf clubs over the Atlantic in a military jet is no ordinary citizen. Anyone who is prepared to work on behalf of our Special Boat Squadron and then accept the opprobrium of our diplomatic service in Washington by recommending an overtly Argie line on Presidential policy is no ordinary citizen. Anyone who gets the American Embassy to phone the length and breadth of the United Kingdom to make what is patently a murder become acceptable as a suicide is no ordinary citizen. Do you get my drift?"

"If you know Zelinsky was murdered, why isn't someone being charged?"

"Because justice caught up with one of his assassins last night."

"Hernandez?"

"The same."

"The message I'm getting loud and clear is that you are no ordinary policeman."

Smith's smile became more expansive and his apple cheeks took on a burnished glow. "How right you are. One of my jobs here - incidentally, I am only here on secondment, in the same way as yourself, I expect - is to keep the lid on something which you and your colleagues have nearly blown sky-high."

"You knew Zelinsky was working for the United States government?"

"Yes, although it took me a little time to pinpoint him. You were much more obliging. You came right into my parlour. Now, you and I have to work out a modus vivendi. It was really very awkward for me when your colleague got himself killed, and then you come along and kill one of my main links. After all, you are on my patch. So I think my priorities should get preference. Your government has wind of something and they want to nip it in the bud. My government knows a little more about it and has a great deal more at stake, and it suits their purpose that the exercise continues a bit further than your government would like. It is our country and we are the host nation, so don't usurp your position here or I'll cause the damnedest diplomatic incident you've ever heard of." Smith's expression almost lost some of its blandness.

"Tell me. Does MacLaren play a part in your organisation?" Glen interrupted.

"Funny you should ask that. I was going to ask you the same question." Almost in the same breath Smith added with his usual urbanity, "That was a delicious cup of coffee. Now, how about getting me back to the nick as we promised?"

The phone rang.

When Glen answered it, a heavily accented eastern-European voice asked, "Dr. Glen?"

"Yes."

"This is Wladyslaw. Father Mackellar said it would be appreciated by you if I telephone to you."

"Right, I sure want to talk with you."

"I am sorry I am not able to come to St Andrews on this Sunday, but I can come tomorrow if we can meet in a between place. Will you suggest Perth?"

"Great. What time will suit you?"

"Morning will be best. I can be there by ten. Where in the town shall we meet?"

"There should be a hotel at the station. We'll meet there. If not, I'll be at the ticket office from ten onwards. If anything delays either of us, we can phone Information and leave a message."

Smith made no attempt to hide the fact that he was paying avid attention to the conversation.

CHAPTER 29

Laxalt mingled with British, German and Scandinavian tourists in the small concourse of Malaga airport. Saturday had been chosen because of the extra holiday traffic.

The headlines of all the Spanish newspapers on the stand at the entrance carried the sensational story of the huge bank raid carried out by his group the previous day. The papers gave a list of the number of robberies in the last ten days and a tally of the total amount stolen. The average estimate was a total of 150 million pesetas. One newspaper suggested that ETA was going to buy an atomic weapon.

The turmoil of his mind did not show in the purposeful mountain stride which carried him to the exit.

Behind a large airport bus, he saw the Mercedes that was to take him to his destination. He held up his case to show the coloured sticker to a watchful driver who recognised it and moved the car up beside him; he jumped out and opened the back door for Laxalt.

"Have you any more luggage, sir?"

"This is all. I'm not staying long."

He held onto his small case and took it into the back with him.

The driver manoeuvred expertly through the urban traffic around the environs of the airport on to the main road south. Despite his deadpan expression, Laxalt never missed a detail of the journey, as they sped past the western outskirts of Torremolinos with its towering hotel blocks hiding the Mediterranean, through Fuengirola and Marbella, swerving once - unsuccessfully - to avoid a stray dog, without stopping to check whether it was dead or injured, through burgeoning concrete, across bridges spanning torrents of dry pebbles, past dazzling displays of myriad coloured pottery, not slowing for anything until the archway of the Atalaya Park loomed on the left.

The Mercedes gave way momentarily to the closest of the eastbound traffic, then surged through the first gap and under the archway.

The landscape was an immediate transformation from the dusty roadside with its thirsty boundary fields, so inimical to Laxalt, to luxuriant verdure and colour under the shade of overhanging trees, pervaded by the perfume of climbing plants and the musty smell of vivid, omnipresent pelargoniums.

Through the luxuriant vegetation peeped the white stucco and pink tiles of expansive villas, which shared the grounds of the prestigious Atalaya Park Hotel.

They drew up beside an imposing iron gate festooned with elaborate figures and intricate designs.

"This is the house, sir," the driver said, but Laxalt could see nothing beyond the impenetrable hedge.

Once inside the gate, there was a fresher atmosphere, for the skilful juxtaposition of light and shade in the design of house and garden induced a constant movement of air, which gave a balmy comfort in sharp contrast to the heat and pressure at the airport.

The driver insisted on taking Laxalt's case from his reluctant grasp and carrying it into the house, while the two men, known to General Lopez in San Sebastian as Don José and Don Ramon, came down the curved flight of marble steps to greet Laxalt with warm handshakes and hearty backslapping.

"Come this way and meet the General. He has been looking forward so much to your arrival," Ramon enthused.

Despite that assurance, the General could hardly bear to look at Laxalt far less welcome him, and could not be induced to shake hands on any account.

Despite this temporary social hiatus, the jubilant spirits of Ramon and José were not to be subdued.

They insisted on going over to the hotel for a celebratory drink and to book their evening meal. The General argued unsuccessfully that both could as easily be accomplished without leaving the villa.

"Don't worry, General," Ramon tried to assure him. "Only foreigners can afford this place. No-one will recognise us together."

"It is an offence to our national pride that we should take second place to foreigners in our own country," General Lopez pronounced, and in spite of Ramon's reasoning, not because of it, he insisted on going to the hotel.

Laxalt observed dryly, "Now you know how we Basques feel in our own country."

"There is all the difference in the world," the General retorted, "between mastering people through one's military superiority and being mastered through one's own slavish avarice."

Marble-floored and marble-walled corridors led from the side door by which they had entered the hotel precinct, past exquisite and exclusive boutiques to the main foyer, but the four conspirators did not follow it all the way along. Instead they turned right, up a long flight of marble stairs, made opulently inviting by a rich maroon carpet, to the diningroom and its adjacent bar.

They sat at a table in the bar savouring French brandy and anticipating the evening meal by perusing the menu so that they could order the a la carte specialities, which required extra preparation for absolute perfection.

Laxalt excused his lack of enthusiasm for the culinary diversions. "Someone else can choose for me. Something plain. The brandy is fine, although I prefer our own Armagnac to Cognac, but I want to keep a clear head for our discussions.

Lopez spoke civilly to Laxalt for the first time. "You are correct. This is enough alcohol for tonight. A little wine does not count. But I firmly believe an army marches on its stomach - especially the generals." And he laughed heartily, affectionately patting his tight jacket buttons.

....

Back in the villa three hours later, with the driver and another three men posted as lookouts within the garden perimeter, the four men got down to business.

José began, "I think we have all to be congratulated on the success of our plan

121

so far. Practically all the funds have been gathered, thanks to the way the General prepared the ground and Laxalt's men have completed the sweeping-up operation."

"I'm not so happy," Laxalt interrupted, "that ETA is getting all the blame. We distributed the raids widely so that they were all outside our normal area of operation. Yet the finger is always pointed at us."

"It was certainly not intended," Ramon tried to console. "It's been the sheer efficiency with which the raids were carried out that makes everyone think it must be the work of ETA. On the plus side it obscures the co-operation which the General so cleverly arranged. It also adds to ETA's notoriety which you aim to make part of your bargaining strength, and it will help to remove suspicion from people in positions of responsibility who have been very helpful."

"It will make reprisals more savage, and official investigations of legitimate complaints against abuses by the authorities even more tardy than they are at present," Laxalt complained bitterly.

"If you go outside the law, you have no right to expect protection from the law," Lopez snapped.

"Gentlemen, gentlemen," Ramon interposed soothingly, "we are after all on the same side. So far we have worked very well together. Don't let us quarrel when victory is within our grasp."

"I don't see," complained the General, "why so much money is necessary. I could accept it as part of a diversionary tactic, but I can't see for the life of me why we need all this cash."

"That does not worry me," said Laxalt, "but I do want to know that my members who are in your custody are absolutely safe, and I must insist on speaking to them before we proceed any further. The General is right. We have accumulated a great deal of money. We have kept our side of the bargain so far."

"But they're miles away. How did you ever expect to be able to speak to them in a place like this?" José protested.

"There is such a thing as a telephone."

José looked at Ramon, who nodded. "Dial from next door."

Ramon disappeared for a few moments and returned to say, "They're on the line now. Use the extension over there so that we can hear you."

Laxalt took the phone and spoke quickly in Basque.

José protested, "Speak in Spanish so that we can understand you."

Laxalt ignored him.

When he had finished, Ramon asked, "Is everything in order?"

"As far as it can be when men are deprived of their freedom. Now, as you promised, I want to know details of the overall plan."

"Exactly what I intend doing now. First, let me answer the General's question about the money that has been gathered. You will all appreciate that success in this kind of operation depends on maximum secrecy and dividing the operation into cells or wings. So far we have kept the wings separate, but now we are going to bring them together in a pincer movement.

"None of us knows how the General made the arrangements for the money to be available and for the opposition to be minimal. None of us cares. It was done through organisation, and organisation costs money. The General knew that and performed his duty. Expenses of mobility and manpower and resources are always high. That is appreciated. This operation is on a very ambitious scale. Hopefully, we shall only need a fraction of what is gathered, but it is vital to have a strategic reserve."

Ramon repeated the need for money so often in so many ways that he almost began to believe it himself, and each time he saw a flicker of doubt in the General's eyes he added a little bit of extra praise for the way the General had done his duty.

When he was reasonably sure that the General would not return to the question, he started to give Laxalt details of the overall strategic plan, sticking in for good measure from time to time the expenses that would be involved.

He omitted to point out that although the plan was elaborate and expensive, most of the resources were to be provided gratis, albeit unwittingly, by government forces.

"And now, I call on General Lopez to give you the military details."

Laxalt asked the General about the strength, distribution and state of preparedness of men on the ground. The insight, incisiveness and intensity of his questioning aroused a grudging respect from the General. As a result he asked Laxalt about his tactics for the exercise. He criticised some proposals and enthused over others. An unusual bond formed between the two.

Their conversation resumed after breakfast while José and Ramon went to play golf.

CHAPTER 30

Glen was waiting on the steps of Perth Station Hotel, a Victorian red sandstone building framed in an outline of contrasting grey stone.

His eye alighted on the man crossing from the station. His grey jacket was more loosely cut at the waist than a British one would normally have been, and his light brown shoes with plain uppers and thick stitching were neither the traditional British style nor the trendy chunky look.

As he came up the steps, head bowed as though he was counting them, Glen noticed that his fair hair was flecked with grey. When he reached the top step he looked up sharply and with his piercing blue eyes caught Glen studying him.

"Dr. Glen?"

"Right first time, and you must be Wladyslaw."

The man smiled. "Wladyslaw Zochowski," he said, giving a formal stiffening of his back and a neat bow as they shook hands.

"Call me Colin. I'm afraid I only knew your first name, and somehow I formed the impression that you were a young student and all I needed was your first name."

"Do not apologise. It is happier that we get to know each other this way."

"I've ordered coffee. Shall we go into the lounge?"

Once they were seated and drinking their coffee, Glen brought the conversation to Zelinsky.

"I wondered if I could do anything to help over the death of Stefan, like write to his family. Someone suggested I should see Father Mackellar, and it was he, as you know, who suggested that I should speak to you. I just wondered what you could tell me about him, so that I can build up a picture and write to his mother in a more personal way. I believe she is his nearest relative."

"Stefan and I, we met at the St Andrews Polish Club. I am told in Glasgow, 'You should visit St Andrews where the Poles have a very strong society. You will be made welcome'. Unfortunately, it is not as simple. I am not welcome by the Polish people in St Andrews. They think I am a government spy. They fear for their families and friends in Poland. May I explain? You want to know about Stefan. You will understand better if I tell you first about myself. Or do I waste your time?"

"By no means. Go right ahead."

"Do you know about the partition of Poland?"

"You mean the Oder-Neise boundary?"

"That is part of it. The boundaries of Poland have changed much in history because it occupies an area of great plains without natural boundaries. It has two powerful and greedy neighbours who all the time want to take our land - the Germans and the Russians. In times past, the Swedes were also predators on our land." And he added wryly, "That is where the colour of my eyes come from, maybe.

"This century, until the end of the First World War, there was no Poland. The Poles were in their land, but the west was ruled by the Kaiser, and the east was ruled by the Tsar, each one of them taking his name from the Caesars of Rome, but we took what mattered from Rome, our religion. Oh, I hope I do not offend you! I mean no ill if you are not a Catholic."

"No offence taken. Please go on."

"Thank you. At the end of World War I, Poland became a nation in law as well as in fact. But that remained so for fewer than twenty years. By 1939, Russia and Germany had agreed to divide Poland between themselves again. They quarrelled, and Poland was taken first by the Germans and then by the Russians.

"Everyone today knows that the Russians control the Polish government, but many do not know, or forget, that Russia moved Poland towards the west. Russia fears Germany. So, to weaken it, Poland was given German territory, but Russia did not want Poland to grow bigger. So, it takes part of Poland in the east. Poland knows it will not take that land back from Russia, so it must keep what Russia has given it from Germany. Therefore Russia has a strong ally between itself and Germany who will help Russia to keep Germany divided.

"Now, I must come to my part in this story. Russia thinks, Germany claimed the Sudetenland because Germans lived in that part of Czechoslovakia. Russia thinks, we must not let Poles say that Poles live in what is now part of Russia. They then moved hundreds of thousands of Polish people from White Russia, Ukraine and Lithuania. Most of them were sent to the new area of Poland between Poznan and the Oder, which has been taken from Germany. To make room for the Poles, the Russians moved hundreds of thousands of Germans to the west of the Oder.

"My own family was among those moved, but we had moved nationalities several times before, sometimes without moving our home. My parents were natives of Kovno on the Nema River. They were Polish-speaking and Catholic. After they married in 1935 they moved to the city of Vilna which by the international treaties after the First World War had become Polish. I was born in March, 1939. By September, 1939, Vilna had become the city of Wilno and part of Lithuania. This was part of the agreement between Russia and Germany. Each one probably thought it would gobble up what had been given to little Lithuania.

"Within a year Lithuania was occupied by the Soviet Union, and again the city changed her name and became Vilnius. We were regarded as foreign intruders and deported to Byelorussia, which is another name for White Russia. My father was forced into the Russian or Soviet army. However, that improved the status of his family, for we were regarded as on the same side as the rest of the families round about. There is no need to say that he was moved away from us very soon. Within a year the Germans had attacked and reached far east of where we were. If you have been counting, you know that when I reached my third birthday, I have three different nationalities. Unlike my parents, I was born a Pole. Then I became Lithuanian. Then I became White Russian.

"My father was so lucky to survive the war, but he was unlucky to be in the Russian army in Poland. You know there was much cruelty there. My father tried to be friends with his own people in Poland. He knew nothing of what happened in Poland. They did not trust him. They said he spoke Polish with a foreign accent. He must be a Russian spy trying to find secrets. This he told us afterwards.

"Two years after the war ended, and my father was back with his family in Byelorussia, we are told, 'You are Poles. You will be evacuated to your own country.' Then my father said he was afraid to go to Poland, for again he would be called a Russian. The Russians say this is an honour and they laugh. We had no choice. After many days of travel under armed guards we were taken off the train at Inowroclaw. We remained there in a transit camp. Then one day my father heard there was work on the canal at Lubiszyn. It was a great risk that we all might starve if we went with him. If we did not go, we might never see him again. We walked the forty kilometres with all our possessions in our hands. There was work when we got there, but it was labouring, not work for an engineer. My father was glad to get work at all, even with not being able to use his skills.

"We survived. I followed my father in my training and became an engineer. I held several posts in different parts of Poland. Then I become a teacher of engineering at the University of Gdansk. There I met people who are probably closer to the influence of the West than anywhere else in Poland. The ideas of Solidarity appealed to me. I talked with my students about it. I believed it was good for our country. In my own work, I believed we would make more progress and have a more meaningful life with greater freedom of action by the workers and the population together.

"I was given the opportunity to come to study trade unions in this country and was attached to the School of Slavonic Studies at Glasgow University because I was able to contribute to teaching and tutorials. Now that Juraselski has come in with harsh treatment on people, it is very difficult for me to go back."

"What was the problem between the St Andrews people and yourself?"

"I came to Scotland and met Poles, but did not say to them, 'Yes, my father was in the Russian army; yes, my birthplace is in the Soviet Union today; yes, I worked for the communist government; no, my father and mother were not born in Poland.' These things I have not said in Poland for many, many years. So many people in Poland today have had the same problem. We do not go about talking about them. Poland has moved forward.

"But I go to the Polish society in Glasgow one week and I am a great friend. Then I come back two weeks later and nobody speaks to me. They turn their backs, but I can see it in their eyes. I say, 'What is wrong? What have I done?' And someone say to me, 'You are Russian. Karola has written his parents, and they say you are Russian.' I say, 'Let me explain', but they say, 'You should have explained when you came here first.' But I say, 'Who wants to listen to my life story now? Do people always give their life story when they come among you? That is unreasonable!'

"So I came to St Andrews. I have been told I will be welcome here. I will tell them my life story from the beginning. But when I arrive they say, 'We know who you are. We have heard from our friends in Glasgow.'

"Now I have told you my story from the beginning. Do you still want to ask me about Stefan, or do you not trust me, either?"

It was the kind of story Glen had heard many times before, a human tragedy repeated time without number, but impossible to attribute to every family that told it of themselves and impossible to relate any quality to any such family whether the story was true or false. The only constant factor was the enormity of human suffering, suffering on a scale, which could distort the truth of anything. At the trivial level, it was also the technique of the salesman wanting to make his pitch on sympathy.

Glen had only one option if he wanted to hear anything about Zelinsky, so, quite objectively, he transferred the value judgement from story to teller.

"You've suffered more than your share. I don't blame you for wanting to try to forget it. I'd be more than happy to hear about Stefan from you. His mother would understand. It would be good for her to know he did not die among strangers, but that he had friends from among her own people."

"Well, what can I tell you about Stefan? He did not worry about what the others said. You see, they remember a different kind of Poland, even from the one I came to. It was new to me in 1947, and I was only a child. But even in that time it was changed, and since then it has changed even more. Stefan was not so attached to it. The young people in St Andrews were not so worried. They were born in Scotland. Stefan was like them. He was born in America. But the young people could not treat me as a friend or even as a Pole because their parents would not allow them to forget that I had not told about my father.

"I used to come through on a Saturday or Sunday and visit Stefan. We did not talk about our countries very much, but we were able to talk about our work. Since I am an engineer, I could understand something about what he was trying to do. He took me to church with him, but I am afraid I have not a habit of going to church. My parents were very attached to the Catholic Church, but it made us look too different from our neighbours during the war.

"He used to go hill-walking a lot on his own. He was kind and friendly, but he worked very hard."

"Do you know what progress he was making in his work?"

"Not as good as he had hoped. Wind energy does not seem as promising as people had estimated. He was, as you say, having his problems."

"Do you think it would have been bad enough to have depressed him so much that he would take his own life?"

Zochowski thought hard. "It's possible. He was deep. Introspective. He could have been a worrier."

"Did he have a girl friend while he was here?"

"Not one of whom he spoke."

"What were his hobbies?"

"All I know is that he went walking in the hills a lot."

"Did you ever go with him?"

"No, he never invited me."

"Did he talk about where he went?"

"No. It was mixed with his work. He had to take wind measurements for locations for his windmills, so he went over the hills. Then he grew to like them and just went walking in them on his own time. He liked being alone on the hills. It could have been part of his depression."

Glen learned very little about Zelinsky from the remainder of the conversation, but it was evident that Zochowski subscribed to the suicide theory, a fact which Glen had to treat with the same kind of circumspection as he accorded to his life story.

"If that is all I can tell you, I shall catch the next train back to Glasgow. I'm sure you are doing something very kind for Stefan's family. Of course the Americans have a world reputation for their kindness."

As they parted, Zochowski said, "Please give my regards to Dr. MacLaren."

"MacLaren? I didn't know you knew him?"

Zochowski's vivid blue eyes glittered. "I met him at the Students' International Society in St Andrews. You are working in his department, are you not?"

....

An hour later, Zochowski emerged from Queen Street Station in Glasgow and walked diagonally across the Sunday quiet of George Square, past the Palladian frontage of the City Chambers and the GPO into one of the narrow streets crowded with old office blocks and names redolent of a great mercantile tradition. He entered one of the buildings and climbed the worn sandstone stairs to the second floor, where he knocked on the door of a small export-import firm and entered the scuffed wooden threshold.

He gave an account of his conversation with Glen to the round-faced, bald man with watery eyes who sat behind the desk in the shabby office.

He concluded, "I am satisfied that his motive is to make himself feel good and to show that the American flag flies piously wherever an American needs support."

He omitted nothing except his message to MacLaren. It was the only time there had been the glimmer of more than a superficial questioning in Glen's eyes. No suggestion of doubt was allowed to appear on Zochowski's face. Otherwise, the dull brown eyes opposite would have recognised an unforgivable reticence and cross-examined relentlessly until a momentary lapse became a capital offence.

CHAPTER 31

As he drove north-east from Perth through the rich red soils of Strathmore past well-drilled ranks of raspberry canes and docile fodder crops, Glen enumerated the points he had made of his interview with Zochowski. One, Zochowski had laid great emphasis on his own bona fides; two, he was subtle in his determination to have Zelinsky's death assumed to be suicide; three, he had told practically nothing about Zelinsky; four, he had come all the way to Perth for no good reason. Observation - unlikely to have been purposeless. Question - what had he done then? Answer - he came, he saw, he conned.

Glen smiled grimly to himself. He had been assessed by Zochowski. He cursed aloud and thumped the driving wheel with the edge of his fist. The damnable thing about this operation was the lack of time. With the Latins, he could usually work at a calculated pace or have the ground prepared well in advance, so that when a crisis like the Falklands blew up he knew where he was at.

Zelinski was an eastern hemisphere watcher, himself a western hemisphere watcher. What the hell were they doing on the same assignment? Was it a Company foul-up? Or had the comrades from the steppes recruited the gauchos from the pampas? It was more than possible. They'd made their first move in Chile and only been frustrated in the overthrow of the Marxist regime by the intervention of the CIA. Goddamnit, were they going to get their revenge this time? But the Russians wouldn't want to get involved in some madcap scheme. The consequences could be too horrific. Unless, of course, the Russians were going to capitalise with a pre-emptive nuclear strike.

Were the Argies hand in glove with the Soviets, or were the Soviets just interested spectators? If they weren't in either team, nothing surer than they'd run on to the pitch at the end of the game and cause havoc.

And what the hell's everyone rushing off to the mountains for?

The modern sweep of the road made driving easy, even if it had to be done on the wrong side. He continued his conversation with himself, but despite every twist and turn of his mind he could come to no satisfactory answer for any of his questions, and he was taken by surprise when his subconscious registered the Edzell road sign just north of Brechin.

He had no difficulty in finding the US Navy's early warning station with its network of aerials stretching around an enormous spherical honeycomb towering above the surrounding buildings.

The guard at the gate checked with his commander, whom Glen could see phoning for approval before giving permission for him to be admitted. When he got through the barrier, the guard commander was still not satisfied. He came out and waved him to stop.

Glen wound down the window. "Hi," he said, relaxing among his fellow-countrymen. "Good to see you." His open, smiling face hid the sharp awareness that he was very much on active service. But he was here to play golf and had to give the impression he was out to enjoy himself.

However, the young lieutenant did not seem prepared to join him in holiday mood as he greeted him, "Good day, sir. If it's alright by you, sir, I'll climb in and show you your way to the Captain."

From the size of the base, there was little need for a guide. Security was tighter than Glen had expected, but he put that down to diMaggio's death.

"Where are you from in the States, Lieutenant?" he asked affably.

"Twin Falls, Idaho, sir."

"No kidding! The Potato State. You sure ought to be at home in this country with all the potatoes in these fields around here!"

"I guess so, sir, but I'm no farming boy," he replied, resentment showing in his voice at the thought of having been taken for some kind of hayseed.

"Ever fish the Snake?"

"Now you're talking! Do you know the Snake?"

"Do I know the Snake? I just about was spawned in it. I was born in Richland, Oregon."

Despite the Lieutenant's objection to being thought a country boy, he demonstrated one of Glen's theories that local sentiment could expose the vulnerability of most young servicemen away from home.

His face lit up and his whole body relaxed.

"Gee!" he exclaimed. "Hardly anyone else has ever heard of Idaho, let alone the Snake and Twin Falls." Then he recovered quickly. "We're at the Captain's, sir."

Glen parked and they both got out.

"That's it over there. The Captain's expecting you."

"Say, I wouldn't mind a chin-wag afterwards with a neighbour from the old Northwest days before I leave. I'll be finished with your skipper about five. Will you be around then?"

"Sorry, sir. I go off duty at 1400. I live off the base with my wife and our little girl. We'd sure like to have you visit with us though. Tell you what, I'll leave a map showing you how to get to our place. Come round when you're through with the Captain. We'll be home all afternoon. Better not tell him I'm stealing his guest, though," he ended with a smile, before throwing a flat-handed naval salute.

Schultz welcomed him warmly. "Good of you to come out all this way. The weather's stayed fair. We should have a fine round. It's not the Old Course, but it's got a good little name for itself. We'll have a fine round."

"I thought for a couple of minutes your boys weren't going to let me in."

Schultz chuckled, "That's young Knudsen. He runs everything by the book. Quite right, of course. We've got to be damned careful about who gets in here."

"What's your poison?"

"Whisky, thanks."

"Are there ever any security buzzes around here?"

"Not since I arrived. diMaggio could have told you anything before that, but he was killed in a climbing accident yesterday. Damned shame, but there you are."

130

"Seamus is late again. What a guy that is! You know, he has his own clan. He's the chief, entitled to wear an eagle's feather in his bonnet. He does too. He sure helped me to get to know a lot of people when I first came to this base. He knows all the men here and makes them feel right at home. He entertains them on his estate only a few miles over the other side of that hill."

"He must know a lot about what goes on here," Glen encouraged.

Schultz chuckled, "He sure does. I sometimes say to him, 'It's lucky we're on the same side.' He knows the base better than I do myself. He knew it before I ever got here. In fact, he showed me round during my first week. Showed me things I'd never have looked for. He doesn't give a damn about anybody.

"Say, would you like to see around some of the place while we're waiting?"

They had almost reached the main gate when they hear a commotion from near the guardhouse.

When they went to investigate, they saw a red-faced Knudsen being harangued by Breck.

"Tell this jumped-up colonial auxiliary to lift this barrier and let me in!" he was yelling at Knudsen from the window of his Range Rover. "I've been coming in here with impunity before you'd even heard of Vietnam."

Knudsen struggled to keep his voice level. "I'm sorry, sir, but we must abide by the rules. You must show your pass to the guard. If you don't have one, he is not permitted to let you through."

On seeing Schultz, Breck bellowed, "This is a conspiracy to prevent me beating you at golf."

Schultz seemed greatly amused and intervened, "It's OK, Lieutenant. The usual rules don't apply to the chief. You know that."

Knudsen stood his ground. "Sir, I have to follow orders."

Breck had left his Range Rover with the engine running to come over and join the Captain and Lieutenant.

He addressed Knudsen in a lofty moral tone. "You must learn to accept defeat like a gentleman, just as your Captain does when I trounce him at golf."

Laughing heartily, he put his arm round Schultz' shoulder and guided him in the direction of his own office, tapping the head of the golf club he was carrying on the grass verge as they walked, oblivious of his abandoned vehicle.

Out of the corner of his eye Glen noticed the sailor who had been on gate duty say something to Knudsen, who was studying the departing figures, his jaw set in determination. He gave an order to the sailor. There was a pause. Then the sound of the engine changed, as it slipped into gear. Wheels screeched and gears grated, as the vehicle was moved about. The engine was switched off, and the quiet of the hills reasserted itself with the fragility of thin oil on water.

Glen looked over his shoulder. The Range Rover was parked well clear of the gate, still on the outside and facing away from the base. Knudsen did not vary orders for anyone.

Inside Schultz' quarters, he and Glen had another whisky, while Breck's exceeded their combined intake for the morning.

When they were in the washroom, Breck brandished the callused palms of his hands.

"Look at these hands. These are the hands of a real campaigner. Let's see yours, Captain, and yours, Glen. Aha! As I thought, the soft hands of gentility. I wouldn't expect any better of a teacher, but fie on you, Captain. How can our allies protect us, when their fighting men have hands as smooth as a baby's bum?"

For the first time, a shadow of resentment flickered across Schultz' bland features.

Glen retorted in the manner which he had observed MacLaren use. "I thought you were a gentleman landowner, only tussling with the occasional recalcitrant rent-payer."

"You know nothing of me," Breck snapped angrily. "Nothing! I work with real people, not books. The people who pay me rents deserve no better. There is only the loyalty of money between us, which is no loyalty. A chief was judged, not by his lands, but by his men. I will be judged by the calibre of the men who will follow my leadership and example.

"I have just come back from three days and nights in the mountains with such men. We have climbed and abseiled, bivouacked in the snow at over 4,000 feet and lived off the land for the entire time."

"In Glencoe?"

"Yes. From Glencoe by Mamore to Ben Nevis and back. But how did you know?"

"Just a guess. It's the only climbing country I've heard of here. Climbing seems to be a more popular sport here than in the States. Did you come across any people from St Andrews University during your hike?"

Breck's eyes glittered, and he paused momentarily before replying, "No, but I wouldn't expect to find any of these fine fellows where we were. Besides I'm not talking about sport. I'm talking about survival."

Although his rumbustuousness did not desert him he was not as acerbic as usual at lunch. He was wary of Glen, but warmed to the attentive audience of Schultz.

After lunch, Glen's offer to drive them to Edzell Golf Club was accepted.

The golf did nothing for international relations. Schultz was one over par at the first, Glen birdied, and Breck was three over. For the rest of the game Breck's performance and temper fed on each other to the detriment of both. He came in such an ignominious third that he did not issue an instant challenge to another game. Having declined a lift back, he remained on his own in the clubhouse.

CHAPTER 32

Knudsen's place turned out to be a tiny wooden bungalow nestling on the edge of a conifer plantation, which stretched halfway up the hill. The narrow, unsurfaced road leading to it was little more than a track whose route was determined by the rough and tumble descent of an energetic mountain stream.

Knudsen came to the door in jeans and plaid shirt. His wife followed him, similarly attired and clutching her baby daughter in her arms.

"Glad you could make it," he called out as he strode forward to welcome Glen. "Come and meet Fran and Julie."

Fran rubbed her hand on the side of her jeans before she stuck it out. "It's great to have a visit from another civilian like myself from back home. Sorry if my hand's wet. I've been washing some lettuce."

Glen chucked Julie under the chin, and she gurgled her welcome. To Fran he said, "I sure appreciate your having me at such short notice, seeing as you have Julie here to look after."

"Oh, Ed's good at helping when he's home. She's no problem. She's a good baby."

Julie was left to explore the living-room floor while the two men talked and Fran went through to the kitchen with the promise, "I'll fix us some coffee."

Ed was a much more relaxed person at home than he had been on base, and his enthusiasm at meeting someone from the closest part of the neighbouring state bubbled over boyishly.

"Fancy coming across someone right here in Scotland who just happened to live right across the river from Idaho! When were you last back in Washington?"

"Some time, I guess. I left Richland with my parents when I was just a kid, but I used to go back and stay with my grandparents right into my college days. When they died, there was no-one left of our family, and I guess life and making a living has kept me away for considerably more than ten years now. I can still remember a lot about it. Why don't you bring me up-to-date?"

"My folks are in business in Twin Falls and I guess I'll go back after I've finished this stint in the Navy. After my bachelor's at Oregon State in Portland, I decided to do my postgraduate experience in the Navy. It might have been useful to have done a master's in business admin. But I decided to get a different insight into working with people. I guess I had enough of being inside as an undergrad. And, let's face it, I wanted to travel.

"Idaho has a lot for the outdoor person. I can fish steelhead or rainbow in the lakes and rivers, shoot big-horn sheep or bears, deer or the occasional cougar. In the winter we have skiing that compares with anywhere in the world. When I go back, Idaho will be my world. So I want to see the outside now instead of being on one campus."

"The services are a better deal now than when I did my draft in Vietnam."

"Travel and mountains. I can't resist them. It must be the Basque blood."

"You have Basque blood?"

"Sure. My mother's father was Basque. He came out to Idaho with his herd of sheep and built up his flock. Nowadays he has a fair-sized ranch with cattle and sheep, but he keeps in touch with his roots as it were, for he still hires shepherds on three-year contracts from Spain. Basques have to move from the family farms because everything is inherited by the first son. That way, their farms have remained viable family units. So the other sons have to find some place new."

"Say, I never knew that! Maybe that's how I met some Basques in the next state, but it still must be pretty unique being a Basque in Idaho."

"Not a bit! There are over twenty thousand in Idaho, mainly drawn by sheep-farming possibilities in the first instance."

Fran brought the coffee. "Is that Ed telling you about his peculiar blood again?" she joked.

"It was no laughing matter when she was on the way," Ed admonished with a nod towards Julie.

"You sure are right. We were pretty worried when I was carrying Julie. We were afraid our blood groups were incompatible, but it turned out OK. Then we discovered that Basque blood has different proportions in its groupings from any other race in Europe. Basques have far more Rhesus 'O' negative blood."

"We're always learning, I guess," Glen philosophised. "But it's a coincidence that this should crop up, for I've just heard of someone else who's half Basque. He's a lecturer at St Andrews University where I am temporarily on a research project. His name's David Johnson. I'd thought he was British, but it turns out that his mother was Basque. Have you ever met him?"

"No, but the name rings a bell. I'm sure that guy, Breck, wanted to bring a David Johnson on to base one time. He wanted to take some of our fellows on a mountaineering expedition and was boasting how much he and Johnson could teach them. He went on about himself and Johnson having mountains in their blood. Is your man a mountaineer?"

"I have it on the best authority that he's fanatical about it."

"If he's a fanatic, he'll make a good buddy for Breck."

"You don't seem to like Breck very much."

"Don't mention that man's name," Fran interposed. "Ed can't stand him."

"Fran's right. I mustn't start on that topic, especially if he's a golfing friend of yours."

"Our relationship's scarcely friendly. I met him and Schultz by chance, and Schultz invited me up here for a game of golf. I wasn't delighted but not really surprised when Breck showed up. I can't figure him at all. He strikes me as a phoney. What do you think of him?"

"Why not blow off some steam about him? It's been building up a real head. You saw the way he tried to barge into the base today. He's getting worse. I'm getting close to the stage of being charged with insubordination. I guess I was pretty near the line today. I have no wish to be disrespectful, but I can't start criticising my commanding officer to his guest. That wouldn't be fair to either of us."

"Schultz and I are only the slightest acquaintances. We met once before and got on well together on the common ground of being Americans and liking golf. Today's outing was not an outstanding social success nor a distinguished sporting encounter, and it won't surprise me if I never meet either of them again. If I do, it certainly won't be by prior arrangement. Does that assure you that your views will go no further?"

"Why are you so interested?"

"I'm an American citizen. Something is obviously worrying you. I don't like the way I saw that man trying to muscle his way onto the base. I didn't like the way Schultz treated security. You were quite right to point out there are no exceptions. I don't want to think that security can get so slack. As an American it makes me feel vulnerable. Last, but not least, I find Breck a thoroughly obnoxious character and I wouldn't trust him as far as I could throw him.

"If you want to talk, you have a friendly and attentive ear; if you don't, there's no harm done." Glen weighed the balance of pressure on Knudsen finely between desire to talk and resolution to keep quiet. He measured the appeal to citizenship and sense of duty onto the same side as personal feelings.

His judgement was vindicated when Knudsen made up his mind to unburden himself.

"It must be pretty obvious that I find the man loathsome. He's a misfit and a throwback, a complete snob in the very worst sense because he makes a fetish of not being a snob. He takes all the advantages of wealth and privilege and pretends that he despises people who do exactly that. He tries to impress people with his coarseness and his overbearing crudeness, which he represents as being the common touch.

"He's taken our enlisted men out to provide so-called hospitality, but usually it's been to get cheap labour out of them for a limited favour. Last August he took them out to shoot grouse - I wasn't here, but diMaggio told me - and began with a complicated story about taking turns at driving the grouse to the guns. Most of them spent their day beating, that is, frightening the birds out of the heather so that they fly towards the butts where the shooters are. He only let the men try when the birds were too tired to fly and there were no people prepared to do the beating. Then he told them they were just poor shots.

"Unfortunately, our previous Captain was easily flattered by being wined and dined in a castle with titled guests. Maybe I shouldn't blame him as much as his wife. She was a natural for the British class system - a southern lady, she called herself. She was just dazzled by Breck and the names he kept dropping. Once Breck had his foot in the door he started throwing his weight around. Schultz landed in a situation Breck had all set up. He's not a social climber, but he's at risk because he regards Breck as an amusing buffoon."

"Why do you say 'risk'?"

"I have no proof, but I have a feeling Breck is up to something. He doesn't particularly like Americans. He makes that perfectly clear often enough. So there must be some reason other than our charming personalities that keeps bringing him around here. He never mentions anything technical, but he tries to move about the camp unescorted if he possibly can. He likes the English even less than he likes us. Question if he likes anyone or anything except his own good opinion of himself as some golden-age Highland chieftain who's due to come into his place in the sun. I can't put it down to anything definite. He sure isn't the kind to be in with the reds or Ruskies, but he's got something up his sleeve alright."

"I'm glad you told me this. You see I've some political contacts through the consultancy work I do," Glen told him truthfully, but incompletely.

"If I'd known that earlier, I wouldn't have felt in a position to speak. It would have sounded like criticism of my superior officers."

"I wouldn't divulge what you have told me without your approval, but you have a sound sense of values, and I'm sure you can quite appreciate that this revelation could be of vital importance to your country. I promised you my confidential treatment of what you had to say. That promise stands. I won't divulge your name, but I ask you very seriously indeed for your approval to tell what I know. I won't allow you to be dragged into any investigation which may be necessary, but you and I must keep in very close contact."

Knudsen received this turn of events with some discomfort. A sense of loyalty to his superior officers was already in conflict with his patriotism, and here was a complete stranger about to take the situation out of his hands.

"If you'll pardon me, I don't think you have any right to do anything of the kind. I've no wish to seem inhospitable, having invited you to my home, but it occurs to me you have a lot of information out of me for precisely nothing in return. All I got from you was a promise which you promptly say in a fancy, dressed-up way you're going to break. You haven't even told me anything about Richland. Anybody could have said about anywhere in the world what you've said about it."

"I can easily put your mind at rest on Richland. I can tell you about the native petroglyphs on the anciently decorated rocks up river from Lewiston, or Hell's Canyon, half as deep again as Grand Canyon, or that the last sturgeon was caught on the Snake in 1956, or lots about the Nez Perce Indians, or Orofino Creek, where gold was first discovered in Idaho thirty years before it became a state in 1890. Shall I go on, or do you want to test me some more?"

"I guess you know Idaho, but that's no reason why I should let you interfere in naval security."

"You're implicated either way. Perhaps you've told me too much. On the other hand, perhaps you've kept back too much.

"You didn't tell me that diMaggio was in interim command before Schultz got here. Nor did you tell me about his relationship with Breck. But I'll tell you. He had inherited a security problem from his previous CO and wasn't going to come into conflict with Breck before Schultz got here. But Schultz let things get into worse shape because he's an electronic whiz kid, not an administrative officer.

"Now I've told you a little of what I know. I had to check you out first. It should be glaringly obvious that you have a duty to update me as of now on every aspect of laxity in security."

Fran, having noticed when she first brought the coffee that the conversation was not the homely chat she had been looking forward to, had taken herself and Julie through to the kitchen where she kept her entertained.

"You know what you're talking about, and I guess you probably knew all I told you already."

"Not everything," Glen conceded with a smile. "And I don't know enough about diMaggio yet. For instance did you discuss these problems with him?"

"I tried. He listened as though he agreed, but he never did anything about it."

Glen continued probing, but despite giving a verification of a security clearance classification far below his actual one, but more than adequate to get Knudsen's complete co-operation, Knudsen was unable to tell anything of significance about diMaggio.

At last he said, "I've got to go now, but I want you to report to me on a daily basis through this number. You may recognise the first part, the Embassy in Grosvenor Square.

"If there's something urgent, leave your message with the number at the Embassy, phone me at one of these numbers." He wrote down his house and office numbers. "Don't say anything except one word, 'Potato'. I'll know it's Idaho calling, and I'll check what message you've left at the Embassy.

"Give my apologies to Fran and love to Julie. Don't scare them, but something's brewing."

137

CHAPTER 33

On his way home Glen made two detours and one brief stop.

His first detour was to the scrambler phone at the Ministry of Defence radio listening post to report on the day's activities and ask for information on some of the new people he had come across, especially Zochowski and Knudsen.

His brief stop was at the Land Rover parked in the quarry beside his house. He slowed as he passed and, because of what he saw, stopped.

Sitting on the ground in front of the radiator was a small saucer-shaped metal disk painted in the same camouflage as the vehicle. Inside were two indistinct figures.

He went up to the driver's window and tapped on it. It opened grudgingly, and a bespectacled face surmounted by a black beret and muffled to its chin in a camouflage field jacket looked blankly at him and uttered one word, "Yes?"

"Forgive my curiosity," he began with the firm politeness of a local civil rights activist, "but I've seen you here several times when I passed and I wondered what you're doing?"

"Do you live here?" the expressionless face demanded.

"Just over there." He pointed vaguely towards Stevenson's house.

"Well, it's because of complaints by people like you. We have to measure the noise of planes taking off to decide whether they're causing a nuisance."

"Oh, I see. I'm only here temporarily. I didn't know. What a good idea!"

"Yes, I hope the bleeding Russians will ask you if the noise of their bombs is disturbing you when they decide to attack."

Glen allowed the sarcasm to roll off his back and asked, "How do you measure the noise?"

"There's a dish aerial in front. It picks up sounds, and we have instruments in here which measure the level, record it and time it so that it can be related to individual planes taking off."

" I'm sorry to have troubled you. I'll leave you to get on with the good work."

"We have to stay all night tonight. The Phantoms are practising night flying. There was a warning in the 'Citizen' - you know, the local paper, - with an apology for any disturbances. Night flying always produces complaints. One of the district councils in Fife has an arrangement with the Russians not to attack at night, but some of us don't trust either of them."

Glen departed with a "Goodnight."

The window closed quickly behind him.

His second detour took him to St James' presbytery.

"I only came to tell you I met Wladyslaw this morning and had a very interesting talk."

"But?" the priest questioned perceptively.

"Why do you say that?"

"You are not entirely satisfied?"

"Correct, but without abusing any privilege further, I want to ask you a simple question."

"The simple questions are often the hardest to answer, but try."

"Simply, did you give him only my house number or did you give him my university number, or did you give him any indication of which department I was working in or with whom I was working?"

"That's four questions, not one. So I'll have to give you four answers: yes, no, no, no. Now, since you're not so good at asking questions, and since its easier for a theologian to ask them than to answer them, I'll pose a few, and you need only give me monosyllabic answers as well.

"First question: do you have a doubt in your mind?"

"Yes."

"You cannot ask me because you know I cannot answer?"

"Yes."

"You wonder if I can get someone to help you?"

"Yes."

"I'll phone someone who knows how good Mrs. MacDonald's baking is."

He lifted the phone, dialled and, when it was answered, said simply, "Zygmunt, we're ready now." He put down the phone and smiled at Glen.

Glen was taken aback. "You had that arranged before I got here," he accused.

"True. Have I done anything wrong?"

"No, but how did you know?"

"I knew your arrangement to meet him this morning. I suspected you would not be satisfied, and I have a good friend who knows a great deal about such matters as you might have discussed. I couldn't tell him a time, but it's good practice as well as good theology to be prepared.

"On the other hand, you could, if you insisted, simply call it inspiration."

"Who is Zygmunt?"

"Zygmunt Wojcik, a very fine man. He fought in the Polish cavalry against German tanks. When Poland was over-run he came over to this country and learned to fly. He was shot down over Germany and spent two years in Colditz. Since the end of the war he has made his home in St Andrews. He is a leading figure not only of the Polish community but also of the total community. He retains many contacts with Poles in exile but also knows a great deal about what is happening in Poland. I should pay a lot of attention to what he has to say."

When Mrs. MacDonald showed Zygmunt in, he was not the dashing cavalry officer Glen had expected. He was about five feet eight inches tall, and, although his body was still neat, his round face with an unfashionably-clipped moustache gave him the appearance of being more rotund than he was. For his military career to have started so far back, he must have been at least sixty-five, but he looked scarcely sixty.

Mackellar stood up and Wojcik took his hand and bowed respectfully to the priest, and when he was introduced to Glen he bowed again.

"Come in, Zygmunt, my son. Won't you join us in some supper?"

Glen noticed for the first time that the tray, brought in before the priest had lifted the phone, had a setting for a third person.

The priest leaned conspiratorially towards his old friend. "It worked out as we thought it would when we spoke about Zochowski after Mass this morning."

Wojcik sat as if there was a ramrod up his back. At the mention of Zochowski his face became stiffer than his back. He looked Glen straight in the eye. "Father Mackellar is such a charitable man, he will not speak ill of people if he cannot speak well of them, but I must speak what I believe of Zochowski.

"He claims to be a member of Solidarity, but he was only an infiltrator. He was put into university to watch and report on Solidarity sympathisers and members.

"He probably told you how his family had been moved around from pillar to post. His family were opportunists out to take advantage of changing political situations, but it is true that they had a difficult time when he was a young child at the beginning of the war.

"However, his father had such a strong sense of survival that not only did he volunteer to join the Red Army but he also managed to join the Communist Party, not as easy in the Soviet Union as it may sound. Consequently he spent part of the war as a political commissar, being responsible for political indoctrination of the troops with every sanction on discipline at his disposal. Executions among his troops were disproportionately high.

"With his Baltic background he was very useful to the Russians in carrying out some of the enforced migrations from those countries. There are rumours that he took over from the Gestapo in Riga and that many of the atrocities attributed to the Germans were actually carried out by him in the confused period after they were driven out.

"As part of the Kremlin plan to subjugate the countries of Eastern Europe, he was sent with his family as refugees to their own country as what you would call sleepers, that is, as agents who would conform completely with the normal life around them for years, to be activated only in event of an emergency or special circumstance. The Russians' first line of attack, of course, consisted of the puppet politicians they pushed into power like Gomulka in Poland, Ulbricht in East Germany, and even people regarded later as relative liberals, like Dubjek in Czechoslovakia. All these men and many others spent the whole period of the war in Moscow being trained to seize power in their own lands and deliver them to the Soviets.

"People like Colonel Zochowski - ah, I see from your expression that his son did not boast to you of his father's high rank - such commendable modesty - were placed to provide another line of attack by disrupting the country, possibly acting mainly as agents provocateurs and informers if the political structure should falter. Ideally, their families would carry on the mission so that some sleepers are indeed slumbering on beyond a generation.

"The very survival of something like Solidarity depends upon knowing as much as it can about such people. There is little point in reforming the government, if the

140

government is not the final arbiter. It has taken us a long time to establish the links of such people, but we are making progress. Like the Jews, we suffered at the hands of both the Germans and the Russians, and we are learning from them how to protect our own until we can avenge them.

"We Poles must be vigilant, for we have been deprived of our national boundaries before. As far as we are concerned there is no difference between a Tsarist Russia and a Communist Russia. They use the same policies of centralisation, secret police, spies and informers. It is their way of controlling their widespread conquests, which they call their state.

"Unfortunately for us, they see Poland as a special risk to them in the West. We form the most populous country in Eastern Europe, with almost twice as many people as the next largest country. We have a relatively advanced industrial society. Because of our ports we are more open to trade and ideas than the land-locked countries. We share with Spain the third largest Catholic population in the whole of Europe and probably the most devout. That represents a huge cultural gulf between us and the Orthodox Church of the Tsars or the atheism of the Soviets. Our language, although it is Slavonic and the second most widely spoken after Russian, uses the Roman alphabet in contrast with the Cyrillic alphabet of Russian. Thus we Poles find it easier to master the languages of Western Europe than do the Russians.

"You can see what a large thorn Poland is in the paw of the Russian bear. Because of the size of our population, our involvement in the war, the position of our country, far more people from Poland fought in the West than from all the other Eastern European countries put together. We also had an element of stability in Britain because of our government in exile in London throughout the war.

"For these reasons, the communists and especially the Soviet Union want to damage the relationship between the Polish people living in the West and Poles still in their own country. That is why we are so vigilant against infiltrators. Refugees from Poland include informers who would betray those with whom they fled and their relatives back home. Similarly, non-communists can be suborned abroad if pressure is put on their families in Poland. One of the aims is to destabilise the established Polish communities such as our one here in St Andrews. Nothing would be more natural than that we should welcome with open arms anyone who came in the name of Solidarity.

"Zochowski is worried because he has no future here as an infiltrator and he knows that the Russians do not continue to make life attractive for those not in a position to repay the investment.

"His only hope would be to try to bring off some success in another direction, perhaps something more ambitious. Or he could have been sent over to be deliberately found as a cover for something worse."

"It's a fearful thing, indeed," lamented Mackellar, "to hear how far man can sink from grace."

Glen's face was set as he said to Wojcik, "Your interpretation of Zochowski's behaviour is as though you had been at our meeting. I share your fear that he may be involved in some other task for his masters."

CHAPTER 34

Shortly after midnight Glen stood at the picture window scrutinising Leuchars RAF Station and trying to piece together the jigsaw in his mind.

A voice from beside his shoulder broke into his trance.

"If I must have an excuse I can give you a massage even if your back is perfect. Think of all that tension to be soothed away."

He could feel Isobel's fingers tingle through his shirt.

He turned and clasped her gently. "My, you have been neglected," he murmured. "Your husband must be punished for this crime against humanity. What shall we devise? Tell him the truth?"

"Ssh. Don't talk about him. He's not interested in me."

"You can say that again. The man must be mad."

"Come through to the bedroom. We've not got much time. I'll have to go before he gets home from bridge."

"I'll follow you."

He watched her shadowy lithe movement appreciatively as she padded gracefully across the room. His keen hearing picked up the slight squeak of a floorboard whose location he knew exactly, then the bedroom door click behind her. He drained his glass and followed her.

He opened the door with one hand and stretched the other one towards the light-switch, but it didn't get there.

A powerful pair of arms grabbed him from behind and pinned his arms to his sides. Another pair locked round his ankles.

Without either of his captors moving, the light was switched on by a third person. In the sudden light he saw Isobel dwarfed and pale in the grip of a large khaki-clad figure, with one hand clamped over her mouth. His own captors were also in khaki combat jackets.

Sitting on the bed, his head resting on the wall above the headboard and his highly polished brogues on the quilt, was a fifth man, the archetypal British army officer, his thin greying moustache stretching to the ends of his mouth at right angles to a large patrician nose which protruded from a lined face with just the correct nuance of surplus claret in the complexion. He regarded Glen balefully through bushy eyebrows.

The large, fresh-faced man who had switched on the light gave Glen a thorough body search with strong, skilled hands that did nothing for Glen's dignity. When he finished he stood up and, looking down on Glen with piercing grey eyes, muttered to no one in particular, "Clean as a whistle."

With heavy sarcasm Glen demanded from the man on the bed, "Now that you're satisfied with my personal hygiene, tell these gorillas to let go of us."

"Oh, how thoughtless of me. Wilson and Harding, you may release Dr Glen now. Shearer, you're much too rough with Mrs. MacLaren. Let her be."

When they released their captives, the men moved to new strategic points, two by the window and two by the door. There was no prospect of escape.

"That's better," Glen acknowledged. "Now what's all this about?"

"Oh!" replied the spokesman, "I thought you were never going to get round to that. I'll put your mind at rest, Dr. Glen. We're not a private detective agency on behalf of an irate husband. Satisfied?"

"That's not called for. Leave her out of it."

"Out of what?"

"Whatever your business is with me. Let her go. She's not involved."

"I'll need guarantees."

"Small town gossip against a respectable pillar of society or a hue and cry for a missing person. At the moment she knows nothing. If she stays she becomes vulnerable for herself, me and possibly you."

Without batting a laconic eyelid at his own blatant blackmail, the spokesman threatened Isobel. "If I let you go now, my dear, do I have your solemn promise not to mention your night excursions to anyone? In exchange, I promise to do likewise. Alternatively, I can construct and substantiate by the devious inventions at my disposal the most lurid background for the delectation of the most unsavoury newspapers. If you stay, the outcome could be worse."

Confused and dishevelled at the moment of erotic anticipation, Isobel looked pleadingly at Glen. "What should I do?"

"Do as he says -exactly."

Isobel hesitated momentarily before saying across the room, oblivious to the other listeners, "I trust you, Colin. If you say so, I'll do it."

It was not obedience, but depth of understanding and genuine commitment.

Her attraction multiplied for Glen with the calm manner in which she accepted the traumatic situation and moved towards the door, saying to her tormentor, "I promise." No tears. No hysterics. No questions. Control. Dignity. Trust.

Shearer made to step outside with her, but Glen snapped, "Not him."

Shearer looked at his leader for a command, and the figure on the bed pursed his lips and gave a slow shake of his head. The door closed quietly behind Isobel before his face had returned to a symmetrical profile.

"OK. This time. What's it all about?" Glen demanded.

"You should know, Doctor. But suppose you tell us why you're here. After all, we're natives of this sceptred isle."

Under protest, Glen gave them an account of himself.

"Ah, Dr. Glen, you haven't even begun to get interesting yet. Perhaps we should jog your memory a little."

"Is this where the rough stuff begins?"

"You do us an injustice. We're all intelligent people. We surely don't have to resort to physical persuasion at such an early stage. No, no. Let me just put a few instances requiring simple recall.

"You were as surprised as the rest of us to find yourself suddenly in Scotland. You were also badly let down by poor Dr. Zelinsky dropping, if you'll pardon the expression, dead so inconveniently. You showed an exceptional interest in his death, convincing yourself that it was neither suicide nor accident and everyone else that it must have been one of these causes. You made a special arrangement to meet Señor Hernandez, and despite having met him and being in an even better position to write one of your famous letters of sympathy to Dr Zelinsky's family, you have ignored the aftermath of his death completely. Am I beginning to get through to you?"

"You've put a few things together, but I don't see where they lead."

"As the Queen of Hearts said to Alice, 'To lose both parents is sheer carelessness.' I say to you, to lose two contacts has its own element of carelessness, or worse."

"I didn't know they linked with each other."

"Ah, then you admit they link with you?"

"You jump too easily to the wrong conclusions."

"Alright. Can you account for some of the company you keep?"

"Like?"

"Breck, Mrs. MacLaren or Smith."

"Smith?"

"Inspector Smith?"

"Look, who are you guys? If you're in something with Hernandez or Johnson, you must be as mad as they are."

"Oh, I do apologise." The voice came from the man who had searched him. "Didn't we introduce ourselves?"

Glen was taken by surprise. He had assumed the man on the bed was the only spokesman.

"I'm Commander Ross of Scotland Yard. Sitting over there is Colonel Sinclair of the Military Police. By the window are Corporals Wilson and Harding and this is Sergeant Shearer, all colleagues of Colonel Sinclair."

For the first time, Sinclair's eyes left Glen and he gave Ross a lugubrious look.

"Why didn't you say so before?"

Ignoring the question, Ross continued, "Since our identity is in the open, yours may as well be too. We know you are a CIA agent and we want to know what you're doing here."

"If I was a CIA agent, you wouldn't expect me to come out and say so."

"It may be much worse for you if you're not with the Arlington Company.

If you're a private citizen we would want to know about your guns. If you're neither, then we may have to remove you entirely. Anyone who disappears so quickly from Florida could disappear just as quickly from St Andrews."

"What do you know about guns?"

"Wilson noticed one bulge under your jacket when you spoke to him earlier this evening. Besides, we'd taken the precaution of X-raying your parcels in the Securicor depot. We watch."

Glen looked again at Wilson. Recognition dawned on his face as he remembered the Land Rover that was supposed to be measuring the decibels produced by the jets taking off. "That was a plausible story. I'd suspected you earlier, but you put me off with that cover."

"And listen," Ross added. "Hence our reluctance to talk in the lounge. That big window lets every blessed word through."

Sinclair caught Harding's eye and gave a minimal gesture with one eyebrow.

Harding led the other two NCOs out.

"Now that's settled, we can continue to assume that you are innocent until proved guilty - innocent, that is, as far as a CIA agent ever can be.

"What I am primarily interested in is your relationship with Inspector Smith. He might claim to be on our side, but he goes about his duties in a very different way from me."

"What you're admitting is that the British left hand doesn't know what its right hand is doing, and you'd like to know which one this American hand is clasping."

"That's about it. I'm like the policeman on the beat. My job is to prevent incidents. Smith watches incidents grow, sometimes helps them along, sometimes even initiates them. It's fair game to use a sprat to catch a mackerel, and I've co-operated with them in the past when his department wanted a sprat to twirl that little bit more tantalisingly to draw the mackerel, but on this occasion I feel they are playing with tackle like a bent pin on a foot-long line when they should be using a harpoon gun. Smith is a good lad, very clever. Loves pitting his wits against the foe, but there are too many waves accompanying this one, and he might get swept away by one.

"Smith and I usually keep each other at arm's length, and we know the length of our arms. However, you've come in between us, and that could be dangerous for the three of us.

"My job is to protect totally the security of this NATO conference. I believe Smith's may be to allow it to be put at risk for political reasons.

"You see what I mean about your presence? You could be a short fuse, a detonator or a dud fuse. For all I know there may be different American departments running around here with their own different priorities. There's only one way I'll tolerate you on the ground. I want all your information on anything that puts the conference at risk and I want it now."

"I don't think you have any authority to make such a demand."

"I have all the authority I need - five to one."

"I'd like to consult my Control, but my line's bugged and I can't do it for hours."

"Use this one. I'll blow down the wire first and clear it for you if you don't want my men to listen."

When Glen finished on the phone he turned to Ross and said, "You've got a deal."

At the end of a long exchange of information and analyses, Ross said, "Russia and Argentina are too far-fetched. Hernandez sounds a psychopath, and Zochowski is desperately trying to avoid being discredited."

"It boils down to the anti-EC and anti-NATO factions in France and Spain. You've good sources in both. Can you tap them?"

"I guess so."

"Fine. What we want to know are indications of any untoward activity in France and Spain concerning propaganda, pressure groups, diplomatic movements and so on to make Spanish entry to EC or NATO more difficult or less popular."

Glen put through the call and asked the necessary questions.

"No, don't wait till morning. Phone back as soon as you've any information at all. I'm at my home number. Don't worry about line security. It's clear."

Then he turned to his uninvited guests and said, "How about a nice cup of coffee while we're waiting? It'll help to keep us awake if nothing else."

He put the percolator on and announced, "Help yourselves when it's ready. I'm going to have a shower. Nobody answer the phone if it rings. Security at the other end will go haywire if the voice doesn't coincide with my profile."

He had just got under the spray when the phone rang, and he rushed through dripping water everywhere.

The expressions of the British security men showed amazement at the efficiency of their American counterparts at the other end of the line.

"Colin Glen here."

It was Isobel. The Brits exchanged cynical smiles.

"Gee, I'm sorry. Is Campbell not home yet?"

Glen listened for a moment.

"On the West Sands with the dog? At this hour?"

Glen raised his eyebrows at her reply.

"You're right. It's daylight outside. I can never keep pace with the short hours of darkness in Scotland, but I didn't realise it was six o'clock already. It's been a busy night.

"They're still here. Everything's fine. Relax. I'll talk to you later."

He hung up.

"Isobel. She thought you were a right bunch of thugs."

A long shower and several cups of coffee later, the phone rang. It was the call Glen had been expecting. Ten minutes later he put the receiver down.

"Spain is so preoccupied with a series of bank raids it has little interest in external affairs. ETA is most likely involved, but never on this scale before," Glen began.

"Probably," Ross cut in. "Could be Falangists. Could be both by coincidence, but if it is, nothing surer than they'll be at each others' throats."

"They seem to accept that it's ETA, but they do say there are two unusual strands to the pattern, the wide geographical distribution of the raids and the huge sums of money taken, as though there's collusion with internal security."

146

"Sounds more like Falangists. They still have influential contacts in the big business world, so we can forget the Basques."

"Only one thing," Glen cautioned with a frown.

"Yes?"

"Hernandez' friend, Johnson, happens to be half Basque, and this afternoon - sorry, yesterday afternoon - I happened to be talking to a US Navy lieutenant who happened to be quarter Basque. These Basque coincidences give me a superstitious feeling of premonition."

"Blast! It was little enough good trying to point the finger at the Falangists, but anything was better than nothing. Back it goes into the melting pot. What about France?" Ross complained.

"The farmers in the Eastern Pyrenees are still stirring it up like mad, but Deuzième Bureau is quiet to the point of dullness."

"What do you make of that?"

"France is waiting for someone else to do their dirty work for them," Glen suggested with a tone of déjà vu.

"Exactly!"

For the first time since Ross had introduced himself Sinclair made a contribution to the conversation. "Thank god I'm only a simple bloody soldier."

"Some of us know better," Ross contradicted.

147

CHAPTER 35

In the Bay of Biscay two trawlers were hove to about a hundred metres apart. Although they were ablaze with lights shining on the deck, where the crew would normally be operating fishing gear or sorting fish, there was no sign of activity. In fact, there were fewer men than usual on board. Each ship, which should have had at least eight men, had only four. They had spent two hours fishing, but now all the catch was in the hold and the gear stowed, the decks scrubbed clean of fish scales and offal.

From each of the trawlers four pairs of eyes gazed intently into the black space of heaving water between them. Simultaneously on each boat there was a gasp of suppressed excitement, as one of the waves rising in the middle did not subside but continued unremittingly upwards. A frill of phosphorescent spray slipped like a ruff collar down the neck of blackness, and the watchers could make out symmetrical shoulders emerge from the deep with a dark outline separating them from the turmoil of the waves.

There was a whispered aspirate of a cheer from the hypnotised watchers, as the white frill suddenly elongated, and the dorsal surface of a submarine's deck provided a horizon to which the conning tower could be related.

Suddenly one of the crew members of the Santa Miranda 'broke ranks at the rail and called urgently to the bridge, "Skipper! Skipper! It's a trick. It's one of ours. It's the Delfin. I've seen her before."

"How do you know?" hissed the skipper.

"Two years ago I was in Majorca. We visited the port of Soller. I saw that submarine. I would know her anywhere. She's the Delfin."

"How are you so sure, Manuel?" the skipper asked nervously, his right hand poised beside the control lever, ready to push the engines to 'Full Ahead'.

"That bump at the bow. It sticks up quite sharply. You can't see clearly because you are looking across the lights, but if you stand at the rail with the light behind you, you can easily see it."

Two figures emerged on the conning tower. One of them held a megaphone. From it came an electronic crackle, and Manuel groaned. The noise cleared, and a voice called, "Ahoy, there!" A look of surprised delight spread across Manuel's face, and he crossed himself fervently.

The megaphone crackled again, and another voice spoke, this time in a Spanish accent that sounded to the fishermen very much as a Boston accent would have sounded to British ears.

"It's good to see you. I hope we didn't keep you waiting. We have several passengers for you. In a few moments we'll launch the rubber dinghies and start ferrying them to you."

In a rush of emotion, Manuel's skipper upbraided him roundly for almost causing a panic.

Manuel apologised. "I'm more relieved than you, skipper, for I was absolutely certain. I still don't understand it, but I can tell you I'm very glad to be wrong."

The skipper of the other trawler doused all lights except his navigation ones, and Manuel's skipper immediately followed suit. In the darkness, the noises from the submarine sounded louder, and the trawlermen listened nervously to the bumping of equipment and the scraping of boots on the submarine's deck. As their eyes grew accustomed to the dark, they could just make out the shadowy shapes of rubber dinghies being slipped into the water and the jostling of men trying to clamber into their unpredictable safety as both they and boats slid up and down the curved hull of the submarine with each movement of the ocean's swell.

To everyone's relief, the squat craft left the submarine's side and glided across the intervening water without a sound except the dip and drip of the paddles. The men on the Santa Miranda could see one dinghy grow slowly as it neared their vessel, while the other receded in the opposite direction towards their companion.

The trawlermen dropped a rope ladder for their passengers to climb up. When five of them were on deck, the two submariners in the dinghy cast off and returned to the submarine.

The newcomers and the fishermen embraced each other with enthusiastic hugs.

The passengers jumped and pranced and swung their legs, and performed abbreviated power walks on the restricted deck. Manuel and his shipmates leaned against the rail and laughed at the antics. They laughed again, partly in relief and partly at the difference between their own accents and the Castilian of Argentina when they started shaking hands and introducing themselves.

Then one of them took it upon himself to go amidships below the low-slung bridge and call up to the skipper, "Thank you, captain, for rescuing us from that iron coffin. We have never been so relieved before to see God's good stars in His heaven and to breathe fresh air."

"It's nothing. No matter how stormy the waves, I always prefer to have them below me than above me."

By this time another load of men had been delivered, and the same performance ensued, this time embellished with more embraces, for the Argentines already aboard the Santa Miranda increased the welcome party with the exception of the man who had spoken to the skipper.

The skipper, not wanting to miss out on the fellowship, pointed to the small steel ladder and invited the Argentine to join him on the bridge. The invitation was accepted with alacrity.

"Manuel," said the skipper, pointing out his deck-hand, "thought the submarine was one of ours. He said that a bump on the bow made it identical to one he had seen at a submarine base in Majorca."

"He wasn't far wrong. One of the few things we were able to do on board was learn about submarines. It seems that one is a French design called the Daphne class. She was built in France for South Africa, but four were built in Spain for your navy. You can tell Manuel he must have cats' eyes."

They stood in the dark, watching the third load of men transfer from the frail rubber craft. This time there were six, making the total sixteen. The same celebrations took place on the now crowded deck of the small trawler. The

Argentine turned to the skipper. "I'm sorry, I should have introduced myself before this. I am Major Rodriguez de Las Verallas."

The skipper removed a stubby cigarette from his mouth with his left hand and shook hands. "How do you do, Major? Luis Azpiazu.

"Yes. We'll just wait until the men are back in the submarine." With that he put the engines ahead to bring his vessel closer to the submarine to watch as the dinghies were stored aboard. He let down the window of his little wheelhouse and yelled, "Good luck!"

Only one man remained in the conning tower. He lifted the megaphone to his lips, but Azpiazu did not wait to listen. He pushed the lever forward, and the powerful marine diesel throbbed noisily in response, thrusting the trawler's bows deeper into the waves before her speed built up enough to lift her stem clear of the water.

With the breeze induced by the boat's movement, the men on deck were beginning to get too much fresh air and were either huddling in bunches or going below.

"How did you all manage to get space on board the submarine?" Azpiazu asked.

"They left twenty of the crew in Tenerife. That meant we had to share accommodation with the remaining twenty-seven crew members. We used the bunks in relays. I'm afraid none of us slept very well. We didn't really get used to life aboard since we joined her off the Canarias four days ago."

"I would have expected a larger submarine to be required to make the journey all the way from South Africa."

"That's the largest they have. They only have three and they all belong to that class. From Cape Town this would have been at the limit of their range if they had travelled at their most economic cruising speed, but that would have been too slow. So they made a call at Walvis Bay and refuelled there. The round trip from Puerto to this rendezvous was well within their range, even allowing for the fact that we travelled fairly fast to reduce the time we had to be on board. Their own fleet auxiliary, the Tafelberg, is somewhere over the horizon. She kept away from Puerto."

"How did you travel to the Canarias?"

"Courtesy of a very wealthy ranchero, a breeder of polo ponies and pedigree bulls. His ocean-going yacht was the last word in luxury. We are to be replaced by royalty for a cruise to Cadiz. A perfect cover, don't you think?"

Sensing from Skipper Azpiazu's amazed expression that he had already said more than enough, Rodriguez quickly changed the subject. "What's the plan now?"

"We want to avoid putting you ashore in a bunch. I'm taking you to another meeting place. I'll transfer one third each to another two trawlers.

"They'll meet smaller boats and transfer again. I'll meet three smaller boats, do another transfer and eventually dock with only two of you to put ashore. You can come home with me. You'll have two days to recover from all your travelling, and then the next stage is up to someone else."

At six hundred hours the 'Santa Miranda' docked at Las Arenas by the mouth of the Rio Nervion. From an hour earlier to an hour later, Argentines were coming ashore from a variety of fishing boats in all the fishing ports of Northern Spain, from Santona in the west to Lequeitio in the east, and each of them reached the comfort and protection of a Basque home to rest for the next forty-eight hours.

The Argentine North Atlantic Task Force was in position.

CHAPTER 36

Allowing for the fact that Spanish travellers were in the minority on the ferry from Santander, there was nothing remarkable about the small Seat car that queued with the returning British tourists for their turn to pass through Customs at Portsmouth. Its three male occupants looked as though they were hardy enough to survive the northern summer with all the camping equipment they had aboard.

The Customs Officer took one look at them. They weren't remotely close to any of the categories he was trained to identify as risks. Perhaps a bit edgy.

That could be put down to their arrival in a foreign country and the prospect of driving on the wrong side of the road. Besides, they didn't look like seasoned tourists. Serious-looking men. They reminded him of the dependable petty officers with sleeves full of good conduct stripes so familiar in that great naval port.

He waved them through.

The three Spanish sergeants from the Corps of Engineers managed to retain their impassive expressions until they were out of the dock area. Then they chortled and laughed and backslapped like raw recruits just finished their basic training square-bashing.

Three days earlier a similar carload had passed along the same route. The men in it had been every bit as relieved to get through Customs, not that they had smuggled drugs, tobacco, alcohol or any such sundries. They had only taken one thing which they should not. Packed carefully into a specially prepared compartment within the upholstery of the back seat was a large quantity of plastic explosives.

It was fresh and in good condition, thanks to General Mendez' careful supervision of his meticulous quartermaster. Together they had ensured that only the best of equipment and materials were available for what they classified as special operations. That didn't entirely prevent some anxiety for the three men who accompanied it in the confined space of their small car over hundreds of miles by road and international ferry.

A third car had arrived the previous day by sea from Lisbon to neighbouring Southampton. The three cars travelled north by different routes.

Since all three vehicles were safely through Customs, the plastic explosives in the diplomatic briefcase padlocked to the wrist of the courier emerging from Heathrow was surplus to requirements, but Mendez preferred to economise in other areas.

In addition to the nine men driving north, thirty-six others had flown in to different airports in Britain over the last three days. They were widely scattered and travelling independently, but all were moving inexorably northwards except the two who had flown into Glasgow. They would visit Loch Lomond before moving east the next day. None of them travelled direct to Edinburgh. That would have been too obvious.

By the evening of 15th July, however, they were all within ten miles of the centre of Edinburgh. No group had tried to contact another. No problems had obliged any of them to contact their control in Scotland. Everything was going according to plan.

Edinburgh was an automatic choice. It was close to the target areas. It is a cosmopolitan city, second in Britain only to London, where overseas visitors and foreign voices are an integral part of the tourist scene throughout the summer.

Despite this, Lopez and Mendez had agreed with their co-ordinator in Scotland that the men should camp and not seek hotel or guest-house accommodation where a fussy landlady or disapproving housekeeper might raise eyebrows at some of the bulky equipment.

Each campsite had been booked in advance to avoid any possible confusion, and each party, as it arrived on its campsite, was handed an envelope which had been waiting for them at Reception.

The contents were identical: a simple notice of a welcome to Scotland on behalf of the Scottish-Hispanic Society, intimating that a weekly introductory lecture would be given at eleven o'clock on Friday mornings in the annexe of Portobello High School in Edinburgh's eastern suburbs. By happy coincidence there would be a meeting the morning after the sappers arrived in Edinburgh.

By a planned coincidence, it was the same morning as the arrival of the Argentines on the Basque coast.

A map in the envelope showed the exact location of the lecture venue with a different route marked from each campsite.

Parking was no problem as the school was on holiday and the Spaniards were provided with the staff parking area.

Upstairs, at the door of one of the north-facing rooms, special identity cards were checked by a civilian, recognised by some of the soldiers as a Major in the Spanish Corps of Engineers. He compared the names and numbers of the cards against a list given to him personally by General Mendez.

When he had accounted for thirty-six men, the Major closed the door and went over to the table at the front of the room, where their two host lecturers were sitting, and whispered to them that everyone was present and correct.

Both were rugged individuals. The bearded one rose and addressed them in Spanish. "Good morning, gentlemen. My name is David Johnson and my companion is Sir Seamus Breck. Some of you may have recognised Major Gonzales who has just taken his seat beside us. I hope you will accept the background music as being essential to confuse anyone trying to listen in.

"Major Gonzales is the chief technical officer. He will also be taking over liaison duties with the strike force in place of Señor Hernandez, who met with an accident. He will allocate duties to each of you.

"Now let's have the lights out and the first slide."

He pressed the button on the control flex and a map leapt onto the screen. It showed a section of Scotland from Stirling to St Andrews and beyond to Fife Ness, bounded by the two great river estuaries, the Tay to the north and the Forth to the south.

"Can everyone see the whole map? If not, move to a better position. If anyone does not know exactly what I am saying, ask immediately. You will be acting independently, and the success of the whole operation depends on meticulous and unsupervised attention to detail."

When he finished, he handed over to Gonzales.

Gonzales first named the team that was to work with Breck. He told the three men grimly, "At least, you'll be able to keep your feet dry."

"That means the rest of you will be spending some time at least in the water. It's a bit different in this part of the world from what you're used to, and therefore we want to make sure we have a little conditioning. So we have arranged a dress rehearsal to help you contend with the cold, the dark waters, and the strong tidal currents against a target which we intend to use as a warning shot against their bows.

"We will rendezvous at 1100 hours at map reference 149793, fully equipped for attack procedure. If anyone is not one hundred per cent fit, he must not jeopardise the operation by taking part. Likewise, you must have nothing on your person when you dive that would lead to any indication of your origins. That's why we have taken so much care with the assembly of your diving equipment.

"Now, let's get down to the details of our objectives."

....

While the irregular Spanish service volunteers were converging on Edinburgh, the official movements of forces tended to be in the opposite direction.

The counter-insurgency squadron, normally based north of Madrid, was put on a tour of the south, providing demonstrations of their strike potential ostensibly to reassure the people throughout the land that Spain was united as one nation and intended to stay that way. The suggestion had been well received by the military brass when it was put forward by one of Colonel Alcazar's closest confidants. They liked the idea of a higher profile for the services, especially when it was an élite commando unit up front. There was some grumbling because of the bank raids. Some argued that ETA had been emboldened by their absence from the north and that they should be returned, but there was too much right wing support for the public relations tour.

According to their advertised programme they were in Algeciras.

Most of the military aircraft had also moved south. One squadron of fighter-bombers was in the Canaries, another in Seville and a third in Cordoba. Two squadrons remained in the north at Bilbao. Of the remaining two squadrons, a high proportion of their planes and equipment were being serviced in accordance with paper-work programmes which had been planned much earlier, and their aircrews were mainly on leave.

One squadron of heavy transport planes was on stand-by at Zaragoza. Apart from that, the only aircraft north of Madrid were training squadrons and search-and-rescue helicopter support squadrons, which had taken over the accommodation left behind by those who had moved south.

One exception to the general exodus southwards was the aircraft carrier, *Dedalo*, cruising northwards from joint manoeuvres off the Canaries with the Marin destroyer squadron, whose ships were breaking off escort duties to return to their separate port, while *Dedalo* continued to her home port of Rota, still a day's sailing to the north.

With her complement of seven Sea Harriers and twenty Sea King helicopters, the latter capable of moving a substantial number of marines within a short time, *Dedalo* represented Spain's most formidable strike force. The only disadvantage of her air power was its short range.

To add further to Spain's vulnerability, her most able and experienced sea-going officer, Captain Almonte, was beached, not punitively, but because he was standing by the new pride of the Spanish fleet, the major capital ship, *Principe de Asturias*. He fretted and fumed at the delays caused by incompetent and inaccurate paperwork.

If Lopez had been sure of his co-operation, his ship could have been commissioned on schedule. But Lopez and his sensitively-placed clique were playing for real as devil's advocate against Spain in their war games exercise.

CHAPTER 37

Having spent the whole day of the Scottish-Hispanic Society's meeting with Ross and Sinclair, Glen was aroused on Saturday morning by the insistent ringing of the phone.

Ross' voice sounded grim at the other end of the line. "We've got a third body for you. I don't think it's anyone you know, but you may be able to help Forensic. Meet me at Edinburgh Royal Infirmary. I'll be there in an hour. It shouldn't take you much longer. Fast as you can."

One hour and ten minutes later he entered the main gate of the hospital, left his car in a place reserved for a consultant, and raced up a flight of steps to the large Victorian doors. A uniformed policeman stood just inside the door.

Glen called to him, "Where can I find Commander Ross?"

"Dr. Glen?"

"Right."

"This way, sir."

The policeman marched swiftly along an anonymous white-tiled tunnel with Glen in tow.

Somehow in that maze of corridors he chose one door, pushed it open for Glen and stood aside.

Glen entered an immaculate room, which seemed at first glance to be an operating theatre. Several green-garbed figures cluttered round a table in the middle of the room. One detached himself. It was Ross. He strode over to Glen.

"This body they're dismantling was fished out of the Forth near Granton at first light this morning. It had nothing to identify it. Nobody can so far say with certainty who manufactured the sub-aqua equipment it was wearing. No identifying tabs or labels. Nobody's reported him missing. No abandoned vehicles have been found. No drifting boats. No marker buoys to indicate where he had begun his dive. These forensics are now delving for internal clues."

"How can I help?" Glen interrupted.

"Over here."

Ross led the way to a marble table with a display of several numbered plastic bags. He handed one to Glen.

"What do you make of that?"

"It looks like a St Christopher."

"That's what we thought at first. Have another look. Look at the tiny writing." He handed him a magnifying glass.

Glen read the motto. "This is Spanish!" he exclaimed.

"I know that. What does it say?"

Glen translated easily, "All to the Greater Glory of God. That's the motto of St Ignatius Loyola. It's the sort of thing a Catholic might have, especially if he had been educated by Jesuits. It's obviously Spanish in origin, but it could have been brought back as a souvenir."

"Would it have any further significance?"

"It looks as though it was being worn instead of a St Christopher medallion. Poor old St Christopher would have done this lad as much good even if he was demoted by the Vatican."

"I was wondering if it would have been more likely to have been worn by a soldier."

"Could be. Loyola was a soldier, and the Jesuits whose Order he founded is run on lines of military discipline. The head of the Order is known as the Vicar General. It could be very appropriate for a soldier if he was going on what might be regarded as a Crusade. I've just thought of something else. Loyola was a Basque."

"Would that rule out Argentina?"

"Not at all. The Basques are among the most mobile of all groups making up the Spanish population. In fact, their involvement overseas is disproportionate to their numbers, but remember Loyola and the Jesuits are international. What else have you to go on?"

"We've confirmed that the man died of drowning. There were no injuries on the body. There was still compressed air in his bottles, which made us wonder why he had taken off his face-mask. A blood test in here showed he'd had malaria. It could have flared up while he was in the water and caused him to remove his mask."

"There are plenty ex-servicemen in this country who have recurring bouts of malaria, but this body was of a man of about forty, which makes him too young to have had British wartime service, and our men are so well protected against it when they're in the tropics nowadays that they rarely contract it. It suggests to me that he'd spent some time in a country where the precautions may not have been as efficient as they are for people from this country. This one caught my fancy, for it was a namesake of my own, Ronald Ross, who identified the anopheles mosquito as the malarial carrier."

"It might be useful if we could have a look at the body."

"As soon as these medics put it together again we'll have a good look. It has all the appearance of a southern European or Latin American: black hair, tanned skin, five-foot-eight tall. He certainly liked Mediterranean-type food. They've separated the contents of his stomach over there: rice, shellfish, peppers, olive oil. That would suggest he'd arrived very recently or had all his meals in a Spanish or Italian-type restaurant. We've already got men out visiting such places in the Edinburgh area with a reconstructed picture of what he would have looked like when alive."

"He could have done his own cooking or shared it with friends, possibly using food he'd brought here with him."

Before Glen had finished talking, Ross had his two-way pocket radio in his hand. He pressed the call button and then the transmit one. Turning his back on the eviscerated cadaver, he spoke quietly into the machine, "Ross here. Granton body case. Extend the questioning to campsites - round Edinburgh first. Then extend it along the shores of the Forth. Get Fife and Central police to co-operate."

"You haven't told me yet why you're so excited about this body."

Ross looked at him grimly. "There was a trace of plastic explosive on the left sleeve of his wet-suit."

"No doubt you've worked out how long he's been in the water and when he died."

"He'd been dead for five to six hours. The body was taken out of the water just after six this morning. That means he died between one and two a.m. The amount of air in his bottles suggested that he had used it for not more than half an hour. The tide was full at three, which means the body could have been carried upstream before slack water. The ebb would have started about three-thirty, and built up to a maximum of four knots. So we could estimate that it moved a maximum of eight miles downstream from the point where death occurred. More realistically, it would have moved downstream a net distance of four to six miles. That takes us to a position between Hound Point and North Queensferry."

"I'm sorry," Glen said, shaking his head, "but you've lost me."

"My fault. I'll show you on a map once we get hold of one. The point I'm trying to make is that it came from the direction of the oil terminal at Hound Point. It's not the sort of place I'd expect anyone to go for pleasure. Frankly, it worries me."

"If you've a strong stomach, we can have a look at what other interesting things they're finding in this fellow's anatomy."

As they crossed to the table where the pathologist's team was absorbed in interpreting the clues which their amazing science revealed, Glen asked, "Have they established the blood group yet?"

"Yes, but it didn't seem to mean much apart from the fact that it wasn't the most common. You'll have to ask the pathologist."

"Rhesus O, negative," the pathologist replied without raising his eyes.

Glen whistled.

"What's the significance?" the pathologist asked, his professional interest aroused.

"It may simply be a coincidence, but that blood group is much more commonly found among Basques than any other ethnic group in Europe."

The expression in the forensic scientist's eyes told Glen that the information had struck a chord in his memory.

....

At midday, a phone call came through to *The Scotsman* office on North Bridge, Edinburgh. It was put direct to the editor's desk.

Unusually, he was wearing his jacket and tie. It had been a quiet day in the office, and it looked as though the biggest stories would be in the sports section covering the arrival of the golfing greats for the Open at St Andrews.

Mr Duncansby was therefore hoping to escape briefly from the office to attend at least part of the literary lunch at which his wife would be speaking about her latest bestseller.

As an experienced newspaper man in charge of one of the oldest and most respected newspapers in the English-speaking world, he didn't often show surprise at anything he heard over the line, but on this occasion he was not only startled but shocked.

"Who is this? No. Wait. How do I know it's the truth?"

But the caller had rung off.

....

Ross' face was set in granite as he turned to Glen and said, "The worst is upon us."

They had just left the forensic experts and were on the point of driving to St Andrews House. Glen was intended to follow in convoy.

"Leave your car. Come in with us. We'll stop at *The Scotsman*. It's on our way."

As the Rover plunged out of the gates and turned right across the path of a taxi travelling west along Lauriston Place, Ross said, hanging on to a roof strap to prevent himself colliding with Glen, "*The Scotsman's* had a phone call saying that a bomb's been planted on an oil-related target. We'll have to visit the editor, as he took the phone call personally. We're going straight there now."

Five minutes later they were ushered into the editor's office. Andrew Duncansby welcomed them warmly. He was a smallish man with aquiline features and eyes to match, not the kind of person to be taken in by a trickster or to be put on a false trail.

Ross opened the conversation. "Would you tell us exactly what was said?"

"The telephonist realised it was an unusual call and she wisely put it straight through to my office. Fortunately, although I'm not usually here on a Saturday, I was in today. The caller said, 'This is a warning to those responsible for the rape of Scotland. The victim is fighting back. Today we strike against a strategic oil target. My call sign will be Alba.' Then he hung up. These were his exact words."

"How are you so sure?"

"I still keep up my shorthand from my cub reporter days. I wrote it down as he was speaking."

"No indication of time? No indication of place?"

"None at all."

"If he's not completely mad, he must give us some indication of those, to avoid loss of life. You're sure it wasn't a hoax?"

"It sounded genuine to me. Obviously I tried to hold him on the line, but he hung up."

"It seems that he's given you a call sign. Next time he phones, if we're lucky, he should give us time and place, but he'll spend a fraction of the time on the phone. However, we have to try to have it traced."

Glen spoke for the first time. "What's the significance, if any, of his call sign?"

Duncansby beat Ross to the answer. "It's the Gaelic name for Scotland. Many would claim it's the correct ancient name of this country."

Ross asked, "Was it a genuine Scottish accent?"

"No doubt about it."

"We're in the hands of the politicians now. I've got to speak to the Secretary of State. Can I use your phone, Andrew, to make a few arrangements?"

Ten minutes later Ross, with Glen beside him, sat fuming at the traffic hold-up as they waited to turn into Waterloo Place at one of the busiest road junctions in the capital.

Once through the logjam, the driver accelerated all the way to St Andrews House, that symmetrical pile of the late bureaucratic derivative of the Odeon School of architecture. Once inside, they were ushered to an empty office. The Secretary of State entered moments later from another door, having been called from his official residence in Charlotte Square. As soon as he put his file on the large empty desk, from which it was instantly whisked by an assistant, his hand went up to flick a troublesome forelock from his high forehead. He looked disapprovingly at Glen as Ross hastily explained he was on special secondment.

"What's this panic about, Commander?" MacEwan demanded, trying to shrug the political pressure that was piling up from his shoulders to those of the policeman.

"I told you everything I know on the phone, sir. In the few minutes since this news broke, I've been trying to think of possible lines of action. First, I think that you would agree we should ask the newspapers not to publish the threat. Second, we must contact Regional Police Forces and oil companies and advise them to be on extra alert. Third, we must run a check on all known political extremists. Fourth, we must step up our efforts to find the connection between the body taken out of the sea at Granton this morning and any activist group.

"With regard to the last, sir, we've a very strong suspicion that he may have been a Spanish national. We're presently checking all campsites around Edinburgh to try to trace his companions. Since the man had been equipped for work in the water, it would seem reasonable to infer that the target threatened is in the water. Considering the location of the body, I believe the target is very probably one of the Forth Bridges or the tanker terminal at Hound Point. To minimise risk, I would therefore suggest that any tanker berthed, or about to berth, should stand off immediately. Grangemouth Refinery is also at risk, and again I would strongly recommend that tankers and any associated shipping be moved from the docks as soon as the tide permits. We're only too familiar with the tricks of the currents in the Forth, and it's not beyond the realms of possibility that the body came from further upstream."

Ross drew a deep breath.

"Other areas of high risk are Finnart and Sullom Voe, but it seems to me that the Forth is the prime target. I intend an examination by our underwater team of the pontoons and piers at Hound Point."

MacEwan had been avidly following Ross' outline of the crisis and his proposed lines of action. As soon as there was a pause, he demanded sharply, "But what about the threat to the editor at The Scotsman and the code-word? We've never had that before. What can they be trying to do?"

"Sir, they're setting up a situation so that when they phone a message in the future we will know it is not from your run-of-the-mill crank, but from a genuine terrorist. This is not a one-off. That's why I'm treating it as deadly serious. They must carry out their threat this time in order to be credible when they come up with whatever demand they're going to make. Their call is unusual in that they have given no time or place, and they've made no demands. To some extent it sounds a bit premature, and I believe that is because they fear we can beat them to it with the evidence we can get from the body. Unfortunately, the first edition of The Evening News is on the streets by now, and the discovery of the body is no doubt on the front page. We'll need to take the editor into our confidence and ask him to make it sound as routine as possible. We'll give him a very dull report."

"I'm glad we're in your capable hands," MacEwan said with a mixture of personal relief and political buck-passing. "Keep me informed as events develop. Be assured that you have my full authority to take initiatives when time does not permit consultation with myself, although I mustn't be kept in the dark a moment longer than necessary. Meanwhile my staff will provide a room for you and Mr Glen while you are in this building."

CHAPTER 38

Ross nodded Glen towards a chair as he lifted the phone from the vacant desk and dialled Colonel Sinclair at Gleneagles. "I'd like to have some help from your stand-by detachment at Redford Barracks, and I must have some sappers. You can get them more quickly than I can by going through channels. We need bomb-disposal and underwater experts. Rendezvous at South Queensferry marina. Extreme urgency."

"Consider it done." Sinclair was a man of few words. He hung up.

The phone rang. Ross lifted the receiver. He listened attentively to the report from Lothian Police that two campsites had reported a party of Spaniards, all male, having left that morning.

Although the air-conditioned room was comfortable for temperature and humidity, and although his face showed no signs of perspiration, Ross rubbed the back of his hand across his brow as though it was streaming with sweat. He thanked the officer at the other end and, turning back to Glen, said, "Not much else we can do here. Let's get to South Queensferry like the hammers of hell. Sinclair will have his men mobilised already. I feel it in my bones that's where the action's going to be."

As the Rover raced along Queen Street, Ross confided in Glen. "I've got us into action at least - nothing worse than waiting - but I still don't see the connection between the phone call and the Spaniard, although I'm certain there is one. I'd have been happier if that body hadn't pointed so strongly to being Spanish, or if the voice had not been genuine Scottish. I can understand either working separately, but I don't understand how they can be connected."

"Perhaps," Glen suggested tentatively, "we should look at the possibility of a connection between extremists in Scotland and Basque separatists, instead of Spanish as such."

You could be onto something there. That's the kind of area in which our friend Smith operates. He can see patterns more complex than interwoven Buchanan and Ogilvie tartans. In fact, I sometimes think he weaves them to his own design."

"What about Sir Seamus Breck?"

"He makes the occasional outrageous remark, but that's just to draw attention to himself. He's part of the Establishment and has no intention of rocking the boat. Investigating someone like that can be very difficult for the ordinary policeman like myself. He and MacEwan served in the same regiment, which makes them even closer than the usual peacetime officer caste, and MacEwan's older brother was in Breck's class at the same boarding school. To get *carte blanche* on Breck requires more than the usual dispensation offered when I'm allowed to take my own initiative. He's another chapter in the same book as Lord Lucan."

"I don't know about Lucan. I'll leave him to you, but I do want to follow up on Breck. You told MacEwan I was seconded, but this is one place I'm going to treat myself to some latitude."

Ross grinned at the response to Lucan. "I won't go into it just now, but Lord Lucan is a by-word for the way in which the powerful social establishment can make life impossible for the police when one of their own number is on the wrong side of the law.

"Forget him just now. I'll try to get a fix on Breck for you. He's got property all over Scotland so there are several places he could be. I'll put out a call right now to Tayside and Grampian police. They'll get in touch with us when they know where he is, and you can go and check him out in your own style."

After a steep descent they reached the shore of the Forth beside the gigantic red sandstone pillars that support the elegant arches leading to the iron cantilever of the original Forth Bridge.

When Ross and Glen got out, the driver moved forward to park at a safe distance from the corner. Leading the way across the road, Ross pointed downstream to the oil terminal.

"Those piers make up the docking facilities for supertankers bringing in North Sea Oil,which is then piped to storage tanks concealed in an old shale bing on the west side of the southern approach to the Road Bridge which you can see over there." He pointed in the opposite direction from Hound Point.

With a roar of heavy tread tyres and a growling of engines in four-wheel low gear, two Land Rovers bounced into sight, each pulling a large rigid inflatable boat bouncing violently on a bobbing trailer.

Ross grinned. "Here come the Royal Engineers - 'first in, last out', as their motto says. Let's hope we'll all be out of this one without too much damage."

An older than average captain jumped out of the front passenger seat of the first vehicle before it had come to a complete halt, looked first at the Rover parked a hundred yards in front of his own machine, noticed Ross beckoning him, and doubled across the road, gave an experienced rather than punctilious salute and introduced himself, "Captain MacTaggart, sir."

"You're very prompt, Captain. My name is Ross, and this is Dr. Glen." The formalities over, Ross got down to business. "What information have you been given?"

"Only to report to you here, sir."

"I'll put you in the picture as clearly as I can. This morning we fished a body out of the Forth near Granton Harbour. It was in a frogman's get-up, and what worries us is that there were traces on it to suggest that the man had been handling plastic explosives. We have since had a threatening phone-call claiming an imminent strike against an oil-related target. My guess is that the terminal out there is the target.

"What you'll be looking for is a sabotage device, probably below the low-water mark. Probably expertly done and maybe booby-trapped. We don't have a time limit on it, but we'll be informed instantly there's further contact from the terrorist. Your radio operator will get the frequency from my driver."

"We'll make sure he keeps an ear wide open on that one, sir," MacTaggart replied evenly. "In the meantime we'll launch the RIBs at the old ferry jetty and go

163

have a look-see. I don't suppose either of you gentlemen wants to keep us company out there? Funny how no-one ever takes up my invitation to inspect a bomb closeup with me. I must ask my dentist about my oral hygiene."

"Don't make us sound so cowardly," scolded Ross with a gallows humour. "All the perfumes of Arabia wouldn't entice me to be near you when you're working." He paused before adding the almost mandatory, "Good luck!"

MacTaggart grinned and, with a salute on the polite side of casual, said, "Don't worry, sir. We'll be careful. Just watch our backs."

As soon as MacTaggart opened the door of his Land Rover, the driver had it in gear and shot away with the RIB, the second Land Rover so close behind that it looked as if it was jostling for first place.

Despite the fact that there was scarcely any distance to the slipway, the drivers raced up the gears; down to second for the right hand turn on to the slipway; up to third and down again to second for the short dash to the water's edge by the full-tide mark.

A quick reversal manoeuvre of the articulated combinations, and both were facing up the slipway towards where they had come from. Almost simultaneously and equally noisily they changed into reverse again. With wheels spinning on the wide smooth stones of the old jetty, they drove backwards until the axles of the trailers were awash.

Eight soldiers emerged from each Land Rover and raced through a highly-organised drill as though they were taking part in the Edinburgh Tattoo. Trailers, being of the break-back variety, were tipped up and the boats launched without unhitching. A soldier was already in the boat manning the big outboard motor in the stern. It roared to life the moment the RIB was afloat.

As the small craft went astern at open throttle, the trailers were brought back into their road-travelling positions and towed above high water mark alongside the sheltering wall on the western side of the slipway, where they were drawn up one behind the other to minimise obstruction.

Two of the men in each boat were in their wet-suits ready to dive. Others were helping with their air cylinders and weights.

It took the same time for Ross and Glen to reach their car. As they separated at the back, each to go in by his own door, the driver leaned out and said to Ross, "Message for you, sir."

Ross lifted the phone before getting into the car. He listened for a moment and then barked, "I want to know when he left, where he's going and how he's travelling - and I want to know fast. Lives already depend on your speed."

He hung up as he slipped into the seat beside Glen, his face like thunder.

"Trouble?" Glen asked.

"Your theory about Breck is becoming more plausible by the minute. Rumour is he's gone abroad, but no one seems to be definite. They'd better be definite fast. Next bit of news: Lothian Police say he's a trustee of a recent group called the Scottish-Hispanic Society, a cultural organisation to improve relations and understanding between the two countries."

164

After ruminating for a minute, he added, "I'll stake my pension he's involved."

MacTaggart's two-boat flotilla was already halfway from the jetty to the terminal.

"Let's get the hell back to Edinburgh. There's nothing we can do here to improve the efficiency of that bunch of fellows."

As the car made a U-turn at the top of the jetty and was facing towards the tanker terminal, Ross said, "Hold it a minute. I want to have a look."

Taking a pair of powerful binoculars from a small locker on top of the drive shaft, he put them to his eyes, commenting, "The first boat has just reached the pier."

The next event was as obvious to Glen and the driver without the benefit of binoculars. For no apparent reason, and in complete silence, the nearest pier of the terminal complex took off like a space shuttle complete with seething energy of burning fuel at its base. Only this time, the foaming plumes were not of fire, but of water, nor were they homogeneous, for the water contained all kinds of flotsam including disintegrating bodies and dismembered limbs.

Six seconds later, Ross pulled the binoculars from his disbelieving eyes, and, before he had laid them on his knees, the car shook with the blast of the explosion.

Farther down the jetty, the drivers jumped from their Land Rovers to see the pier, now shattered into a myriad of components, return to the sea in a widely distributed pattern of assorted splashes, the largest first, the smallest seconds later.

Recovering his senses first, but not his normal voice, Ross ordered the driver, "Get the Royal Navy at Rosyth to send rescue boats immediately. It's just across the water. Pinpoint the location for them. Then tell Flag Officer, Scotland, at Pitreavie Castle. Who knows? They must have seen it. They'll co-ordinate rescue services, not that it looks as though anyone will be left to be rescued after that lot." His normal healthy glow had turned to ash-grey and the very flesh of his face disappeared in a sudden gauntness.

Automatically, the driver began to comply before Ross had finished and was already speaking into his radio.

Ross muttered to Glen, "They'll have rescue helicopters from Leuchars in a few minutes."

But Glen was already halfway out of the car. "Let's find out what emergency drill applies."

He raced to where the two army drivers were standing on the edge of the jetty in a vain gesture of being as close as possible to their stricken companions.

"Come on, you guys! Have you nothing better to do? Let's get out there!"

They stared dumbly at him.

"Right! Let's commandeer something! This is war!" he screamed at them.

Nothing caught his eye in the immediate vicinity. He leapt onto the bonnet of a Land Rover, scrambled onto its cab roof and looked over the high wall beside which it was parked. He saw what he wanted.

"Let's go!"

He leapt to the ground and sprinted to the top of the jetty before disappearing round the corner. The drivers, converted from numbed shock to pounding adrenaline, charged after him. When they caught up with him, he was untying the painter of a fibreglass speedboat temporarily moored to an iron ring just below road level in the retaining wall.

He undid the clove hitch, but left the rope running freely through the ring. Holding the loose end of the rope, he clambered down the wall and jumped the last few feet onto the small fore deck. He slipped one half hitch round a cleat, stepped over the small windscreen onto the dashboard top and into the cockpit.

At the stern he opened the hatch behind the padded seat, checked the fuel-tank was three-quarters full and pumped the bulbous rubber primer. The boat rocked, as one soldier landed on the deck, and then changed to a different rhythm as his companion followed him with a bump.

The change in motion almost caught Glen wrong-footed as he stepped over the back seat and into the engine-well at the stern to drop the Yamaha 85 outboard from its stowed position into the water.

"Shift that gear lever into neutral," he yelled over his shoulder.

Someone must have obeyed, for the moment he dropped the engine it clicked into place as it automatically fastened onto the fixed bracket on the stern. When he turned round, the second soldier was about to step over the windscreen.

"Wait where you are," Glen ordered. To the other soldier he said, "Can you operate this boat?"

"Yes, sir. The key's been left in the ignition."

"That'll save us a lot of time in short-circuiting the starting motor. Let's go. And you," he said to the man in the bow, "cast off the moment that engine fires."

Above them a voice cried, "Hang on!"

When they looked up they saw Ross bending between the railings.

"No! Don't come," Glen ordered unceremoniously. "It's more important you remain ashore. Keep the operation going. Besides, there may be another charge out there."

Hesitating briefly before returning to the landward side of the railing, Ross was assailed by a new voice "Hey! What d'you think you're on? That's my boat!"

By the time the irate owner had finished his brief statement, the speedboat was already rising into its angle of plane as the engine pushed straight into full power.

Within four minutes of calling on the engine for everything it had, the soldier was already throttling back as they approached the first of the floating debris. Because of their low position in the water, they did not have an adequate view of what lay among the subsiding waves. There was an unspoken consensus among the men that they would not spend time on anything inanimate or inert. From the nature of everything they saw in the first five minutes there appeared little prospect of their ever having to stop.

While one soldier continued as coxswain, his companion stood upright beside him, scanning as much of the sea's surface as he could. Glen did the same thing from the stern.

Suddenly the uniformed lookout broke the funereal silence. "Over there!" He pointed to the starboard quarter. "Something moving."

The coxswain coaxed the boat slightly faster through the flotsam. Fifty yards away a black figure feebly lifted an appealing hand. The boat eased gently to approach the figure on the lee side to avoid being blown on top of him.

The man was in his wet suit. Together the two soldiers began to haul him from the water as gently as they knew how. One released the buckle holding on his harness, and the compressed air cylinders slipped from his back and disappeared under the surface, thus enabling his rescuers to lift him clear of the water and into the confined space of the sports boat.

All that Glen knew was that the man was not MacTaggart, but his comrades recognised him. One asked him in anguished tones, "What the bloody hell happened, Taff?"

Taff pointed languidly to his ear and whispered, "I'm deaf. Help me to get this off." He tugged ineffectually at his close-fitting helmet.

As soon as it was removed, the filigree of blood from his ear told them why he was deaf. More blood trickled from his nose. As he lay exhausted from the effort of having his helmet removed, his breath rasped painfully through his heaving chest.

With spasmodic gasps he tried to explain. "I was ... in the water ... first ... dived ... felt crushed ... surfaced ... nothing but this ... mess." The final sibilants continued involuntarily until they subsided in a burbling red foam trickling from his mouth.

His two erstwhile companions looked stunned until Glen broke the silence.

"He was crushed by the shock waves under the surface. The only reason he survived so long was that he escaped the full blast in the air which killed all the others still in the dinghies."

The explanation also accounted for Taff having been kept relatively in one piece.

As they propped Taff's body in the stern seat, powerful engines throbbed towards them. Looking up, Glen saw a naval patrol boat bearing down on them, the line of its wake forming a V, its open end widening towards the Royal Naval Dockyards on the distant Fife shore.

"There's nothing left for us to do here that the Navy can't do better," he told his companions. "We'd better go ashore and leave it to them."

The coxswain pushed the combined throttle and gear lever forward, and they were beginning to pick up speed when the lieutenant in command of the patrol boat hailed them from his wheelhouse. "What's been going on here?"

"An explosion!" Glen yelled back. "We came out to see if we could help. We have one body on board. It's the nearest thing to a survivor we've seen."

"Thanks!" the lieutenant called back. "The authorities will take it off your hands when you get ashore. We won't waste time taking it on board."

With throttle open they returned to the jetty, but despite the high speed, their journey lacked the dash of their outward trip.

Taff's body was manhandled out of the small craft and covered with blankets before being hastily bundled into a waiting ambulance.

Some spectators tried to offer comfort to the would-be rescuers. Glen struggled free from all their well-meaning embraces and forged his way through the gathering crowds to where Ross was standing, his face as hard as the stonework behind him.

Staring fixedly to the front, Ross grated, "I've just had a call from Duncansby at *The Scotsman*. Alba called. 'Somebody guessed well,' he said, 'but wasn't clever enough. These men were killed needlessly."

"He goes on, 'An empty tanker was due at five tomorrow morning. Its bulk would have absorbed the explosion as it touched the pier. The crew would have been warned. Don't try to outsmart us again. You know we mean business.'"

The anguish in his voice spoke volumes for the bitterness he felt against himself for having sent the men to their deaths.

Glen offered some practical consolation. "Don't forget. We've wrong-footed the enemy. His calculations are now at least twelve hours out and we are ahead of him by that time. We now have to apply our minds to his next move. Remember, in relation to the sixteen lives lost today, our ultimate objective is the future of NATO and the protection of hundreds of millions of lives."

"You're right, of course. It's easier to admire an individual like MacTaggart than think of faceless millions. That conference assembles tomorrow and we've still got a job to do. I'm going back to Gleneagles. You cover Leuchars and see if you can get any trace of what's happened to Breck. He holds one key to this mystery, and Smith holds another."

CHAPTER 39

Bilbao civil airport, which lies in the flat valley of the Rio Asua five kilometres north of the city centre, was a hive of military activity with a canvas village set up on the southern perimeter as far as possible from the road and rail access points. The accommodation was provided for the aircrews and ground crews who made up the 121 and 122 Squadrons of the EdA, as the Spanish Air Force is known. The aircrews of both squadrons had flown in their MacDonald-Douglas F-4C Phantoms at dusk from their normal base at Torrejon. The other personnel had been carried, along with their stores and spares, by two Douglas C-54s of 35 Wing Transport, which had returned to their base at Getafe, near Madrid, as soon as they had unloaded.

The encampment was in darkness apart from the lighting provided by mobile generators. No leave was being allowed during the exercise.

They were all pawns in the giant game of chess being played, with Spain as the board and its airborne forces as the pieces. The purpose of the game, of which Lopez was the Grand Master, was to move all effective elements of the Spanish Air Force and Spain's only operational aircraft-carrier as far as possible from the north of the country. The few elements moved north consisted of machines chosen for a special role.

Because the overall distribution of aircraft remained relatively even, nothing was seen to be amiss by senior officers not privy to Lopez' plan.

301 Squadron of Transport Wing had flown their two Lockheed C-130 Hercules north from Valenzuela into Zaragoza Airport with its unusual pair of parallel runways running north-west along the Ebro Valley. Unlike the fighter squadrons in Bilbao, their personnel were housed in the permanent barracks of the EdA at the airport, and no leave restrictions had been placed on them.

These were the only three squadrons under the control of Zaragoza Air Region, the most northerly of Spain's four military air regions. Two squadrons of Mirage F1Cs from Albacete, 150 miles south-east of Madrid, had joined the other two squadrons with the same type of plane at Los Llanos in La Palma, Canaries, to take part in exercises with the aircraft carrier *Dedalo*.

111 Squadron and 112 Squadron remained at their own base of Manises near Valencia.

The three Army Mobile Air Force units from Tablada had joined the third unit of the Force at Moron de la Frontera, south-east of Seville, for a combined training exercise, part of which was to harass *Dedalo* as she returned to Rota, her home port across the bay from Cadiz, and part to raise the morale at La Linea in face of the British fortress on Gibraltar.

The net result was that Air Regions Las Palmas and Seville contained most of Spain's air power, and a gap yawned between the extreme north and the far south of the country. This was not serious, for, provided they remained operational and in the right hands, the squadrons at Bilbao and Zaragoza retained a reasonable balance.

The Hercules transports were on a crew conversion course. One plane had been converted to a mid-air tanker. The squadron was to practise rendezvous over the

169

Bay of Biscay with the two Phantom Squadrons from Bilbao. Each day a different crew would man the tanker, while the other Hercules accompanied it on a simulation exercise.

....

At four a.m., through the blanket of mist rising from the river, small groups of purposeful, determined-looking men could be discerned converging on the southern side of Bilbao Airport. They were unarmed.

A few miles east of Bilbao, a truck drew up in the middle of the straight stretch of road between Larrabezua and the Airport, about one kilometre west of the village of Zamudio, where a tributary on the left bank joins the Rio Asua, at the point where the river begins to turn south-west and away from the road. Three men from the cab joined two who jumped out of the back. Together they drew out of the back of the truck an already inflated rubber dinghy and carried it to the river, where they launched it before securing it by its painter to a wooden boundary post. Quickly and silently each man made three or four return trips between truck and dinghy and in so doing transferred a veritable arsenal of guns and ammunition from road transport to river transport.

Four men scrambled on board as the driver cast off from the shore with a whispered farewell, "I gora Euzkadi - Long live the Basques!" as he gave the laden craft a gentle push towards mid-stream and into the enveloping mist.

He returned to his truck and drove off to uplift some more mundane load.

Crouching low, the four men in the dinghy dipped their paddles furtively into the water to push the craft along the slow-moving current.

Minutes later they froze into immobility as the headlights of an approaching vehicle bore towards them across the flat valley floor. At what appeared the inevitable moment of impact, the headlights suddenly jerked skywards and the large truck roared above them, lifted upwards by the bridge which carried the Bilbao-Munguia road across the river. The men sighed heavily as the protective darkness of the bridge engulfed them.

Twenty minutes later the boat was deliberately run ashore on the right bank just before an undercut, as the river took a sharp turn to the south-west. The minutely abrasive sound, as the craft grounded on the soft silt, was picked up clearly by several acutely attuned pairs of ears.

Immediately, heads and figures of earlier arrivals began to rise from their hiding-places close to the river. By a pre-arranged signal, the men crawled and scrambled towards the dinghy in such a way that there was a constant stream of bodies arriving empty-handed and departing fully-armed from the dinghy. There was never any congestion, queuing or breaks in the continuity of the activity.

When all the weapons and ammunition had been distributed, the crew deflated the dinghy and stowed it in a space behind the roots of a tree whose soil had been eroded by the river during times of flood.

In response to a hand signal from close to the perimeter fence, the force of thirty men moved towards the fence and passed through it by a space made by two comrades wearing thick leather gloves as they strained to provide a gap by holding two of the lower strands of barbed wire as far apart as possible. It would have been easier to have cut the wire, but that would have left dangerous evidence for any patrol.

The ETA attackers flitted like shadows past the drugged guards to the tents occupied by the aircrews. On the dot of five they crept into the tents and wakened the fliers very gently, apart, that is, from the fact that each airman recognised the cold muzzle of a gun in his face as he awoke. They dressed meekly as instructed.

An engine shattered the dawn stillness as it sprang into life in the vehicle pool beyond the lines of canvas quarters. With a change of noise and a rasping of gears the vehicle approached the officers' tents.

In each tent, an ETA spokesman told his captives, "A coach is outside to take you for a short journey. There are two airmen standing at the door of the coach and two sitting at the back. They are wearing uniforms, but be in no doubt. They are not on your side. Each one is well armed, sharp-eyed and trigger-happy. Don't give the slightest provocation. You'll only be detained for a short time while we help the government reassess its programme. Your co-operation will ensure that neither you nor anyone else in Spain is harmed in any way."

The ETA kidnappers, knowing that, despite a socialist government, officers and other ranks in the Spanish services lead very separate lives, found the officers' tents separate from those of other ranks, with their doors faced away from them. One by one the tent flaps were lifted, the kidnappers entered and an enlarged group emerged from each tent and entered the coach at exact intervals.

When all the fliers were on the bus, the driver turned round to face them and let them see the sub-machine gun on his lap. He gave them a huge smile.

At the same time, the two guards from the coach door walked one to each end of the line of tents and watched for any movement from the rest of the camp, while their ETA colleagues filed quickly and quietly onto the coach.

The other ranks showed no interest in the arrival of a vehicle. As far as they were concerned, officers were a law unto themselves. They were welcome to arrive back late or early. In any case, they'd had a tiring day the day before and wanted to enjoy the remnants of their sleep.

The guards returned to the coach when everyone else was on board, closed the door, and stood facing their captives with their machine pistols at the ready. The driver, with an ominous click, snapped on the safety-catch of his gun and laid it down beside him. He revved the engine noisily and slapped it into gear before juddering across the grass to the main exit.

When they reached the security control at the exit, the coach stopped and one of the guards went out to report, closing the door carefully behind him. He saluted smartly and asked the Civil Guard officer to check the numbers on the coach.

The officer was not concerned about people leaving the base. "There's no need. I'll count them when they come back. That's much more important."

"I'm sorry, sir, but these are my orders. Part of our manoeuvre involves mobilising aircrews quickly and they will not have time for checks on the return journey. That is why it is essential for you as well as the EdA guard to check now.

All that is necessary is a head count to make sure that no-one extra comes onto the protected military zone of the airport."

The captain grumbled again, but ordered his senior NCO, "Go and do as he asks, Manuel, just to keep him happy."

The ETA guard stood smartly to attention and gave a cheerful salute. "Thank you, sir."

Then he led the sleepy-eyed sergeant round the outside of the bus, counting the heads all covered with uniform hats so that little of their individual features were discernible, something which the sergeant neither realised nor worried about, as he muttered, "Fifty-two. That's the lot."

"Fifty-three," corrected the ETA guard. "Don't forget me. I'll be on the coach when we get back. I don't want to end up in the guardhouse."

The sergeant grunted. He was more interested in getting off duty within the next half-hour.

"Please make sure it's recorded, so that there's no foul-up when we get back, or you and I will share the responsibility for delaying a carefully planned operation."

"You're a most officious beggar," the sergeant complained, "but don't worry. We're tops at our job. There'll be no hitches on our part. When will you be back?"

"1000 hours."

With that, the freedom fighter returned to the coach, half of whose occupants were hiding below the level of the windows, their guns trained on their captives who were thereby constrained to keep their faces well averted from the windows in case they gave a signal to the Civil Guard.

Once clear of the security formalities, the coach fairly tore along the road towards Larrabezua.

After only six kilometres it turned sharp left and took the winding road up the hill to Basabilotra. It drove right through the small town and followed the single-track road that led to the forest and an abandoned sawmill.

They didn't stop until they were inside the ramshackle wooden walls that had given shelter to the now dismantled machinery.

Most of the ETA men got out of the coach, leaving five guards behind with the prisoners.

They crossed the muddy yard to the wooden hut, which had housed the loggers and sawmill workers in the past.

The bunkhouse was crowded before they reached it, for waiting to greet them were the thirty-two Argentine airmen brought ashore from the South African submarine two nights before. There were subdued greetings and exchanges of questions and answers.

Laxalt asserted his authority over the company. "There are forty-eight EdA officers across the yard, all dressed up in their uniforms. By the time you get over there, they'll be in a nice straight line, tallest to the right, smallest to the left. Pick out someone about your own height and weight, and persuade him to lend you his uniform. You can promise to return it by tonight."

172

The Spanish fliers were not amused at the prospect of lending their uniforms to the motley crew who suggested the idea to them. They were little mollified by the prospect of adorning themselves in the variety of clothes offered, however brief the duration of the exchange, but the serious faces of the guards persuaded them that excessive modesty and propriety would not be rewarding.

In addition to those taken by the Argentines, the balance of the uniforms were donned by several of Laxalt's men who had been briefed to do so.

The newly uniformed men looked every bit as smart as the original owners. The Argentines easily assumed their new military roles, although there was the slight inconvenience that badges of rank did not match the status of those whom they now embellished. Major Rodriguez was acutely aware of the dilemma, since he had been reduced to the rank of second lieutenant.

"We must be careful," he warned, "that an Argentine major dressed as a Spanish lieutenant doesn't give orders to one of our captains in the uniform of a Spanish major in front of anyone outside our own group."

Laxalt had to issue a reminder to his own men. "Forget the clowning around in these uniforms. Treat them seriously whether you like them or not, and behave like regular servicemen."

All the uniformed men except the four guards and the driver of the coach returned to the bunkhouse for a final briefing by Major Rodriguez.

"Don't look too excited," he concluded. "The people we're replacing weren't going into real action, so don't betray your feelings, and take care your accents aren't too obvious. Let's go."

When the coach reached the edge of the forest, the road was blocked by an ancient truck. As the coach drew up, the driver of the truck scrambled out of his rusty cab and approached them aggressively.

"What's the meaning of this?" he demanded, pointing an indignant finger at a smartly-painted sign erected on new wooden posts by the side of the road.

The coach driver first tried reading the writing in his side mirror, and then opened his window and twisted his head round.

The notice had an official EdA badge and proclaimed in large letters:

'DANGER

- LIVE AMMUNITION -

- SURVIVAL COURSE -

- THIS ROAD CLOSED FOR 24 HOURS -

by order EdA.'

He tried to console the angry old peasant. "You're better out of there today. They even have a field hospital. You should see the ambulances going through Fica on the other road out of the forest. It's the Army Mobile Air Force. They're all mad, you know. When you see what they do to their own people, you shudder at the thought of what they might do to strangers."

But the old man was non-plussed. "I may as well be dead if I can't get firewood to sell. I depend on nothing else."

"Don't worry," the driver tried to reassure him. "Tomorrow they have to be in ..." - and he chose the name deliberately - "Donostia."

The old man looked at him sharply, and to make sure the Spanish serviceman had used the Basque name for the town, he corrected him, "You mean, San Sebastian?"

The driver nodded. "Yes, Donostia."

"In that case, I'll get out of your way at once," he said obligingly, and then added, "I gora."

And the driver whispered, "Euzkadi."

The old man ambled quickly to his decrepit vehicle and reversed downhill to the nearest entrance to a field, nipped out, opened the gate and backed his vehicle in. It was no mean feat of navigation, for not only did he have to contend with the ruts in the road which jerked his steering wheel in all directions, but he had also to find his way through clouds of smoke belching from the remnants of his exhaust system. He waved cheerfully as the coach lumbered past.

At one minute to ten the coach drew up at the Civil Guard post beside the barrier they had passed earlier. The same man got out to report to the guard, who nodded and said, "Yes, we were told to expect you. I believe you're a great man for numbers."

He pushed past and entered the coach. Walking slowly up and down the passage, he counted fifty-two, and, as he came down the steps, pointed an accusing finger at the freedom-fighter, paused, and said, "Fifty-three," grinned and gave a hand signal to a companion to raise the barrier.

CHAPTER 40

At the moment the ETA guerrillas entered the tents in Bilbao, their Spanish compatriots were stirring in Scotland.

Because of Scotland's more northerly position, however, the sky was already lighter than in Bilbao, making stealthy movement conspicuous.

Three men left the small campsite in Strathmartine on the northern edge of Dundee. They walked a hundred metres along Strathmartine Road to a car parked on a piece of waste ground. They got in and drove through the hushed roads on the long descent through the silent city to the small deserted dock formerly used by the ferry-boats made redundant by the Tay Road Bridge. The car stopped long enough for two of the men to get out with their equipment.

They slipped off jeans and anoraks and stood in wetsuits. They threw their clothes into the back of the car, an inconspicuous Ford Escort, hired mainly for the convenience of its British number plates while their own Seat languished under a pile of larch branches and twigs in an obscure corner of Drumsuldry Wood.

The third man drove the car from the dock to the car park beside the Leisure Centre, got out and stripped down to his wetsuit. He locked the car, slipped the string to which the keys were attached over his head and tucked it under his collarless jacket.

When he rejoined his companions, they were already at the edge of the water, and his gear was neatly laid out for him. The small pleasure steamer, now converted to a floating restaurant, cast a shadow which gave them confidence to move fast without drawing unwanted attention from the sleeping city's insomniacs.

The steamer's hull enabled them to submerge unseen before entering the estuary with their deadly burden of explosives. The still water of the dock gave way to the strong ebb current of the river, which carried them inexorably towards the Road Bridge.

By swimming towards the opposite shore, their net movement brought them to the fourth set of piers from the northern landfall of the bridge.

Despite the force of the current, they worked quickly and deftly to attach the explosives where the charge would do most damage.

Their final task was the priming of the radio-controlled detonator. When everything had been double-checked, they allowed themselves to be swept away by the increasing strength of the current as the momentum of the ebb built up.

Two-and-a-half miles downstream they swam towards the smooth pebbles below Grassy Beach, a favourite site for sailing dinghies and water-skiers. They crawled ashore, gradually adjusting to their loss of buoyancy. Giving themselves the minimum time for recovery from the unaccustomed cold, they staggered through the double gates which allowed access over the railway line, and shambled to a parked Ford Sierra. The man who had parked the Escort at the Leisure Centre took the same string from round his neck and used a different key on the door of the Sierra. It worked.

They took the towels from the back seat and dried themselves vigorously before dressing in the jeans, sweatshirts and anoraks which lay waiting in the boot.

On their drive back to the city centre they diverted towards the river and drew up at the entrance to the disused Carolina Port Power Station. One man got out, coded the correct numbers into the electronic door-lock, and admitted himself.

Quickly finding his way to a vantage point high in the south-west corner of the building, he settled in comfortably to watch the bridge and switched on his hand-held phone.

Meanwhile the other two continued on their way to the Leisure Centre.

The man who emerged from the passenger door carried a large white towel over his left arm and went over to the parked Escort. He laid the towel across the roof of the car as he fiddled in the lock with his key.

An alert pair of eyes behind a third-floor bedroom window in the Tay Centre Hotel saw the signal. The hidden observer crossed to the phone beside his bed and dialled before the Spaniards had driven away in the two hired cars.

The Perth number answered immediately with one word, "Alba."

The voice in the hotel bedroom said, "Team eight complete."

In a disused salmon-fishermen's bothy, Johnson hung up the phone and said to Breck and Gonzales, "Five down. Three to go."

Breck crossed to the map pinned to the wall. It covered the same area as had been shown on the first slide at the introductory lecture at Portobello High School Annexe. From a small box lying on the table he took a round, self-adhesive label about a quarter of an inch in diameter and pressed it onto the map right in the middle of the Tay Road Bridge, where it joined five identical markers, similarly symmetrically placed on the Tay Rail Bridge, the Forth Road Bridge, the Forth Rail Bridge and Kincardine Bridge.

He muttered to himself, "They'll never believe about the Forth Rail Bridge. The others maybe, but it's so bloody strong."

Gonzales answered him, whether or not he was meant to, "If they don't believe you, I will give them the technical details. We could never have tackled the bases of the cantilevers, but the intervening spans were the weakest points. We only had to prepare one, but it was a bigger risk than working in the water. Your nights are far too short for saboteurs. Don't worry. It will blow sky-high if it has to."

The phone clicked as though it was going to ring, and Johnson lifted it.

"Alba," he said quietly, nodded and hung up.

"Friarton," he informed the others.

"Friarton," echoed Breck. "What the hell's been keeping them?"

He stuck another red label on the map, this time in the middle of Friarton Bridge, which carried the dual carriageway from Dundee to the complex motorway intersection at Craigend.

Then, although everyone else was moving with cat-like stealth, he stomped over to the window, which was covered with a square of muslin cloth. As his hand twitched impatiently at the bottom corner, it was frozen by a hissed command from Johnson, "Don't move that screen."

Breck complied with bad grace and concentrated on gazing out towards the river. Despite the cloth, he was able to see clearly, especially since the sun was shining strongly onto the north bank of the Tay and the wooded cliffs of Kinnoull Hill beyond. Slightly to the left, he could see Friarton Bridge, whose demolition team had just reported, and as he moved his head from left to right he had an uninterrupted view over two miles of the approach road along the north side of the river before it started to rise on viaduct legs to the bridge proper.

He began to chortle, his heavy shoulders shrugging with increasing speed. "It's perfect," he told himself delightedly. Then, turning to Gonzales, he ordered, "Admit it. I got the perfect site for these headquarters."

"They are excellent from a strategic point of view. We could not have asked for better."

The bothy stood on its own at the edge of the water with an uninterrupted view of the north bank. Behind it, a single track road led up the steep slope. Despite its apparent isolation, it was less than a mile from the M90 Motorway to which it had access at the Craigend Intersection, Scotland's rural spaghetti junction.

The phone rang again. As he hung up, Johnson reported monosyllabically, "Perth."

Hastening back to his beloved map, Breck put a red marker on the two road bridges across the Tay in the middle of Perth city and on the railway bridge, which vaulted across the river by Moncrieffe Island.

The next time the phone began to ring he had two stickers already in his hand before Johnson had uttered, "Alba", and his hand trembled over the map as he twisted to watch Johnson's face. The expression told him everything. His hand pressed one marker on the A9 and the railway where almost contiguous bridges carried them across the Forth on the northern edge of Stirling. The other marker obliterated Intersection 10, where the M9 took both the A84 and the Forth in its stride.

Breck's exuberance was boundless, as he declaimed, "This part of Scotland hasn't been so cut off since the Battle of Stirling Bridge. We'll have it to ourselves."

Johnson's appraisal was much more objective, as he reminded Breck, "Your men may still have to seal the bridges across the Earn and the Almond."

"They'll do it. Never fear. Reinforcements will take hours to come round by the only detours left. We'd have plenty warning, and all that's needed are heavy vehicles to block the bridges. They're all standing by. Lookout posts, radios and telephones are all manned. It can't fail."

"In that case," said Johnson, "we have only to wait for our radio checks to confirm that all's ready."

At 0830 brief radio signals came in pre-arranged sequence from ten observer points - Stirling and Perth had two each for the separate bridge locations.

Johnson fine-tuned his receiver, listened attentively and then sent out his own signal.

Ironically, the only observer who needed any adjustment was one whose position in a small allotment hut on Moncrieffe Island was almost within view of the bothy headquarters.

Johnson now had overall control of all the bridge access to what was potentially an isolated peninsula in the heart of Scotland. Stirling Bridge had effectively the same strategic value as in the days of Sir William Wallace himself, almost seven centuries earlier.

Johnson addressed his companions. "You realise that we also control the radio waves. The authorities will have to believe me when I tell them we've several strategically-placed radio detonators, and they mustn't use any frequencies except those we declare open. In that way they'll not be able to risk transmitting any message which we can't listen to. On the other hand, not only have I separate wavelengths for our people, but I shall also be using my unique form of code."

To Breck he added, "It's time for you to take your road gang out now."

Breck swung into ferocious action to cover his seething resentment at Johnson's position of command. "Come on, lads, kit up."

Six men wearing heavy boots and working clothes donned fluorescent orange safety vests and safety helmets before following Breck outside and piling into the back of a truck bearing the insignia of a well-known international civil engineering contractor. Breck climbed into the cab beside the driver, yelling, "We're on our way!"

It was 0900 hours.

CHAPTER 41

Glen parked his car in North Street, a few doors from the Police Station. He was lucky to find a place, as the traffic for the Final of the Open was everywhere.

Striding across the wide road to the university entrance, he caught sight of the familiar figure of Father Mackellar waiting for him on the opposite kerb.

"Good morning, my son."

"Good morning, Father. You're up early this morning. It's barely nine o'clock."

"Oh, I'm always up and working much earlier than this. I admit I'm usually back from chapel by this time and tucking into a good breakfast in the presbytery, but I couldn't settle this morning and had no appetite. I've just come out for a walk between services."

"Nothing wrong, I hope?"

"Have you heard the news of that dreadful explosion in the Forth yesterday?"

"Yes. A terrible business."

"I realise these things are going on all the time, and one should be a neighbour to all one's fellow-humans, but I felt yesterday's incident most acutely. I was at a meeting in Edinburgh organised by the Polish Ex-Combatants League for all priests with significant numbers of Poles in their parishes, to confer about the relationship between the Church in Poland and Solidarity, following the Holy Father's latest visit to his homeland. It was a most stimulating meeting, for I could feel that we were neighbours in a much larger community than I am usually conscious of at my own selfish, parochial level.

"Then I returned home in the early evening, and from the Forth Bridge I could see the fleet of rescue craft still searching for the pieces of these poor boys' dismembered bodies. I think I had the same kind of feeling as you experienced on Stefan's death."

"Which reminds me. I saw your friend, Wladyslaw."

"At your meeting?"

"Hardly. I'm afraid his presence would not have been very welcome to his compatriots. No. He was walking on the Forth Bridge. I'm sorry to say quite a crowd had been attracted by the grisly spectacle.

"I was travelling north when I caught a glimpse of him walking in the same direction. The funny thing is that most people were on the southbound side to watch the activity."

"Did he see you?"

"No. I couldn't stop on the bridge, so when I got to the end I pulled into the lay-by and walked back, but I could see that he had stopped and was leaning on the rail. I was afraid at first that he might be contemplating something dreadful, but then I saw he had something in his hand like a camera or binoculars, for he seemed to be taking a sighting."

"What could he have been looking at?"

"It's mainly an industrial landscape, not a scenic one at all. It could have been Grangemouth Refinery or Rosyth Royal Naval dockyard."

....

Glen's brow was furrowed as he checked the mail in his office. Zochowski had ceased to figure in his calculations, and now he had re-emerged as a threatening complication.

He got back to his car and drove along North Street past streams of cars converging on the Golf Links for the Open Final.

At Guardbridge he was held up by a policeman on point duty, who found it inconvenient to let him turn across the steady flow of traffic.

After a similar delay at the next intersection, he eventually swung into Leuchars Air Base, where the usual barrier and guardhouse were augmented by Ferret armoured cars, one on each side of the entrance, manned by tough-looking crews.

Beyond the barrier stood another pair of mute sentinels from earlier eras, a long retired Spitfire and a more recently retired Lightning.

The barrier and guardhouse swarmed with men of the RAF Regiment. Glen jumped out of his car and asked the first man, "Squadron Leader Carrington. He's expecting me. Colin Glen."

The man spoke to a sergeant who disappeared into the guardhouse. When Glen tried to follow him, two burly members of the RAF Regiment who had been standing on either side of the door moved closer together. With their shoulders almost touching, it was impossible for him to pass.

The sergeant returned with a corporal and said to Glen, "Corporal Williams will take you round to the Squadron Leader, but first you'll have to park your car at the Sergeants' Mess on the opposite side of the road. The corporal will wait for you here."

When Glen was ushered into Carrington's office, the Squadron Leader stood up. He was a tall, gaunt figure whose height made him appear to be of slighter build than he actually was. His face flexed like wiry biceps every time he smiled, and the tight skin stretched translucent-white across the ridge of his nose. He was all muscle and sinew.

"Thanks for letting me in," Glen began.

"Not at all. I appreciate all the help I can get today. Besides, Colonel Sinclair describes you as a man brimful of information with a capacity for intuitive thinking. From someone like Sinclair that's praise indeed."

"That sure is a surprise!"

"He's a shrewd old bird. He soaks in everything he sees, but only says the minimum. That's why I lay so much store by his character reference."

"We can all make mistakes, I guess," Glen joked at his own expense. "Now, how do you read the present situation?"

For a second or two Carrington rallied his thoughts before he began. "There's trouble brewing. I can assure you nothing is going to go wrong on the Station. It's virtually ringed with steel. Beyond the perimeter we have a high density of men on the ground. NASA has put up a geostatic satellite right over our heads. Using heat sensitive sensors, it will pinpoint any weapon larger than a .38 calibre pistol the moment it fires one round. If there is someone out there in the woods with a rocket-launcher, he'll never get a second chance. We'll be on his top in seconds. There'll be two Puma helicopters out there with devices to draw heat-seeking missiles.

"Gleneagles is a fortress for the next few days. The only vulnerable part is the road journey, but I reckon if Ross can deliver people like that through London time after time, he can do it through the countryside with his hands tied behind his back."

"What do you make of yesterday's explosion on the Forth?"

"Could have been caused by a build-up of combustibles from some leak that's gone unnoticed, as the papers are suggesting. One thing that worries me, however, was the mention in the early evening paper of an unidentified frogman's body being found. There was no follow-up anywhere else - not even in later editions of the same paper, which I checked out of curiosity. It's the kind of news that's relatively big for the evening papers, but they dropped it. My guess is Ross suspects a connection between the two events and got the media to co-operate."

"You guessed right. Ross asked me to put you in the picture. We believe the oil terminal was sabotaged, and we further believe there is a connection with Spanish-speaking terrorists ..."

"You mean Cubans?"

Glen paused thoughtfully before he replied, "That's a possibility I'd neglected. It would make sense because their friends from the other side of the Iron Curtain are sniffing around. It could also explain the efficiency of yesterday's outrage. I may have been barking up the wrong tree. There were leads that pointed to Argentina, but then Che Gevara was originally from there. Why shouldn't Castro have other Argentine followers?"

After filling in Carrington on the events of the previous day, Glen asked suddenly, "What's special about Rosyth?"

Carrington's eyes almost popped, as his facial skin tightened. "Only that it's the Royal Navy's most important nuclear submarine base. That's where the subs are serviced. Apart from that, it's the HQ of the Scottish Fishery Protection Fleet, the Forth Mine-sweeping Squadron and home for various veterans of the Falklands War."

"How vulnerable is it?"

"Apart from a nuclear attack for which it could be a prime target along with ourselves, it's virtually impregnable. I should know. We do unannounced simulation infiltrations on each other. I've probed every possible weakness. They have dozens of intermeshing procedures to trigger intricate warning systems and a tip-top team. Why do you ask?"

"Just something nagging at the back of my mind."

CHAPTER 42

At 1000 hours two Lockheed Hercules C-130s took off from Zaragoza Airport.

Thirty minutes later and two hundred miles to the north-west, the pilot of the conventional transport reported a malfunction of his navigational equipment. Zaragoza Air Region control told him that, as he was more than half-way to Bilbao, he should land there for an emergency repair, but issued a firm warning to the converted tanker that, because of its load of fuel, it must under no circumstances attempt to land at the shorter Bilbao runway.

Half an hour later the tanker flew over Bilbao, while its companion peeled off formation and began its landing circuit. The tanker flew on to the coast where it began a slow waiting pattern.

As soon as the Hercules touched down, a team of mechanics raced to meet it in a bay set apart from civilian aircraft. A coach drove up, and Major Rodriguez emerged. He invited the crew to come and relax in the Mess until their aircraft was ready for take-off.

From the coach the jovial and companionable major led them into a marquee where they were confronted by a ring of stern-looking men armed with distinctly unfriendly machine pistols. To their surprise and consternation, Rodriguez took the whole thing in his stride and further confused them with his profuse apologies for the inconvenience and the sudden unexpected turn of events.

"No harm will come to you," he promised them, "provided you do exactly as you are told. We are all officers together, and you are more than welcome to any hospitality we can offer. But you have just lost a large and valuable aeroplane belonging to the government. It could be very unpleasant for you if the government were to find out. That is only one of the difficulties we would ensure for you if you do not obey us absolutely."

The twelve-man crew had no option but to comply.

Half-an-hour later the huge plane thundered down the runway and eased itself into the air in time to leave a few inches between its undercarriage and the roof of a train stopped at the level-crossing to the north-west of the airport.

It spiralled up to join its companion twenty thousand feet above the Bay of Biscay. The pilot, doing his best to disguise his Argentine accent, radioed to the tanker, "A change of order came through on the ground. The rendezvous are farther away than originally detailed, and we are to return to base separately. We'll refuel before parting company. The next refuelling will be at 1430 hours, ten kilometres west of Malin More. Stand by for exact co-ordinates."

The tanker pilot acknowledged the message, and a few minutes later confirmed the co-ordinates. He asked his flight engineer to estimate their fuel requirements for the extra distance.

The flight engineer did a few calculations before replying, "Taking into account the time we spent over the coast already, just waiting, I reckon we have a margin of two hundred miles for our return trip to Zaragoza. We'll have plenty of time, provided the wind speed and direction remain as forecast and nothing unexpected happens."

"Sounds fine," the pilot retorted.

The crews of the two aircraft settled back for the unremarkable journey over the monotonous sea, but only the official crew relaxed, oblivious to the fact that their transport companion had a completely different complement and mission from when they had taken off from Zaragoza for a routine training flight.

....

An Aeroflot Illushyn descending for touchdown at Shannon Airport picked them up in its radar abeam Innishvickillane at thirteen-thirty hours. In accordance with his instructions, the pilot radioed the information to Moscow.

From Moscow a coded message reached the Soviet Embassy in Kensington Gardens, London, where a not-insignificant member of staff was interrupted at his lunch to have the message whispered in his ear. On the strength of his reply, a call was made to a St Andrews number.

Isobel MacLaren didn't rush from the shower to answer the incessant ringing. She took her time and dried herself carefully in her favourite fluffy pink towel. The phone continued to ring. She picked up her perfumed talc, hesitated and put it down with a sigh. She stepped daintily across her bedroom and sat on the edge of the bed, admiring her reflection in the large mirror as she picked up the insistent instrument.

She listened to the brief message.

"Yes. I'll see he gets it right away. He's been expecting to hear from you."

She depressed the phone rest with her right index finger, released it, and dialled a Dunfermline number.

Campbell was called to the phone from a meeting of the Trustees of the Carnegie Foundation to whom he was a consultant.

....

At 1330 hours, the Phantoms of 121 Squadron of EdA thundered down the Bilbao runway. The pilots were flying in earnest.

They had been cooped up for days in a submarine, lived in strange surroundings with an atmosphere of apprehension and excitement, travelled in a variety of vehicles to a clandestine meeting at a tumble-down sawmill, been smuggled into Bilbao Airport, been party to the kidnap of a Hercules aircrew, and shamed thousands of miles away by an ignominious defeat in which they had been betrayed by their leaders. All their pent-up frustration and nervous energy was released, as they accelerated down the runway and took off into a climb that became almost vertical, as the after-burners roared their defiance at gravity.

The Spanish onlookers, even those accustomed to airport sights and sounds, had never seen planes flown with such verve and aggression.

The pilots were in their element, but the ETA members accompanying them were having serious misgivings about the whereabouts of some of the components of their digestive tracts.

Major Rodriguez knew what was good for his men's morale and the need to keep their adrenaline throbbing through their muscles and brains for the next couple of hours. He led them straight to 62,000 feet where they levelled out, still pushing their machines to their utmost as they watched their air speed climb through and beyond mach 2.

As soon as the physical exhilaration began to subside and they were able to regard their instruments objectively, as the speed rose to mach 2.1 and then touched mach 2.2, he led them in a long descent which brought a new sense of speed, as they levelled out again at three hundred feet above the waves, a hundred miles to the west of the Isles of Scilly. Rodriguez made sure that even if a ship spotted them it would not be in a position to interpret the roundels or other identification marks on the planes.

Despite brilliant evasive navigation and a hawk-like alert, Rodriguez' success in avoiding all visual or radar recognition was to little avail, since the complete progress of 121 Squadron from take-off was being carefully monitored by a Soviet satellite and less carefully monitored by an American one. Although the American satellite was as meticulous and accurate as the Soviet one, its supervisors were much less interested in the information it was relaying than were the Soviets. It was particularly satisfying to the latter, since the activity was as had been predicted.

The Squadron's eventual rendezvous with the lone Hercules tanker was exactly on time, as Rodriguez nudged the refuelling probe in his plane's nose into the drogue weaving gently at the end of the hose dangling from the belly of the Hercules.

The posse of planes bobbed around as close to the waves as they dared in face of the tricky manoeuvre, which they were carrying out at a dangerously low level in order to take maximum advantage of the western mountains of Donegal to prevent detection by radar.

The low speed after the earlier supersonic race was soporific in its soothing smoothness behind the tanker.

As soon as the last Phantom had drunk its fill and released the mammary cord, the whole Squadron accelerated and dodged with the precision of a flight of hedge sparrows tantalising the unwary motorist in country lanes. The Hercules rose with a clumsy gracefulness and swung slowly seawards to begin its return journey and fulfil its assignation en route with 122 Squadron.

From the point of view of the Phantoms, their own speed caused it to recede as rapidly as if it was being sucked into a black hole in space.

Visual confirmation from another Aeroflot Illushyn taking off from Shannon, the Soviet Airline's busiest destination outside the Eastern Block, reached the same ultimate destination in Moscow as previous information.

122 Squadron lurked in support behind the Cliffs of Moher.

After refuelling the planes made no attempt to follow 121, but contained themselves in a holding configuration a hundred miles off the Connemara coast.

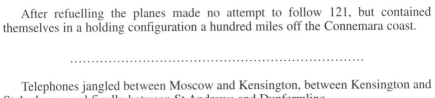

Telephones jangled between Moscow and Kensington, between Kensington and St Andrews, and finally between St Andrews and Dunfermline.

The coded messages would have meant as little to any eavesdropper as they did to Isobel MacLaren.

As she passed the third message within the last half-hour to her husband, she chided, "Campbell, dear, I wish you would ask your veteran friends to phone when you're going to be at home."

"Don't worry, Isobel. I'm going to put an end to this soon. I'll get someone else to take over as organising secretary."

"That's a change," she murmured to herself as she hung up. "He's never suggested that before."

The transport Hercules, having separated from the tanker at Malin More, flew round Northern Ireland, hugging the coast to Fair Head before lunging across the North Channel at top speed for the first time on its flight from Bilbao.

The pilot took a great risk in skimming the waves in his unwieldy-looking aircraft to avoid detection from the NATO Air Base at Machrihanish just beyond the lump of land that formed Mull of Kintyre. It crossed the Scottish coast at Girvan, flew inland to New Cumnock, and turned south-east into Nithsdale, thence across country to Teviotdale, in the shadow of the Lammermuir Hills, to emerge at the coast over the cliffs of St Abbs Head.

121 Squadron, minutes behind the Hercules, skipped from the Giant's Causeway in Northern Ireland through the Scottish coast by West Loch Tarbert and north to the head of Loch Fyne at a maximum height of one hundred feet, leaving behind a blast of swirling air to fan the faces of the irate isolated householders as they rushed out of their homes in alarm at the supersonic cacophony.

By the time skipper Jackson had put his pipe back in his mouth aboard the Village Belle in Tarbert, the Squadron was glissading down the mountainside at the northern end of Loch Lomond and screaming along Glen Dochart to follow the defile of Loch Tay and the Tay Valley to Dunkeld, whence it was a quick dash over the Sidlaws to clear the East Coast at Carnoustie.

Glen and Carrington had moved over from the latter's office to the control tower, where they were at the centre of the communications network for both air traffic and ground forces.

185

The three Benelux ministers had landed at 1330 in a British Aerospace 146, several of which had been put at the disposal of the NATO organiser by the British government in an effort to bring the qualities of the new plane to as many potential customers as possible.

The ministers of Norway, Denmark and Greece accepted the offer of the plane and arrived in quick succession.

Not surprisingly, the United States and France had made it clear from the outset that they would be arriving courtesy of their own technology.

By 1350, the fourteen ministers of the NATO countries and their Spanish counterpart were assembled in the hangar, temporarily converted into a cross between a municipal flower show and a motor showroom with its floral decorations and its gleaming line-up of Volvo coaches.

Despite the reluctance of important politicians to being ushered about rather brusquely, the military managed to adhere meticulously to a strict timetable and had all the ministers aboard the coaches five minutes before the deadline.

On the dot of fourteen hundred hours, the two leading Land Rovers, with their full complement of Sinclair's Military Police aboard, moved smoothly out of the hangar.

On the outside of the barrier at the guardhouse a BMW police patrol car faced the road, its engine purring with the patience of inbred confidence.

As soon as the driver saw the first Land Rover in his mirror he said to his companion, "Here they come."

The latter pressed the transmit button on the radio and self-consciously gave the call-sign, "Nessie moving."

As he released the button and listened for the acknowledgement, he muttered to the driver, "Who thought up that code-word? Fancy working on an operation named after a monster!"

"Just keep your fingers crossed that this one remains as quiet as Nessie when there's people about. I've never seen top brass so jumpy."

With that, the order came to move out, and they pulled forward in the convoy pilot position.

CHAPTER 43

Gleneagles had a different air about it. For one thing, no vehicles were parked alongside the access roads or even in the car parks adjacent to the hotel. Any transport required had to be summoned by radio from the vehicle pool beside the King's Course.

The time-share homes had been vacated and were under twenty-four-hour guard. The owners for that week had been found alternative accommodation through their time-share international organisation.

A cordon sanitaire had been thrown round the whole complex, with an unbroken military ring along perimeter roads on three sides and cutting across the famous golf courses on the fourth. Colonel Sinclair was responsible for all security within that area, which he controlled from a nerve-centre within the building.

Likewise, Carrington was responsible for all internal security at Leuchars.

Between the two, Ross was at the nerve centre of convoy control at the headquarters of Perth Division of Tayside Police in Perth City. He had taken direct responsibility for the co-ordination of the convoy and had overall responsibility for the total operation.

In the windowless confines of the communications control room, where all the detailed planning for the convoy had been committed to the memory of the traffic computer, Ross was anxiously watching the plan unfold on the map display unit. The moment the lead car left Leuchars, the screen had started to chatter and change the patterns in its electronic glow.

....

In the control tower, Carrington put down the phone. "The convoy has cleared the station. It's over to Ross now."

His sinewy physique began to relax, as the load of responsibility slipped from his shoulders.

But Glen had seen something a fraction of a second ahead of Carrington - the startled expression in the eyes of one of the radio-monitoring RAF Corporals.

Ignoring Carrington's remark, he demanded, "What is it?"

"A very strong signal coming through in some crazy language, sir!"

"Let's hear."

She removed her headphones and handed them to him.

All eyes were upon him as he put them on.

His grave face told them it was trouble.

"Get me US Naval Station, Edzell, immediately. I must get Lieutenant Knudsen on the line. This is a red alert."

Within seconds he was connected. He snatched the phone.

"That you, Ed? Colin Glen here. Get your radio tuned into this frequency now." He looked over the RAF Corporal's shoulder and read out her radio dials to Knudsen. "They're talking Basque. Give me an instantaneous translation."

The control tower was under the command of a pretty WRAF Flight Lieutenant. He shook his head dolefully at her. "Trouble brewing. Get an amplifier on this earpiece so that everyone knows what these fellows are saying to each other."

An unexpected yelp came from a mature-looking, grey-haired Flight Sergeant in front of the short-range radar screen. "Unidentified aircraft bearing zero-eight-five approaching fast. They must be touching the waves, they're so low. They're passing the Bell Rock now. They'll be visible any second."

An Observer Flying Officer snatched up a pair of binoculars and gazed out towards the sea end of the runway.

"Got them!" he shouted, and then, with admiration in his voice, added, "They're flying beautifully. What a tight formation at that altitude!"

"There's something else on the screen," interrupted the Flight Sergeant, "behind the first blimp."

The Flying Officer moved his sights marginally.

"Yes, it looks like a Hercules. I'd say the chaps in front could be Phantoms."

An element of relief showed on the anxious faces at the thought that the approaching planes were not Russian.

But Glen did not share the new mood.

"We've made the classic blunder," he said to Carrington. "It's the typical Singapore situation."

"What do you mean?"

"Our guns are pointing the wrong way. We were expecting an attack from the land. In fact, it's an airborne one coming in from the sea, - the opposite of what happened in Singapore, which could have withstood any attack from the sea, but the Japs sneaked in by the back door through the jungle. Those boys out there are coming in by the front door."

Knudsen's voice crackled hesitantly over the amplifier.

The draught from the wheels of Rodriguez' leading Phantom produced two furrows in the sand at the top of the beach seconds before the screaming rubber made its first tentative contact with the concrete of the runway.

....

A telephone jangled. A shirt-sleeved constable answered it and looked at Ross in consternation. "For you, sir."

Ross bent over and took the receiver from the man. "Ross here," and felt the colour drained from his ruddy face as he heard the first word.

"Alba."

"What do you want?"

"Just listen. We have several radio-controlled explosive devices set to detonate unless you restrict all communications to the following frequencies." The voice gave three sets of figures, and the phone went dead in Ross' hand.

He had no option but to give the message to the Inspector in charge of communications and order him to obey the instructions immediately.

"The blighter'll be able to hear everything we say. We can't resort to phones while we have to keep in contact with a convoy."

The phone rang again, and Ross beat the constable to it.

"Alba," the same voice said. "Glad you have the time to answer yourself, Commander. I'll tell you now where our charges are placed, but first let me warn you that I have a sensitive instrument in front of me which will tell me immediately there is any attempted interference with our line. I took the precaution of making certain arrangements in advance to ensure that I would have direct access to your phone. It doesn't take much ingenuity or technical expertise to give oneself an uninterrupted line, if you know the right manhole covers to lift.

"Now that your mind will not be distracted by thoughts of how you can trap me, you can concentrate on listening.

"We're going to display a little bit of force shortly and I want you to appreciate from the outset two basic facts: first, you are completely outmanoeuvred and outgunned; second, you cannot possibly call on any reinforcements. The simple fact is that every major route ... Are you still with me, Commander?"

"I'm listening," Ross gritted through clenched teeth.

"As I was saying, every major route which could carry reinforcements has to cross water, and every bridge is mined. There is a watch scrutinising every one of these bridges and the first hint of any breach of my instructions will cause a nervous little finger to press a destructive button."

The voice paused.

"Your mind is wandering, Commander. You are wondering how you can warn your convoy, but that would be very dangerous. It might be on the middle of a bridge when you tune into the wrong radio channel. You wouldn't want to blow them all sky-high. Don't worry. We won't harm them - unless provoked. Just be patient." The phone clicked.

Ross had always disciplined himself and his men to concentrate on the possible, but it was difficult under such pressure. However, he forced himself to look at the chattering computer. He'd been through rehearsals so often that an incongruity struck his eye immediately. The convoy was approaching Kinfauns Castle, exactly according to timetable. The information about road conditions for the next two miles showed on the screen. It was not as he remembered it should be.

"What's been rescheduled at Craigend?" he demanded sharply.

The Inspector stepped over to the console. "Oh, that's alright, sir. The bridge engineer is testing the stress on the bearing points of the fly-over. It's had clearance from the Scottish Office Development Department."

"But not from me!" Ross thundered. "For purposes of this exercise, I am the

189

Scottish Office and God Almighty, if it comes to that. If I haven't cleared it, it's a threat. Why wasn't I informed?"

The seventeen stone inspector quailed before Ross' fury.

"What company got this clearance?"

The Inspector stammered a name, which would have been recognised on half the major building sites in Britain and many overseas, from the Persian Gulf to the Amazon jungle.

"Would I be far out if I suggested that Sir Seamus Breck might be a shareholder?"

The Inspector swallowed hard. "He's a director, sir."

Ross nodded, his eyes blazing. "Here we are with all the sophisticated equipment money can buy, and one dumb inspector who doesn't have the capacity of a one-bead abacus builds up a disaster for us because his genteel mind cannot conceive of treachery behind a title.

"Haven't you heard of Sir Anthony Blount, for one?

"Get men to that intersection and arrest everyone in sight. I just bloody well hope it's not too late."

....

The chubby Inspector Smith stood bareheaded in the open air not a hundred yards from the police radio aerial on which Ross had a few minutes earlier expected to depend for all his confidential links with his men and vehicles. He was just inside the north-eastern corner of the wood on Kirkton Hill. His outward calmness belied the effort with which he was concentrating his binoculars on the opposite wood at the other side of Craigend intersection, carved into canyons and fly-overs from the ancient volcanic rock.

He had already recognised Breck with the work-party on the road. None of the faces with him rang a bell as being among the more hot-headed nationalists that it was Smith's responsibility to compromise so that the anti-devolutionary elements, who held the ascendancy in Westminster, would not be pestered by what they regarded as a political aberration.

Smith, like many others before him from Daniel Defoe onwards, wore the mantle of agent provocateur. He and his kind had to facilitate, if not actually foment nationalistic disquiet, bring it to some inconclusive crisis of violence and so alienate the electorate at large from nationalist sympathisers.

He smiled quietly to himself. Things were going well. There would be a bit of an ambush. That hothead Breck was going to be involved. It would be convenient to allow him to escape the net. He had far too many influential friends to make an arrest worthwhile and he was always easy to watch on future occasions. Thank goodness he'd warned that snooping American off. Blasted cheek! What right had they to interfere in the internal politics of a friendly ally?

He watched Breck and his crew disguised as workmen withdraw from the bridges where they had been working, and scramble their way quickly towards the shelter of the wood.

What he did not know was that Breck had been warned over his handset by Johnson from his observation post in the bothy by the river that the convoy had swung into view in front of Kinfauns Castle and would be at the cutting within two minutes.

....

Having left his meeting with the Carnegie Trustees, MacLaren had driven south from Dunfermline, stopping only to pick up Zochowski and two surly companions at Rosyth railway halt, two hundred yards from the entrance to Pitreavie Castle, Headquarters of the Flag Officer (Scotland) with responsibility for, among other things, Rosyth Royal Naval Dockyard and its nuclear submarine base ...

One mile from the Dockyard entrance he slowed down to let the car behind catch up.

CHAPTER 44

Eight Phantoms came tearing along the runway with little attempt to slow down over the first two miles. Only as they approached the main buildings did they decelerate noticeably. Then, instead of turning onto an apron in an organised pattern, they did the reverse and fanned outwards so that they pointed themselves and their rockets at several chosen targets, including the control tower.

Within the control tower the radio monitors picked up the limited conversation between the planes in the unfamiliar tongue.

Knudsen's translation was relayed to them in its attractive western drawl, "The leader says the landing is a complete success. They've met no opposition. He's now giving instructions to another group to get out and go for the helicopters. He's handing over to someone else now."

A clear voice spoke on the monitor in slightly accented English, "It was good of you to allow us in at such short notice. I regret that we must impose further on your hospitality by borrowing your nice yellow helicopters. There are some people we must rescue. To keep matters on a friendly basis, I must advise you not to interfere with us. As you can see, we have the control tower, arms dumps and fuel stores lined up in our sights. We are unlikely to miss with our rockets at this range."

The polite tone faded and the voice became much harsher. "Get your station commander on the radio to talk to me."

Glen surprised no one as he took charge of the situation. Indicating the amplifier, he said, "Turn that off in the meantime."

Then he switched the radio to transmit and demanded, "What do you want?"

The accented voice replied, "Some passengers landed here by mistake. We are going to take them to their correct destination. That is all."

By now the Hercules had trundled to a halt. The great drawbridge-type door at the rear of the fuselage lowered, and twenty heavily-armed men emerged. They formed a screen between all the occupied buildings and the line of helicopters.

They stood with feet apart and guns pointing challengingly outwards. The moment they were in position, the navigators' canopies of all eight Phantoms were thrown back, and the men in the cockpits scrambled out and down the sides of their machines. As soon as their feet touched the ground, they sprinted to the helicopters.

Within seconds the mesmerised observers in the tower could see the great rotors on the yellow Wessex rescue machines swing slowly round before gradually building up their centrifugal force. Only ten minutes after the departure of the coaches, the helicopters rose like giant crane-flies and fluttered westwards.

The radio crackled, and Glen held up his hand for silence. The ancient Basque language once more resonated through the electronic ether. Then another voice replied in Basque, which, despite the technological modifications to the accent, Glen instantly recognised as Johnson's.

Glen made a winding sign with his finger to the man beside the amplifier to increase the volume again, and Knudsen's voice came through clearly.

"The flier has just reported to someone on the ground that the helicopters have taken off. The man on the ground says that all bridges have been mined. The area is completely cut off from all help. Observer number seven has reported that the convoy is exactly on time. The passengers will be ready for helicopters in under ten minutes."

The voices stopped.

Glen turned to Carrington. "Where will the convoy be ten minutes from now?"

Carrington consulted the map for a moment before replying, "Perth southern by-pass."

Glen put his next question to the WRAF Flight Lieutenant. "Ten minutes to Perth for the helicopters?"

"Easily."

"You've got to hand it to them for organisation," he admired grudgingly.

The phone rang. A worried-looking WRAF Sergeant answered it. "Commander Ross for you," she told Glen.

"Colin, we've been boxed in. All the bridges are threatened by explosives controlled by radio. This has effectively prohibited the use of radio except for channels left open courtesy of the opposition, who can listen to everything we say. An attack is imminent at Craigend intersection. I believe the convoy is going to be ambushed there within the next couple of minutes. We must have reinforcements to prevent a getaway, which would be disastrous. The only place from which we can get personnel is the Navy at Rosyth. Get on to them at once. We're totally dependent on you. Sinclair is just as hemmed in as I am. This phone is tapped. So all this is known to the enemy."

"I'll do all I can. Depend on it."

The phone went dead.

"Carrington, if we called on support from Rosyth, we'd need to take men who were on duty. We couldn't wait even ten minutes for the off-duty ones. In your experience, what would be the effect on the security of the base if the guards were taken off for even half an hour?"

"If even a small group of men made a determined effort to get in they could cause a disaster to our defensive system which would have repercussions for decades. There are electronic and nuclear secrets worth enormous investment in time, money and brains. Sabotage would also be a risk, possibly causing a long-term reaction. The worst would be a release of radio-active substances, either accidental or contrived."

"Just what I feared."

To the Flight Lieutenant he said, "Get me a line to the Admiral in command there."

The connection was made in seconds.

As Glen was on the point of speaking into the phone, he noticed out of the corner of his eye a handsomely-uniformed Group Captain enter quickly but calmly. His arrival was greeted with relief. It seemed that his subordinates had high hopes of

193

what he could accomplish now that he had returned from the diplomatic niceties of greeting his important, if transient, ministerial guests.

Glen's reaction was immediate and pragmatic. Here was the best man to speak to the Admiral. "Will you confirm to the Royal Navy that this is a genuine message in an extremely grave situation?" He asked authoritatively, but courteously. "My instructions must be followed to the letter."

His eyes almost glazed with sincerity as they protruded from their tight-fitting sockets, Carrington affirmed, "Dr. Glen knows more about what is happening than anyone. He'll explain as we go along, but please do as he asks right away, sir."

Group Captain Dow had not reached his present rank and responsible position without knowing how to sum up a situation quickly and come to an effective decision. He took the phone. "Station Commander, Leuchars, here. Put me through to the Flag Officer. This is an emergency."

Holding his hand over the mouthpiece, he raised his eyebrows at Glen and said, "Give it to me as briefly as you can, and I'll pass it on to the Admiral."

He repeated Glen's words into the phone verbatim without batting an eyelid.

"A terrorist attack has been mounted to kidnap NATO Defence Ministers. The Russians know, and are preparing to use it as a cover for a quite separate raid on Rosyth. It may be espionage or sabotage. In either event, it would be much more damaging than what is going on here, but they must be convinced that their ruse is working so that we can flush them into the open.

"Get drivers for all the personnel vehicles you can muster and only enough men to take up places where they can be seen, so that the vehicles look packed. Use stewards, clerks and so on. Send them towards the M9 to head north as far as the Kinross Service Area. Clear every guard out of sight except one at the gate and have them withdraw to the most vulnerable parts of the base. They can expect infiltrators within minutes. These men must be captured."

Through the earpiece Admiral Palmer's bland tones were as unruffled as ever, even if his words were slightly faster, as he asked only one question, "Is this an exercise or the real thing?"

"The real thing!"

"No sooner said than done." Palmer hung up.

Still gripping the phone and looking very pensive, Dow asked, "Now perhaps someone can tell me what's going on outside? I can see for myself by their roundels that these are Spanish planes. Have their pilots gone mad?"

"The planes have been hijacked, sir," Carrington explained. They have rockets pointed at vulnerable targets and in a few minutes they're going to have some important hostages, unless Ross can prevent them. They've isolated us from all possible reinforcements by threatening to blow up all the bridges along the Forth and Tay. Rosyth was our only hope, but, as you've just heard, we can't risk taking men from there."

"Why don't we get the Marines?"

"Where from?" Glen demanded in surprise.

"Arbroath!" Carrington broke in.

"Of course," Dow confirmed. "We have 45 Royal Marine Commando at Condor Base in Arbroath virtually on our door-step. They're equipped with small, high-speed invasion craft. They can be here in minutes."

The WRAF Flight Lieutenant, having already dialled a number, was holding the phone towards Dow.

He took it and said into it, "Station Commander, Leuchars. Put me through to the CO or adjutant."

After a pause, he continued. "Martin? We're having a spot of bother here. Would you care to send some of your more violent friends as a matter of some urgency?"

While he was still speaking, he and others in the room could hear terse instructions issuing from Lieutenant-Colonel Martin Lloyd-Morgan.

Then his deceptively mellifluous Welsh tones lilted to them, "Allow me two sentences before I leave this phone. I need the exercise, so I'll be joining the lads on this one. Then fill me in by radio as we scoot across."

"Can't be done. Risk of detonating explosive charges."

"Use the local radio station, Radio Tay, on VHF frequency 95.8. Charges can't have been set on that one. We'll be afloat in five minutes."

Glen spoke to Knudsen, "Ed, use your gear to jam VHF 95.8. We have to use it. Keep it out of action for ten minutes at least."

....

In the fisherman's bothy by the river Johnson carefully timed the convoy over a marked mile with his stopwatch, and quickly calculated its speed and the moment it would reach Craigend intersection. He spoke over a simple two-way radio to Breck, hidden with his Spanish 'workmen' and thirty assorted Scots, recruited as mercenaries, all equipped with armalite rifles. Their artillery consisted of two hand-held rocket-launchers.

Breck started his stopwatch and held it in front of himself and Major Gonzales. At thirty seconds exactly, the police pilot car appeared under the first flyover, which carried traffic from Friarton Bridge to the M90 Perth bypass.

At thirty-three seconds, Gonzales pressed a button on his detonator.

A small puff of smoke appeared at each corner of the fly-over.

Inspector Smith, who was watching the wood instead of the road, was taken completely by surprise when the shock waves reached his ears. Even the men around Gonzales and Breck winced, although they had anticipated the noise.

The front wheels of the pilot car caught the full impact of the explosion. Disintegrating metal was the only solid remnant. Rubber and plastic were reduced to smoke, and bodies to ooze.

The first Land Rover flew across the opening chasm, unscathed until it struck the solid concrete upright with such force that the cement-work was impregnated with the driver's blood.

The driver of the second Land Rover was ultimately no more fortunate. Although he had succeeded in slewing his vehicle so that it went over the brink sideways, the only advantage to him was that he lived a fraction of a second longer than his front-seat passenger, who hit the ground that much sooner.

Gonzales' perfection in explosives and timing markedly reduced the risk factor for Breck's mercenaries in the forthcoming confrontation. The first coach, carrying press and minor permanent staff of various governments, braked in time to produce a much more graceful parabola, as its front wheels screeched noisily over the edge and the rear wheels rolled freely and obligingly after them.

The most important coach with the intended kidnap victims came to a juddering halt on the edge of the gap, at the same time as the Rhynie flyover and the flyover from the entrance to Friarton Detention Centre collapsed on the Land Rovers bringing up the rear of the convoy. Even if the pyrotechnics were not entirely as precise as those under the leading police car, they were nevertheless effective. Although some of the soldiers survived in the screaming mayhem, none of them would ever be able again to engage in anything remotely approximating what is militarily understood as combat.

Whether he was encouraged or outraged by the lack of prospect of battle, Breck led a bloodcurdling charge of non-plussed, circumspect professionals who were neither impressed nor chilled by the carnage before them.

Before they reached their goal, the middle section of a second-tier flyover was brought down by Gonzalez' index finger with a slice as delicate through concrete as a scalpel through a cadaver.

Breck reached the only intact vehicle ahead of any of his men. Shocked, grey faces stared out at the wild figure yanking furiously at the jammed door. The driver lay slumped over his wheel in a faint, but the noise of Breck's frenzied attack on the door roused him from his torpor and he leaned over to release the door by the lever at his side.

Breck stepped up into the bus, waving his service revolver and gesticulating wildly in accompaniment to his hysterical commands to get out at once.

The assorted politicians, like most successful members of their calling, were able to distinguish that a sudden revision of priorities was called for. They fought and struggled with those whose good opinions they had been cultivating moments earlier.

About a hundred yards of the motorway access road on which they were standing remained uncluttered. Breck, brandishing his revolver like a fetish, was in an ecstasy of passion as he ordered the defence ministers to stand close to the rear of the coach while he yelled a mixture of abuse and confused religious slogans at his army.

Recovering slightly from the bloodbath before his eyes, a shocked Smith emerged from the shelter of the woods and began slipping and sliding down the grassy slope, calling out to the ambushers to lay down their arms and surrender.

Breck, noticing him for the first time, when he was only fifty yards away, screamed at one of his troops. The man knelt, took careful aim, squeezed the trigger, and sent Smith spinning down the steep embankment with a bullet through his throat.

His two assistants, on the point of following him, hastily retraced their steps into the wood and hid among the branches, which covered the conifers down to the ground. Such flimsy cover was to no avail.

The same marksman turned towards where they had disappeared, aimed at the last point of movement in the trees and fired. The second detective dropped, pierced through the spine.

Without any support now, his companion switched on his radio to call for reinforcements. The signal was immediately answered by a plume of smoke and an earth-shattering explosion, as Friarton Bridge crumpled to the bed of the river.

To the deafening accompaniment, three helicopters skipped over the opposite hill. With wheels stretching downwards like umbilical antennae they felt their way to the roadway as though guided by a sense of touch.

The dumbfounded ministers were ushered aboard the helicopters, five to each aircraft, which whisked them aloft with greater confidence than they had descended. Within a minute they had disappeared over the crest of the hill and on eastwards to their violated home base and its usurpers.

Breck's irregulars began piling their weapons in the middle of the road. Gonzales put a small charge of plastic explosives on top and placed the rockets and ammunition around it. Then everyone, excluding Breck and Gonzales, scattered in different directions to preselected spots where a variety of dependable cars had been parked. As they drove away, Gonzales pressed his small radio transmitter and detonated the ammunition dump in the middle of the road.

His latest explosion took with it the unfortunate driver, secretaries and interpreters who had been locked in the coach. As dangerous witnesses, their deaths had been one of the preconditions demanded by the mercenaries.

Breck drove north alone in his favourite machismo machine, a Mercedes 350SL. To absorb the adrenaline surging through his body still aquiver with the ecstasy of violence, he pressed the accelerator to the floor. His heart sang. Today he had led an army, a fighting unit, not a ceremonial throw-back like that of his distant neighbour, the Duke of Atholl, with his toy-town army to drill, not command under fire. Although he could not share his great secret with anyone, in his own eyes he was as heroic as any of his ancestors and infinitely more heroic than any of his contemporaries in regiment or club.

He wallowed in the satisfaction of driving the fast smooth car, so smooth today that he was oblivious to road noise of any kind. He was flying along. He was. Not along. Downwards. What had happened to Friarton Bridge? It had not been part of the plan to destroy it.

From the road, observers watched as a car plunged into the water.

CHAPTER 45

Glen studied the hostile Phantoms for several minutes before asking Carrington, "Do you notice any weakness in the way these planes are fanned out?"

"We're the weak ones. We're properly sewn up."

"Look again. They have a real vulnerable situation when a plane is at such an angle that it can't be totally observed by one of its companions. They can beat us in fire-power, but they can't combat stealth."

Carrington's facial muscles bulged as he searched his mind to think of a way in which he could exploit this chink in his tormentor's armour.

"Perhaps," the WRAF Flight Lieutenant speculated tentatively and with increasing embarrassment as she drew attention to herself, "perhaps the armourers could disarm the planes in some way."

"Brilliant, Flight Lieutenant!" Dow complimented soberly.

At first it sounded sarcastic. Then doubt was dispelled when they saw the glitter in his eye as he started issuing orders.

"Get the armourers to stand by under cover. We've got to wait for these guerrillas to get back into the Hercules. They won't do that till the choppers return. Squadron-Leader, organise your men to give maximum cover to the armourers, but make sure no activity's spotted from the planes."

"By disabling the Phantoms," Glen intervened, "we aren't preventing the abduction of the ministers. As soon as the other terrorists turn up with their hostages, we're as badly off as when they're pointing their rockets at the arms dumps."

"Let's take one point at a time. We can disarm four Phantoms if we work very quickly. There are also two which have got themselves into a corner they can't get out of without assistance. They may have made a mistake, or they may be intending to abandon them on the basis that they don't need fighter cover when they have a Hercules full of hostages."

"Could their weapons be booby-trapped?" Glen asked.

"It's possible, but not likely," Dow retorted, "because they may have to use them at any minute. What could be tricky, however, is that they made their minds up in advance to abandon the Phantoms. They could have a device to switch to a timed fuse to cause maximum chaos as the Hercules takes off. We must have a team of top armourers ready to go to each Phantom at a moment's notice. Get them to study the planes for the few minutes that remain so that they know every nut and bolt and piece of wire before they leave cover."

A WRAF Corporal interrupted politely, but urgently. "Colonel Lloyd-Morgan on the radio for you, sir."

Dow hesitated momentarily, then said to Glen, "You talk to him. You know more than I do. I'll help Carrington prepare."

Glen went to the radio. "Group Captain Dow has asked me to liaise with you, Colonel."

Lloyd-Morgan's voice came over amid a cacophony of pop music and other piercing whines. "We've got two companies afloat. Give me the disposition and strength of the enemy and your own proposed action. I'll work something out for us."

Glen condensed the situation into three short sentences.

Suddenly the background noises switched off. Radio Tay had stopped broadcasting on its VHF waveband. For almost a minute there was silence. Then Lloyd-Morgan's voice came over again. "We'll do a pincer. I'll land one company at Shelly Point and the other at Cable House Point. Get at least twenty of the RAF Regiment into Reres Wood. Only one problem about coming up the estuary. Our outboards make a helluva racket. Get some jets warming up so that no one'll notice us. Keep this frequency permanently open."

Another phone rang. "Dr Glen," a corporal called.

Glen took it.

Knudsen's voice sounded exasperated. "I keep yelling at you on that phone you're supposed to be manning."

"Sorry. It's a bit hectic here at the moment. Have you anything new?"

"The choppers're on their way back. They have Basque radio-operators. They've been speaking to a Major Rodriguez who seems to be in command of the planes at your end. From what I hear their enterprise was a complete success, but casualties to the convoy were very heavy. Their ground control tells them he still has complete monitor coverage of all your radio communications. Friarton Bridge has been blown sky-high, but not by the terrorists. So it could be true about the radio-controlled detonators. Don't take any risks with any wave-lengths."

"Not good news, but you're doing a great job, Ed. I'll make sure there's an ear stuck fast to this instrument for as long as it takes."

He spoke to a young WRAF Corporal and handed her the phone.

Dow was in intense conversation with Carrington and another officer carrying the same two-and-a-half rings of Squadron Leader. None of them paid any attention to Glen as he came over to eavesdrop, but he learned little, for the newcomer was going into the technical intricacies of removing rockets from bellies of belligerent Phantoms.

With a laconic look at the senior armaments officer, Dow said quietly, "What's impossible now must be possible within five minutes, because that's all we have."

Without another word the Squadron Leader turned tail and virtually ran for the exit.

"Sorry to pile on the agony, sir," Glen began, "but the Marines are asking if we can run a jet to provide noise cover for their outboards coming up the Eden."

"We can't just nip out and start up a jet. The madmen in these Spanish Phantoms would think we were having a go at them. They'd fire their rockets right away. That might make a diversionary noise alright, but it wouldn't help anyone." For the first time in the crisis Dow betrayed some of the strain he was under.

"I realise that's impossible. I passed the message verbatim. All the Marines want is a distraction."

"Got it!" Dow snapped his fingers. "We've a muffler in the engine room to reduce the noise when we're testing serviced engines. We'll start an engine in there without the muffler. That'll make so much noise, even the Marines won't hear their outboards."

No sooner had Dow shouted the necessary orders than the Flight Sergeant at the radar screen called out, "Looks as though the Wessexes are coming back."

All available binoculars focused on the skyline above the steep slopes on which nestled the picturesque red pantile roofs of Balmullo village, a haven of rural bliss, and home to many of the personnel on the station. It was ironic that wives and children could be looking down on the base, believing that all was normal.

Several people at once saw the yellow of the helicopters that distinguished the humanity of their rescue role in the service.

The room filled with new apprehension.

The WRAF Corporal holding Knudsen's phone link nodded and said something into the mouthpiece.

Glen demanded sharply, "What's that about?"

She flushed as she replied, "He only said the helicopters have visual contact with base. You knew that already, so I didn't bother you."

He nodded.

The Hercules' engines, which had remained turning roared, as the pilot opened the throttle. It began to move laboriously in the turning area at the western end of the runway. The guards outside it moved jerkily, trying to retain their spacing among themselves and form a defensive ring around the lumbering giant at the same time.

The three helicopters whirled low over the village of other-rank housing and vaulted the public road and perimeter fence. The Hercules drew forward onto the runway, leaving room for the helicopters to tuck in as close as they could behind her fuselage like yellow chicks gathering close to a gloomy mother hen.

A movement on the far side of the airfield caught Glen's attention and he turned his binoculars on it. A truck was moving out there. He watched it and distinguished the name. It belonged to the main contractor for the nuclear shelters. This was strange. Carrington had told him the men had been given a holiday for the weekend to make sure that they were off the base during the security build-up. Many of the men had been annoyed at losing Saturday and Sunday overtime.

As he watched, the truck began to move away from the building site and was following the road towards the runway.

Realisation dawned on his face. The noise that the Marines had requested had been provided intentionally by the racket from the jet engine undergoing tests, but also unintentionally from the helicopters and Hercules. The truck was coming from where one company of Marines would have landed.

A shout from the WRAF Corporal on Knudsen's line startled him.

"Dr. Glen, they've noticed a truck approaching. They might fire."

Glen spoke to Lloyd-Morgan. "You've been spotted. Keep it slow. We'll stall."

There was no acknowledgement, but the truck did slow down.

Rodriguez' clipped English came over the radio. "Stop that truck before we have to."

"What truck?" Glen asked into the mouthpiece.

"Out there. You can't miss it. Look."

"Oh, that's the civilian contractor from the far side of the airfield. They resumed work after their siesta."

"No matter whose truck. Stop it."

"We have no way of contacting it. Somebody will have to signal to it by hand."

The terrorist guards were reducing their circle and withdrawing closer to the helicopters, some of them helping the aircrews hustle their reluctant guests towards the Hercules which had again lowered its loading door.

As the Marines saw what was happening, their driver put his foot to the floor and changed his line of direction straight for the Hercules. The terrorists scrambled for the safety it offered, but their prisoners were not moving as fast as they wanted. Fifty yards away the truck slewed round to a stop. Marines spilled over the side with no protection except their ability to squeeze themselves into the ground while they opened fire.

In desperation to fulfil his mission, the pilot started to draw forward before the ramp was clear of the ground. Several terrorists dropped their weapons as they grappled to get inside. The Marines, seeing the confusion, moved surprisingly quickly for men on their bellies.

While everyone's attention was thus diverted, a large bulldozer was racing at incongruous speed north-east along the second runway, at approximately forty-five degrees to the main runway. Almost at the last moment, the pilot realised the driver's intention. He was racing to block the Hercules' take-off right in front of the control tower.

The door was snapped shut, despite the fact that a terrorist was hanging outside, his wrist trapped by the pulping force of the massive hydraulics. He hung there screaming until his convulsions helped the door complete its scissors effect. He was the seventh casualty among the terrorists since the Marines had started firing.

Amazingly, the bulldozer looked as though it was bound to reach the intersection ahead of the Hercules, but the pilot had one chance, and he took it. Regardless of adding to the discomfort of his passengers already reeling about inside the barn of a cargo hold, he swung the great machine to port, thus enabling him to take advantage of the extra width afforded by the secondary runway on the north side of the main runway.

In the nick of time, he swung the Hercules back on to the main runway and pushed just enough extra acceleration out of its mighty engines to persuade its forward momentum to overcome, by the merest fraction, the force of the incipient spin, which would have carried it off the runway altogether.

The section of Marines who had hitched a ride on the bulldozer fired their rifles at the engines and tanks of the plane to try to prevent its take-off.

RAF Regiment marksmen tried the same thing from Reres Wood on the opposite side. All carefully avoided the fuselage for fear of hitting a hostage.

The increased stink of fuel and the heavier than usual trail of exhaust fumes convinced the men on the ground that at least one fuel tank had been pierced.

The general mêlée made it easier for the armourers to get to work underneath four of the Phantoms. The two pilots, whose planes had no chance of take-off without help to taxi out from the corner, snapped back their canopies, one after the other, and sprinted towards two of the planes whose navigators, having gone with the helicopters, had been forced to board the Hercules because of the intervention by the Marines. The first one reached a plane as yet unattended by an armourer and got safely on board. But the second one, as he reached the Phantom's wingtip, saw a MasterSergeant beavering away.

Without a word, he pulled his pistol from his pocket, but before he could aim it, was felled by a bullet from a stern-faced youngster whose shoulder-flash proudly proclaimed, 'RAF Regiment'. The pilot sprawled below the wing, unseen by Rodriguez in the cockpit above.

The six planes that were in a position to manoeuvre began to follow the Hercules down the runway. Rodriguez reminded the tower not to interfere because of the risk to the hostages.

But Knudsen spoiled things for him by excitedly telling the WRAF Corporal that he had just picked up a rendezvous position for the Hercules.

She passed on the message to Glen, who took an instant decision and made a suggestion to Carrington, on whose order a hand-held rocket-launcher was aimed at one of the two Phantoms not yet disarmed. The aim was careful and the most vulnerable target chosen.

A white sheet of flame from below the wing of the plane erupted and engulfed the Phantom as it passed the control tower. Fortunately for those in the tower, the plane's inertia carried it for another hundred yards before its fuel tanks ignited and converted the plane into a mobile inferno.

A furious Rodriguez ordered his pilots to fire their rockets at random, by which time the RAF Regiment's lethal marksman had his rocket-launcher aimed at the only other missile that remained intact. As he squeezed the trigger, the first aggressive pilot pressed his firing button and was rewarded with the anticlimax of a click, and the sound of his unprimed missiles fall harmlessly to the tarmac.

Glen's ruse had worked. All the planes were harmless, including the second one which the armourers had been unable to tackle, for the Regiment's rocket reached the plane's port missile a full second before the pilot got into exactly the position he wanted - facing directly towards the control tower. He heard the explosion which was his own death knell, while his finger hovered harmlessly in mid-air, at least six inches from the firing button.

Cursing the incompetence of the Spanish ground-crew, Rodriguez ordered his squadron to take off in a tighter formation than the one in which they had landed, for the simple reason that there were only four of the original eight planes left. Or at least there were, until the bulldozer lunged to life again at the last minute and clipped the starboard wing of the unfortunate who came too close because he was hemmed in by his comrades.

When the Marines, who had landed at Shelly Point, reached the edge of the runway in time to open fire at the approaching planes, the unfortunate pilot they hit ensured his own fatality by accelerating his plane so enthusiastically that he doubled the effective velocity of the bullet that hit him between the eyes.

His dead hands jerked back on the stick to induce a loop which at that speed and elevation had only one possible outcome - an inverted pancake. When things start to go wrong, they can only get worse. The dead pilot pancaked not on the ground, but on top of the Phantom next to him.

Only Rodriguez took to the air.

CHAPTER 46

Rodriguez' luck continued to desert him at a geometric rate. His erstwhile radio-operator and interim helicopter navigator was rattling around inside the cavernous hold of the Hercules, deriving no comfort from the fact that he was sharing his hardship with distinguished company. Meanwhile, the Basque-speaking radio-operator aboard the Hercules was pouring forth a stream of vital information, which impressed itself upon Rodriguez' uncomprehending mind as meaningless babble.

The injustices that the fates were visiting upon Rodriguez were compounded by the fact that Knudsen was giving an instantaneous translation to Glen and his companions, who were transforming it into action.

The Hercules was heading for a pre-arranged rendezvous at 55° 50' north, 8° 30' west. Everyone in the tower except Glen seemed to find that location very puzzling.

When Glen asked why, the little WRAF Corporal looked up at him innocently and said, "It's in the middle of the sea."

"They must have a ship, or more likely a submarine out there waiting to pick them up," he exclaimed.

"But a Hercules can't land in the sea," she protested.

"Oh, yes it can," Dow interrupted. "Not if it wants to take off again, of course, but our friends seem to regard aircraft as expendable as yesterday's newspaper.

"We'll get an anti-submarine Nimrod out there and ask NATO at Machrihanish to scramble their Tornadoes. Even if there's only one Phantom leaving here, so many unexpected things have happened today, I don't want to be caught out again. There's no point in our sending Phantoms to catch a Phantom.

"It's up to the Admiralty to get some help out there in the form of ships. We'd better find out what's been happening at Pitreavie Castle. Let's see if your theory's right, Dr. Glen."

He took the direct line to Pitreavie from the WRAF NCO who had put him through. Everyone watched him attentively, but none more so than Glen, as Dow's intelligent face reflected interest, anticipation, relief and pleasure. He then passed on all the information he had and asked the Navy to send ships to the designated meeting-place.

As soon as he put the phone down he addressed the WRAF Flight Lieutenant. "My request to RAF Kinloss to station a Nimrod at this map reference. Then an emergency to Machrihanish. While you're doing that you can eavesdrop on what I tell the others, if you can hear anything above the noise these fire-engines are making outside.

"This place is in some mess. It's a curse when you consider how long we spent bulling it up for those blasted NATO ministers. We've got quite a few casualties heading for hospital too, I see. I hope there aren't many of our lads or Marines among them.

"You were right, Dr. Glen. It appears that six men broke into the Royal Naval Dockyard. They seemed to expect that they would have the place to themselves. So they were allowed to penetrate as deeply as they could, to make sure there were no arguments later that they'd been stray passers-by, and also to find out how well they were informed about the place. That would have given counter-espionage an idea of where leaks could have come from.

"Beyond that, the Admiralty will only say that they've had some very interesting revelations. We can only hope that the value of that capture can in some way offset the mayhem and havoc we've seen here.

"In the meantime, it's up to us to continue with this ingenious listening post you've contrived, Dr. Glen, and to do whatever we can to retrieve the situation."

....

The Hercules flew back to the Atlantic Coast by the same route as it had come. Rodriguez overtook it as it swooped westwards over Tinto Hill to provide its sole escort.

Its return journey was watched closely by radar control at Machrihanish, Prestwick and Belfast. This was no worse than had been planned. What was not known was that the Basque messages had been interpreted from the moment they had landed at Leuchars.

The sense of achievement aboard the Hercules was modified by the news from Rodriguez of the disastrous departure of the Phantoms.

It was an accepted risk that fighters would have been scrambled, but the kidnappers still had three aces: the hostages, 122 Squadron and their alternative transport to safety.

....

An AEW Mk3 Nimrod on a training flight from RAF Waddington, Lincolnshire, to RAF Kinloss, Moray, was approaching Barra Head when it received orders to divert eighty miles to the south-west to bring it to the Hercules' projected destination half-an-hour before the latter's estimated time of arrival.

Even without the aid of the three fluorescent orange marker buoys forming a triangle with quarter-mile-long sides, the Nimrod, using its Doppler pulsed radar system, picked out a submarine one mile to the east of the triangle ten fathoms below the surface.

Despite its attempts to jam the Nimrod's radar, its electronics came nowhere near to the sophistication necessary to baffle the Doppler, whose anti-jamming devices were superior to most electronic counter-measures.

The Nimrod glided towards the submarine at sea level and dropped a sonar buoy beside the hull before spiralling upwards to watch and listen.

At forty thousand feet it levelled out, shut off two of its Rolls Royce Spey Turbofan engines and floated like a bird of prey, except that no bird of prey ever kept such a sharp or hungry look-out. That was hardly surprising, as no bird of prey had six pairs of eyes and ears glued to the tactical display and impulses feeding a stream of automatically-filtered data from the intricate environment that was this creature's element.

One console operator, concentrating on the submarine, was amazed to hear through the sonar buoy a conversation in English within the vessel. Although no friendly submarine was supposed to be in the area, he checked again on his computer, but before it could answer, there was a snapped command on board the boat. The conversation stopped. There was a pause. Then the same voices continued in German-sounding whispers.

Meanwhile, another console having picked up the Hercules and the Phantom, their configuration on the screen like a shark accompanied by a solitary pilot fish, stayed exclusively with the two Spanish planes.

....

Two Panavia Tornado F Mk2s stood together at the beginning of the runway at Machrihanish, pilots and navigators poised for immediate action. The talon-like clamps beneath the fuselages gripped four Sky Flash missiles, whilst those under each wing clenched two Sidewinders.

As zero approached for take-off, the pilots increased power in their Mk 103 Turbofan engines, scarcely a year in service with the RAF. The youthful engines screamed their impatience.

Zero. Brakes off. Full throttle.

Four minutes later, side by side, the planes were eleven miles above the Atlantic and still climbing.

Within another two minutes their Type 72 Doppler Foxhunter radar systems had used their Kalman filtering and inertial inputs to bring the planes with undeviating accuracy to a point exactly five miles above the Nimrod.

From their moment of take-off, another console on the Nimrod had been devoted to the two Tornadoes.

The three remaining consoles fed back information from the continuing sky-searching probes pulsing from the clumsy, bulbous appendages at each end of the fuselage.

It did not take them long to find the Phantoms of 122 Squadron, divided into two flights of four, one lurking low behind Aran Island and the other off Bloody Island. Each flight was assigned to a separate monitor, leaving one monitor to continue its random search.

Selected information was transmitted from the Nimrod to the two Tornadoes who fed it into their nose-mounted Ferranti laser ranger and marked target receivers.

Considering that the Nimrod was jamming all radar on the Hercules and Phantoms, they were blind victims at the mercy of the Tornadoes' missiles, already locked on to their targets with an inevitability restricted only by the lock of the steel talons.

The Hercules, with its single escort, reached the area of splashdown, the pilot aware that it was under electronic surveillance, but relieved that there were no hostile aircraft in sight.

Despite the intervention by the Marines, it was on schedule. The pilot flew over the triangle of buoys, noting from the small bunting on one of them that the wind was from due west.

He banked and completed a low-level circuit as though for a normal landing.

With undercarriage retracted, the pilot made his final approach from three miles. He passed over the submarine at one hundred feet. Seconds later, the great belly of the plane touched the crest of a wave, which produced the right amount of drag to convert a forward momentum of one hundred knots into a perfect decelerating hydro-plane effect, at the end of which the Hercules settled snugly and stably in the waves, its side-doors at an ideal height above the sheltered water on the lee side as the pilot turned the plane's nose south.

Inside there was frantic activity to launch liferafts. The well-rehearsed exercise succeeded largely because of the gentleness of the Atlantic swell. With everyone on board, six large dinghies began to drift eastwards, looking from the air like a string of orange icebergs being calved from an Arctic glacier.

By the time the last one had cleared the tail of the Hercules, the submarine had surfaced, presenting her port beam to the diminutive convoy.

That was the moment at which both submariners and survivors became aware of company, as the Nimrod flew south towards the conning tower at an altitude of less than fifty feet, giving the commander the benefit of internationally-recognised signals that his presence was regarded as hostile and he should remove himself and his ship immediately or he would be fired upon.

To emphasise the point, the pilot gave him a view of the Stingray torpedoes, one of which could sink the submarine before the survival dinghies reached it. The Nimrod did a tight turn to starboard, then another to bring its sights in line with the Hercules, now wallowing deeper in the waves beyond all prospect of salvage.

One Stingray was released.

The disintegration of the Hercules electrified the submarine commander and crew into frantic activity.

Under instructions to use maximum stealth and avoid all confrontation, Commander Zeitsmann ordered emergency dive procedures.

Abandoned in their life rafts, the terrorists were in their weakest bargaining position.

Rodriguez's unarmed attempt to buzz the Nimrod raised a cheer from his compatriots, but as the other Phantoms of 122 Squadron raced in from the west to join him, the futility of their action became apparent, as the two vastly superior Tornadoes streaked in between the unsuspecting flights with devastating precision.

Rodriguez, recognising the odds against them and their depleting fuel, ordered 122 Squadron to break off the engagement and return to Bilbao.

Regardless of the integrity of Ireland's air space, they took the most direct route.

Observing the niceties of international law, the Tornadoes did not follow, but were waiting for them off the Scilly Isles to hustle them across the Bay of Biscay.

The Nimrod remained on station. Having cut back to two engines again, it glided above the waves in a figure-of-eight pattern which intersected over the middle of the bedraggled life-rafts, until one of the large new Fishery Protection ships hove to and drew the first of the rafts alongside.

To continue with the niceties of protocol, the ship had been slightly delayed while the Secretary of State was ferried aboard by helicopter from Prestwick after being whisked from Gleneagles.

As armed crew segregated VIPs from former captors on deck, MacEwan presided over the preparation of hospitality for the NATO Ministers in the wardroom.

CHAPTER 47

There was a knock on Glen's office door.

Glen called, "Come in."

Professor Gainsborough, head of the department, entered, his upswept bushy grey hair giving his worried blue eyes a startled look.

"Forgive me for intruding," he began, "but it's my job to ensure that the department keeps rolling along in spite of whatever members of staff happen to get up to."

He leaned against the narrow windowsill, his back to the monochrome view of slates.

"Who would have thought it of MacLaren?" he mused. "The personification of rectitude. But, mind you, when you think about it, certain threads begin to weave into place."

"How has his wife taken the news?" Glen enquired.

"Philosophically."

"They were both very kind to me. I think I should visit her today."

"That's very kind of you, and since you're of a generous disposition, I'll come straight to the point. I know you have a lot on your plate, but three of MacLaren's research students have been left rather in the lurch, and I was wondering if you would be prepared to take them under your wing for the duration of your stay. Naturally, I'd be glad to do what I can to have it extended if that would help."

"It's an attractive proposition. I've a lot of loose ends to tie up here. Without any promise of a commitment I may not be able to keep, I'll give all the help I can."

"That's good enough in the circumstances. We'll discuss it one day next week when things are settling down a bit."

After Gainsborough had gone, Glen phoned Isobel and invited himself round.

When she opened the door, she warned him, "I have two Special Branch detectives in the lounge. They arrived after you phoned. Would you rather come back later?"

Her clear blue eyes looked calm, but the corners of her mouth seemed lower and the muscles between them and the delicate chin more mobile than normal.

"I'll just wait, if it's alright with you."

The relief showed in her face, and she closed her eyes tightly to bring her tear ducts under control.

Her eyes shone as she looked into Glen's and said, "Yes, please."

The detectives resented Glen's arrival, and relations deteriorated when he pointed out that Mrs. MacLaren was entitled to have her lawyer present, whatever they claimed about the Official Secrets Act.

They reacted by insisting on searching MacLaren's study again.

As soon as she and Glen were alone, Isobel sighed, "Poor Campbell. I knew we were on different wavelengths, but I had no idea how far apart we were. No wonder there was nothing between us. His heart and mind were elsewhere."

"They believe he was brainwashed in Korea. All those old pal calls were from communist sympathisers and espionage contacts. I wish I'd kept a closer record of them.

"I'll stand by him as a sort of domestic colleague. That's all I ever was to him, and it's probably a lot more than he expects. You'll be leaving Scotland now, I expect."

"Not immediately."

He gave an account of the arrangement he and Gainsborough had made that morning and waited with her until the two Special Branch men left.

His parting words were, "You know you have a lot of talent to make a neglected man very happy."

His next call was at the R&A Clubhouse.

Because of the activity surrounding the Open, he had made no further attempt to contact officials after his first visit with MacLaren.

At the porter's box he asked for the Secretary.

After a brief exchange on the intercom, the porter asked him to wait in the lounge as Mr. Mackinnon was engaged, but would join him as soon as he could.

In the timeless lounge it was hard to believe that a world-focusing sports event had climaxed outside its windows the day before.

The battles with the invaders seemed even more remote in this tranquil sanctuary.

He picked up a newspaper.

'Mock Battle Mocks Open' screamed the headline. Below it Glen read, 'Influential members of that haven of privilege, the Royal and Ancient Golf Club of St Andrews, are hopping mad. For the first time the Old Course was played on the Sabbath. Golf's greatest were in the final of the £70,000 classic.

'But that was the day another Royal - the Royal Air Force - chose also to disrupt the Scottish day of rest and carry out a mock battle for the benefit of visiting Ministers of Defence from our NATO allies.

'The noise that followed spoiled concentration for players and pleasure for spectators.

'Such a blatant disregard for the rights of civilians deserves an enquiry at the highest level in the Ministry of Defence.

'At least the Russians do all they can to encourage sport.

'If the Air Force is pretending to protect us from attacks by Russians, we must ask, who is going to protect us from the Air Force?'

In a corner of the page, he read, 'Highland Laird Dies - Sir Seamus Breck was involved in a fatal accident when his car plunged from the damaged Friarton Bridge.'

He put down the paper in disgust and took up another one whose more modest headline stated, 'Soviet Diplomats Expelled.'

Below, it stated, 'The Soviet Ambassador was summoned to the Foreign Office late on Sunday evening. The Foreign Secretary demanded the immediate return to the Soviet Union of four accredited members of the Embassy staff for activities incompatible with their status as diplomats - a formula of words for saying that they have been spying.

'A Polish citizen on a temporary work-permit has been deported, and a British academic, Dr. Campbell MacLaren, is helping police with their enquiries.'

On an inside page was a photograph of the Secretary of State for Scotland, beaming in the midst of some bemused foreign defence ministers.

The caption read, 'Secretary of State MacEwan was on hand to play a personal role when NATO defence ministers were given a practical display of Britain's air defences. It is the first time a Scottish Secretary has played such a prominent role in a conference of this nature. Rumours of Mr. MacEwan's prospects of moving to a very senior Cabinet post in the Prime Minister's imminent reshuffle would seem to be well-founded.'

His concentration was broken by a voice at his side saying, "So sorry. I didn't mean to keep you waiting." It was the R&A Secretary.

"Ah, I see you've been reading about us in the paper. We got marvellous coverage this year from the Press, but that carry-on at Leuchars almost spoiled everything. The television people almost stopped transmission for a time, but I kicked up such a fuss. Told them they'd never get our facilities again.

"I can tell you the Ministry of Defence is up to its neck in hot water this morning. We've contacted every MP who plays golf. Those who are members of the R&A have been phoning in ever since the first noises came over, spoiling the transmission."

Then he added unexpectedly, "Didn't that Spaniard have a brilliant victory?"

Glen was startled. "What do you mean?"

"Seve." Then, after a moment's pause he added, "Ballesteros."

When no flicker of comprehension dawned on Glen's face, the Secretary of the R&A added incredulously, "You know. The Champion. He won the Open yesterday."

Glen nodded at last.

His host added quickly, "Look. This is a bad day for me. Could we have lunch tomorrow? Things will be more settled then. Though I must admit life is never quiet in this job. I have a lot to make up to you for our mistake in filing your Fellowship details."

....

Glen spent most of the afternoon trying to contact Ross. Eventually his efforts were rewarded when Ross was brought to a phone in Gleneagles.

"I believe your men had a bloody time," Glen began. "I'm sorry."

"We lost more than we should have done, but we got off remarkably lightly as far as our honoured guests were concerned, and our political masters are relatively happy. That counts for a lot in this job."

211

"Was much material damage done?"

"A bit. Most of it will be attributed in the Press tomorrow to structural failure. High-tensile steel in reinforced concrete can go off with a helluva bang, you know. We saved all the bridges except Friarton. They really were mined. We managed to pick up most of the people involved, including Johnson. We don't have extradition treaties with Spain, but we're going to send their chaps back under escort.

"We can use that as a lever for repatriation of some of our crooks from the Costa Del Sol. The Spanish government will find it useful to get these people back. They'll get a lot out of them on the right-wing underground. That's now been smashed in the services. It's destroyed it more than any official purge could have done."

"What about the Basques? They'll hardly get a fair hearing."

"They shouldn't have taken on the big boys. If they can't get power in Spain, they needn't think it's a good idea to bloody the nose of the whole of NATO. Somebody conned them into doing the dirty work."

"I've been reading the papers. Nothing I've seen so far is very accurate. What happens when the truth begins to come out?"

"We'll slap a 'D Notice' on it.

....

From one of their adjoining luxury villas in Acapulco, Don José and Don Ramon contemplated the sunset over the Pacific and lamented that South Africa had inexplicably upset the price of gold by selling the largest amount ever to the United Kingdom at a price well below the prevailing one, at which they had bought their bullion the previous week.

Don Ramon said, "The politicians may be disappointed, but they were playing for very high stakes, and as businessmen, we are entitled to our commission."

....

Glen's first thought in the morning was for Isobel. He dialled her number.